A century before the term "crossover" became a buzzword in popular culture, Edgar Rice Burroughs created the first expansive, fully cohesive literary universe. Coexisting in this vast cosmos was a pantheon of immortal heroes and heroines—Tarzan of the Apes™, Jane Porter®, John Carter®, Dejah Thoris®, Carson Napier™, and David Innes™ being only the best known among them. In Burroughs' 80-plus novels, their epic adventures transported them to the strange and exotic worlds of Barsoom®, Amtor™, Pellucidar®, Caspak™, and Va-nah™, as well as the lost civilizations of Earth and even realms beyond the farthest star. Now the Edgar Rice Burroughs Universe expands in both new definitive editions of Burroughs' classic works and an adventure-filled series of canonical novels written by today's talented authors!

THE SEMINAL WORKS OF EDGAR RICE BURROUGHS

EDGAR RICE BURROUGHS UNIVERSE™

The Edgar Rice Burroughs Universe is the interconnected and cohesive literary cosmos created by the Master of Adventure and continued in new canonical works authorized by Edgar Rice Burroughs, Inc., the corporation based in Tarzana, California, that was founded by Burroughs in 1923. Unravel the mysteries and explore the wonders of the Edgar Rice Burroughs Universe alongside the pantheon of heroes and heroines that inhabit it in both classic tales of adventure penned by Burroughs and brand-new epics from today's talented authors.

TARZAN® SERIES

Tarzan of the Apes
The Return of Tarzan
The Beasts of Tarzan
The Son of Tarzan
Tarzan and the Jewels of Opar
Jungle Tales of Tarzan
Tarzan the Untamed
Tarzan the Terrible
Tarzan and the Golden Lion
Tarzan and the Ant Men
Tarzan, Lord of the Jungle
Tarzan and the Lost Empire
Tarzan at the Earth's Core
Tarzan the Invincible
Tarzan Triumphant
Tarzan and the City of Gold
Tarzan and the Lion Man
Tarzan and the Leopard Men
Tarzan's Quest
Tarzan and the Forbidden City
Tarzan the Magnificent
Tarzan and "The Foreign Legion"
Tarzan and the Madman
Tarzan and the Castaways
Tarzan and the Tarzan Twins
Tarzan: The Lost Adventure (with Joe R. Lansdale)

BARSOOM® SERIES

A Princess of Mars
The Gods of Mars
The Warlord of Mars
Thuvia, Maid of Mars
The Chessmen of Mars
The Master Mind of Mars
A Fighting Man of Mars
Swords of Mars
Synthetic Men of Mars
Llana of Gathol
John Carter of Mars

PELLUCIDAR® SERIES

At the Earth's Core
Pellucidar
Tanar of Pellucidar
Tarzan at the Earth's Core
Back to the Stone Age
Land of Terror
Savage Pellucidar

AMTOR™ SERIES

Pirates of Venus
Lost on Venus
Carson of Venus
Escape on Venus
The Wizard of Venus

ERBUniverse.com

Swords of Eternity Super-Arc

Carson of Venus: The Edge of All Worlds
by Matt Betts

Tarzan: Battle for Pellucidar
by Win Scott Eckert

John Carter of Mars: Gods of the Forgotten
by Geary Gravel

Victory Harben: Fires of Halos
by Christopher Paul Carey

The Dead Moon Super-Arc

*Korak at the Earth's Core**
by Win Scott Eckert

* Releasing 2023

Other ERB Universe Books

Cosmic Epics: The Seminal Works of Edgar Rice Burroughs (*A Princess of Mars*, *The Moon Maid*, and *Pirates of Venus*)
by Edgar Rice Burroughs

*A Princess of Mars: Shadow of the Assassins***
by Ann Tonsor Zeddies

Tarzan and the Forest of Stone
by Jeffrey J. Mariotte

** Releasing 2024

Mahars of Pellucidar
by John Eric Holmes

Red Axe of Pellucidar
by John Eric Holmes

Tarzan and the Forest of Stone
by Jeffrey J. Mariotte

Tarzan and the Dark Heart of Time
by Philip José Farmer

Tarzan and the Valley of Gold
by Fritz Leiber

EDGAR RICE BURROUGHS UNIVERSE™

SAVAGE EPICS

THE SEMINAL WORKS OF EDGAR RICE BURROUGHS

TARZAN® OF THE APES™
AT THE EARTH'S CORE™
THE LAND THAT TIME FORGOT®

Illustrations by
ZDENĚK BURIAN, FRANK FRAZETTA, MICHAEL HERRING,
JOE JUSKO, AND J. ALLEN ST. JOHN

EDGAR RICE BURROUGHS, INC.
Publishers

TARZANA   CALIFORNIA

To Steven K. Dowd,
for the generous support he has provided for both
this book and the legacy of Edgar Rice Burroughs.

CONTENTS

PREFACE
EDGAR RICE BURROUGHS: MASTER OF ADVENTURE

CHRISTOPHER PAUL CAREY

I T IS NOT AN EXAGGERATION to state that Edgar Rice Burroughs was cast out of the same mold as the ancient Greek bards and the other great oral storytellers who have enchanted audiences since the dawn of humanity. Although Burroughs is, of course, renowned for the eighty-some books of genre-influencing science fiction, fantasy, and romance that he penned during his highly successful career as a writer, he cut his storytelling teeth improvising tall tales and other yarns to friends, classmates, relatives, and later at the bedside of his young children. There, often acting out the antics of the outlandish characters he created, he would regale his little ones with fantastical stories about such things as interplanetary heroes mixed up in perilous plots and predicaments, beset by malevolent monsters and dastardly villains on weird, distant worlds. Without needing to write a word, he honed essential storytelling skills such as characterization, pacing, narrative, and world building, while he simultaneously mastered the art of the cliffhanger, stopping his tales just at the most captivating part and forcing his rapt audience to wait on pins and needles until he resumed the next tantalizing chapter the following evening.

Something primal and powerful comes out of the best oral storytelling, a kind of magic that cannot be learned from a literature seminar—a type of wizardry abounding with archetypes, and moral lessons, and the rhythmic thrum of mythology, and yet that somehow seems alive and fresh and new. It is raw and organic, and it hits us straight in the heart. It is this same oral storytelling alchemy that the thirty-five-year-old Edgar Rice Burroughs both instinctively and skillfully transferred to the printed page when, after having failed utterly at numerous business ventures as he strove to support his expectant wife and their two young children, he decided to pick up his pen and take up the craft of writing.

Burroughs hit the ground running with his debut novel, "Under the Moons of Mars," serialized in *The All-Story* magazine in 1912, and published in hardcover in 1917 by A. C. McClurg & Co. under the title *A Princess of Mars*. Readers of the magazine immediately demanded a sequel, and the story struck such a chord that legions of imitators sprang up almost instantly, before long leading to the birth of the sword and planet subgenre in the field of literature that would eventually become known as "science fiction."*

Most writers would have been content to rest on their laurels after such an achievement, but not so our intrepid storyteller, who was bursting at the seams to chronicle his next tale. While looking for a publisher for his second novel, a medieval romance titled *The Outlaw of Torn*, Burroughs struck literary gold with the publication *Tarzan of the Apes* in the October 1912 issue of *The All-Story*. The story of an orphaned boy raised by great apes in the heart of the African jungle was an instant sensation, with, once again, readers clamoring for a sequel, this time even more passionately. The sheer power of the mythic storytelling in the novel birthed not only an entire literary series**; it also launched one of the most popular multimedia franchises of the twentieth century, ultimately imprinting Burroughs' famous ape-man on the worldwide psyche. More than a century after the Lord of the Jungle first appeared in print, who today doesn't instantly recognize Tarzan's mighty yell, made famous by actor and Olympic athlete Johnny Weissmuller when he played the ape-man in numerous films in the 1930s and '40s?

With the creation of Tarzan, Edgar Rice Burroughs achieved literary and pop-culture immortality. But like the bards of ages past, he had so many more stories to tell, so many tales of unbounded imagination with which he yearned to entertain his audience. Two of his best are collected

---

* *A Princess of Mars* may be found in the present book's companion volume, *Cosmic Epics: The Seminal Works of Edgar Rice Burroughs* (Edgar Rice Burroughs, Inc., 2023), which collects the first novels in Burroughs major science fiction series, including *The Moon Maid* and *Pirates of Venus*.

** All twenty-four original novels in the Tarzan series are now available in the Edgar Rice Burroughs Authorized Library at EdgarRiceBurroughs.com or wherever fine books are sold.

in this book alongside his acclaimed *Tarzan of the Apes*, and they too left a lasting impression on readers across the world, and across generations. They too are genre-defining classics, and they too abound with archetypes and feel alive and fresh while yet thrumming with the primordial heartbeat of myth and legend. *At the Earth's Core*, with its proto-steampunk "iron mole" digging machine that drills its way to the savage inner world of Pellucidar, where humanity has been enslaved by a race of cold-blooded, telepathic reptiles. And *The Land That Time Forgot*, with its wayward World War I submarine crew stranded on a lost continent of dinosaurs and primeval people, where they must solve a mystery that will unlock the secrets of time-lost Caspak. Both novels captivated readers' imaginations, and like *Tarzan of the Apes* they both spawned series of popular sequels, as well as comic books and motion pictures.

But I have said enough. Now it is time to leave behind the hustle and bustle of modern life, to sit back and allow ourselves to be swept away by Edgar Rice Burroughs' mythic storytelling as he summons his Muse and spins his savage epics like only the Master of Adventure can.

Christopher Paul Carey
Tarzana, California
June 2023

CHRISTOPHER PAUL CAREY *is the Director of Publishing and Creative Director of the ERB Universe at Edgar Rice Burroughs, Inc. He is the author of the ERB Universe novel* Victory Harben: Fires of Halos *as well as* Swords Against the Moon Men, *an authorized sequel to Edgar Rice Burroughs' classic science fantasy novel* The Moon Maid. *He has scripted several comic books set in Mr. Burroughs' worlds, including* Pellucidar: Across Savage Seas, Pellucidar: Dark of the Sun, *and* Carson of Venus: The Flames Beyond. *He holds a master's degree in Writing Popular Fiction from Seton Hill University, and has edited more than ninety novels, anthologies, and collections for a variety of publishers. He lives in Southern California.*

INTRODUCTION
ERB AND THE SAVAGE EPIC
GARYN G. ROBERTS, PH.D.

AVID COLLECTORS, SCHOLARS, AND FANS ALIKE have considered and analyzed Edgar Rice Burroughs' (September 1, 1875–March 19,1950) life work from an array of perspectives with a range of methodologies. For more than a century, both zealots and academics have contemplated underpinning themes of politics, race and ethnicity, rival societies at war, characterization, gender roles, settings, mortality, and morality found in Burroughs' storytelling. Publishing history is considered, as is popular literary and sociohistorical context.

One important approach to understanding and appreciating the savage epics of Edgar Rice Burroughs like *Tarzan of the Apes*, *At the Earth's Core*, and *The Land That Time Forgot* is to consider these adventures as definitive models or archetypes. Most often, archetypes have both predecessors and imitators. This is the case with Edgar Rice Burroughs' savage epics collected in this volume.

ARCHETYPE. Not necessarily the first, but the ultimate model—an archetype is the "gold standard" by which all similar forms are measured, evaluated, and considered. In the case of storytelling and literature, archetypes are a synthesis of conventional, established traditions expanded with inventions derived from then contemporary history and culture, and then solidified into that ultimate model.

In regard to story genres today broadly deemed "fantasy" and "science fiction"—listed under a number of other categories in years past—Mary Wollstonecraft Shelley (1797–1851) provided and articulated some of our penultimate archetypes of all time in her *Frankenstein; Or, The Modern Prometheus* (1818; revised edition 1831). Here, in the archetypal *Frankenstein*,

xvii

Shelley synthesized and expanded then existing "scientific romance" and "science fiction," "dark fantasy" and "horror," "gothicism," and "moral allegory." Although Boris Karloff's (1887–1969) portrayal of the tragic mutation in the Universal Studios' *Frankenstein* is the image that has remained since 1931, Shelley's original tale is much more detailed and complex than the fun, even admirable, portrayal by Karloff. Of course, "Frankenstein" references Dr. Frankenstein the scientist, not his monstrous creation.

The quintessential archetypal non-motion-picture depiction of Frankenstein's monster was provided by Norman Saunders (1907–89) in his painting for the *Classics Illustrated* #26 (1958) comic book cover. (This comic book adapts Shelley's archetypal novel.)

In her archetypal novel, Mary Shelley addressed, in a very progressive and open fashion, the moral and social issues of her day. These dilemmas and issues, which are still relevant today, include reanimation of human flesh, genetic engineering, cloning, the nature and quality of life, love, compassion, mortality and morality.

There is probably no other individual storyteller more responsible for contributing to story archetypes—"gothic," "dark fantasy/horror," "science fiction" and "detective fiction"—than Edgar Allan Poe (1809–49). As was the case with Mary Shelley, Poe was by no means the first person to tell tales of "fantasy" and "science fiction." Yet both Shelley and Poe solidified and advanced traditions of these existing story forms and created master patterns or models—archetypes—that stand tall in contemporary fiction. Unlike Mary Shelley, Edgar Allan Poe did not produce one single novel-length masterpiece that defines him to this day. Instead, he wrote and published a number of very pointed stories (of varying lengths) about the horrors and uncertainties of life, about the human psyche, and about the possibilities of science.

Poe's "The Fall of the House of Usher" (*Burton's Gentleman's Magazine*, September 1839) is the archetype for the "gothic haunted house" story. Gothic haunted house stories are defined by a central symbol, an icon, that is an architectural structure or building such as a haunted house, decaying castle, or moldering old estate. Within the confines of the mysterious building are found long, decadent, incestuous family histories and atrocities augmented by elements of the supernatural. This setting provides the vehicle for fictions that examine the inner workings of the individual and society alike.

To further detail the concept of the larger Gothic "archetype," consider some elements and terms associated with Gothic stories, which include: abandoned houses, abbeys, asylums, bats, bell towers (belfries), big winding staircases, bodysnatching, candlelight, castles, chandeliers, churches and houses of worship, clock towers, coffins/caskets, creaking doors, crows, crypts, dumb waiters, dungeons, dusty cloth-covered furniture ghosts, elevators, fireplaces, ghosts, gnarled old trees, gramophones, gravestones, graveyards and cemeteries, Hansom cabs, hidden rooms, horse–drawn carriages, insanity/madness, laboratories, long winding staircases, mad scientists, mausoleums, mirrors, mobs of people, monasteries, moors, mortuaries, motes, moth-eaten draperies, noises, old family history, old homes, organs and harpsichords, owls, paintings, pipe organs, portraits (old family), rats (plague, disease, big teeth), ravens, secret passages, secret walls, shadows, spider webs/cobwebs, tapestries, thunderstorms and lightning, torches, towers, tunnels, vaults, and windmills. Some adjectives and adverbs often associated with the Gothic archetype are atmospheric, crumbling, dank, dark, decaying, foggy, gloomy, hazy, lurid, misty, mo(u)ldy, mo(u)ldering, nighttime, rainy, supernatural, and weird.

Examples of landmark Gothic fiction contribute to the overall archetype. An incomplete list of these legendary works is Horace Walpole's *The Castle of Otranto* (1764), Ann Radcliffe's *The Mysteries of Udolpho* (1794), Mary Shelley's *Frankenstein; Or the Modern Prometheus* (1818; 1831), Edgar Allan Poe's "The Fall of the House of Usher" (1839), Henry James' *The Turn of the Screw* (1898), Bram Stoker's *Dracula* (1897), stories by H. P. Lovecraft (1890–1937), the Batman franchise (begun in *Detective Comics #27*, 1940), Robert Bloch's "A Feast in the Abbey" (*Weird Tales*, January 1935), *Psycho* (1959 novel by Robert Bloch [1917–94]; 1960 Hitchcock movie), *The Ghost and Mr. Chicken* (1966), the *Dark Shadows* television series (1966–71), Robert Bloch's *American Gothic* (1974), Stephen King's *The Shining* (1977), Peter Straub's *Ghost Story* (1979), Robert McCammon's *Usher's Passing* (1984), the Harry Potter novels and movies (begun in 1997), and Douglas Preston and Lincoln Child's *The Cabinet of Curiosities* (2002, and their Dr. Leng stories).

James Fenimore Cooper's (1789–1851) Leatherstocking series of frontier romances (*The Pioneers* [1823], *The Last of the Mohicans* [1826], *The Prairie* [1827], *The Pathfinder* [1840], and *The Deer Slayer* [1841]) solidified the American frontier or Western story. At first designed by

Cooper to be a buffoon, a parody, Natty Bumppo developed into a serious character and became the archetype of the "Leatherstocking"— the Western hero literally named for his clothing.

Edgar Rice Burroughs solidified and articulated several archetypes in his extensive, wide-ranging, and literary writing career. *Cosmic Epics: The Seminal Works of Edgar Rice Burroughs* collects three legendary archetypes of scientific romance. Our collection here celebrates three more archetypes, this time in the area of savage epics.

Authors and stories that predicted and set up Edgar Rice Burroughs' savage epics most notably include Jules Verne's (1828–1905) *Journey to the Centre of the Earth* (1864 as *Voyage au centre dela Terre*), masterpiece of a genre we might literally term "journeys to inner Earth." Similarly, Verne's *Twenty Thousand Leagues under the Sea* (serialized between March 1869 and June 1870 in the French periodical *Magasin d'éducation et de récréation* as *Vingt mille lieues sous les mers*) was not the first fictional underwater adventure, but it remains the archetype of such tales. Did Verne invent the submarine or underwater travel? No, not at all. In 1776 Revolutionary War America, the Patriots first employed the "Turtle"—an early rudimentarily functional real-life submarine. In recent decades the works of Clive Cussler (1931–2020) and Tom Clancy (1947–2013) are great grandchildren of Verne's tale of the deep seas fantastique, or "deep-seas adventures."

In nineteenth-century Victorian and imperialist England, Sir Henry Rider Haggard (1856–1925) was the chief purveyor of romantic adventures. *King Solomon's Mines* (1885)—probably Haggard's most famous single work—was one of the first stories of the African adventure genre. Allan Quatermain, introduced in *King Solomon's Mines*, became the archetypal world adventure hero of the second half of the 1800s. Haggard followed this novel with *She: A History of Adventure* (1887).

England's own H. G. Wells (1866–1946) provided savage epics most notably in the Morlocks of *The Time Machine* (1895) and the title mad scientist in *The Island of Doctor Moreau* (1896).

Sir Arthur Conan Doyle's (1859–1930) Sherlock Holmes, who debuted in "A Study in Scarlet" (*Beeton's Christmas Annual*, 1887), was not the first fictional detective by any means, but Doyle's Holmes became the archetype of the "Consulting Detective" literary form or genre. Likewise, Arthur Conan Doyle's Professor Challenger stories—*The Lost World* (1912), *The Poison Belt*

(1913), *The Land of Mist* (1926), "When the World Screamed" (1928 short story), and "The Disintegration Machine" (1929 short story)—became archetypes of the "scientist explorer" variant of savage epics.

There exist further profound archetypes of storytelling, literature, and the popular media. Robert E. Howard's (1906–36) Conan the Barbarian (who debuted in the December 1932 issue of *Weird Tales* in the story "The Phoenix and the Sword") is the archetype of "barbarian fantasy" or "sword and sorcery."

John Huston's (1906–87) motion-picture adaption, *The Maltese Falcon* (Warner Brothers, 1941), based on Dashiell Hammett's (1894–1961) novel of the same title originally serialized in the pages of (*The*) *Black Mask* pulpwood (or "pulp") magazine (first published in a five-part serial, September 1929 to January 1930) is the archetype of the "private investigator" (P.I.) story in motion-picture history. In addition, (*The*) *Black Mask* (1920–51) is the archetype, the gold standard, of "hard-boiled" or private investigator periodicals.

Among the contemporaries and followers of Edgar Rice Burroughs' savage epics and adventures number J. U. Giesy (1877–1947), Charles B. Stillson (1880–1932), A. Merritt (1884–1943), Frances Stevens (pseudonym for Gertrude Barrows Bennett, 1884–1948), Austin Hall (1885–1933) and Homer Eon Flint (1888–1924), Ray Cummings (1887–1957), Otis Albert Kline (1891–1946), Murray Leinster (pseudonym for William Fitzgerald Jenkins, 1896–1975), Edmond Hamilton (1904–77), William L. Chester (1907–71), Fritz Leiber (1910–92), Leigh Brackett (1915–78), Ray Bradbury (1920–2012), and most recently, Michael Crichton (1942–2008).

Beyond Frank A. Munsey's (1854–1925) *Argosy*, *The All-Story*, and similar titles, pulp magazines showcasing works that imitated and expanded upon Edgar Rice Burroughs' savage epics included *Short Stories* (1890-1959), (*The*) *Blue Book* (1905–75), *Adventure* (1910–71), *Weird Tales* (1923–53, and several reincarnations even since), *Amazing Stories* (1926–2021), (*Thrilling*) *Wonder Stories* (1929–55), *Thrilling Adventures* (1931–43), and *Jungle Stories* (1938–54).

The first appearance of Edgar Rice Burroughs' ***Tarzan of the Apes—A Romance of the Jungle*** in The Frank A. Munsey Company's *The All-Story* (October 1912. Vol. XXIV, No. 2, 241–372, later reprinted in hardcover by A. C. McClurg & Co. in 1914) features one of the greatest and most revered covers of all pulp magazines. (Walter) Clinton Pettee (1872–1937) painted the original cover for this issue. According to David Saunders— in my mind, the world's top pulp magazine art scholar and authority— Pettee's "cover for the October 1912 issue of the *The All-Story* featured the world's first published image of Tarzan. Collectors have long considered this landmark issue the most valuable of all pulp magazines."*

Ultimately, Edgar Rice Burroughs produced twenty-three more volumes of Tarzan stories beyond *Tarzan of the Apes*. These begin with *The Return of Tarzan* (1913) and conclude with *Tarzan and the Castaways* (1964). In addition, he wrote two juvenile Tarzan tales—*The Tarzan Twins* (P. F. Volland, 1927) and *Tarzan and the Tarzan Twins with Jad-bal-ja, the Golden Lion* (Whitman Publishing Company, 1936)—and left behind an unfinished manuscript that was completed by Joe R. Lansdale under the title *Tarzan: The Lost Adventure* (Dark Horse Books, 1995). The publishing history of all these stories is definitively chronicled and beautifully detailed in two volumes published by Edgar Rice Burroughs, Inc. These are Robert B. Zeuschner's *Edgar Rice Burroughs: The Bibliography* (2016) and B. J. Lukes' *Edgar Rice Burroughs: The Descriptive Bibliography of the Grosset & Dunlap Reprints* (2017). (Though I have said it before, and will say it other places: Zeuschner's and Lukes' works are not only critical, must-have, essential volumes of Edgar Rice Burroughs and his literary history; they are cornerstones of all twentieth-century literature study.)

In *Tarzan of the Apes*, Edgar Rice Burroughs provided archetypal work in the areas of savage epic, heroic fantasy, and jungle adventure. In its magazine appearance, the novel used the "Edgar Rice Burroughs" byline. (Norman Bean—the byline Burroughs used for *A Princess of Mars* a few months earlier—appeared in parentheses after "Edgar Rice Burroughs.")

Like *A Princess of Mars*, *Tarzan of the Apes* was an important bridge between the dime novel and pulpwood eras. The story begins with a voyage on "the *Fuwulda*, a barkentine [ship, vessel] of about 100 tons." At this time in human history, of course, travel by ship was the only means of

---

* Important to note here is that Frank A. Munsey would often alter the titles of his periodicals over time. For example, *The All-Story* morphed into *All-Story Weekly* and *Argosy* into *Argosy All-Story*. I believe that these title changes are accounted for correctly in my writing here, but the definitive authority on this topic and related Edgar Rice Burroughs stories in Munsey periodicals is Robert B. Zeuschner.

transcontinental travel across the Atlantic and Pacific Oceans. (The *Titanic* sank April 15, 1912.)

Some of the staples of savage epics, heroic fantasies, and jungle adventures include: bows and arrows; caravans and journeys in quest of monetary treasure such as ivory and gold; extensive vines, plant life, and jungle growth; extremes of climate and weather like wind, rain and storms, heat, humidity, and aridity (dryness); gender stereotypes (beautiful women in various states of distress; strong women leaders such as princesses; heroic men; and adolescent boys following in the footsteps of the hero); insects; knives; machetes for clearing jungle undergrowth and for hunting and defense; stereotypical ethic and racial groups (Black natives, wealthy unscrupulous White European imperialists, Black slaves, and naïve, out-of-place White people); "thunder-sticks" and various sorts of guns; trees large enough to live in, tree houses; and wild animals (lions, other big cats, apes, monkeys, hyenas, snakes, elephants, crocodiles, and predatory fish). In many ways the savage epic is a close cousin to the American Western because the hero is caught between the worlds of "savagery" and "civilization" and features a heritage with strong elements of both.

Beyond its lead Edgar Rice Burroughs' Tarzan novel, other features found in the October 1912 issue of *The All-Story* were and are four serials, six short stories, and an editorial page. Of the four serial stories, "The Magical Bath-Tub," Part II, by J. Earl Clauson, is my favorite of all these secondary works, being really very funny, inventive and entertaining. (I am in quest of the other installments of this serial.) "Enter the Hero," Part I, by Robert Simpson, is good, entertaining, pretty standard fare today, but certainly rewarding given the context of 1912. "The Living Past," Part III, by Richard Duffy, is a romantic melodrama with a sort of soap opera feel. And "The Wreck of the Lauderdale," Part V, by William Patterson White, is a fun high-seas adventure featuring sunken treasure.

The six short stories found in the October 1912 issue of *The All-Story* are: "The Spaniard," by Frank Comstock (a short short Western with a sort of surprise twist ending); "Doorway Forty-Nine' by Frank Condon (a sort of "tall tale"); "The Goat of Dolores Valdez" by John D. Swain (a tall tale that features a play on words), "Sleepy Sweeny" by Jack Brant (a short Western tall tale); "Crossed Wires" by R. A. Ellis (featuring "Jimsie

Dale"); and "On the Zodiac Turnpike" by Ella B. Argo (a lighthearted mythic fairy tale fantasy).

Period ethnic and gender stereotypes abound in several of these serial installments and stories. Though probably a coincidence, the main character of "Crossed Wires," one "Jimsie Dale," predates a very famous pulp character and mystery series by Frank L. Packard (1866–1923) that featured "Jimmie Dale" (begun in 1914).

Also included in the October 1912 installment of *The All-Story* is a feature entitled "All-Story Table-Talk"— an editorial page with letters to the editor, and previews of the next issue's stories.

At the Earth's Core (first published in Munsey's *All-Story Weekly* in four parts, April 4, 11, 18, and 25, 1914; McClurg hardcover 1922) is the first in Edgar Rice Burroughs' fabled Pellucidar series. It is followed by:

2. *Pellucidar* (*All-Story Weekly* serial, May 1, 8, 15, 22, and 29, 1915; McClurg hardcover, 1923);

3. *Tanar of Pellucidar* (*The Blue Book* serial, March to August 1929; Metropolitan hardcover, 1930);

4. *Tarzan at the Earth's Core* (*The Blue Book* serial, September 1929 to March 1930; Metropolitan hardcover, 1930);

5. *Back to the Stone Age* (*Argosy Weekly* serial, as *Seven Worlds to Conquer*, January 9, 16, 23, and 30, February 6 and 13, 1937; Edgar Rice Burroughs, Inc., hardcover, 1937);

6. *Land of Terror* (Edgar Rice Burroughs, Inc., hardcover, 1944);

7. *Savage Pellucidar* (published in four parts as "The Return to Pellucidar," *Amazing Stories*, February 1942; "Men of the Bronze Age," *Amazing Stories*, March 1942; "Tiger Girl," *Amazing Stories*, April 1942; and "Savage Pellucidar," *Amazing Stories*, November 1963; Canaveral Press hardcover, 1963)

At the Earth's Core is a lost world fantasy, a hollow Earth adventure, and a savage epic.

In this first Pellucidar novel, mining heir David Innes and his inventor friend Abner Perry create what they deem an "iron mole" and break through 500 miles of Earth's crust into the inner world of Pellucidar. (David Innes and Abner Perry remind me of Tom Swift and his pal, Ned Newton.) Burroughs' ability to create a very detailed, colorful, senses-filling, and exotic world in Pellucidar pulls his readers through his narrative. A tremendously imaginative and creative man, Edgar Rice Burroughs is at or near his zenith in terms of detailed scientific romance in the pages of *At the Earth's Core*. Certainly, the author was working in a literary palette that influenced the great A. Merritt a few years later.

Archetypal elements found in Edgar Rice Burroughs' *At the Earth's Core* include, but are not limited to: a beautiful damsel in distress; creatures in need of help; incredibly beautiful settings; explorations, journeys, and quests; heroes and heroines; intruding humans; potential victims; prehistoric animals such as dinosaurs and other monstrous creatures; prehistoric native people and cultures; primitive, barbaric, exotic, untouched savagery; and a theme of "good versus evil."

First published in 1914, *At the Earth's Core* is influenced by the real-life events of World War I.

Beginning in the era of the scientific romance and savage epics of Verne, Wells, and Burroughs, another significant subgenre and eventually larger genre emerged that is very popular to this day. This was and is "steampunk." There was a resurgence of steampunk in the 1980s and the years that followed, and two of its primary practitioners are James P. Blaylock and Rudy Rucker. These two uniquely talented and highly regarded science fantasy and steampunk authors are literary direct descendants of Edgar Rice Burroughs. Note the back cover blurbs of their respective paperbacks, *The Digging Leviathan* (1984) and *The Hollow Earth* (1990).

From Blaylock's novel:

"Giles Peach is unique. He was born with a neat set of gills along either side of his neck—and webbed fingers. Giles Peach loves to read and he has the power to make all his fantasies come true. Unfortunately, his favorite author is Edgar Rice Burroughs . . ."

And then from Rucker's novel:

"In the year 1836, Mason Algiers Reynolds leaves his daddy's Virginia farm to seek his fortune. But misfortune brands him a murderer and forces him to seek sanctuary with his literary hero, Edgar Allan Poe, who soon has young Mason roped into an extraordinary balloon journey . . . and plummeting down to the unexplored center of the hollow Earth—crossing the gateway into a remarkable parallel world of strange wormlike creatures and unusual civilizations on an adventure more bizarre that anyone, even Poe, could possibly imagine."

In the creative genres of scientific romance, scientifiction, science fantasy and savage epics, Edgar Rice Burroughs stories are indeed archetypal fare.

The Land That Time Forgot (first published in the September 1918 issue of McCall's *The Blue Book Magazine*) is the first of the Caspak trilogy. "Caspak" is the name of the fictional setting, the South Pacific island on which the novel takes place. The remaining installments of the Caspak trilogy are as follows:

2. *The People That Time Forgot* (*The Blue Book Magazine*, October 1918); and

3. *Out of Time's Abyss* (*The Blue Book Magazine*, December 1912). All three novels of the Caspak trilogy were first collected together in the 1924 McClurg hardcover.

This epic adventure, this archetype, is defined by prehistoric men and beasts; ancient, prehistoric settings; complex civilizations; nature; evolution and metamorphosis; hostile natives; friendly natives in need of help; tribal life; privileged aristocrats; plots that involve trying to survive (finding food, water, and shelter); class and slavery structure; and trying to return to the "civilization" from which the travelers have come.

The story begins as an acutely danger-fraught World War I maritime adventure, and then evolves into a lost world fantasy reminiscent of Verne (*Journey to the Center of the Earth*, 1864; *The Mysterious Island*, 1874), Wells (*The Time Machine*, 1895); and Conan Doyle (Professor Challenger stories, 1912–1929). As is the case in his *At the Earth's Core*, Edgar Rice Burroughs provides colorfully inventive ideas, plotting, character types, and world building that expand the lost world fantasy genre in *The Land That Time Forgot*. H. P. Lovecraft's (1890–1937) *At the Mountains of Madness* showcases many thematic similarities to *The Land That Time Forgot*. For example, Burroughs' fictional island of Caspak is geographically located near Antarctica, the setting for *At the Mountains of Madness*. (Lovecraft's story first appeared in a heavily edited and compromised state in the February, March, and April 1936 issues of *Astounding Stories* pulp magazine.) In both stories there is an overriding thread that claims that the past never totally goes away.

Captured enemy Germans of World War I are also part of the complications of *The Land That Time Forgot*. The story begins as American Bowen J. Tyler, Jr., is on a vessel that is sunk by a German U-boat in the English Channel. Tyler and a woman, Lys La Rue (who becomes Tyler's love interest), are rescued by the British and the tale is underway.

The savage epics of Edgar Rice Burroughs, like the author's cosmic epics, provide profound archetypes that to this day define the very broad, multifaceted world of fantasy and science fiction storytelling and literature. The significance of Burroughs' archetypal contributions to barbarian fantasy, sword and sorcery, jungle adventure, and lost world fantasy—savage epics—is monumental.

Most importantly, these tales remain timeless, socially significant—and perhaps most importantly—entertaining to this day. In terms of fast-paced, captivating plotting, colorful characters, exotic locales, and pure entertainment and escapism, there really are no contemporary equivalents in the world of popular literature to the savage epics of Edgar Rice Burroughs' *Tarzan of the Apes*, *At the Earth's Core*, and *The Land That Time Forgot*.

GARYN G. ROBERTS, PH.D., *is a multi-awarded college and university professor, and author. Among his longtime interests and pursuits is the history of the pulp magazine (1896–1960). Roberts was presented with the Munsey Award in 2013 for his work in this field. He has authored, edited, and appeared in many hundreds of books and periodicals worldwide.*

Roberts lives in what was once a remote woodland and lake country of northern Wisconsin with his wife, Virginia, and two Golden Retriever dogs, Teddy and Spenser. He loves his grown children, David, Lauryn, and Morgan, as much as any dad ever has, and he misses them very much even though they have grown up and are thriving as highly talented and tremendously big-hearted people.

Born on President Dwight D. Eisenhower's birthday when Ike was President in 1958, Roberts read his first Edgar Rice Burroughs books in the 1960s. His life has never been the same since, and he shares a lifelong love of Edgar Rice Burroughs with his late friend and soul brother, Ray Bradbury (1920–2012). Roberts has lived in Wisconsin, Ohio, Minnesota, and Michigan.

TARZAN®
OF THE APES™
FRAZETTA

*With lightning speed an arm
that was banded layers of
iron muscle encircled the
huge neck, and the great
beast was raised from
behind, roaring and pawing
the air...*

Contents

To
EMMA HULBERT BURROUGHS

CHAPTER ONE
OUT TO SEA

I HAD THIS STORY from one who had no business to tell it to me, or to any other. I may credit the seductive influence of an old vintage upon the narrator for the beginning of it, and my own skeptical incredulity during the days that followed for the balance of the strange tale.

When my convivial host discovered that he had told me so much, and that I was prone to doubtfulness, his foolish pride assumed the task the old vintage had commenced, and so he unearthed written evidence in the form of musty manuscript, and dry official records of the British Colonial Office to support many of the salient features of his remarkable narrative.

I do not say the story is true, for I did not witness the happenings which it portrays, but the fact that in the telling of it to you I have taken fictitious names for the principal characters quite sufficiently evidences the sincerity of my own belief that it *may* be true.

The yellow, mildewed pages of the diary of a man long dead, and the records of the Colonial Office dovetail perfectly with the narrative of my convivial host, and so I give you the story as I painstakingly pieced it out from these several various agencies.

If you do not find it credible you will at least be as one with me in acknowledging that it is unique, remarkable, and interesting.

From the records of the Colonial Office and from the dead man's diary we learn that a certain young English nobleman, whom we shall call John Clayton, Lord Greystoke, was commissioned to make a peculiarly delicate investigation of conditions in a British West Coast African Colony from whose simple native inhabitants another European power was known to be recruiting soldiers for its native army, which it used solely for the forcible collection of rubber and ivory from the indigenous tribes along the Congo and the Aruwimi.

The natives of the British Colony complained that many of their young men were enticed away through the medium of fair and glowing promises, but that few if any ever returned to their families.

The Englishmen in Africa went even further, saying that these poor natives were held in virtual slavery, since when their terms of enlistment expired their ignorance was imposed upon by their white officers, and they were told that they had yet several years to serve.

And so the Colonial Office appointed John Clayton to a new post in British West Africa, but his confidential instructions centered on a thorough investigation of the unfair treatment of black British subjects by the officers of a friendly European power. Why he was sent, is, however, of little moment to this story, for he never made an investigation, nor, in fact, did he ever reach his destination.

Clayton was the type of Englishman that one likes best to associate with the noblest monuments of historic achievement upon a thousand victorious battlefields—a strong, virile man—mentally, morally, and physically.

In stature he was above the average height; his eyes were gray, his features regular and strong; his carriage that of perfect, robust health influenced by his years of army training.

Political ambition had caused him to seek transference from the army to the Colonial Office and so we find him, still young, entrusted with a delicate and important commission in the service of the Queen.

When he received this appointment he was both elated and appalled. The preferment seemed to him in the nature of a well-merited reward for painstaking and intelligent service, and as a stepping-stone to posts of greater importance and responsibility; but, on the other hand, he had been married to the Hon. Alice Rutherford for scarce a three months, and it was the thought of taking this fair young girl into the dangers and isolation of tropical Africa that dismayed and appalled him.

For her sake he would have refused the appointment, but she would not have it so. Instead she insisted that he accept, and, indeed, take her with him.

There were mothers and brothers and sisters, and aunts and cousins to express various opinions on the subject, but as to what they severally advised history is silent.

We know only that on a bright May morning in 1888, John, Lord Greystoke, and Lady Alice sailed from Dover on their way to Africa.

A month later they arrived at Freetown where they chartered a small sailing vessel, the *Fuwalda*, which was to bear them to their final destination.

And here John, Lord Greystoke, and Lady Alice, his wife, vanished from the eyes and from the knowledge of men.

Two months after they weighed anchor and cleared from the port of Freetown a half-dozen British war vessels were scouring the south Atlantic for trace of them or their little vessel, and it was almost immediately that the wreckage was found upon the shores of St. Helena which convinced the world that the *Fuwalda* had gone down with all on board, and hence the search was stopped ere it had scarce begun; though hope lingered in longing hearts for many years.

The *Fuwalda*, a barkentine of about one hundred tons, was a vessel of the type often seen in coastwise trade in the far southern Atlantic, their crews composed of the offscourings of the sea—unhanged murderers and cutthroats of every race and every nation.

The *Fuwalda* was no exception to the rule. Her officers were swarthy bullies, hating and hated by their crew. The captain, while a competent seaman, was a brute in his treatment of his men. He knew, or at least he used, but two arguments in his dealings with them—a belaying pin and a revolver—nor is it likely that the motley aggregation he signed would have understood aught else.

So it was that from the second day out from Freetown John Clayton and his young wife witnessed scenes upon the deck of the *Fuwalda* such as they had believed were never enacted outside the covers of printed stories of the sea.

It was on the morning of the second day that the first link was forged of what was destined to form a chain of circumstances ending in a life for one then unborn such as has probably never been paralleled in the history of man.

Two sailors were washing down the decks of the *Fuwalda*, the first mate was on duty, and the captain had stopped to speak with John Clayton and Lady Alice.

The men were working backwards toward the little party who were facing away from the sailors. Closer and closer they came, until one of them was directly behind the captain. In another moment he would have passed by and this strange narrative had never been recorded.

But just that instant the officer turned to leave Lord and Lady Greystoke, and, as he did so, tripped against the sailor and sprawled headlong upon the deck, overturning the water-pail so that he was drenched in its dirty contents.

For an instant the scene was ludicrous; but only for an instant. With a volley of awful oaths, his face suffused with the scarlet of mortification and rage, the captain regained his feet, and with a terrific blow felled the sailor to the deck.

The man was small and rather old, so that the brutality of the act was thus accentuated. The other seaman, however, was neither old nor small—a huge bear of a man, with fierce black mustachios, and a great bull neck set between massive shoulders.

As he saw his mate go down he crouched, and, with a low snarl, sprang upon the captain, crushing him to his knees with a single mighty blow.

From scarlet the officer's face went white, for this was mutiny; and mutiny he had met and subdued before in his brutal career. Without waiting to rise he whipped a revolver from his pocket, firing point-blank at the great mountain of muscle towering before him; but, quick as he was, John Clayton was almost as quick, so that the bullet which was intended for the sailor's heart lodged in the sailor's leg instead, for Lord Greystoke had struck down the captain's arm as he had seen the weapon flash in the sun.

Words passed between Clayton and the captain, the former making it plain that he was disgusted with the brutality displayed toward the crew, nor would he countenance anything further of the kind while he and Lady Greystoke remained passengers.

The captain was on the point of making an angry reply, but, thinking better of it, turned on his heel and black and scowling, strode aft.

He did not care to antagonize an English official, for the Queen's mighty arm wielded a punitive instrument which he could appreciate, and which he feared—England's far-reaching navy.

The two sailors picked themselves up, the older man assisting his wounded comrade to rise. The big fellow, who was known among his mates as Black Michael, tried his leg gingerly, and, finding that it bore his weight, turned to Clayton with a word of gruff thanks.

Though the fellow's tone was surly, his words were evidently well meant. Ere he had scarce finished his little speech he had turned and was limping off toward the forecastle with the very apparent intention of forestalling any further conversation.

They did not see him again for several days, nor did the captain vouchsafe them more than the surliest of grunts when he was forced to speak to them.

They messed in his cabin, as they had before the unfortunate occurrence;

but the captain was careful to see that his duties never permitted him to eat at the same time.

The other officers were coarse, illiterate fellows, but little above the villainous crew they bullied, and were only too glad to avoid social intercourse with the polished English noble and his lady, so that the Claytons were left very much to themselves.

This in itself accorded perfectly with their desires, but it also rather isolated them from the life of the little ship so that they were unable to keep in touch with the daily happenings which were to culminate so soon in bloody tragedy.

There was in the whole atmosphere of the craft that undefinable something which presages disaster. Outwardly, to the knowledge of the Claytons, all went on as before upon the little vessel; but that there was an undertow leading them toward some unknown danger both felt, though they did not speak of it to each other.

On the second day after the wounding of Black Michael, Clayton came on deck just in time to see the limp body of one of the crew being carried below by four of his fellows while the first mate, a heavy belaying pin in his hand, stood glowering at the little party of sullen sailors.

Clayton asked no questions—he did not need to—and the following day, as the great lines of a British battleship grew out of the distant horizon, he half determined to demand that he and Lady Alice be put aboard her, for his fears were steadily increasing that nothing but harm could result from remaining on the lowering, sullen *Fuwalda*.

Toward noon they were within speaking distance of the British vessel, but when Clayton had about decided to ask the captain to put them aboard her, the obvious ridiculousness of such a request became suddenly apparent. What reason could he give the officer commanding her majesty's ship for desiring to go back in the direction from which he had just come!

Faith, what if he told them that two insubordinate seamen had been roughly handled by their officers? They would but laugh in their sleeves and attribute his reason for wishing to leave the ship to but one thing—cowardice.

John Clayton, Lord Greystoke, did not ask to be transferred to the British man-of-war, and late in the afternoon he saw her upper works fade below the far horizon, but not before he learned that which confirmed his greatest fears, and caused him to curse the false pride which had restrained him from seeking safety for his young wife a few short hours before, when safety was within reach—a safety which was now gone forever.

It was midafternoon that brought the little old sailor, who had been felled by the captain a few days before, to where Clayton and his wife stood by the ship's side watching the ever diminishing outlines of the great battleship. The old fellow was polishing brasses, and as he came edging along until close to Clayton he said, in an undertone:

"'Ell's to pay, sir, on this 'ere craft, an' mark my word for it, sir. 'Ell's to pay."

"What do you mean, my good fellow?" asked Clayton.

"Wy, hasn't ye seen wats goin' on? Hasn't ye 'eard that devil's spawn of a capting an' 'is mates knockin' the bloomin' lights outen 'arf the crew?

"Two busted 'eads yeste'day, an' three today. Black Michael's as good as new agin an' 'e's not the bully to stand fer it, not 'e; an' mark my word for it, sir."

"You mean, my man, that the crew contemplates mutiny?" asked Clayton.

"Mutiny!" exclaimed the old fellow. "Mutiny! They means murder, sir, an' mark my word for it, sir."

"When?"

"Hit's comin,' sir; hit's comin' but I'm not a-sayin' wen, an' I've said too damned much now, but ye was a good sort t'other day an' I thought it no more'n right to warn ye. But keep a still tongue in yer 'ead an' when ye 'ear shootin' git below an' stay there.

"That's all, only keep a still tongue in yer 'ead, or they'll put a pill between yer ribs, an' mark my word for it, sir," and the old fellow went on with his polishing, which carried him away from where the Claytons were standing.

"Deuced cheerful outlook, Alice," said Clayton.

"You should warn the captain at once, John. Possibly the trouble may yet be averted," she said.

"I suppose I should, but yet from purely selfish motives I am almost prompted to 'keep a still tongue in my 'ead.' Whatever they do now they will spare us in recognition of my stand for this fellow Black Michael, but should they find that I had betrayed them there would be no mercy shown us, Alice."

"You have but one duty, John, and that lies in the interest of vested authority. If you do not warn the captain you are as much a party to whatever follows as though you had helped to plot and carry it out with your own head and hands."

"You do not understand, dear," replied Clayton. "It is of you I am thinking—there lies my first duty. The captain has brought this condition upon himself, so why then should I risk subjecting my wife to unthinkable horrors in a probably futile attempt to save him from his own brutal folly? You have no conception, dear, of what would follow were this pack of cutthroats to gain control of the *Fuwalda*."

"Duty is duty, my husband, and no amount of sophistries may change it. I would be a poor wife for an English lord were I to be responsible for his shirking a plain duty. I realize the danger which must follow, but I can face it with you—face it much more bravely than I could face the dishonor of always knowing that you might have averted a tragedy had you not neglected your duty."

"Have it as you will then, Alice," he answered, smiling. "Maybe we are borrowing trouble. While I do not like the looks of things on board this ship, they may not be so bad after all, for it is possible that the 'Ancient Mariner' was but voicing the desires of his wicked old heart rather than speaking of real facts.

"Mutiny on the high sea may have been common a hundred years ago, but in this good year 1888 it is the least likely of happenings.

"But there goes the captain to his cabin now. If I am going to warn him I might as well get the beastly job over for I have little stomach to talk with the brute at all."

So saying he strolled carelessly in the direction of the companionway through which the captain had passed, and a moment later was knocking at his door.

"Come in," growled the deep tones of that surly officer. And when Clayton had entered, and closed the door behind him:

"Well?"

"I have come to report the gist of a conversation I heard today, because I feel that, while there may be nothing to it, it is as well that you be fore-armed. In short, the men contemplate mutiny and murder."

"It's a lie!" roared the captain. "And if you have been interfering again with the discipline of this ship, or meddling in affairs that don't concern you, you can take the consequences, and be damned. I don't care whether you are an English lord or not. I'm captain of this here ship, and from now on you keep your meddling nose out of my business."

As he reached this peroration, the captain had worked himself up to such a frenzy of rage that he was fairly purple of face, and he shrieked the last words at the top of his voice, emphasizing his remarks by a loud thumping of the table with one huge fist, and shaking the other in Clayton's face.

Greystoke never turned a hair, but stood eyeing the excited man with level gaze.

"Captain Billings," he drawled finally, "if you will pardon my candor, I might remark that you are something of an ass, don't you know."

Whereupon he turned and left the captain with the same indifferent ease that was habitual with him, and which was more surely calculated to raise the ire of a man of Billings' class than a torrent of invective.

So, whereas the captain might easily have been brought to regret his hasty speech had Clayton attempted to conciliate him, his temper was now irrevocably set in the mold in which Clayton had left it, and the last chance of their working together for their common good and preservation of life was gone.

"Well, Alice," said Clayton, as he rejoined his wife, "if I had saved my breath I should likewise have saved myself a bit of a calling. The fellow proved most ungrateful. Fairly jumped at me like a mad dog.

"He and his blasted old ship may go hang, for aught I care; and until we are safely off the thing I shall spend my energies in looking after our own welfare. And I rather fancy the first step to that end should be to go to our cabin and look over my revolvers. I am sorry now that we packed the larger guns and the ammunition with the stuff below."

They found their quarters in a bad state of disorder. Clothing from their open boxes and bags strewed the little apartment, and even their beds had been torn to pieces.

"Evidently someone was more anxious about our belongings than we," said Clayton. "By jove, I wonder what the bounder was after. Let's have a look around, Alice, and see what's missing."

A thorough search revealed the fact that nothing had been taken but Clayton's two revolvers and the small supply of ammunition he had saved out for them.

"Those are the very things I most wish they had left us," said Clayton, "and the fact that they wished for them and them alone is the most sinister circumstance of all that have transpired to endanger us since we set foot on this miserable hulk."

"What are we to do, John?" asked his wife. "I shall not urge you to go again to the captain for I cannot see you affronted further. Possibly our best chance for salvation lies in maintaining a neutral position.

"If the officers are able to prevent a mutiny, we have nothing to fear, while if the mutineers are victorious our one slim hope lies in not having attempted to thwart or antagonize them."

"Right you are, Alice. We'll keep in the middle of the road."

As they fell to in an effort to straighten up their cabin, Clayton and his wife simultaneously noticed the corner of a piece of paper protruding from beneath the door of their quarters. As Clayton stooped to reach for it he was amazed to see it move further into the room, and then he realized that it was being pushed inward by someone from without.

Quickly and silently he stepped toward the door, but, as he reached for the knob to throw it open, his wife's hand fell upon his wrist.

"No, John," she whispered. "They do not wish to be seen, and so we cannot afford to see them. Do not forget that we are keeping to the middle of the road."

Clayton smiled and dropped his hand to his side. Thus they stood watching the little bit of white paper until it finally remained at rest upon the floor just inside the door.

Then Clayton stooped and picked it up. It was a bit of grimy, white paper roughly folded into a ragged square. Opening it they found a crude message printed in uncouth letters with many evidences of an unaccustomed task.

Translated, it was a warning to the Claytons to refrain from reporting the loss of the revolvers, or from repeating what the old sailor had told them—to refrain on pain of death.

"I rather imagine we'll be good," said Clayton with a rueful smile. "About all we can do is to sit tight and wait for whatever may come."

CHAPTER TWO
THE SAVAGE HOME

NOR DID THEY HAVE TO WAIT, for the next morning as Clayton was emerging on deck for his accustomed walk before breakfast, a shot rang out, and then another, and another.

The sight which met his eyes confirmed his worst fears. Facing the little knot of officers was the entire motley crew of the *Fuwalda*, and at their head stood Black Michael.

At the first volley from the officers the men ran for shelter, and from points of vantage behind masts, wheelhouse and cabin they returned the fire of the five men who represented the hated authority of the ship.

Two of their number had gone down before the captain's revolver. They lay where they had fallen between the combatants.

Presently the first mate lunged forward upon his face, and at a cry of command from Black Michael the bloodthirsty ruffians charged the remaining four. The crew had been able to muster but six firearms, so most of them were armed with boat hooks, axes, hatchets, and crowbars.

The captain had emptied his revolver and was reloading as the charge was made. The second mate's gun had jammed, and so there were but two weapons opposed to the mutineers as they rapidly approached the officers, who now started to give back before the infuriated rush of their men.

Both sides were cursing and swearing in a frightful manner, which, together with the reports of the firearms and the screams and groans of the wounded, turned the deck of the *Fuwalda* to the likeness of a madhouse.

Before the officers had taken a dozen backward steps the men were upon them. An ax in the hands of a burly sailor cleft the captain from forehead to chin, and an instant later the others were down; dead or wounded from dozens of blows and bullet wounds.

Short and grisly had been the work of the mutineers of the *Fuwalda*, and through it all John Clayton had stood leaning carelessly beside the companionway puffing meditatively upon his pipe as though he had been but watching an indifferent cricket match.

As the last officer went down he bethought him that it was time that he returned to his wife lest some members of the crew find her alone below.

Though outwardly calm and indifferent, Clayton was inwardly apprehensive and wrought up, for he feared for his wife's safety at the hands of these ignorant half-brutes into whose hands fate had so remorselessly thrown them.

As he turned to descend the ladder he was surprised to see his wife standing on the steps almost at his side.

"How long have you been here, Alice?"

"Since the beginning," she replied. "How awful, John. Oh, how awful! What can we hope for at the hands of such as those?"

"Breakfast, I hope," he answered, smiling bravely in an attempt to allay her fears.

"At least," he added, "I'm going to ask them. Come with me, Alice. We must not let them think we expect any but courteous treatment."

The men had by this time surrounded the dead and wounded officers, and without either partiality or compassion proceeded to throw both living and dead over the sides of the vessel. With equal heartlessness they disposed of their own wounded and the bodies of the three sailors to whom a merciful Providence had vouchsafed instant death before the bullets of the officers.

Presently one of the crew spied the approaching Claytons, and with a cry of: "Here's two more for the fishes," rushed toward them with uplifted ax.

But Black Michael was even quicker, so that the fellow went down with a bullet in his back before he had taken a half-dozen steps.

With a loud roar, Black Michael attracted the attention of the others, and, pointing to Lord and Lady Greystoke, cried:

"These here are my friends, and they are to be left alone. D'ye understand?

"I'm captain of this ship now, an' what I says goes," he added, turning to Clayton. "Just keep to yourselves, and nobody'll harm ye," and he looked threateningly on his fellows.

The Claytons heeded Black Michael's instructions so well that they saw but little of the crew and knew nothing of the plans the men were making.

Occasionally they heard faint echoes of brawls and quarreling among the mutineers, and on two occasions the vicious bark of firearms rang out on the still air. But Black Michael was a fit leader for this heterogenous band of cutthroats, and, withal, held them in fair subjection to his rule.

On the fifth day following the murder of the ship's officers, land was sighted by the lookout. Whether island or mainland, Black Michael did not know, but he announced to Clayton that if investigation showed that the place was habitable he and Lady Greystoke were to be put ashore with their belongings.

"You'll be all right there for a few months," he explained, "and by that time we'll have been able to make an inhabited coast somewheres and scatter a bit. Then I'll see that yer gover'ment's notified where you be an' they'll soon send a man-o'-war to fetch ye off.

"You may be all right, but it would be a hard matter to land you in civilization without a lot o' questions being asked, an' none o' us here has any very convincin' answers up our sleeves."

Clayton remonstrated against the inhumanity of landing them upon an unknown shore to be left to the mercies of savage beasts, and, possibly, still more savage men.

But his words were of no avail, and only tended to anger Black Michael, so he was forced to desist and make the best he could of a bad situation.

About three o'clock in the afternoon they came about off a beautiful wooded shore opposite the mouth of what appeared to be a landlocked harbor.

Black Michael sent a small boat filled with men to sound the entrance in an effort to determine if the *Fuwalda* could be safely worked through the entrance.

In about an hour they returned and reported deep water through the passage as well as far into the little basin.

Before dark the barkentine lay peacefully at anchor upon the bosom of the still, mirrorlike surface of the harbor.

The surrounding shores were beautiful with semitropical verdure, while in the distance the country rose from the ocean in hill and tableland, almost uniformly clothed by primeval forest.

No signs of habitation were visible, but that the land might easily support human life was evidenced by the abundant bird and animal life of which the watchers on the *Fuwalda*'s deck caught occasional glimpses, as well as by the shimmer of a little river which emptied into the harbor, insuring fresh water in plentitude.

As darkness settled upon the earth, Clayton and Lady Alice still stood by the ship's rail in silent contemplation of their future abode. From the dark shadows of the mighty forest came the wild calls of savage beasts—the deep roar of the lion, and, occasionally, the shrill scream of a panther.

The woman shrank closer to the man in terror-stricken anticipation of the horrors lying in wait for them in the awful blackness of the nights to come, when the two should be alone upon that wild and lonely shore.

Later in the evening Black Michael joined them long enough to instruct them to make their preparations for landing on the morrow. They tried to persuade him to take them to some more hospitable coast near enough to civilization so that they might hope to fall into friendly hands. But no pleas, or threats, or promises of reward could move him.

"I am the only man aboard who would not rather see ye both safely dead, and, while I know that's the sensible way to make sure of our own necks, yet Black Michael's not the man to forget a favor. Ye saved my life once, and in return I'm goin' to spare yours, but that's all I can do.

"The men won't stand for any more, and if we don't get ye landed pretty quick they may even change their minds about giving ye that much show. I'll put all yer stuff ashore with you as well as cookin' utensils an' some old sails for tents, an' enough grub to last you until you can find fruit and game.

"So that with your guns for protection, you ought to be able to live here easy enough until help comes. When I get safely hid away I'll see to it that the British gover'ment learns about where you be; for the life of me I couldn't tell 'em exactly where, for I don't know myself. But they'll find you all right."

After he had left them they went silently below, each wrapped in gloomy forebodings.

Clayton did not believe that Black Michael had the slightest intention of notifying the British government of their whereabouts, nor was he any too sure but that some treachery was contemplated for the following day when they should be on shore with the sailors who would have to accompany them with their belongings.

Once out of Black Michael's sight any of the men might strike them down, and still leave Black Michael's conscience clear.

And even should they escape that fate was it not but to be faced with far graver dangers? Alone, he might hope to survive for years; for he was a strong, athletic man.

But what of Alice, and that other little life so soon to be launched amidst the hardships and grave dangers of a primeval world?

The man shuddered as he meditated upon the awful gravity, the fearful helplessness, of their situation. But it was a merciful Providence which prevented him from foreseeing the hideous reality which awaited them in the grim depths of that gloomy wood.

Early next morning their numerous chests and boxes were hoisted on deck and lowered to waiting small boats for transportation to shore.

There was a great quantity and variety of stuff, as the Claytons had expected a possible five to eight years' residence in their new home, so that, in addition to the many necessities they had brought, there were also many luxuries.

Black Michael was determined that nothing belonging to the Claytons should be left on board. Whether out of compassion for them, or in furtherance of his own self-interests, it were difficult to say.

There is no question but that the presence of property of a missing British official upon a suspicious vessel would have been a difficult thing to explain in any civilized port in the world.

So zealous was he in his efforts to carry out his intentions that he insisted upon the return of Clayton's revolvers to him by the sailors in whose possession they were.

Into the small boats were also loaded salt meats and biscuit, with a small supply of potatoes and beans, matches, and cooking vessels, a chest of tools, and the old sails which Black Michael had promised them.

As though himself fearing the very thing which Clayton had suspected, Black Michael accompanied them to shore, and was the last to leave them when the small boats, having filled the ship's casks with fresh water, were pushed out toward the waiting *Fuwalda*.

As the boats moved slowly over the smooth waters of the bay, Clayton and his wife stood silently watching their departure—in the breasts of both a feeling of impending disaster and utter hopelessness.

And behind them, over the edge of a low ridge, other eyes watched—close-set, wicked eyes, gleaming beneath shaggy brows.

As the *Fuwalda* passed through the narrow entrance to the harbor and out of sight behind a projecting point, Lady Alice threw her arms about Clayton's neck and burst into uncontrolled sobs.

Bravely had she faced the dangers of the mutiny; with heroic fortitude she had looked into the terrible future; but now that the horror of absolute solitude was upon them, her overwrought nerves gave way, and the reaction came.

He did not attempt to check her tears. It were better that nature have her way in relieving these long-pent emotions, and it was many minutes before the girl—little more than a child she was—could again gain mastery of herself.

"Oh, John," she cried at last, "the horror of it. What are we to do? What are we to do?"

"There is but one thing to do, Alice," and he spoke as quietly as though they were sitting in their snug living room at home, "and that is work. Work must be our salvation. We must not give ourselves time to think, for in that direction lies madness.

"We must work and wait. I am sure that relief will come, and come quickly, when once it is apparent that the *Fuwalda* has been lost, even though Black Michael does not keep his word to us."

"But John, if it were only you and I," she sobbed, "we could endure it I know; but—"

"Yes, dear," he answered, gently, "I have been thinking of that, also; but we must face it, as we must face whatever comes, bravely and with the utmost confidence in our ability to cope with circumstances whatever they may be.

"Hundreds of thousands of years ago our ancestors of the dim and distant past faced the same problems which we must face, possibly in these same primeval forests. That we are here today evidences their victory.

"What they did may we not do? And even better, for are we not armed with ages of superior knowledge, and have we not the means of protection, defense, and sustenance which science has given us, but of which they were totally ignorant? What they accomplished, Alice, with instruments and weapons of stone and bone, surely that may we accomplish also."

"Ah, John, I wish that I might be a man with a man's philosophy, but I am but a woman, seeing with my heart rather than my head, and all that I can see is too horrible, too unthinkable to put into words.

"I only hope you are right, John. I will do my best to be a brave primeval woman, a fit mate for the primeval man."

Clayton's first thought was to arrange a sleeping shelter for the night; something which might serve to protect them from prowling beasts of prey.

He opened the box containing his rifles and ammunition, that they might both be armed against possible attack while at work, and then together they sought a location for their first night's sleeping place.

A hundred yards from the beach was a little level spot, fairly free of trees; here they decided eventually to build a permanent house, but for the time being they both thought it best to construct a little platform in the trees out of reach of the larger of the savage beasts in whose realm they were.

To this end Clayton selected four trees which formed a rectangle about eight feet square, and cutting long branches from other trees he constructed a framework around them, about ten feet from the ground, fastening the ends of the branches securely to the trees by means of rope, a quantity of which Black Michael had furnished him from the hold of the *Fuwalda*.

Across this framework Clayton placed other smaller branches quite close together. This platform he paved with the huge fronds of elephant's ear which grew in profusion about them, and over the fronds he laid a great sail folded into several thicknesses.

Seven feet higher he constructed a similar, though lighter platform to serve as roof, and from the sides of this he suspended the balance of his sailcloth for walls.

When completed he had a rather snug little nest, to which he carried their blankets and some of the lighter luggage.

It was now late in the afternoon, and the balance of the daylight hours were devoted to the building of a rude ladder by means of which Lady Alice could mount to her new home.

All during the day the forest about them had been filled with excited birds of brilliant plumage, and dancing, chattering monkeys, who watched these new arrivals and their wonderful nest-building operations with every mark of keenest interest and fascination.

Notwithstanding that both Clayton and his wife kept a sharp outlook they saw nothing of larger animals, though on two occasions they had seen their little simian neighbors come screaming and chattering from the nearby ridge, casting affrighted glances back over their little shoulders, and evincing as plainly as though by speech that they were fleeing some terrible thing which lay concealed there.

Just before dusk Clayton finished his ladder, and, filling a great basin with water from the nearby stream, the two mounted to the comparative safety of their aerial chamber.

As it was quite warm, Clayton had left the side curtains thrown back over the roof, and as they squatted, like Turks, upon their blankets, Lady Alice, straining her eyes into the darkening shadows of the wood, suddenly reached out and grasped Clayton's arms.

"John," she whispered, "look! What is it, a man?"

As Clayton turned his eyes in the direction she indicated, he saw silhouetted dimly against the shadows beyond, a great figure standing upright upon the ridge.

For a moment it stood as though listening and then turned slowly, and melted into the shadows of the jungle.

"What is it, John?"

"I do not know, Alice," he answered gravely, "it is too dark to see so far, and it may have been but a shadow cast by the rising moon."

"No, John, if it was not a man it was some huge and grotesque mockery of man. Oh, I am afraid."

He gathered her in his arms, whispering words of courage and love into her ears, for the greatest pain of their misfortunes, to Clayton, was the mental anguish of his young wife. Himself brave and fearless, yet was he able to appreciate the awful suffering which fear entails—a rare gift, though but one of many which had made the young Lord Greystoke respected and loved by all who knew him.

Soon after, he lowered the curtain walls, tying them securely to the trees so that, except for a little opening toward the beach, they were entirely enclosed.

As it was now pitch dark within their tiny aerie they lay down upon their blankets to try to wrest, through sleep, a brief respite of forgetfulness.

Clayton lay facing the opening at the front, a rifle and a brace of revolvers at his hand.

Scarcely had they closed their eyes than the terrifying cry of a panther rang out from the jungle behind them. Closer and closer it came until they could hear the great beast directly beneath them. For an hour or more they heard it sniffing and clawing at the trees which supported their platform, but at last it roamed away across the beach, where Clayton could see it clearly in the brilliant moonlight—a great, handsome beast, the largest he had ever seen.

During the long hours of darkness they caught but fitful snatches of sleep, for the night noises of a great jungle teeming with myriad animal life kept their overwrought nerves on edge, so that a hundred times they were startled to wakefulness by piercing screams, or the stealthy moving of great bodies beneath them.

CHAPTER THREE
LIFE AND DEATH

MORNING FOUND THEM but little, if at all refreshed, though it was with a feeling of intense relief that they saw the day dawn.

As soon as they had made their meager breakfast of salt pork, coffee, and biscuit, Clayton commenced work upon their house, for he realized that they could hope for no safety and no peace of mind at night until four strong walls effectually barred the jungle life from them.

The task was an arduous one and required the better part of a month, though he built but one small room. He constructed his cabin of small logs about six inches in diameter, stopping the chinks with clay which he found at the depth of a few feet beneath the surface soil.

At one end he built a fireplace of small stones from the beach. These also he set in clay and when the house had been entirely completed he applied a coating of the clay to the entire outside surface to the thickness of four inches.

In the window opening he set small branches about an inch in diameter both vertically and horizontally, and so woven that they formed a substantial grating that could withstand the strength of a powerful animal. Thus they obtained air and proper ventilation without fear of lessening the safety of their cabin.

The A-shaped roof was thatched with small branches laid close together and over these long jungle grass and palm fronds, with a final coating of clay.

The door he built of pieces of the packing-boxes which had held their belongings, nailing one piece upon another, the grain of contiguous layers running transversely, until he had a solid body some three inches thick and of such great strength that they were both moved to laughter as they gazed upon it.

Here the greatest difficulty confronted Clayton, for he had no means whereby to hang his massive door now that he had built it. After two days' work, however, he succeeded in fashioning two massive hardwood hinges, and with these he hung the door so that it opened and closed easily.

The stuccoing and other final touches were added after they moved into the house, which they had done as soon as the roof was on, piling their boxes before the door at night and thus having a comparatively safe and comfortable habitation.

The building of a bed, chairs, table, and shelves was a relatively easy matter, so that by the end of the second month they were well settled, and, but for the constant dread of attack by wild beasts and the ever growing loneliness, they were not uncomfortable or unhappy.

At night great beasts snarled and roared about their tiny cabin, but, so accustomed may one become to oft-repeated noises, that soon they paid little attention to them, sleeping soundly the whole night through.

Thrice had they caught fleeting glimpses of great manlike figures like that of the first night, but never at sufficiently close range to know positively whether the half-seen forms were those of man or brute.

The brilliant birds and the little monkeys had become accustomed to their new acquaintances, and as they had evidently never seen human beings before they presently, after their first fright had worn off, approached closer and closer, impelled by that strange curiosity which dominates the wild creatures of the forest and the jungle and the plain, so that within the first month several of the birds had gone so far as even to accept morsels of food from the friendly hands of the Claytons.

One afternoon, while Clayton was working upon an addition to their cabin, for he contemplated building several more rooms, a number of their grotesque little friends came shrieking and scolding through the trees from the direction of the ridge. Ever as they fled they cast fearful glances back of them, and finally they stopped near Clayton jabbering excitedly to him as though to warn him of approaching danger.

At last he saw it, the thing the little monkeys so feared—the man-brute of which the Claytons had caught occasional fleeting glimpses.

It was approaching through the jungle in a semi-erect position, now and then placing the backs of its closed fists upon the ground—a great anthropoid ape, and, as it advanced, it emitted deep guttural growls and an occasional low barking sound.

Clayton was at some distance from the cabin, having come to fell a particularly perfect tree for his building operations. Grown careless from months of continued safety, during which time he had seen no dangerous animals during the daylight hours, he had left his rifles and revolvers all within the little cabin, and now that he saw the great ape crashing through the underbrush directly toward him, and from a direction which practically cut him off from escape, he felt a vague little shiver play up and down his spine.

He knew that, armed only with an ax, his chances with this ferocious monster were small indeed—and Alice; O God, he thought, what will become of Alice?

There was yet a slight chance of reaching the cabin. He turned and ran toward it, shouting an alarm to his wife to run in and close the great door in case the ape cut off his retreat.

Lady Greystoke had been sitting a little way from the cabin, and when she heard his cry she looked up to see the ape springing with almost incredible swiftness, for so large and awkward an animal, in an effort to head off Clayton.

With a low cry she sprang toward the cabin, and, as she entered, gave a backward glance which filled her soul with terror, for the brute had intercepted her husband, who now stood at bay grasping his ax with both hands ready to swing it upon the infuriated animal when he should make his final charge.

"Close and bolt the door, Alice," cried Clayton. "I can finish this fellow with my ax."

But he knew he was facing a horrible death, and so did she.

The ape was a great bull, weighing probably three hundred pounds. His nasty, close-set eyes gleamed hatred from beneath his shaggy brows, while his great canine fangs were bared in a horrid snarl as he paused a moment before his prey.

Over the brute's shoulder Clayton could see the doorway of his cabin, not twenty paces distant, and a great wave of horror and fear swept over him as he saw his young wife emerge, armed with one of his rifles.

She had always been afraid of firearms, and would never touch them, but now she rushed toward the ape with the fearlessness of a lioness protecting its young.

"Back, Alice," shouted Clayton, "for God's sake, go back."

But she would not heed, and just then the ape charged, so that Clayton could say no more.

The man swung his ax with all his mighty strength, but the powerful brute seized it in those terrible hands, and tearing it from Clayton's grasp hurled it far to one side.

With an ugly snarl he closed upon his defenseless victim, but ere his fangs had reached the throat they thirsted for, there was a sharp report and a bullet entered the ape's back between his shoulders.

Throwing Clayton to the ground the beast turned upon his new enemy. There before him stood the terrified girl vainly trying to fire another bullet into the animal's body; but she did not understand the mechanism of the firearm, and the hammer fell futilely upon an empty cartridge.

Screaming with rage and pain, the ape flew at the delicate woman, who went down beneath him to merciful unconsciousness.

Almost simultaneously Clayton regained his feet, and without thought of the utter hopelessness of it, he rushed forward to drag the ape from his wife's prostrate form.

With little or no effort he succeeded, and the great bulk rolled inertly upon the turf before him—the ape was dead. The bullet had done its work.

A hasty examination of his wife revealed no marks upon her, and Clayton decided that the huge brute had died the instant he had sprung toward Alice.

Gently he lifted his wife's still unconscious form, and bore her to the little cabin, but it was fully two hours before she regained consciousness.

Her first words filled Clayton with vague apprehension. For some time after regaining her senses, Alice gazed wonderingly about the interior of the little cabin, and then, with a satisfied sigh; said:

"O, John, it is so good to be really home! I have had an awful dream, dear. I thought we were no longer in London, but in some horrible place where great beasts attacked us."

"There, there, Alice," he said, stroking her forehead, "try to sleep again, and do not worry your head about bad dreams."

That night a little son was born in the tiny cabin beside the primeval forest, while a leopard screamed before the door, and the deep notes of a lion's roar sounded from beyond the ridge.

Lady Greystoke never recovered from the shock of the great ape's attack, and, though she lived for a year after her baby was born, she was never again outside the cabin, nor did she ever fully realize that she was not in England.

Sometimes she would question Clayton as to the strange noises of the nights; the absence of servants and friends, and the strange rudeness of the furnishings within her room, but, though he made no effort to deceive her, never could she grasp the meaning of it all.

In other ways she was quite rational, and the joy and happiness she took in the possession of her little son and the constant attentions of her husband made that year a very happy one for her, the happiest of her young life.

That it would have been beset by worries and apprehension had she been in full command of her mental faculties Clayton well knew; so that while he suffered terribly to see her so, there were times when he was almost glad, for her sake, that she could not understand.

Long since had he given up any hope of rescue, except through accident. With unremitting zeal he had worked to beautify the interior of the cabin.

Skins of lion and panther covered the floor. Cupboards and bookcases lined the walls. Odd vases made by his own hand from the clay of the region held beautiful tropical flowers. Curtains of grass and bamboo covered the windows, and, most arduous task of all, with his meager assortment of tools he had fashioned lumber to neatly seal the walls and ceiling and lay a smooth floor within the cabin.

That he had been able to turn his hands at all to such unaccustomed labor was a source of mild wonder to him. But he loved the work because it was for her and the tiny life that had come to cheer them, though adding a hundredfold to his responsibilities and to the terribleness of their situation.

During the year that followed, Clayton was several times attacked by the great apes which now seemed to continually infest the vicinity of the cabin; but as he never again ventured outside without both rifle and revolvers he had little fear of the huge beasts.

He had strengthened the window protections and fitted a unique wooden lock to the cabin door, so that when he hunted for game and fruits, as it was constantly necessary for him to do to insure sustenance, he had no fear that any animal could break into the little home.

At first he shot much of the game from the cabin windows, but toward the end the animals learned to fear the strange lair from whence issued the terrifying thunder of his rifle.

In his leisure Clayton read, often aloud to his wife, from the store of books he had brought for their new home. Among these were many for little children—picture books, primers, readers—for they had known that their little child would be old enough for such before they might hope to return to England.

At other times Clayton wrote in his diary, which he had always been accustomed to keep in French, and in which he recorded the details of their strange life. This book he kept locked in a little metal box.

A year from the day her little son was born Lady Alice passed quietly away in the night. So peaceful was her end that it was hours before Clayton could awake to a realization that his wife was dead.

The horror of the situation came to him very slowly, and it is doubtful that he ever fully realized the enormity of his sorrow and the fearful responsibility that had devolved upon him with the care of that wee thing, his son, still a nursing babe.

The last entry in his diary was made the morning following her death, and there he recites the sad details in a matter-of-fact way that adds to the pathos of it; for it breathes a tired apathy born of long sorrow and hopelessness, which even this cruel blow could scarcely awake to further suffering:

My little son is crying for nourishment—O Alice, Alice, what shall I do?

And as John Clayton wrote the last words his hand was destined ever to pen, he dropped his head wearily upon his outstretched arms where they rested upon the table he had built for her who lay still and cold in the bed beside him.

For a long time no sound broke the deathlike stillness of the jungle midday save the piteous wailing of the tiny man-child.

CHAPTER FOUR
THE APES

IN THE FOREST OF THE TABLELAND a mile back from the ocean old
Kerchak the Ape was on a rampage of rage among his people.

The younger and lighter members of his tribe scampered to the
higher branches of the great trees to escape his wrath; risking their lives
upon branches that scarce supported their weight rather than face old
Kerchak in one of his fits of uncontrolled anger.

The other males scattered in all directions, but not before the infuriated
brute had felt the vertebra of one snap between his great, foaming jaws.

A luckless young female slipped from an insecure hold upon a high
branch and came crashing to the ground almost at Kerchak's feet.

With a wild scream he was upon her, tearing a great piece from her
side with his mighty teeth, and striking her viciously upon her head and
shoulders with a broken tree limb until her skull was crushed to a jelly.

And then he spied Kala, who, returning from a search for food with
her young babe, was ignorant of the state of the mighty male's temper
until suddenly the shrill warnings of her fellows caused her to scamper
madly for safety.

But Kerchak was close upon her, so close that he had almost grasped
her ankle had she not made a furious leap far into space from one tree to
another—a perilous chance which apes seldom if ever take, unless so closely
pursued by danger that there is no alternative.

She made the leap successfully, but as she grasped the limb of the further
tree the sudden jar loosened the hold of the tiny babe where it clung
frantically to her neck, and she saw the little thing hurled, turning and
twisting, to the ground thirty feet below.

With a low cry of dismay Kala rushed headlong to its side, thoughtless
now of the danger from Kerchak; but when she gathered the wee, mangled
form to her bosom life had left it.

With low moans, she sat cuddling the body to her; nor did Kerchak
attempt to molest her. With the death of the babe his fit of demoniacal
rage passed as suddenly as it had seized him.

Kerchak was a huge king ape, weighing perhaps three hundred and fifty pounds. His forehead was extremely low and receding, his eyes bloodshot, small and close set to his coarse, flat nose; his ears large and thin, but smaller than most of his kind.

His awful temper and his mighty strength made him supreme among the little tribe into which he had been born some twenty years before.

Now that he was in his prime, there was no simian in all the mighty forest through which he roved that dared contest his right to rule, nor did the other and larger animals molest him.

Old Tantor, the elephant, alone of all the wild savage life, feared him not—and he alone did Kerchak fear. When Tantor trumpeted, the great ape scurried with his fellows high among the trees of the second terrace.

The tribe of anthropoids over which Kerchak ruled with an iron hand and bared fangs, numbered some six or eight families, each family consisting of an adult male with his wives and their young, numbering in all some sixty or seventy apes.

Kala was the youngest wife of a male called Tublat, meaning broken nose, and the child she had seen dashed to death was her first; for she was but nine or ten years old.

Notwithstanding her youth, she was large and powerful—a splendid, clean-limbed animal, with a round, high forehead, which denoted more intelligence than most of her kind possessed. So, also, she had a great capacity for mother love and mother sorrow.

But she was still an ape, a huge, fierce, terrible beast of a species closely allied to the gorilla, yet more intelligent; which, with the strength of their cousin, made her kind the most fearsome of those awe-inspiring progenitors of man.

When the tribe saw that Kerchak's rage had ceased they came slowly down from their arboreal retreats and pursued again the various occupations which he had interrupted.

The young played and frolicked about among the trees and bushes. Some of the adults lay prone upon the soft mat of dead and decaying vegetation which covered the ground, while others turned over pieces of fallen branches and clods of earth in search of the small bugs and reptiles which formed a part of their food.

Others, again, searched the surrounding trees for fruit, nuts, small birds, and eggs.

They had passed an hour or so thus when Kerchak called them together, and, with a word of command to them to follow him, set off toward the sea.

They traveled for the most part upon the ground, where it was open, following the path of the great elephants whose comings and goings break the only roads through those tangled mazes of bush, vine, creeper, and tree. When they walked it was with a rolling, awkward motion, placing the knuckles of their closed hands upon the ground and swinging their ungainly bodies forward.

But when the way was through the lower trees they moved more swiftly, swinging from branch to branch with the agility of their smaller cousins, the monkeys. And all the way Kala carried her little dead baby hugged closely to her breast.

It was shortly after noon when they reached a ridge overlooking the beach where below them lay the tiny cottage which was Kerchak's goal.

He had seen many of his kind go to their deaths before the loud noise made by the little black stick in the hands of the strange white ape who lived in that wonderful lair, and Kerchak had made up his brute mind to own that death-dealing contrivance, and to explore the interior of the mysterious den.

He wanted, very, very much, to feel his teeth sink into the neck of the queer animal that he had learned to hate and fear, and because of this, he came often with his tribe to reconnoiter, waiting for a time when the white ape should be off his guard.

Of late they had quit attacking, or even showing themselves; for every time they had done so in the past the little stick had roared out its terrible message of death to some member of the tribe.

Today there was no sign of the man about, and from where they watched they could see that the cabin door was open. Slowly, cautiously, and noiselessly they crept through the jungle toward the little cabin.

There were no growls, no fierce screams of rage—the little black stick had taught them to come quietly lest they awaken it.

On, on they came until Kerchak himself slunk stealthily to the very door and peered within. Behind him were two males, and then Kala, closely straining the little dead form to her breast.

Inside the den they saw the strange white ape lying half across a table, his head buried in his arms; and on the bed lay a figure covered by a sailcloth, while from a tiny rustic cradle came the plaintive wailing of a babe.

Noiselessly Kerchak entered, crouching for the charge; and then John Clayton rose with a sudden start and faced them.

The sight that met his eyes must have frozen him with horror, for there, within the door, stood three great bull apes, while behind them crowded many more; how many he never knew, for his revolvers were hanging on the far wall beside his rifle, and Kerchak was charging.

When the king ape released the limp form which had been John Clayton, Lord Greystoke, he turned his attention toward the little cradle; but Kala was there before him, and when he would have grasped the child she snatched it herself, and before he could intercept her she had bolted through the door and taken refuge in a high tree.

As she took up the little live baby of Alice Clayton she dropped the dead body of her own into the empty cradle; for the wail of the living had answered the call of universal motherhood within her wild breast which the dead could not still.

High up among the branches of a mighty tree she hugged the shrieking infant to her bosom, and soon the instinct that was as dominant in this fierce female as it had been in the breast of his tender and beautiful mother—the instinct of mother love—reached out to the tiny man-child's half-formed understanding, and he became quiet.

Then hunger closed the gap between them, and the son of an English lord and an English lady nursed at the breast of Kala, the great ape.

In the meantime the beasts within the cabin were warily examining the contents of this strange lair.

Once satisfied that Clayton was dead, Kerchak turned his attention to the thing which lay upon the bed, covered by a piece of sailcloth.

Gingerly he lifted one corner of the shroud, but when he saw the body of the woman beneath he tore the cloth roughly from her form and seized the still, white throat in his huge, hairy hands.

A moment he let his fingers sink deep into the cold flesh, and then, realizing that she was already dead, he turned from her, to examine the contents of the room; nor did he again molest the body of either Lady Alice or Sir John.

The rifle hanging upon the wall caught his first attention; it was for this strange, death-dealing thunder-stick that he had yearned for months; but now that it was within his grasp he scarcely had the temerity to seize it.

Cautiously he approached the thing, ready to flee precipitately should it speak in its deep roaring tones, as he had heard it speak before, the last words to those of his kind who, through ignorance or rashness, had attacked the wonderful white ape that had borne it.

Deep in the beast's intelligence was something which assured him that the thunder-stick was only dangerous when in the hands of one who could manipulate it, but yet it was several minutes ere he could bring himself to touch it.

Instead, he walked back and forth along the floor before it, turning his head so that never once did his eyes leave the object of his desire.

Using his long arms as a man uses crutches, and rolling his huge carcass from side to side with each stride, the great king ape paced to and fro, uttering deep growls, occasionally punctuated with the ear-piercing scream, than which there is no more terrifying noise in all the jungle.

Presently he halted before the rifle. Slowly he raised a huge hand until it almost touched the shining barrel, only to withdraw it once more and continue his hurried pacing.

It was as though the great brute by this show of fearlessness, and through the medium of his wild voice, was endeavoring to bolster up his courage to the point which would permit him to take the rifle in his hand.

Again he stopped, and this time succeeded in forcing his reluctant hand to the cold steel, only to snatch it away almost immediately and resume his restless beat.

Time after time this strange ceremony was repeated, but on each occasion with increased confidence, until, finally, the rifle was torn from its hook and lay in the grasp of the great brute.

Finding that it harmed him not, Kerchak began to examine it closely. He felt of it from end to end, peered down the black depths of the muzzle, fingered the sights, the breech, the stock, and finally the trigger.

During all these operations the apes who had entered sat huddled near the door watching their chief, while those outside strained and crowded to catch a glimpse of what transpired within.

Suddenly Kerchak's finger closed upon the trigger. There was a deafening roar in the little room and the apes at and beyond the door fell over one another in their wild anxiety to escape.

Kerchak was equally frightened, so frightened, in fact, that he quite forgot to throw aside the author of that fearful noise, but bolted for the door with it tightly clutched in one hand.

As he passed through the opening, the front sight of the rifle caught upon the edge of the in-swung door with sufficient force to close it tightly after the fleeing ape.

When Kerchak came to a halt a short distance from the cabin and discovered that he still held the rifle, he dropped it as he might have dropped a red-hot iron, nor did he again attempt to recover it—the noise was too much for his brute nerves; but he was now quite convinced that the terrible stick was quite harmless by itself if left alone.

It was an hour before the apes could again bring themselves to approach the cabin to continue their investigations, and when they finally did so, they found to their chagrin that the door was closed and so securely fastened that they could not force it.

The cleverly constructed latch which Clayton had made for the door had sprung as Kerchak passed out; nor could the apes find means of ingress through the heavily barred windows.

After roaming about the vicinity for a short time, they started back for the deeper forests and the higher land from whence they had come.

Kala had not once come to earth with her little adopted babe, but now Kerchak called to her to descend with the rest, and as there was no note of anger in his voice she dropped lightly from branch to branch and joined the others on their homeward march.

Those of the apes who attempted to examine Kala's strange baby were repulsed with bared fangs and low menacing growls, accompanied by words of warning from Kala.

When they assured her that they meant the child no harm she permitted them to come close, but would not allow them to touch her charge.

It was as though she knew that her baby was frail and delicate and feared lest the rough hands of her fellows might injure the little thing.

Another thing she did, and which made traveling an onerous trial for her. Remembering the death of her own little one, she clung desperately to the new babe, with one hand, whenever they were upon the march.

The other young rode upon their mothers' backs; their little arms tightly clasping the hairy necks before them, while their legs were locked beneath their mothers' armpits.

Not so with Kala; she held the small form of the little Lord Greystoke tightly to her breast, where the dainty hands clutched the long black hair which covered that portion of her body. She had seen one child fall from her back to a terrible death, and she would take no further chances with this.

CHAPTER FIVE
THE WHITE APE

TENDERLY KALA NURSED HER LITTLE WAIF, wondering silently why it did not gain strength and agility as did the little apes of other mothers. It was nearly a year from the time the little fellow came into her possession before he would walk alone, and as for climbing—my, but how stupid he was!

Kala sometimes talked with the older females about her young hopeful, but none of them could understand how a child could be so slow and backward in learning to care for itself. Why, it could not even find food alone, and more than twelve moons had passed since Kala had come upon it.

Had they known that the child had seen thirteen moons before it had come into Kala's possession they would have considered its case as absolutely hopeless, for the little apes of their own tribe were as far advanced in two or three moons as was this little stranger after twenty-five.

Tublat, Kala's husband, was sorely vexed, and but for the female's careful watching would have put the child out of the way.

"He will never be a great ape," he argued. "Always will you have to carry him and protect him. What good will he be to the tribe? None; only a burden.

"Let us leave him quietly sleeping among the tall grasses, that you may bear other and stronger apes to guard us in our old age."

"Never, Broken Nose," replied Kala. "If I must carry him forever, so be it."

And then Tublat went to Kerchak to urge him to use his authority with Kala, and force her to give up little Tarzan, which was the name they had given to the tiny Lord Greystoke, and which meant "White-Skin."

But when Kerchak spoke to her about it Kala threatened to run away from the tribe if they did not leave her in peace with the child; and as this is one of the inalienable rights of the jungle folk, if they be dissatisfied among their own people, they bothered her no more, for Kala was a fine clean-limbed young female, and they did not wish to lose her.

As Tarzan grew he made more rapid strides, so that by the time he was ten years old he was an excellent climber, and on the ground could do many wonderful things which were beyond the powers of his little brothers and sisters.

In many ways did he differ from them, and they often marveled at his superior cunning, but in strength and size he was deficient; for at ten the great anthropoids were fully grown, some of them towering over six feet in height, while little Tarzan was still but a half-grown boy.

Yet such a boy!

From early infancy he had used his hands to swing from branch to branch after the manner of his giant mother, and as he grew older he spent hour upon hour daily speeding through the treetops with his brothers and sisters.

He could spring twenty feet across space at the dizzy heights of the forest top, and grasp with unerring precision, and without apparent jar, a limb waving wildly in the path of an approaching tornado.

He could drop twenty feet at a stretch from limb to limb in rapid descent to the ground, or he could gain the utmost pinnacle of the loftiest tropical giant with the ease and swiftness of a squirrel.

Though but ten years old he was fully as strong as the average man of thirty, and far more agile than the most practiced athlete ever becomes. And day by day his strength was increasing.

His life among these fierce apes had been happy; for his recollection held no other life, nor did he know that there existed within the universe aught else than his little forest and the wild jungle animals with which he was familiar.

He was nearly ten before he commenced to realize that a great difference existed between himself and his fellows. His little body, burned brown by exposure, suddenly caused him feelings of intense shame, for he realized that it was entirely hairless, like some low snake, or other reptile.

He attempted to obviate this by plastering himself from head to foot with mud, but this dried and fell off. Besides it felt so uncomfortable that he quickly decided that he preferred the shame to the discomfort.

In the higher land which his tribe frequented was a little lake, and it was here that Tarzan first saw his face in the clear, still waters of its bosom.

It was on a sultry day of the dry season that he and one of his cousins had gone down to the bank to drink. As they leaned over, both little faces were mirrored on the placid pool; the fierce and terrible features of the ape beside those of the aristocratic scion of an old English house.

Tarzan was appalled. It had been bad enough to be hairless, but to own such a countenance! He wondered that the other apes could look at him at all.

That tiny slit of a mouth and those puny white teeth! How they looked beside the mighty lips and powerful fangs of his more fortunate brothers!

And the little pinched nose of his; so thin was it that it looked half starved. He turned red as he compared it with the beautiful broad nostrils of his companion. Such a generous nose! Why it spread half across his face! It certainly must be fine to be so handsome, thought poor little Tarzan.

But when he saw his own eyes; ah, that was the final blow—a brown spot, a gray circle, and then blank whiteness! Frightful! not even the snakes had such hideous eyes as he.

So intent was he upon this personal appraisement of his features that he did not hear the parting of the tall grass behind him as a great body pushed itself stealthily through the jungle; nor did his companion, the ape, hear either, for he was drinking and the noise of his sucking lips and gurgles of satisfaction drowned the quiet approach of the intruder.

Not thirty paces behind the two she crouched—Sabor, the huge lioness—lashing her tail. Cautiously she moved a great padded paw forward, noiselessly placing it before she lifted the next. Thus she advanced; her belly low, almost touching the surface of the ground—a great cat preparing to spring upon its prey.

Now she was within ten feet of the two unsuspecting little play-fellows—carefully she drew her hind feet well up beneath her body, the great muscles rolling under the beautiful skin.

So low she was crouching now that she seemed flattened to the earth except for the upward bend of the glossy back as it gathered for the spring.

No longer the tail lashed—quiet and straight behind her it lay.

An instant she paused thus, as though turned to stone, and then, with an awful scream, she sprang.

Sabor, the lioness, was a wise hunter. To one less wise the wild alarm of her fierce cry as she sprang would have seemed a foolish thing, for could she not more surely have fallen upon her victims had she but quietly leaped without that loud shriek?

But Sabor knew well the wondrous quickness of the jungle folk and their almost unbelievable powers of hearing. To them the sudden scraping of one blade of grass across another was as effectual a warning as her loudest cry, and Sabor knew that she could not make that mighty leap without a little noise.

Her wild scream was not a warning. It was voiced to freeze her poor victims in a paralysis of terror for the tiny fraction of an instant which would suffice for her mighty claws to sink into their soft flesh and hold them beyond peradventure of escape.

So far as the ape was concerned, Sabor reasoned correctly. The little fellow crouched trembling just an instant, but that instant was quite long enough to prove his undoing.

Not so, however, with Tarzan, the man-child. His life amidst the dangers of the jungle had taught him to meet emergencies with self-confidence, and his higher intelligence resulted in a quickness of mental action far beyond the powers of the apes.

So the scream of Sabor, the lioness, galvanized the brain and muscles of little Tarzan into instant action.

Before him lay the deep waters of the little lake, behind him certain death; a cruel death beneath tearing claws and rending fangs.

Tarzan had always hated water except as a medium for quenching his thirst. He hated it because he connected it with the chill and discomfort of the torrential rains, and he feared it for the thunder and lightning and wind which accompanied them.

The deep waters of the lake he had been taught by his wild mother to avoid, and further, had he not seen little Neeta sink beneath its quiet surface only a few short weeks before never to return to the tribe?

But of the two evils his quick mind chose the lesser ere the first note of Sabor's scream had scarce broken the quiet of the jungle, and before the great beast had covered half her leap Tarzan felt the chill waters close above his head.

He could not swim, and the water was very deep; but still he lost no particle of that self-confidence and resourcefulness which were the badges of his superior being.

Rapidly he moved his hands and feet in an attempt to scramble upward, and, possibly more by chance than design, he fell into the stroke that a dog uses when swimming, so that within a few seconds his nose was above water and he found that he could keep it there by continuing his strokes, and also make progress through the water.

He was much surprised and pleased with this new acquirement which had been so suddenly thrust upon him, but he had no time for thinking much upon it.

He was now swimming parallel to the bank and there he saw the cruel beast that would have seized him crouching upon the still form of his little playmate.

The lioness was intently watching Tarzan, evidently expecting him to return to shore, but this the boy had no intention of doing.

Instead he raised his voice in the call of distress common to his tribe, adding to it the warning which would prevent would-be rescuers from running into the clutches of Sabor.

Almost immediately there came an answer from the distance, and presently forty or fifty great apes swung rapidly and majestically through the trees toward the scene of tragedy.

In the van was Kala, for she had recognized the tones of her best beloved, and with her was the mother of the little ape who lay dead beneath cruel Sabor.

Though more powerful and better equipped for fighting than the apes, the lioness had no desire to meet these enraged adults, and with a snarl of hatred she sprang quickly into the brush and disappeared.

Tarzan now swam to shore and clambered quickly upon dry land. The feeling of freshness and exhilaration which the cool waters had imparted to him filled his little being with grateful surprise, and ever after he lost no opportunity to take a daily plunge in lake or stream or ocean when it was possible to do so.

For a long time Kala could not accustom herself to the sight; for though her people could swim when forced to it, they did not like to enter water, and never did so voluntarily.

The adventure with the lioness gave Tarzan food for pleasurable memories, for it was such affairs which broke the monotony of his daily life— otherwise but a dull round of searching for food, eating, and sleeping.

The tribe to which he belonged roamed a tract extending, roughly, twenty-five miles along the seacoast and some fifty miles inland. This they traversed almost continually, occasionally remaining for months in one locality; but as they moved through the trees with great speed they often covered the territory in a very few days.

Much depended upon food supply, climatic conditions, and the prevalence of animals of the more dangerous species; though Kerchak often led them on long marches for no other reason than that he had tired of remaining in the same place.

At night they slept where darkness overtook them, lying upon the ground, and sometimes covering their heads, and more seldom their bodies, with the great leaves of the elephant's ear. Two or three might lie cuddled in each other's arms for additional warmth if the night were chill, and thus Tarzan had slept in Kala's arms nightly for all these years.

That the huge, fierce brute loved this child of another race is beyond question, and he, too, gave to the great, hairy beast all the affection that would have belonged to his fair young mother had she lived.

When he was disobedient she cuffed him, it is true, but she was never cruel to him, and was more often caressing than chastising him.

Tublat, her husband, always hated Tarzan, and on several occasions had come near ending his youthful career.

Tarzan on his part never lost an opportunity to show that he fully reciprocated his foster father's sentiments, and whenever he could safely annoy him or make faces at him or hurl insults upon him from the safety of his mother's arms, or the slender branches of the higher trees, he did so.

His superior intelligence and cunning permitted him to invent a thousand diabolical tricks to add to the burdens of Tublat's life.

Early in his boyhood he had learned to form ropes by twisting and tying long grasses together, and with these he was forever tripping Tublat or attempting to hang him from some overhanging branch.

By constant playing and experimenting with these he learned to tie rude knots, and make sliding nooses; and with these he and the younger apes amused themselves. What Tarzan did they tried to do also, but he alone originated and became proficient.

One day while playing thus Tarzan had thrown his rope at one of his fleeing companions, retaining the other end in his grasp. By accident the noose fell squarely about the running ape's neck, bringing him to a sudden and surprising halt.

Ah, here was a new game, a fine game, thought Tarzan, and immediately he attempted to repeat the trick. And thus, by painstaking and continued practice, he learned the art of roping.

Now, indeed, was the life of Tublat a living nightmare. In sleep, upon the march, night or day, he never knew when that quiet noose would slip about his neck and nearly choke the life out of him.

Kala punished, Tublat swore dire vengeance, and old Kerchak took notice and warned and threatened; but all to no avail.

Tarzan defied them all, and the thin, strong noose continued to settle about Tublat's neck whenever he least expected it.

The other apes derived unlimited amusement from Tublat's discomfiture, for Broken Nose was a disagreeable old fellow, whom no one liked, anyway.

In Tarzan's clever little mind many thoughts revolved, and back of these was his divine power of reason.

If he could catch his fellow apes with his long arm of many grasses, why not Sabor, the lioness?

It was the germ of a thought, which, however, was destined to mull around in his conscious and subconscious mind until it resulted in magnificent achievement.

But that came in later years.

CHAPTER SIX
JUNGLE BATTLES

THE WANDERINGS OF THE TRIBE brought them often near the closed and silent cabin by the little landlocked harbor. To Tarzan this was always a source of never-ending mystery and pleasure.

He would peek into the curtained windows, or, climbing upon the roof, peer down the black depths of the chimney in vain endeavor to solve the unknown wonders that lay within those strong walls.

His little childish imagination pictured wonderful creatures within, and the very impossibility of forcing entrance added a thousandfold to his desire to do so.

He would clamber about the roof and windows for hours attempting to discover means of ingress, but to the door he paid little attention, for this was apparently as solid as the walls.

It was in the next visit to the vicinity, following the adventure with old Sabor, that, as he approached the cabin, Tarzan noticed that from a distance the door appeared to be an independent part of the wall in which it was set, and for the first time it occurred to him that this might prove the means of entrance which had so long eluded him.

He was alone, as was often the case when he visited the cabin, for the apes had no love for it; the story of the thunder-stick having lost nothing in the telling during these ten years had quite surrounded the white man's deserted abode with an atmosphere of weirdness and terror for the simians.

The story of his own connection with the cabin had never been told him. The language of the apes had so few words that they could talk but little of what they had seen in the cabin, having no words to accurately describe either the strange people or their belongings, and so, long before Tarzan was old enough to understand, the subject had been forgotten by the tribe.

Only in a dim, vague way had Kala explained to him that his father had been a strange white ape, but he did not know that Kala was not his own mother.

On this day, then, he went directly to the door and spent hours examining it and fussing with the hinges, the knob, and the latch. Finally he stumbled upon the right combination, and the door swung creakingly open before his astonished eyes.

For some minutes he did not dare venture within, but finally, as his eyes became accustomed to the dim light of the interior he slowly and cautiously entered.

In the middle of the floor lay a skeleton, every vestige of flesh gone from the bones to which still clung the mildewed and moldered remnants of what had once been clothing. Upon the bed lay a similar gruesome thing, but smaller, while in a tiny cradle nearby was a third, a wee mite of a skeleton.

To none of these evidences of a fearful tragedy of a long-dead day did little Tarzan give but passing heed. His wild jungle life had inured him to the sight of dead and dying animals, and had he known that he was looking upon the remains of his own father and mother he would have been no more greatly moved.

The furnishings and other contents of the room it was which riveted his attention. He examined many things minutely—strange tools and weapons, books, paper, clothing—what little had withstood the ravages of time in the humid atmosphere of the jungle coast.

He opened chests and cupboards, such as did not baffle his small experience, and in these he found the contents much better preserved.

Among other things he found a sharp hunting knife, on the keen blade of which he immediately proceeded to cut his finger. Nothing daunted he continued his experiments, finding that he could hack and hew splinters of wood from the table and chairs with this new toy.

For a long time this amused him, but finally tiring he continued his explorations. In a cupboard filled with books he came across one with brightly colored pictures—it was a child's illustrated alphabet—

> A is for Archer
> Who shoots with a bow.
> B is for Boy,
> His first name is Joe.

The pictures interested him greatly.

There were many apes with faces similar to his own, and further over in the book he found, under "M," some little monkeys such as he saw daily flitting through the trees of his primeval forest. But nowhere was pictured any of his own people; in all the book was none that resembled Kerchak, or Tublat, or Kala.

At first he tried to pick the little figures from the leaves, but he soon saw that they were not real, though he knew not what they might be, nor had he any words to describe them.

The boats, and trains, and cows and horses were quite meaningless to him, but not quite so baffling as the odd little figures which appeared beneath and between the colored pictures—some strange kind of bug he thought they might be, for many of them had legs though nowhere could he find one with eyes and a mouth. It was his first introduction to the letters of the alphabet, and he was over ten years old.

Of course he had never before seen print, or ever had spoken with any living thing which had the remotest idea that such a thing as a written language existed, nor ever had he seen anyone reading.

So what wonder that the little boy was quite at a loss to guess the meaning of these strange figures.

Near the middle of the book he found his old enemy, Sabor, the lioness, and further on, coiled Histah, the snake.

Oh, it was most engrossing! Never before in all his ten years had he enjoyed anything so much. So absorbed was he that he did not note the approaching dusk, until it was quite upon him and the figures were blurred.

He put the book back in the cupboard and closed the door, for he did not wish anyone else to find and destroy his treasure, and as he went out into the gathering darkness he closed the great door of the cabin behind him as it had been before he discovered the secret of its lock, but before he left he had noticed the hunting knife lying where he had thrown it upon the floor, and this he picked up and took with him to show to his fellows.

He had taken scarce a dozen steps toward the jungle when a great form rose up before him from the shadows of a low bush. At first he thought it was one of his own people but in another instant he realized that it was Bolgani, the huge gorilla.

So close was he that there was no chance for flight and little Tarzan knew that he must stand and fight for his life; for these great beasts were the deadly enemies of his tribe, and neither one nor the other ever asked or gave quarter.

Had Tarzan been a full-grown bull ape of the species of his tribe he would have been more than a match for the gorilla, but being only a little English boy, though enormously muscular for such, he stood no show against his cruel antagonist. In his veins, though, flowed the blood of the best of a race of mighty fighters, and back of this was the training of his short lifetime among the fierce brutes of the jungle.

He knew no fear, as we know it; his little heart beat the faster but from the excitement and exhilaration of adventure. Had the opportunity presented itself he would have escaped, but solely because his judgment told him he was no match for the great thing which confronted him. And since reason showed him that successful flight was impossible he met the gorilla squarely and bravely without a tremor of a single muscle, or any sign of panic.

In fact he met the brute midway in its charge, striking its huge body with his closed fists and as futilely as he had been a fly attacking an elephant. But in one hand he still clutched the knife he had found in the cabin of his father, and as the brute, striking and biting, closed upon him the boy accidentally turned the point toward the hairy breast. As the knife sank deep into its body the gorilla shrieked in pain and rage.

But the boy had learned in that brief second a use for his sharp and shining toy, so that, as the tearing, striking beast dragged him to earth he plunged the blade repeatedly and to the hilt into its breast.

The gorilla, fighting after the manner of its kind, struck terrific blows with its open hand, and tore the flesh at the boy's throat and chest with its mighty tusks.

For a moment they rolled upon the ground in the fierce frenzy of combat. More and more weakly the torn and bleeding arm struck home with the long sharp blade, then the little figure stiffened with a spasmodic jerk, and Tarzan, the young Lord Greystoke, rolled lifeless upon the dead and decaying vegetation which carpeted his jungle home.

A mile back in the forest the tribe had heard the fierce challenge of the gorilla, and, as was his custom when any danger threatened, Kerchak called his people together, partly for mutual protection against a common enemy, since this gorilla might be but one of a party of several, and also to see that all members of the tribe were accounted for.

It was soon discovered that Tarzan was missing, and Tublat was strongly opposed to sending assistance. Kerchak himself had no liking for the strange little waif, so he listened to Tublat, and, finally, with a shrug of his shoulders, turned back to the pile of leaves on which he had made his bed.

But Kala was of a different mind; in fact, she had not waited but to learn that Tarzan was absent ere she was fairly flying through the matted branches toward the point from which the cries of the gorilla were still plainly audible.

Darkness had now fallen, and an early moon was sending its faint light to cast strange, grotesque shadows among the dense foliage of the forest.

Here and there the brilliant rays penetrated to earth, but for the most part they only served to accentuate the Stygian blackness of the jungle's depths.

Like some huge phantom, Kala swung noiselessly from tree to tree; now running nimbly along a great branch, now swinging through space at the end of another, only to grasp that of a farther tree in her rapid progress toward the scene of the tragedy her knowledge of jungle life told her was being enacted a short distance before her.

The cries of the gorilla proclaimed that it was in mortal combat with some other denizen of the fierce wood. Suddenly these cries ceased, and the silence of death reigned throughout the jungle.

Kala could not understand, for the voice of Bolgani had at the last been raised in the agony of suffering and death, but no sound had come to her by which she possibly could determine the nature of his antagonist.

That her little Tarzan could destroy a great bull gorilla she knew to be improbable, and so, as she neared the spot from which the sounds of the struggle had come, she moved more warily and at last slowly and with extreme caution she traversed the lowest branches, peering eagerly into the moon-splashed blackness for a sign of the combatants.

Presently she came upon them, lying in a little open space full under the brilliant light of the moon—little Tarzan's torn and bloody form, and beside it a great bull gorilla, stone dead.

With a low cry Kala rushed to Tarzan's side, and gathering the poor, blood-covered body to her breast, listened for a sign of life. Faintly she heard it—the weak beating of the little heart.

Tenderly she bore him back through the inky jungle to where the tribe lay, and for many days and nights she sat guard beside him, bringing him food and water, and brushing the flies and other insects from his cruel wounds.

Of medicine or surgery the poor thing knew nothing. She could but lick the wounds. and thus she kept them cleansed, that healing nature might the more quickly do her work.

At first Tarzan would eat nothing, but rolled and tossed in a wild delirium of fever. All he craved was water, and this she brought him in the only way she could, bearing it in her own mouth.

No human mother could have shown more unselfish and sacrificing devotion than did this poor, wild brute for the little orphaned waif whom fate had thrown into her keeping.

At last the fever abated and the boy commenced to mend. No word of complaint passed his tight-set lips, though the pain of his wounds was excruciating.

A portion of his chest was laid bare to the ribs, three of which had been broken by the mighty blows of the gorilla. One arm was nearly severed by the giant fangs, and a great piece had been torn from his neck, exposing his jugular vein, which the cruel jaws had missed but by a miracle.

With the stoicism of the brutes who had raised him he endured his suffering quietly, preferring to crawl away from the others and lie huddled in some clump of tall grasses rather than to show his misery before their eyes.

Kala, alone, he was glad to have with him, but now that he was better she was gone longer at a time, in search of food; for the devoted animal had scarcely eaten enough to support her own life while Tarzan had been so low, and was in consequence reduced to a mere shadow of her former self.

CHAPTER SEVEN
THE LIGHT OF KNOWLEDGE

AFTER WHAT SEEMED AN ETERNITY to the little sufferer he was able to walk once more, and from then on his recovery was so rapid that in another month he was as strong and active as ever.

During his convalescence he had gone over in his mind many times the battle with the gorilla, and his first thought was to recover the wonderful little weapon which had transformed him from a hopelessly outclassed weakling to the superior of the mighty terror of the jungle.

Also, he was anxious to return to the cabin and continue his investigations of its wondrous contents.

So, early one morning, he set forth alone upon his quest. After a little search he located the clean-picked bones of his late adversary, and close by, partly buried beneath the fallen leaves, he found the knife, now red with rust from its exposure to the dampness of the ground and from the dried blood of the gorilla.

He did not like the change in its former bright and gleaming surface; but it was still a formidable weapon, and one which he meant to use to advantage whenever the opportunity presented itself. He had in mind that no more would he run from the wanton attacks of old Tublat.

In another moment he was at the cabin, and after a short time had again thrown the latch and entered. His first concern was to learn the mechanism of the lock, and this he did by examining it closely while the door was open, so that he could learn precisely what caused it to hold the door, and by what means it released at his touch.

He found that he could close and lock the door from within, and this he did so that there would be no chance of his being molested while at his investigations.

He commenced a systematic search of the cabin; but his attention was soon riveted by the books which seemed to exert a strange and powerful influence over him, so that he could scarce attend to aught else for the lure of the wondrous puzzle which their purpose presented to him.

Among the other books were a primer, some child's readers, numerous picture books, and a great dictionary. All of these he examined, but the pictures caught his fancy most, though the strange little bugs which covered the pages where there were no pictures excited his wonder and deepest thought.

Squatting upon his haunches on the tabletop in the cabin his father had built—his smooth, brown, naked little body bent over the book which rested in his strong slender hands, and his great shock of long, black hair falling about his well-shaped head and bright, intelligent eyes—Tarzan of the apes, little primitive man, presented a picture filled, at once, with pathos and with promise—an allegorical figure of the primordial groping through the black night of ignorance toward the light of learning.

His little face was tense in study, for he had partially grasped, in a hazy, nebulous way, the rudiments of a thought which was destined to prove the key and the solution to the puzzling problem of the strange little bugs.

In his hands was a primer opened at a picture of a little ape similar to himself, but covered, except for hands and face, with strange, colored fur, for such he thought the jacket and trousers to be. Beneath the picture were three little bugs—

BOY.

And now he had discovered in the text upon the page that these three were repeated many times in the same sequence.

Another fact he learned—that there were comparatively few individual bugs; but these were repeated many times, occasionally alone, but more often in company with others.

Slowly he turned the pages, scanning the pictures and the text for a repetition of the combination *b-o-y*. Presently he found it beneath a picture of another little ape and a strange animal which went upon four legs like the jackal and resembled him not a little. Beneath this picture the bugs appeared as:

A BOY AND A DOG.

There they were, the three little bugs which always accompanied the little ape.

And so he progressed very, very slowly, for it was a hard and laborious task which he had set himself without knowing it—a task which might seem to you or me impossible—learning to read without having the slightest knowledge of letters or written language, or the faintest idea that such things existed.

He did not accomplish it in a day, or in a week, or in a month, or in a year; but slowly, very slowly, he learned after he had grasped the possibilities which lay in those little bugs, so that by the time he was fifteen he knew the various combinations of letters which stood for every pictured figure in the little primer and in one or two of the picture books.

Of the meaning and use of the articles and conjunctions, verbs and adverbs and pronouns he had but the faintest and haziest conception.

One day when he was about twelve he found a number of lead pencils in a hitherto undiscovered drawer beneath the table, and in scratching upon the tabletop with one of them he was delighted to discover the black line it left behind it.

He worked so assiduously with this new toy that the tabletop was soon a mass of scrawly loops and irregular lines and his pencil-point worn down to the wood. Then he took another pencil, but this time he had a definite object in view.

He would attempt to reproduce some of the little bugs that scrambled over the pages of his books.

It was a difficult task, for he held the pencil as one would grasp the hilt of a dagger, which does not add greatly to ease in writing nor to the legibility of the results.

But he persevered for months, at such times as he was able to come to the cabin, until at last by repeated experimenting he found a position in which to hold the pencil that best permitted him to guide and control it, so that at last he could roughly reproduce any of the little bugs.

Thus he made a beginning at writing.

Copying the bugs taught him another thing—their number; and though he could not count as we understand it, yet he had an idea of quantity, the base of his calculations being the number of fingers upon one of his hands.

His search through the various books convinced him that he had discovered all the different kinds of bugs most often repeated in combination, and these he arranged in proper order with great ease because of the frequency with which he had perused the fascinating alphabet picture book.

His education progressed; but his greatest finds were in the inexhaustible storehouse of the huge illustrated dictionary, for he learned more through the medium of pictures than text, even after he had grasped the significance of the bugs.

When he discovered the arrangement of words in alphabetical order he delighted in searching for and finding the combinations with which he was familiar, and the words which followed them, their definitions, led him still further into the mazes of erudition.

By the time he was seventeen he had learned to read the simple, child's primer and had fully realized the true and wonderful purpose of the little bugs.

No longer did he feel shame for his hairless body or his human features, for now his reason told him that he was of a different race from his wild and hairy companions. He was a M-A-N, they were A-P-E-S, and the little apes which scurried through the forest top were M-O-N-K-E-Y-S. He knew, too, that old Sabor was a L-I-O-N-E-S-S, and Histah a S-N-A-K-E, and Tantor an E-L-E-P-H-A-N-T. And so he learned to read.

From then on his progress was rapid. With the help of the great dictionary and the active intelligence of a healthy mind endowed by inheritance with more than ordinary reasoning powers he shrewdly guessed at much which he could not really understand, and more often than not his guesses were close to the mark of truth.

There were many breaks in his education, caused by the migratory habits of his tribe, but even when removed from recourse to his books his active brain continued to search out the mysteries of his fascinating avocation.

Pieces of bark and flat leaves and even smooth stretches of bare earth provided him with copy books whereon to scratch with the point of his hunting knife the lessons he was learning.

Nor did he neglect the sterner duties of life while following the bent of his inclination toward the solving of the mystery of his library.

He practiced with his rope and played with his sharp knife, which he had learned to keep keen by whetting upon flat stones.

The tribe had grown larger since Tarzan had come among them, for under the leadership of Kerchak they had been able to frighten the other tribes from their part of the jungle so that they had plenty to eat and little or no loss from predatory incursions of neighbors.

Hence the younger males as they became adult found it more comfortable to take wives from their own tribe, or if they captured one of another tribe to bring her back to Kerchak's band and live in amity with him rather than attempt to set up new establishment of their own, or fight with the redoubtable Kerchak for supremacy at home.

Occasionally one more ferocious than his fellows would attempt this latter alternative, but none had come yet who could wrest the palm of victory from the fierce and brutal ape.

Tarzan held a peculiar position in the tribe. They seemed to consider him one of them and yet in some way different. The older males either ignored him entirely or else hated him so vindictively that but for his wondrous agility and speed and the fierce protection of the huge Kala he would have been dispatched at an early age.

Tublat was his most consistent enemy, but it was through Tublat that, when he was about thirteen, the persecution of his enemies suddenly ceased and he was left severely alone, except on the occasions when one of them ran amuck in the throes of one of those strange, wild fits of insane rage which attacks the males of many of the fiercer animals of the jungle. Then none was safe.

On the day that Tarzan established his right to respect, the tribe was gathered about a small natural amphitheater which the jungle had left free from its entangling vines and creepers in a hollow among some low hills.

The open space was almost circular in shape. Upon every hand rose the mighty giants of the untouched forest, with the matted undergrowth banked so closely between the huge trunks that the only opening into the little, level arena was through the upper branches of the trees.

Here, safe from interruption, the tribe often gathered. In the center of the amphitheater was one of those strange earthen drums which the anthropoids build for the queer rites the sounds of which men have heard in the fastnesses of the jungle, but which none has ever witnessed.

Many travelers have seen the drums of the great apes, and some have heard the sounds of their beating and the noise of the wild, weird revelry of these first lords of the jungle, but Tarzan, Lord Greystoke, is, doubtless, the only human being who ever joined in the fierce, mad, intoxicating revel of the Dum-Dum.

From this primitive function has arisen, unquestionably, all the forms and ceremonials of modern church and state, for through all the countless ages, back beyond the uttermost ramparts of a dawning humanity our fierce, hairy forebears danced out the rites of the Dum-Dum to the sound of their earthen drums, beneath the bright light of a tropical moon in the depth of a mighty jungle which stands unchanged today as it stood on that long-forgotten night in the dim, unthinkable vistas of the long-dead past when our first shaggy ancestor swung from a swaying bough and dropped lightly upon the soft turf of the first meeting place.

On the day that Tarzan won his emancipation from the persecution that had followed him remorselessly for twelve of his thirteen years of life, the tribe, now a full hundred strong, trooped silently through the lower terrace of the jungle trees and dropped noiselessly upon the floor of the amphitheater.

The rites of the Dum-Dum marked important events in the life of the tribe—a victory, the capture of a prisoner, the killing of some large fierce denizen of the jungle, the death or accession of a king, and were conducted with set ceremonialism.

Today it was the killing of a giant ape, a member of another tribe, and as the people of Kerchak entered the arena two mighty bulls might have been seen bearing the body of the vanquished between them.

They laid their burden before the earthen drum and then squatted there beside it as guards, while the other members of the community curled themselves in grassy nooks to sleep until the rising moon should give the signal for the commencement of their savage orgy.

For hours absolute quiet reigned in the little clearing, except as it was broken by the discordant notes of brilliantly feathered parrots, or the screeching and twittering of the thousand jungle birds flitting ceaselessly amongst the vivid orchids and flamboyant blossoms which festooned the myriad, moss-covered branches of the forest kings.

At length as darkness settled upon the jungle the apes commenced to bestir themselves, and soon they formed a great circle about the earthen drum. The females and young squatted in a thin line at the outer periphery of the circle, while just in front of them ranged the adult males. Before the drum sat three old females, each armed with a knotted branch fifteen or eighteen inches in length.

Slowly and softly they began tapping upon the resounding surface of the drum as the first faint rays of the ascending moon silvered the encircling treetops.

As the light in the amphitheater increased the females augmented the frequency and force of their blows until presently a wild, rhythmic din pervaded the great jungle for miles in every direction. Huge, fierce brutes stopped in their hunting, with uppricked ears and raised heads, to listen to the dull booming that betokened the Dum-Dum of the apes.

Occasionally one would raise his shrill scream or thunderous roar in answering challenge to the savage din of the anthropoids, but none came near to investigate or attack, for the great apes, assembled in all the power of their numbers, filled the breasts of their jungle neighbors with deep respect.

As the din of the drum rose to almost deafening volume Kerchak sprang into the open space between the squatting males and the drummers.

Standing erect he threw his head far back and looking full into the eye of the rising moon he beat upon his breast with his great hairy paws and emitted his fearful roaring shriek.

One—twice—thrice that terrifying cry rang out across the teeming solitude of that unspeakably quick, yet unthinkably dead, world.

Then, crouching, Kerchak slunk noiselessly around the open circle, veering far away from the dead body lying before the altar-drum, but, as he passed, keeping his little, fierce, wicked, red eyes upon the corpse.

Another male then sprang into the arena, and, repeating the horrid cries of his king, followed stealthily in his wake. Another and another followed in quick succession until the jungle reverberated with the now almost ceaseless notes of their bloodthirsty screams.

It was the challenge and the hunt.

When all the adult males had joined in the thin line of circling dancers the attack commenced.

Kerchak, seizing a huge club from the pile which lay at hand for the purpose, rushed furiously upon the dead ape, dealing the corpse a terrific blow, at the same time emitting the growls and snarls of combat. The din of the drum was now increased, as well as the frequency of the blows, and the warriors, as each approached the victim of the hunt and delivered his bludgeon blow, joined in the mad whirl of the Death Dance.

Tarzan was one of the wild, leaping horde. His brown, sweat-streaked, muscular body, glistening in the moonlight, shone supple and graceful among the uncouth, awkward, hairy brutes about him.

None more craftily stealthy in the mimic hunt, none more ferocious than he in the wild ferocity of the attack, nor none who leaped so high into the air in the Dance of Death.

As the noise and rapidity of the drumbeats increased the dancers apparently became intoxicated with the wild rhythm and the savage yells. Their leaps and bounds increased, their bared fangs dripped saliva, and their lips and breasts were flecked with foam.

For half an hour the weird dance went on, until, at a sign from Kerchak, the noise of the drums ceased, the female drummers scampering hurriedly through the line of dancers toward the outer rim of squatting spectators. Then, as one man, the males rushed headlong upon the thing which their terrific blows had reduced to a mass of hairy pulp.

Flesh seldom came to their jaws in satisfying quantities, so a fit finale to their wild revel was a taste of fresh-killed meat, and it was to the purpose of devouring their late enemy that they now turned their attention.

Great fangs sunk into the carcass tearing away huge hunks, the mightiest of the apes obtaining the choicest morsels, while the weaker circled the outer edge of the fighting, snarling pack awaiting their chance to dodge in and snatch a dropped titbit or filch a remaining bone before all was gone.

Tarzan, more than the apes, craved and needed flesh. Descended from a race of meat eaters, never in his life, he thought, had he once satisfied his appetite for animal food; and so now his agile little body wormed its way far into the mass of struggling, rending apes in an endeavor to obtain a share which his strength would have been unequal to the task of winning for him.

At his side hung the hunting knife of his unknown father in a sheath self-fashioned in copy of one he had seen among the pictures of his treasure-books.

At last he reached the fast-disappearing feast and with his sharp knife slashed off a more generous portion than he had hoped for, an entire hairy forearm, where it protruded from beneath the feet of the mighty Kerchak, who was so busily engaged in perpetuating the royal prerogative of hogging that he failed to note the act of *lèse-majesté*.

So little Tarzan wriggled out from beneath the struggling mass, clutching his grisly prize close to his breast.

Among those circling futilely the outskirts of the banqueters was old Tublat. He had been among the first at the feast, but had retreated with a goodly share to eat in quiet, and was now forcing his way back for more.

So it was that he spied Tarzan as the boy emerged from the clawing, pushing throng with that hairy forearm hugged firmly to his body.

Tublat's little, close-set, bloodshot, pig eyes shot wicked gleams of hate as they fell upon the object of his loathing. In them, too, was greed for the toothsome dainty the boy carried.

But Tarzan saw his archenemy as quickly, and divining what the great beast would do he leaped nimbly away toward the females and the young, hoping to hide himself among them. Tublat, however, was close upon his heels, so that he had no opportunity to seek a place of concealment, but saw that he would be put to it to escape at all.

Swiftly he sped toward the surrounding trees and with an agile bound gained a lower limb with one hand, and then, transferring his burden to his teeth, he climbed rapidly upward, closely followed by Tublat.

Up, up he went to the waving pinnacle of a lofty monarch of the forest where his heavy pursuer dared not follow him. There he perched, hurling taunts and insults at the raging, foaming beast fifty feet below him.

And then Tublat went mad.

With horrifying screams and roars he rushed to the ground, among the females and young, sinking his great fangs into a dozen tiny necks and tearing great pieces from the backs and breasts of the females who fell into his clutches.

In the brilliant moonlight Tarzan witnessed the whole mad carnival of rage. He saw the females and the young scamper to the safety of the trees. Then the great bulls in the center of the arena felt the mighty fangs of their demented fellow, and with one accord they melted into the black shadows of the overhanging forest.

There was but one in the amphitheater beside Tublat, a belated female running swiftly toward the tree where Tarzan perched, and close behind her came the awful Tublat.

It was Kala, and as quickly as Tarzan saw that Tublat was gaining on her he dropped with the rapidity of a falling stone, from branch to branch, toward his foster mother.

Now she was beneath the overhanging limbs and close above her crouched Tarzan, waiting the outcome of the race.

She leaped into the air grasping a low-hanging branch, but almost over the head of Tublat, so nearly had he distanced her. She should have been safe now but there was a rending, tearing sound, the branch broke and precipitated her full upon the head of Tublat, knocking him to the ground.

Both were up in an instant, but as quick as they had been Tarzan had been quicker, so that the infuriated bull found himself facing the man-child who stood between him and Kala.

Nothing could have suited the fierce beast better, and with a roar of triumph he leaped upon the little Lord Greystoke. But his fangs never closed in that nut-brown flesh.

A muscular hand shot out and grasped the hairy throat, and another plunged a keen hunting knife a dozen times into the broad breast. Like lightning the blows fell, and only ceased when Tarzan felt the limp form crumple beneath him.

As the body rolled to the ground Tarzan of the Apes placed his foot upon the neck of his lifelong enemy and, raising his eyes to the full moon, threw back his fierce young head and voiced the wild and terrible cry of his people.

One by one the tribe swung down from their arboreal retreats and formed a circle about Tarzan and his vanquished foe. When they had all come Tarzan turned toward them.

"I am Tarzan," he cried. "I am a great killer. Let all respect Tarzan of the Apes and Kala, his mother. There be none among you as mighty as Tarzan. Let his enemies beware."

Looking full into the wicked, red eyes of Kerchak, the young Lord Greystoke beat upon his mighty breast and screamed out once more his shrill cry of defiance.

CHAPTER EIGHT
THE TREETOP HUNTER

THE MORNING AFTER THE DUM-DUM the tribe started slowly back through the forest toward the coast.

The body of Tublat lay where it had fallen, for the people of Kerchak do not eat their own dead.

The march was but a leisurely search for food. Cabbage palm and gray plum, pisang and scitamine they found in abundance, with wild pineapple, and occasionally small mammals, birds, eggs, reptiles, and insects. The nuts they cracked between their powerful jaws, or, if too hard, broke by pounding between stones.

Once old Sabor, crossing their path, sent them scurrying to the safety of the higher branches, for if she respected their number and their sharp fangs, they on their part held her cruel and mighty ferocity in equal esteem.

Upon a low-hanging branch sat Tarzan directly above the majestic, supple body as it forged silently through the thick jungle. He hurled a pineapple at the ancient enemy of his people. The great beast stopped and, turning, eyed the taunting figure above her.

With an angry lash of her tail she bared her yellow fangs, curling her great lips in a hideous snarl that wrinkled her bristling snout in serried ridges and closed her wicked eyes to two narrow slits of rage and hatred.

With back-laid ears she looked straight into the eyes of Tarzan of the Apes and sounded her fierce, shrill challenge.

And from the safety of his overhanging limb the ape-child sent back the fearsome answer of his kind.

For a moment the two eyed each other in silence, and then the great cat turned into the jungle, which swallowed her as the ocean engulfs a tossed pebble.

But into the mind of Tarzan a great plan sprang. He had killed the fierce Tublat, so was he not therefore a mighty fighter? Now would he track down the crafty Sabor and slay her likewise. He would be a mighty hunter, also.

At the bottom of his little English heart beat the great desire to cover his nakedness with *clothes* for he had learned from his picture books that all *men* were so covered, while *monkeys* and *apes* and every other living thing went naked.

Clothes therefore, must be truly a badge of greatness; the insignia of the superiority of *man* over all other animals, for surely there could be no other reason for wearing the hideous things.

Many moons ago, when he had been much smaller, he had desired the skin of Sabor, the lioness, or Numa, the lion, or Sheeta, the leopard to cover his hairless body that he might no longer resemble hideous Histah, the snake; but now he was proud of his sleek skin for it betokened his descent from a mighty race, and the conflicting desires to go naked in prideful proof of his ancestry, or to conform to the customs of his own kind and wear hideous and uncomfortable apparel found first one and then the other in the ascendency.

As the tribe continued their slow way through the forest after the passing of Sabor, Tarzan's head was filled with his great scheme for slaying his enemy, and for many days thereafter he thought of little else.

On this day, however, he presently had other and more immediate interests to attract his attention.

Of a sudden it became as midnight; the noises of the jungle ceased; the trees stood motionless as though in paralyzed expectancy of some great and imminent disaster. All nature waited—but not for long.

Faintly, from a distance, came a low, sad moaning. Nearer and nearer it approached, mounting louder and louder in volume.

The great trees bent in unison as though pressed earthward by a mighty hand. Further and further toward the ground they inclined, and still there was no sound save the deep and awesome moaning of the wind.

Then, suddenly, the jungle giants whipped back, lashing their mighty tops in angry and deafening protest. A vivid and blinding light flashed from the whirling, inky clouds above. The deep cannonade of roaring thunder belched forth its fearsome challenge. The deluge came—all hell broke loose upon the jungle.

The tribe huddled, shivering from the cold rain, at the bases of great trees. The lightning, darting and flashing through the blackness, showed wildly waving branches, whipping streamers, and bending trunks.

Now and again some ancient patriarch of the woods, rent by a flashing bolt, would crash in a thousand pieces among the surrounding trees, carrying down numberless branches and many smaller neighbors to add to the tangled confusion of the tropical jungle.

Branches, great and small, torn away by the ferocity of the tornado, hurtled through the wildly waving verdure, carrying death and destruction to countless unhappy denizens of the thickly peopled world below.

For hours the fury of the storm continued without surcease, and still the tribe huddled close in shivering fear. In constant danger from falling trunks and branches and paralyzed by the vivid flashing of lightning and the bellowing of thunder they crouched in pitiful misery until the storm passed.

The end was as sudden as the beginning. The wind ceased, the sun shone forth—nature smiled once more.

The dripping leaves and branches, and the moist petals of gorgeous flowers glistened in the splendor of the returning day. And, so—as Nature forgot, her children forgot also. Busy life went on as it had been before the darkness and the fright.

But to Tarzan a dawning light had come to explain the mystery of *clothes*. How snug he would have been beneath the heavy coat of Sabor! And so was added a further incentive to the adventure.

For several months the tribe hovered near the beach where stood Tarzan's cabin, and his studies took up the greater portion of his time, but always when journeying through the forest he kept his rope in readiness, and many were the smaller animals that fell into the snare of the quick-thrown noose.

Once it fell about the short neck of Horta, the boar, and his mad lunge for freedom toppled Tarzan from the overhanging limb where he had lain in wait and from whence he had launched his sinuous coil.

The mighty tusker turned at the sound of his falling body, and, seeing only the easy prey of a young ape, he lowered his head and charged madly at the surprised youth.

Tarzan, happily, was uninjured by the fall, alighting catlike upon all fours far outspread to take up the shock. He was on his feet in an instant and, leaping with the agility of the monkey he was, he gained the safety of a low limb as Horta, the boar, rushed futilely beneath.

Thus it was that Tarzan learned by experience the limitations as well as the possibilities of his strange weapon.

He lost a long rope on this occasion, but he knew that had it been Sabor who had thus dragged him from his perch the outcome might have been very different, for he would have lost his life, doubtless, into the bargain.

It took him many days to braid a new rope, but when, finally, it was done he went forth purposely to hunt, and lie in wait among the dense foliage of a great branch right above the well-beaten trail that led to water.

Several small animals passed unharmed beneath him. He did not want such insignificant game. It would take a strong animal to test the efficacy of his new scheme.

At last came she whom Tarzan sought, with lithe sinews rolling beneath shimmering hide; fat and glossy came Sabor, the lioness.

Her great padded feet fell soft and noiseless on the narrow trail. Her head was high in ever alert attention; her long tail moved slowly in sinuous and graceful undulations.

Nearer and nearer she came to where Tarzan of the Apes crouched upon his limb, the coils of his long rope poised ready in his hand.

Like a thing of bronze, motionless as death, sat Tarzan. Sabor passed beneath. One stride beyond she took—a second, a third, and then the silent coil shot out above her.

For an instant the spreading noose hung above her head like a great snake, and then, as she looked upward to detect the origin of the swishing sound of the rope, it settled about her neck. With a quick jerk Tarzan snapped the noose tight about the glossy throat, and then he dropped the rope and clung to his support with both hands.

Sabor was trapped.

With a bound the startled beast turned into the jungle, but Tarzan was not to lose another rope through the same cause as the first. He had learned from experience. The lioness had taken but half her second bound when she felt the rope tighten about her neck; her body turned completely over in the air and she fell with a heavy crash upon her back. Tarzan had fastened the end of the rope securely to the trunk of the great tree on which he sat.

Thus far his plan had worked to perfection, but when he grasped the rope, bracing himself behind a crotch of two mighty branches, he found that dragging the mighty, struggling, clawing, biting, screaming mass of iron-muscled fury up to the tree and hanging her was a very different proposition.

The weight of old Sabor was immense, and when she braced her huge paws nothing less than Tantor, the elephant, himself, could have budged her.

The lioness was now back in the path where she could see the author of the indignity which had been placed upon her. Screaming with rage she suddenly charged, leaping high into the air toward Tarzan, but when her huge body struck the limb on which Tarzan had been, Tarzan was no longer there.

Instead he perched lightly upon a smaller branch twenty feet above the raging captive. For a moment Sabor hung half across the branch, while Tarzan mocked, and hurled twigs and branches at her unprotected face.

Presently the beast dropped to the earth again and Tarzan came quickly to seize the rope, but Sabor had now found that it was only a slender cord that held her, and grasping it in her huge jaws severed it before Tarzan could tighten the strangling noose a second time.

Tarzan was much hurt. His well-laid plan had come to naught, so he sat there screaming at the roaring creature beneath him and making mocking grimaces at it.

Sabor paced back and forth beneath the tree for hours; four times she crouched and sprang at the dancing sprite above her, but she might as well have clutched at the illusive wind that murmured through the treetops.

At last Tarzan tired of the sport, and with a parting roar of challenge and a well-aimed ripe fruit that spread soft and sticky over the snarling face of his enemy, he swung rapidly through the trees, a hundred feet above the ground, and in a short time was among the members of his tribe.

Here he recounted the details of his adventure, with swelling chest and so considerable swagger that he quite impressed even his bitterest enemies, while Kala fairly danced for joy and pride.

CHAPTER NINE
MAN AND MAN

TARZAN OF THE APES lived on in his wild, jungle existence with little change for several years, only that he grew stronger and wiser, and learned from his books more and more of the strange worlds which lay somewhere outside his primeval forest.

To him life was never monotonous or stale. There was always Pisah, the fish, to be caught in the many streams and the little lakes, and Sabor, with her ferocious cousins to keep one ever on the alert and give zest to every instant that one spent upon the ground.

Often they hunted him, and more often he hunted them, but though they never quite reached him with those cruel, sharp claws of theirs, yet there were times when one could scarce have passed a thick leaf between their talons and his smooth hide.

Quick was Sabor, the lioness, and quick were Numa and Sheeta, but Tarzan of the Apes was lightning.

With Tantor, the elephant, he made friends. How? Ask not. But this is known to the denizens of the jungle, that on many moonlit nights Tarzan of the Apes and Tantor, the elephant, walked together, and where the way was clear Tarzan rode, perched high upon Tantor's mighty back.

All else of the jungle were his enemies, except his own tribe, among whom he now had many friends.

Many days during these years he spent in the cabin of his father, where still lay, untouched, the bones of his parents and the little skeleton of Kala's baby. At eighteen he read fluently and understood nearly all he read in the many and varied volumes on the shelves.

Also could he write, with printed letters, rapidly and plainly, but script he had not mastered, for though there were several copy books among his treasure, there was so little written English in the cabin that he saw no use for bothering with this other form of writing, though he could read it, laboriously.

Thus, at eighteen, we find him, an English lordling, who could speak no English, and yet who could read and write his native language. Never had he seen a human being other than himself, for the little area traversed by his tribe was watered by no greater river to bring down the natives of the interior.

High hills shut it off on three sides, the ocean on the fourth. It was alive with lions and leopards and poisonous snakes. Its untouched mazes of matted jungle had as yet invited no hardy pioneer from the human beasts beyond its frontier.

But as Tarzan of the Apes sat one day in the cabin of his father delving into the mysteries of a new book, the ancient security of his jungle was broken forever.

At the far eastern confine a strange cavalcade strung, in single file, over the brow of a low hill.

In advance were fifty black warriors armed with slender wooden spears with ends hard baked over slow fires, and long bows and poisoned arrows. On their backs were oval shields, in their noses huge rings, while from the hair on their heads protruded tufts of gay feathers.

Across their foreheads were tattooed three parallel lines of color, and on each breast three concentric circles. Their yellow teeth were filed to sharp points, adding to the ferocity of their appearance.

Following them were several hundred women and children, the former bearing upon their heads great burdens of cooking pots, household utensils, and ivory. In the rear were a hundred warriors, similar in all respects to the advance guard.

That they more greatly feared an attack from the rear than whatever unknown enemies lurked in their advance was evidenced by the formation of the column; and such was the fact, for they were fleeing from the white man's soldiers who had so harassed them for rubber and ivory that they had turned upon their conquerors one day and massacred a white officer and a small detachment of his black troops.

For many days they had gorged themselves on meat, but eventually a stronger body of troops had come and fallen upon their village by night to revenge the death of their comrades.

That night the black soldiers of the white man had had meat aplenty, and this little remnant of a once powerful tribe had slunk off into the gloomy jungle toward the unknown, and freedom.

But what meant freedom and the pursuit of happiness to these fierce warriors meant consternation and death to many of the wild denizens of their new home.

For three days the little cavalcade marched slowly through the heart of this unknown and untracked forest, until finally, early in the fourth day, they came upon a little spot near the banks of a small river, which seemed less thickly overgrown than any ground they had yet encountered.

Here they set to work to build a new village, and in a month a great clearing had been made, huts and palisades erected, plantains, yams, and maize planted, and they had taken up their old life in their new home. Here there were no white men, no soldiers, nor any rubber or ivory to be gathered for cruel and thankless taskmasters.

Several moons passed by ere the party ventured far into the territory surrounding their new village. Several had already fallen prey to old Sabor, and because the jungle was so infested with these fierce and bloodthirsty cats, and with lions and leopards, the ebony warriors hesitated to trust themselves far from the safety of their palisades.

But one day, Kulonga, a son of the old king, Mbonga, wandered far into the dense mazes to the west. Warily he stepped, his slender lance ever ready, his long oval shield firmly grasped in his left hand close to his sleek ebony body.

At his back his bow, and in the quiver upon his shield many slim, straight arrows, well smeared with the thick, dark, tarry substance that rendered deadly their tiniest needle prick.

Night found Kulonga far from the palisades of his father's village, but still headed westward, and climbing into the fork of a great tree he fashioned a rude platform and curled himself for sleep.

Three miles to the west of him slept the tribe of Kerchak.

Early the next morning the apes were astir, moving through the jungle in search of food. Tarzan, as was his custom, prosecuted his search in the direction of the cabin so that by leisurely hunting on the way his stomach was filled by the time he reached the beach.

The apes scattered by ones, and twos, and threes in all directions, but ever within sound of a signal of alarm.

Kala had moved slowly along an elephant track toward the east, and was busily engaged in turning over rotted limbs and logs in search of succulent bugs and fungi, when the faintest shadow of a strange noise brought her to startled attention.

For fifty yards before her the trail was straight, and down this leafy tunnel she saw the stealthy advancing figure of a strange and fearful creature.

It was Kulonga.

Kala did not wait to see more, but, turning, moved rapidly back along the trail. She did not run; but, after the manner of her kind when not aroused, sought rather to avoid than to escape.

Close after her came Kulonga. Here was meat. He could make a killing and feast well this day. On he hurried, his spear poised for the throw.

At a turning of the trail he came in sight of her again upon another straight stretch. His spear hand went far back, the muscles rolled, lightning-like, beneath the sleek hide. Out shot the arm, and the spear sped toward Kala.

A poor cast. It but grazed her side.

With a cry of rage and pain the she-ape turned upon her tormentor. In an instant the trees were crashing beneath the weight of her hurrying fellows, swinging rapidly toward the scene of trouble in answer to Kala's scream.

As she charged, Kulonga unslung his bow and fitted an arrow with almost unthinkable quickness. Drawing the shaft far back he drove the poisoned missile straight into the heart of the great anthropoid.

With a horrid scream Kala plunged forward upon her face before the astonished members of her tribe.

Roaring and shrieking the apes dashed toward Kulonga, but that wary savage was fleeing down the trail like a frightened antelope.

He knew something of the ferocity of these wild, hairy men, and his one desire was to put as many miles between himself and them as he possibly could.

They followed him, racing through the trees, for a long distance, but finally one by one they abandoned the chase and returned to the scene of the tragedy.

None of them had ever seen a man before, other than Tarzan, and so they wondered vaguely what strange manner of creature it might be that had invaded their jungle.

On the far beach by the little cabin Tarzan heard the faint echoes of the conflict and knowing that something was seriously amiss among the tribe he hastened rapidly toward the direction of the sound.

When he arrived he found the entire tribe gathered jabbering about the dead body of his slain mother.

Tarzan's grief and anger were unbounded. He roared out his hideous challenge time and again. He beat upon his great chest with his clenched fists, and then he fell upon the body of Kala and sobbed out the pitiful sorrowing of his lonely heart.

To lose the only creature in all one's world who ever had manifested love and affection for one is a great bereavement indeed.

What though Kala was a fierce and hideous ape! To Tarzan she had been kind, she had been beautiful.

Upon her he had lavished, unknown to himself, all the reverence and respect and love that a normal English boy feels for his own mother. He had never known another, and so to Kala was given, though mutely, all that would have belonged to the fair and lovely Lady Alice had she lived.

After the first outburst of grief Tarzan controlled himself, and questioning the members of the tribe who had witnessed the killing of Kala he learned all that their meager vocabulary could vouchsafe him.

It was enough, however, for his needs. It told him of a strange, hairless, black ape with feathers growing upon its head, who launched death from a slender branch, and then ran, with the fleetness of Bara, the deer, toward the rising sun.

Tarzan waited no longer, but leaping into the branches of the trees sped rapidly through the forest. He knew the windings of the elephant trail along which Kala's murderer had flown, and so he cut straight through the jungle to intercept the black warrior who was evidently following the tortuous detours of the trail.

At his side was the hunting knife of his unknown sire, and across his shoulders the coils of his own long rope. In an hour he struck the trail again, and coming to earth examined the soil minutely.

In the soft mud on the bank of a tiny rivulet he found footprints such as he alone in all the jungle had ever made, but much larger than his. His heart beat fast. Could it be that he was trailing a MAN—one of his own race?

There were two sets of imprints pointing in opposite directions. So his quarry had already passed on his return along the trail. As he examined the newer spoor a tiny particle of earth toppled from the outer edge of one of the footprints to the bottom of its shallow depression—ah, the trail was very fresh, his prey must have but scarcely passed.

Tarzan swung himself to the trees once more, and with swift noiselessness sped along high above the trail.

He had covered barely a mile when he came upon the black warrior standing in a little open space. In his hand was his slender bow to which he had fitted one of his death dealing arrows.

Opposite him across the little clearing stood Horta, the boar, with lowered head and foam-flecked tusks, ready to charge.

Tarzan looked with wonder upon the strange creature beneath him—so like him in form and yet so different in the particulars of its appearance. His books had portrayed *man*, but how different had been the dull, dead print to this sleek thing, pulsing with life.

As the man stood there with taut-drawn bow Tarzan recognized him as the *Archer* of his picture book—

A stands for Archer

How wonderful! Tarzan almost betrayed his presence in the deep excitement of his discovery.

But things were commencing to happen below him. The warrior's sinewy arm had drawn the shaft far back; Horta, the boar, was charging, and then the archer released the little poisoned arrow, and Tarzan saw it fly with the quickness of thought and lodge in the bristling neck of the boar.

Scarcely had the shaft left his bow ere Kulonga had fitted another to it, but Horta, the boar, was upon him so quickly that he had no time to discharge it. With a bound the man leaped entirely over the rushing beast and turning with incredible swiftness planted a second arrow in Horta's back.

Then Kulonga sprang into a nearby tree.

Horta wheeled to charge his enemy once more; a dozen steps he took, then he staggered and fell upon his side. For a moment his muscles stiffened and relaxed convulsively, then he lay still.

Kulonga came down from his tree.

With a knife that hung at his side he cut several large pieces from the boar's body, and in the center of the trail he built a fire, cooking and eating as much as he wanted. The rest he left where it had fallen.

Tarzan was an interested spectator. His desire to kill burned fiercely in his wild breast, but his desire to learn was even greater. He would follow this savage creature for a while and know from whence he came. He could kill him at his leisure later, when the bow and deadly arrows were laid aside.

When Kulonga had finished his repast and disappeared beyond a near turning of the path, Tarzan dropped quietly to the ground. With his knife he severed many strips of meat from Horta's carcass, but he did not cook them.

He had seen fire, but only when Ara, the lightning, had destroyed some great tree. That any creature of the jungle could produce the red-and-yellow fangs which devoured wood and left nothing but fine dust surprised Tarzan greatly, and why the black warrior had ruined his delicious repast by plunging it into the blighting heat was quite beyond him. Possibly Ara was a friend with whom the Archer was sharing his food.

But, be that as it may, Tarzan would not ruin good meat in any such foolish manner, so he gobbled down a great quantity of the raw flesh, burying the balance of the carcass beside the trail where he could find it upon his return.

And then Lord Greystoke wiped his greasy fingers upon his naked thighs and took up the trail of Kulonga, the son of Mbonga, the king; while in far-off London another Lord Greystoke, the younger brother of the real Lord Greystoke's father, sent back his chops to the club's *chef* because they were underdone, and when he had finished his repast he dipped his finger-ends into a silver bowl of scented water and dried them upon a piece of snowy damask.

All day Tarzan followed Kulonga, hovering above him in the trees like some malign spirit. Twice more he saw him hurl his arrows of destruction—once at Dango, the hyena, and again at Manu, the monkey. In each instance the animal died almost instantly, for Kulonga's poison was very fresh and very deadly.

Tarzan thought much on this wondrous method of slaying as he swung slowly along at a safe distance behind his quarry. He knew that alone the tiny prick of the arrow could not so quickly dispatch these wild things of the jungle, who were often torn and scratched and gored in a frightful manner as they fought with their jungle neighbors, yet as often recovered as not.

No, there was something mysterious connected with these tiny slivers of wood which could bring death by a mere scratch. He must look into the matter.

That night Kulonga slept in the crotch of a mighty tree and far above him crouched Tarzan of the Apes.

When Kulonga awoke he found that his bow and arrows had disappeared. The warrior was furious and frightened, but more frighted than furious. He searched the ground below the tree, and he searched the tree above the ground; but there was no sign of either bow or arrows or of the nocturnal marauder.

Kulonga was panic-stricken. His spear he had hurled at Kala and had not recovered; and, now that his bow and arrows were gone, he was defenseless except for a single knife. His only hope lay in reaching the village of Mbonga as quickly as his legs would carry him.

That he was not far from home he was certain, so he took the trail at a rapid trot.

From a great mass of impenetrable foliage a few yards away emerged Tarzan of the Apes to swing quietly in his wake.

Kulonga's bow and arrows were securely tied high in the top of a giant tree from which a patch of bark had been removed by a sharp knife near to the ground, and a branch half cut through and left hanging about fifty feet higher up. Thus Tarzan blazed the forest trails and marked his caches.

As Kulonga continued his journey Tarzan closed up on him until he traveled almost over the man's head. He was almost ready for the kill.

The moment was delayed only because Tarzan was anxious to ascertain the warrior's destination, and presently he was rewarded, for they came suddenly in view of a great clearing, at one end of which lay many strange lairs.

Tarzan was directly over Kulonga, as he made the discovery. The forest ended abruptly and beyond lay two hundred yards of planted fields between the jungle and the village.

Tarzan must act quickly or his prey would be gone; but Tarzan's life training left so little space between decision and action when an emergency confronted him that there was not even room for the shadow of a thought between.

So it was that as Kulonga emerged from the shadow of the jungle a keen-eyed enemy crouched upon the lowest branch of a mighty tree directly upon the edge of the fields of Mbonga, and ere the king's son had taken a half-dozen steps into the clearing his fate was sealed.

So quickly did Tarzan of the Apes draw up his prey into the sheltering verdure of the tree that Kulonga could utter no cry of alarm. Without hesitation the ape-man plunged his hunting knife into Kulonga's heart. Kala was avenged.

Tarzan examined the man minutely, never had he seen any other human being. The knife with its sheath and belt caught his eye; he appropriated them. A copper anklet also took his fancy, and this he transferred to his own leg.

He examined and admired the tattooing on the forehead and breast. He marveled at the sharp filed teeth. He investigated and appropriated the feathered headdress, and then he prepared to get down to business, for Tarzan of the Apes was hungry, and here was meat; meat of the kill, which jungle ethics permitted him to eat.

How may we judge him, by what standards, this ape-man with the heart and head and body of an English gentleman, and the training of a wild beast?

Tublat, whom he had hated and who had hated him, he had killed in a fair fight, and yet never had the thought of eating Tublat's flesh entered his head. It would have been as revolting to him as is cannibalism to us.

But who was Kulonga that he might not be eaten as fairly as Horta, the boar, or Bara, the deer? Was he not simply another of the countless wild things of the jungle who preyed upon one another to satisfy the cravings of hunger?

Of a sudden, a strange doubt stayed his hand. Had not his books taught him that he was a man? And was not The Archer a man, also?

Did men eat men? Alas, he did not know. Why, then, this hesitancy! Once more he essayed the effort, but of a sudden a qualm of nausea overwhelmed him. He did not understand.

All he knew was that he could not eat the flesh of this man, and thus hereditary instinct, ages old, usurped the functions of his untaught mind and saved him from transgressing a worldwide law of whose very existence he was ignorant.

Quickly he lowered Kulonga's body to the ground and took to the trees again.

CHAPTER TEN
THE FEAR-FANTOM

FROM A LOFTY PERCH Tarzan viewed the village of thatched huts across the intervening plantation.

He saw that at one point the forest touched the village, and to this spot he made his way, lured by a fever of curiosity to behold animals of his own kind, and to learn more of their ways and view the strange lairs in which they lived.

His savage life among the fierce wild brutes of the jungle left no opening for any thought that these could be aught else than enemies. Similarity of form led him into no erroneous conception of the welcome that would be accorded him should he be discovered by these, the first of his own kind he had ever seen.

Tarzan of the Apes was no sentimentalist. He knew nothing of the brotherhood of man. All things outside his own tribe were his deadly enemies, with the few exceptions of which Tantor, the elephant, was a marked example.

And he realized all this without malice or hatred. To kill was the law of the wild world he knew. Few were his primitive pleasures, but the greatest of these was to hunt and kill, and so he accorded to others the right to cherish the same desires as he, even though he himself might be the object of their hunt.

His strange life had left him neither morose nor bloodthirsty. That he joyed in killing, and that he killed with a joyous laugh upon his handsome lips, betokened no innate cruelty. He killed for food most often, but, being a man, he sometimes killed for pleasure, a thing which no other animal does; for it has remained for man alone among all creatures to kill senselessly and wantonly for the mere pleasure of inflicting suffering and death.

And when he killed for revenge, or in self-defense, he did that also without hysteria, but it was a very businesslike proceeding which admitted of no levity.

So it was that now, as he cautiously approached the village of Mbonga, he was quite prepared either to kill or be killed should he be discovered. He proceeded with unwonted stealth, for Kulonga had taught him great respect for the little sharp splinters of wood which dealt death so swiftly and unerringly.

At length he came to a great tree, heavy laden with thick foliage and loaded with pendent loops of giant creepers. From this almost impenetrable bower above the village he crouched, looking down upon the scene below him, wondering over every feature of this new, strange life.

There were naked children running and playing in the village street. There were women grinding dried plantain in crude stone mortars, while others were fashioning cakes from the powdered flour. Out in the fields he could see still other women hoeing, weeding, or gathering.

All wore strange protruding girdles of dried grass about their hips and many were loaded with brass and copper anklets, armlets, and bracelets. Around many a neck hung curiously coiled strands of wire, while several were further ornamented by huge nose rings.

Tarzan of the Apes looked with growing wonder at these strange creatures. Dozing in the shade he saw several men, while at the extreme outskirts of the clearing he occasionally caught glimpses of armed warriors apparently guarding the village against surprise from an attacking enemy.

He noticed that the women alone worked. Nowhere was there evidence of a man tilling the fields or performing any of the homely duties of the village.

Finally his eyes rested upon a woman directly beneath him.

Before her was a small cauldron standing over a low fire and in it bubbled a thick, reddish, tarry mass. On one side of her lay a quantity of wooden arrows the points of which she dipped into the seething substance, then laying them upon a narrow rack of boughs which stood upon her other side.

Tarzan of the Apes was fascinated. Here was the secret of the terrible destructiveness of The Archer's tiny missiles. He noted the extreme care which the woman took that none of the matter should touch her hands, and once when a particle spattered upon one of her fingers he saw her plunge the member into a vessel of water and quickly rub the tiny stain away with a handful of leaves.

Tarzan of the Apes knew nothing of poison, but his shrewd reasoning told him that it was this deadly stuff that killed, and not the little arrow, which was merely the messenger that carried it into the body of its victim.

How he should like to have more of those little death-dealing slivers. If the woman would only leave her work for an instant he could drop down, gather up a handful, and be back in the tree again before she drew three breaths.

As he was trying to think out some plan to distract her attention he heard a wild cry from across the clearing. He looked and saw a warrior standing beneath the very tree in which he had killed the murderer of Kala an hour before.

The fellow was shouting and waving his spear above his head. Now and again he would point to something on the ground before him.

The village was in an uproar instantly. Armed men rushed from the interior of many a hut and raced madly across the clearing toward the excited sentry. After them trooped the old men, and the women and children, until, in a moment, the village was deserted.

Tarzan of the Apes knew that they had found the body of his victim, but that interested him far less than the fact that no one remained in the village to prevent his taking a supply of the arrows which lay below him.

Quickly and noiselessly he dropped to the ground beside the cauldron of poison. For a moment he stood motionless, his quick, bright eyes scanning the interior of the palisade.

No one was in sight. His eyes rested upon the open doorway of a nearby hut. He would take a look within, thought Tarzan, and so, cautiously, he approached the low thatched building.

For a moment he stood without, listening intently. There was no sound, and he glided into the semidarkness of the interior.

Weapons hung against the walls—long spears, strangely shaped knives, a couple of narrow shields. In the center of the room was a cooking pot, and at the far end a litter of dry grasses covered by woven mats which evidently served the owners as beds and bedding. Several human skulls lay upon the floor.

Tarzan of the Apes felt of each article, hefted the spears, smelled of them, for he "saw" largely through his sensitive and highly trained nostrils. He determined to own one of these long, pointed sticks, but he could not take one on this trip because of the arrows he meant to carry.

One by one, as he took each article from the walls, he placed it in a pile in the center of the room, and on top of all he placed the cooking pot, inverted, and on top of this he laid one of the grinning skulls, upon which he fastened the headdress of the dead Kulonga.

Then he stood back, surveyed his work, and grinned. Tarzan of the Apes was a joker.

But now he heard, outside, the sounds of many voices, and long mournful howls, and mighty wailing. He was startled. Had he remained too long? Quickly he reached the doorway and peered down the village street toward the village gate.

The natives were not yet in sight, though he could plainly hear them approaching across the plantation. They must be very near.

Like a flash he sprang across the opening to the pile of arrows. Gathering up all he could carry under one arm, he overturned the seething cauldron with a kick, and disappeared into the foliage above just as the first of the returning natives entered the gate at the far end of the village street. Then he turned to watch the proceeding below, poised like some wild bird ready to take swift wing at the first sign of danger.

The natives filed up the street, four of them bearing the dead body of Kulonga. Behind trailed the women, uttering strange cries and weird lamentation. On they came to the portals of Kulonga's hut, the very one in which Tarzan had wrought his depredations.

Scarcely had half a dozen entered the building ere they came rushing out in wild, jabbering confusion. The others hastened to gather about. There was much excited gesticulating, pointing, and chattering; then several of the warriors approached and peered within.

Finally an old fellow with many ornaments of metal about his arms and legs, and a necklace of dried human hands depending upon his chest, entered the hut.

It was Mbonga, the king, father of Kulonga.

For a few moments all was silent. Then Mbonga emerged, a look of mingled wrath and fear writ upon his countenance. He spoke a few words to the assembled warriors, and in an instant the men were flying through the little village searching minutely every hut and corner within the palisades.

Scarcely had the search commenced than the overturned cauldron was discovered, and with it the theft of the poisoned arrows. Nothing more they found, and it was a thoroughly awed and frightened group of villagers which huddled around their king a few moments later.

Mbonga could explain nothing of the strange events that had taken place. The finding of the still warm body of Kulonga—on the very verge of their fields and within easy earshot of the village—knifed and stripped at the door of his father's home, was in itself sufficiently mysterious, but these last awesome discoveries within the village, within the dead Kulonga's own hut, filled their hearts with dismay, and conjured in their brains only the most frightful of superstitious explanations.

They stood in little groups, talking in low tones, and ever casting affrighted glances behind them.

Tarzan of the Apes watched them for a while from his lofty perch in the great tree. There was much in their demeanor which he could not understand, for of superstition he was ignorant, and of fear of any kind he had but a vague conception.

The sun was high in the heavens. Tarzan had not broken fast this day, and it was many miles to where lay the toothsome remains of Horta the boar.

So he turned his back upon the village of Mbonga and melted away into the leafy fastness of the forest.

CHAPTER ELEVEN
"KING OF THE APES"

IT WAS NOT DARK YET when he reached the tribe, though he stopped to exhume and devour the remains of the wild boar he had cached the preceding day, and again to take Kulonga's bow and arrows from the treetop in which he had hidden them.

It was a well-laden Tarzan who dropped from the branches into the midst of the tribe of Kerchak.

With swelling chest he narrated the glories of his adventure and exhibited the spoils of conquest.

Kerchak grunted and turned away, for he was jealous of this strange member of his band. In his little evil brain he sought for some excuse to wreak his hatred upon Tarzan.

The next day Tarzan was practicing with his bow and arrows at the first gleam of dawn. At first he lost nearly every bolt he shot, but finally he learned to guide the little shafts with fair accuracy, and ere a month had passed he was no mean shot; but his proficiency had cost him nearly his entire supply of arrows.

The tribe continued to find the hunting good in the vicinity of the beach, and so Tarzan of the Apes varied his archery practice with further investigation of his father's choice though little store of books.

It was during this period that the young English lord found hidden in the back of one of the cupboards in the cabin a small metal box. The key was in the lock, and a few moments of investigation and experimentation were rewarded with the successful opening of the receptacle.

In it he found a faded photograph of a smooth-faced young man, a golden locket studded with diamonds, linked to a small gold chain, a few letters, and a small book.

Tarzan examined these all minutely.

The photograph he liked most of all, for the eyes were smiling, and the face was open and frank. It was his father.

The locket, too, took his fancy, and he placed the chain about his neck in imitation of the ornamentation he had seen to be so common among the native villagers he had visited. The brilliant stones gleamed strangely against his smooth, brown hide.

The letters he could scarcely decipher for he had learned little or nothing of script, so he put them back in the box with the photograph and turned his attention to the book.

This was almost entirely filled with fine script, but while the little bugs were all familiar to him, their arrangement and the combinations in which they occurred were strange, and entirely incomprehensible.

Tarzan had long since learned the use of the dictionary, but much to his sorrow and perplexity it proved of no avail to him in this emergency. Not a word of all that was writ in the book could he find, and so he put it back in the metal box, but with a determination to work out the mysteries of it later on.

Poor little ape-man! Had he but known it that tiny, baffling mystery held between its sealed covers the key to his origin—the answer to the strange riddle of his strange life.

It was the diary of John Clayton, Lord Greystoke—kept in French, as had always been his custom.

Tarzan replaced the box in the cupboard, but always thereafter he carried the features of the strong, smiling face of his father in his heart, and in his head a fixed determination to solve the mystery of the strange words in the little black book.

At present he had more important business in hand, for his supply of arrows was exhausted, and he must needs journey to the village and renew it.

Early the following morning he set out, and, traveling rapidly, he came before midday to the clearing. Once more he took up his position in the great tree, and, as before, he saw the women in the fields and the village street, and the cauldron of bubbling poison directly beneath him.

For hours he lay awaiting his opportunity to drop down unseen and gather up the arrows for which he had come; but nothing now occurred to call the villagers away from their homes. The day wore on, and still Tarzan of the Apes crouched above the unsuspecting woman at the cauldron.

Presently the workers in the fields returned. The hunting warriors emerged from the forest, and when all were within the palisade the gates were closed and barred.

Many cooking pots were now in evidence about the village. Before each hut a woman presided over a boiling stew, while little cakes of plantain, and cassava puddings were to be seen on every hand.

Suddenly there came a hail from the edge of the clearing.

Tarzan looked.

It was a party of belated hunters returning from the north, and among them they half led, half carried a struggling animal.

As they approached the village the gates were thrown open to admit them, and then, as the people saw the victim of the chase, a savage cry rose to the heavens, for the quarry was a man.

As he was dragged, still resisting, into the village street, the women and children set upon him with sticks and stones, and Tarzan of the Apes, young and savage beast of the jungle, wondered at the cruel brutality of his own kind.

Sheeta, the leopard, alone of all the jungle folk, tortured his prey. The ethics of all the others meted a quick and merciful death to their victims.

Tarzan had learned from his books but scattered fragments of the ways of human beings.

When he had followed Kulonga through the forest he had expected to come to a city of strange houses on wheels, puffing clouds of black smoke from a huge tree stuck in the roof of one of them—or to a sea covered with mighty floating buildings which he had learned were called, variously, ships and boats and steamers and craft.

He had been sorely disappointed with the poor little village, hidden away in his own jungle, and with not a single house as large as his own cabin upon the distant beach.

He saw that these people were more wicked than his own apes, and as savage and cruel as Sabor, herself. Tarzan began to hold his own kind in low esteem.

Now they had tied their poor victim to a great post near the center of the village, directly before Mbonga's hut, and here they formed a dancing, yelling circle of warriors about him, alive with flashing knives and menacing spears.

In a larger circle squatted the women, yelling and beating upon drums. It reminded Tarzan of the Dum-Dum, and so he knew what to expect. He wondered if they would spring upon their meat while it was still alive. The Apes did not do such things as that.

The circle of warriors about the cringing captive drew closer and closer to their prey as they danced in wild and savage abandon to the maddening music of the drums. Presently a spear reached out and pricked the victim. It was the signal for fifty others.

Eyes, ears, arms, and legs were pierced; every inch of the poor writhing body that did not cover a vital organ became the target of the cruel lancers.

The women and children shrieked their delight. The warriors licked their hideous lips in anticipation of the feast to come, and vied with one another in the savagery and loathsomeness of the cruel indignities with which they tortured the still conscious prisoner.

Then it was that Tarzan of the Apes saw his chance. All eyes were fixed upon the thrilling spectacle at the stake. The light of day had given place to the darkness of a moonless night, and only the fires in the immediate vicinity of the orgy had been kept alight to cast a restless glow upon the restless scene.

Gently the lithe boy dropped to the soft earth at the end of the village street. Quickly he gathered up the arrows—all of them this time, for he had brought a number of long fibers to bind them into a bundle.

Without haste he wrapped them securely, and then, ere he turned to leave, the devil of capriciousness entered his heart. He looked about for some hint of a wild prank to play upon these strange, grotesque creatures that they might be again aware of his presence among them.

Dropping his bundle of arrows at the foot of the tree, Tarzan crept among the shadows at the side of the street until he came to the same hut he had entered on the occasion of his first visit.

Inside all was darkness, but his groping hands soon found the object for which he sought, and without further delay he turned again toward the door.

He had taken but a step, however, ere his quick ear caught the sound of approaching footsteps immediately without. In another instant the figure of a woman darkened the entrance of the hut.

Tarzan drew back silently to the far wall, and his hand sought the long, keen hunting knife of his father. The woman came quickly to the center of the hut. There she paused for an instant feeling about with her hands for the thing she sought. Evidently it was not in its accustomed place, for she explored ever nearer and nearer the wall where Tarzan stood.

So close was she now that the ape-man felt the animal warmth of her naked body. Up went the hunting knife, and then the woman turned to one side and soon a guttural "ah" proclaimed that her search had at last been successful.

Immediately she turned and left the hut, and as she passed through the doorway Tarzan saw that she carried a cooking pot in her hand.

He followed closely after her, and as he reconnoitered from the shadows of the doorway he saw that all the women of the village were hastening to and from the various huts with pots and kettles. These they were filling with water and placing over a number of fires near the stake where the dying victim now hung, an inert and bloody mass of suffering.

Choosing a moment when none seemed near, Tarzan hastened to his bundle of arrows beneath the great tree at the end of the village street. As on the former occasion he overthrew the cauldron before leaping, sinuous and catlike, into the lower branches of the forest giant.

Silently he climbed to a great height until he found a point where he could look through a leafy opening upon the scene beneath him.

The women were now preparing the prisoner for their cooking pots, while the men stood about resting after the fatigue of their mad revel. Comparative quiet reigned in the village.

Tarzan raised aloft the thing he had pilfered from the hut, and, with aim made true by years of fruit and coconut throwing, launched it toward the group of villagers.

Squarely among them it fell, striking one of the warriors full upon the head and felling him to the ground. Then it rolled among the women and stopped beside the half-butchered thing they were preparing to feast upon.

All gazed in consternation at it for an instant, and then, with one accord, broke and ran for their huts.

It was a grinning human skull which looked up at them from the ground. The dropping of the thing out of the open sky was a miracle well aimed to work upon their superstitious fears.

Thus Tarzan of the Apes left them filled with terror at this new manifestation of the presence of some unseen and unearthly evil power which lurked in the forest about their village.

Later, when they discovered the overturned cauldron, and that once more their arrows had been pilfered, it commenced to dawn upon them that they had offended some great god who ruled this part of the jungle by placing their village there without propitiating him. From then on an offering of food was daily placed below the great tree from whence the arrows had disappeared in an effort to conciliate the mighty one.

But the seed of fear was deep sown, and had he but known it, Tarzan of the Apes had laid the foundation for much future misery for himself and his tribe.

That night he slept in the forest not far from the village, and early the next morning set out slowly on his homeward march, hunting as he traveled. Only a few berries and an occasional grub worm rewarded his search, and he was half famished when, looking up from a log he had been rooting beneath, he saw Sabor, the lioness, standing in the center of the trail not twenty paces from him.

The great yellow eyes were fixed upon him with a wicked and baleful gleam, and the red tongue licked the longing lips as Sabor crouched, worming her stealthy way with belly flattened against the earth.

Tarzan did not attempt to escape. He welcomed the opportunity for which, in fact, he had been searching for days past, now armed not only with a rope of grass.

Quickly he unslung his bow and fitted a well-daubed arrow, and as Sabor sprang, the tiny missile leaped to meet her in midair. At the same instant Tarzan of the Apes jumped to one side, and as the great cat struck the ground beyond him another death-tipped arrow sunk deep into Sabor's loin.

With a mighty roar the beast turned and charged once more, only to be met with a third arrow full in one eye; but this time she was too close to the ape-man for the latter to sidestep the onrushing body.

Tarzan of the Apes went down beneath the great body of his enemy, but with gleaming knife drawn and striking home. For a moment they lay there, and then Tarzan realized that the inert mass lying upon him was beyond power ever again to injure man or ape.

With difficulty he wriggled from beneath the great weight, and as he stood erect and gazed down upon the trophy of his skill, a mighty wave of exultation swept over him.

With swelling breast, he placed a foot upon the body of his powerful enemy, and throwing back his fine young head, roared out the awful challenge of the victorious bull ape.

The forest echoed to the savage and triumphant paean. Birds fell still, and the larger animals and beasts of prey slunk stealthily away, for few there were of all the jungle who sought for trouble with the great anthropoids.

And in London another Lord Greystoke was speaking to *his* kind in the House of Lords, but none trembled at the sound of his soft voice.

Sabor proved unsavory eating even to Tarzan of the Apes, but hunger served as a most efficacious disguise to toughness and rank taste, and ere long, with well-filled stomach, the ape-man was ready to sleep again. First, however, he must remove the hide, for it was as much for this as for any other purpose that he had desired to encompass the destruction of Sabor.

Deftly he removed the great pelt, for he had practiced often on smaller animals. When the task was finished he carried his trophy to the fork of a high tree, and there, curling himself securely in a crotch, he fell into deep and dreamless slumber.

What with loss of sleep, arduous exercise, and a full belly, Tarzan of the Apes slept the sun around, awakening about noon of the following day. He straightway repaired to the carcass of Sabor, but was angered to find the bones picked clean by other hungry denizens of the jungle.

Half an hour's leisurely progress through the forest brought to sight a young deer, and before ever the little creature knew that an enemy was near a tiny arrow had lodged in its neck.

So quickly the virus worked that at the end of a dozen leaps the deer plunged headlong into the undergrowth, dead. Again did Tarzan feast well, but this time he did not sleep.

Instead, he hastened on toward the point where he had left the tribe, and when he had found them proudly exhibited the skin of Sabor, the lioness.

"Look!" he cried, "Apes of Kerchak. See what Tarzan, the mighty killer, has done. Who else among you has ever killed one of Numa's people? Tarzan is mightiest amongst you for Tarzan is no ape. Tarzan is—" But here he stopped, for in the language of the anthropoids there was no word for man, and Tarzan could only write the word in English; he could not pronounce it.

The tribe had gathered about to look upon the proof of his wondrous prowess, and to listen to his words.

Only Kerchak hung back, nursing his hatred and his rage.

Suddenly something snapped in the wicked little brain of the anthropoid. With a frightful roar the great beast sprang among the assemblage.

Biting, and striking with his huge hands, he killed and maimed a dozen ere the balance could escape to the upper terraces of the forest.

Frothing and shrieking in the insanity of his fury, Kerchak looked about for the object of his greatest hatred, and there, upon a nearby limb, he saw him sitting.

"Come down, Tarzan, great killer," cried Kerchak. "Come down and feel the fangs of a greater! Do mighty fighters fly to the trees at the first approach of danger?" And then Kerchak emitted the volleying challenge of his kind.

Quietly Tarzan dropped to the ground. Breathlessly the tribe watched from their lofty perches as Kerchak, still roaring, charged the relatively puny figure.

Nearly seven feet stood Kerchak on his short legs. His enormous shoulders were bunched and rounded with huge muscles. The back of his short neck was as a single lump of iron sinew which bulged beyond the base of his skull, so that his head seemed like a small ball protruding from a huge mountain of flesh.

His back-drawn, snarling lips exposed his great fighting fangs, and his little, wicked, bloodshot eyes gleamed in horrid reflection of his madness.

Awaiting him stood Tarzan, himself a mighty muscled animal, but his six feet of height and his great rolling sinews seemed pitifully inadequate to the ordeal which awaited them.

His bow and arrows lay some distance away where he had dropped them while showing Sabor's hide to his fellow apes, so that he confronted Kerchak now with only his hunting knife and his superior intellect to offset the ferocious strength of his enemy.

As his antagonist came roaring toward him, Lord Greystoke tore his long knife from its sheath, and with an answering challenge as horrid and bloodcurdling as that of the beast he faced, rushed swiftly to meet the attack. He was too shrewd to allow those long hairy arms to encircle him, and just as their bodies were about to crash together, Tarzan of the Apes grasped one of the huge wrists of his assailant, and, springing lightly to one side, drove his knife to the hilt into Kerchak's body, below the heart.

Before he could wrench the blade free again, the bull's quick lunge to seize him in those awful arms had torn the weapon from Tarzan's grasp.

Kerchak aimed a terrific blow at the ape-man's head with the flat of his hand, a blow which, had it landed, might easily have crushed in the side of Tarzan's skull.

The man was too quick, and, ducking beneath it, himself delivered a mighty one, with clenched fist, in the pit of Kerchak's stomach.

The ape was staggered, and what with the mortal wound in his side had almost collapsed, when, with one mighty effort he rallied for an instant—just long enough to enable him to wrest his arm free from Tarzan's grasp and close in a terrific clinch with his wiry opponent.

Straining the ape-man close to him, his great jaws sought Tarzan's throat, but the young lord's sinewy fingers were at Kerchak's own before the cruel fangs could close on the sleek brown skin.

Thus they struggled, the one to crush out his opponent's life with those awful teeth, the other to close forever the windpipe beneath his strong grasp the while he held the snarling mouth from him.

The greater strength of the ape was slowly prevailing, and the teeth of the straining beast were scarce an inch from Tarzan's throat when, with a shuddering tremor, the great body stiffened for an instant and then sank limply to the ground.

Kerchak was dead.

Withdrawing the knife that had so often rendered him master of far mightier muscles than his own, Tarzan of the Apes placed his foot upon the neck of his vanquished enemy, and once again, loud through the forest rang the fierce, wild cry of the conqueror.

And thus came the young Lord Greystoke into the kingship of the Apes.

CHAPTER TWELVE
MAN'S REASON

THERE WAS ONE OF THE TRIBE OF TARZAN who questioned his authority, and that was Terkoz, the son of Tublat, but he so feared the keen knife and the deadly arrows of his new lord that he confined the manifestation of his objections to petty disobediences and irritating mannerisms; Tarzan knew, however, that he but waited his opportunity to wrest the kingship from him by some sudden stroke of treachery, and so he was ever on his guard against surprise.

For months the life of the little band went on much as it had before, except that Tarzan's greater intelligence and his ability as a hunter were the means of providing for them more bountifully than ever before. Most of them, therefore, were more than content with the change in rulers.

Tarzan led them by night to the fields of the villagers, and there, warned by their chief's superior wisdom, they ate only what they required, nor ever did they destroy what they could not eat, as is the way of Manu, the monkey, and of most apes.

So, while the villagers were wroth at the continued pilfering of their fields, they were not discouraged in their efforts to cultivate the land, as would have been the case had Tarzan permitted his people to lay waste the plantation wantonly.

During this period Tarzan paid many nocturnal visits to the village, where he often renewed his supply of arrows. He soon noticed the food always standing at the foot of the tree which was his avenue into the palisade, and after a little, he commenced to eat whatever the villagers put there.

When the awestruck natives saw that the food disappeared overnight they were filled with consternation and dread, for it was one thing to put food out to propitiate a god or a devil, but quite another thing to have the spirit really come into the village and eat it. Such a thing was unheard of and it clouded their minds with all manner of vague fears.

Nor was this all. The periodic disappearance of their arrows, and the strange pranks perpetrated by unseen hands, had wrought them to such a state that life had become a veritable burden in their new home, and now it was that Mbonga and his headmen began to talk of abandoning the village and seeking a site farther on in the jungle.

Presently the warriors began to strike farther and farther south into the heart of the forest when they went to hunt, looking for a site for a new village.

More often was the tribe of Tarzan disturbed by these wandering huntsmen. Now was the quiet, fierce solitude of the primeval forest broken by new, strange cries. No longer was there safety for bird or beast. Man had come.

Other animals passed up and down the jungle by day and by night—fierce, cruel beasts—but their weaker neighbors only fled from their immediate vicinity to return again when the danger was past.

With man it is different. When he comes many of the larger animals instinctively leave the district entirely, seldom if ever to return; and thus it has always been with the great anthropoids. They flee man as man flees a pestilence.

For a short time the tribe of Tarzan lingered in the vicinity of the beach because their new chief hated the thought of leaving the treasured contents of the little cabin forever. But when one day a member of the tribe discovered the villagers in great numbers on the banks of a little stream that had been their watering place for generations, and in the act of clearing a space in the jungle and erecting many huts, the apes would remain no longer; and so Tarzan led them inland for many marches to a spot as yet undefiled by the foot of a human being.

Once every moon Tarzan would go swinging rapidly back through the swaying branches to have a day with his books, and to replenish his supply of arrows. This latter task was becoming more and more difficult, for the villagers had taken to hiding their supply away at night in granaries and living huts.

This necessitated watching by day on Tarzan's part to discover where the arrows were being concealed. Twice had he entered huts at night while the inmates lay sleeping upon their mats, and stolen the arrows from the very sides of the warriors.

These various escapades again so terrorized the villagers that, had it not been for the monthly respite between Tarzan's visits, in which they had opportunity to renew hope that each fresh incursion would prove the last, they soon would have abandoned their new village.

The villagers had not as yet come upon Tarzan's cabin on the distant beach, but the ape-man lived in constant dread that, while he was away with the tribe, they would discover and despoil his treasure. So it came that he spent more and more time in the vicinity of his father's last home, and less and less with the tribe. Presently the members of his little community began to suffer on account of his neglect, for disputes and quarrels constantly arose which only the king might settle peaceably.

At last some of the older apes spoke to Tarzan on the subject, and for a month thereafter he remained constantly with the tribe.

The duties of kingship among the anthropoids are not many or arduous.

In the afternoon comes Thaka, possibly, to complain that old Mungo has stolen his new wife. Then must Tarzan summon all before him, and if he finds that the wife prefers her new lord he commands that matters remain as they are, or possibly that Mungo give Thaka one of his daughters in exchange.

Whatever his decision, the apes accept it as final, and return to their occupations satisfied.

Then comes Tana, shrieking and holding tight her side from which blood is streaming. Gunto, her husband, has cruelly bitten her! And Gunto, summoned, says that Tana is lazy and will not bring him nuts and beetles, or scratch his back for him.

So Tarzan scolds them both and threatens Gunto with a taste of the death-bearing slivers if he abuses Tana further, and Tana, for her part, is compelled to promise better attention to her wifely duties.

And so it goes, little family differences for the most part, which, if left unsettled would result finally in greater factional strife, and the eventual dismemberment of the tribe.

But Tarzan tired of it, as he found that kingship meant the curtailment of his liberty. He longed for the little cabin and the sun-kissed sea—for the cool interior of the well-built house, and for the never-ending wonders of the many books.

As he had grown older, he found that he had grown away from his people. Their interests and his were far removed. They had not kept pace with him, nor could they understand aught of the many strange and wonderful dreams that passed through the active brain of their human king. So limited was their vocabulary that Tarzan could not even talk with them of the many new truths, and the great fields of thought that his reading had opened up before his longing eyes, or make known ambitions which stirred his soul.

Among the tribe he no longer had friends and cronies as of old. A little child may find companionship in many strange and simple creatures, but to a grown man there must be some semblance of equality in intellect as the basis for agreeable consociation.

Had Kala lived, Tarzan would have sacrificed all else to remain near her, but now that she was dead, and the playful friends of his childhood grown into fierce and surly brutes he felt that he much preferred the peace and solitude of his cabin to the irksome duties of leadership amongst a horde of wild beasts.

The hatred and jealousy of Terkoz, son of Tublat, did much to counteract the effect of Tarzan's desire to renounce his kingship among the apes, for, stubborn young Englishman that he was, he could not bring himself to retreat in the face of so malignant an enemy.

That Terkoz would be chosen leader in his stead he knew full well, for time and again the ferocious brute had established his claim to physical supremacy over the few bull apes who had dared resent his savage bullying.

Tarzan would have liked to subdue the ugly beast without recourse to knife or arrows. So much had his great strength and agility increased in the period following his maturity that he had come to believe that he might master the redoubtable Terkoz in a hand-to-hand fight were it not for the terrible advantage the anthropoid's huge fighting fangs gave him over the poorly armed Tarzan.

The entire matter was taken out of Tarzan's hands one day by force of circumstances, and his future left open to him, so that he might go or stay without any stain upon his savage escutcheon.

It happened thus:

The tribe was feeding quietly, spread over a considerable area, when a great screaming arose some distance east of where Tarzan lay upon his belly beside a limpid brook, attempting to catch an elusive fish in his quick, brown hands.

With one accord the tribe swung rapidly toward the frightened cries, and there found Terkoz holding an old female by the hair and beating her unmercifully with his great hands.

As Tarzan approached he raised his hand aloft for Terkoz to desist, for the female was not his, but belonged to a poor old ape whose fighting days were long over, and who, therefore, could not protect his family.

Terkoz knew that it was against the laws of his kind to strike the woman of another, but being a bully, he had taken advantage of the weakness of the female's husband to chastise her because she had refused to give up to him a tender young rodent she had captured.

When Terkoz saw Tarzan approaching without his arrows, he continued to belabor the poor woman in a studied effort to affront his hated chieftain.

Tarzan did not repeat his warning signal, but instead rushed bodily upon the waiting Terkoz.

Never had the ape-man fought so terrible a battle since that long-gone day when Bolgani, the great king gorilla, had so horribly manhandled him ere the newfound knife had, by accident, pricked the savage heart.

Tarzan's knife on the present occasion but barely offset the gleaming fangs of Terkoz, and what little advantage the ape had over the man in brute strength was almost balanced by the latter's wonderful quickness and agility.

In the sum total of their points, however, the anthropoid had a shade the better of the battle, and had there been no other personal attribute to influence the final outcome, Tarzan of the Apes, the young Lord Greystoke, would have died as he had lived—an unknown savage beast in equatorial Africa.

But there was that which had raised him far above his fellows of the jungle—that little spark which spells the whole vast difference between man and brute—Reason. This it was which saved him from death beneath the iron muscles and tearing fangs of Terkoz.

Scarcely had they fought a dozen seconds ere they were rolling upon the ground, striking, tearing, and rending—two great savage beasts battling to the death.

Terkoz had a dozen knife wounds on head and breast, and Tarzan was torn and bleeding—his scalp in one place half torn from his head so that a great piece hung down over one eye, obstructing his vision.

But so far the young Englishman had been able to keep those horrible fangs from his jugular and now, as they fought less fiercely for a moment to regain their breath, Tarzan formed a cunning plan. He would work his way to the other's back and, clinging there with tooth and nail, drive his knife home until Terkoz was no more.

The maneuver was accomplished more easily than he had hoped, for the stupid beast, not knowing what Tarzan was attempting, made no particular effort to prevent the accomplishment of the design.

But when, finally, he realized that his antagonist was fastened to him where his teeth and fists alike were useless against him, Terkoz hurled himself about upon the ground so violently that Tarzan could but cling desperately to the leaping, turning, twisting body, and ere he had struck a blow the knife was hurled from his hand by a heavy impact against the earth, and Tarzan found himself defenseless.

During the rollings and squirmings of the next few minutes, Tarzan's hold was loosened a dozen times until finally an accidental circumstance of those swift and ever-changing evolutions gave him a new hold with his right hand, which he realized was absolutely unassailable.

His arm was passed beneath Terkoz's arm from behind and his hand and forearm encircled the back of Terkoz's neck. It was the half nelson of modern wrestling which the untaught ape-man had stumbled upon, but superior reason showed him in an instant the value of the thing he had discovered. It was the difference to him between life and death.

And so he struggled to encompass a similar hold with the left hand, and in a few moments Terkoz's bull neck was creaking beneath a full nelson.

There was no more lunging about now. The two lay perfectly still upon the ground, Tarzan upon Terkoz's back. Slowly the bullet head of the ape was being forced lower and lower upon his chest.

Tarzan knew what the result would be. In an instant the neck would break. Then there came to Terkoz's rescue the same thing that had put him in these sore straits—a man's reasoning power.

"If I kill him," thought Tarzan, "what advantage will it be to me? Will it not but rob the tribe of a great fighter? And if Terkoz be dead, he will know nothing of my supremacy, while alive he will ever be an example to the other apes."

"*Ka-goda?*" hissed Tarzan in Terkoz's ear, which, in ape tongue, means, freely translated: "Do you surrender?"

For a moment there was no reply, and Tarzan added a few more ounces of pressure, which elicited a horrified shriek of pain from the great beast.

"*Ka-goda?*" repeated Tarzan.

"*Ka-goda!*" cried Terkoz.

"Listen," said Tarzan, easing up a trifle, but not releasing his hold. "I am Tarzan, King of the Apes, mighty hunter, mighty fighter. In all the jungle there is none so great.

"You have said: '*Ka-goda*' to me. All the tribe have heard. Quarrel no more with your king or your people, for next time I shall kill you. Do you understand?"

"*Huh,*" assented Terkoz.

"And you are satisfied?"

"*Huh,*" said the ape.

Tarzan let him up, and in a few minutes all were back at their vocations, as though naught had occurred to mar the tranquility of their primeval forest haunts.

But deep in the minds of the apes was rooted the conviction that

Tarzan was a mighty fighter and a strange creature. Strange because he had had it in his power to kill his enemy, but had allowed him to live—unharmed.

That afternoon as the tribe came together, as was their wont before darkness settled on the jungle, Tarzan, his wounds washed in the limpid waters of the little stream, called the old males about him.

"You have seen again today that Tarzan of the Apes is the greatest among you," he said.

"Huh," they replied with one voice, "Tarzan is great."

"Tarzan," he continued, "is not an ape. He is not like his people. His ways are not their ways, and so Tarzan is going back to the lair of his own kind by the waters of the great lake which has no farther shore. You must choose another to rule you, for Tarzan will not return."

And thus young Lord Greystoke took the first step toward the goal which he had set—the finding of others like himself.

CHAPTER THIRTEEN
HIS OWN KIND

THE FOLLOWING MORNING, Tarzan, lame and sore from the wounds of his battle with Terkoz, set out toward the west and the seacoast.

He traveled very slowly, sleeping in the jungle at night, and reaching his cabin late the following morning.

For several days he moved about but little, only enough to gather what fruit and nuts he required to satisfy the demands of hunger.

In ten days he was quite sound again, except for a terrible, half-healed scar, which, starting above his left eye ran across the top of his head, ending at the right ear. It was the mark left by Terkoz when he had torn the scalp away.

During his convalescence Tarzan tried to fashion a mantle from the skin of Sabor, which had lain all this time in the cabin. But he found the hide had dried as stiff as a board, and as he knew naught of tanning, he was forced to abandon his cherished plan.

Then he determined to filch what few garments he could from one of the men of Mbonga's village, for Tarzan of the Apes had decided to mark his evolution from the lower orders in every possible manner, and nothing seemed to him a more distinguishing badge of manhood than ornaments and clothing.

To this end, therefore, he collected the various arm and leg ornaments he had taken from the warriors, and donned them all after the way he had seen them worn.

About his neck hung the golden chain from which depended the diamond encrusted locket of his mother, the Lady Alice. At his back was a quiver of arrows slung from a leathern shoulder belt, another piece of loot from some vanquished warrior of the village.

About his waist was a belt of tiny strips of rawhide fashioned by himself as a support for the homemade scabbard in which hung his father's hunting knife. The long bow which had been Kulonga's hung over his left shoulder.

The young Lord Greystoke was indeed a strange and warlike figure, his mass of black hair falling to his shoulders behind and cut with his hunting knife to a rude bang upon his forehead, that it might not fall before his eyes.

His straight and perfect figure, muscled as the best of the ancient Roman gladiators must have been muscled, and yet with the soft and sinuous curves of a Greek god, told at a glance the wondrous combination of enormous strength with suppleness and speed.

A personification, was Tarzan of the Apes, of the primitive man, the hunter, the warrior.

With the noble poise of his handsome head upon those broad shoulders, and the fire of life and intelligence in those fine, clear eyes, he might readily have typified some demigod of a wild and warlike bygone people of his ancient forest.

But of these things Tarzan did not think. He was worried because he had not clothing to indicate to all the jungle folks that he was a man and not an ape, and grave doubt often entered his mind as to whether he might not yet become an ape.

Was not hair commencing to grow upon his face? All the apes had hair upon theirs but those of the black men were entirely hairless, with very few exceptions.

True, he had seen pictures in his books of men with great masses of hair upon lip and cheek and chin, but, nevertheless, Tarzan was afraid.

Almost daily he whetted his keen knife and scraped and whittled at his young beard to eradicate this degrading emblem of apehood.

And so he learned to shave—rudely and painfully, it is true—but, nevertheless, effectively.

When he felt quite strong again, after his bloody battle with Terkoz, Tarzan set off one morning toward Mbonga's village. He was moving carelessly along a winding jungle trail, instead of making his progress through the trees, when suddenly he came face to face with a black warrior.

The look of surprise on the man's face was almost comical, and before Tarzan could unsling his bow the fellow had turned and fled down the path crying out in alarm as though to others before him.

Tarzan took to the trees in pursuit, and in a few moments came in view of the men desperately striving to escape.

There were three of them, and they were racing madly in single file through the dense undergrowth.

Tarzan easily distanced them, nor did they see his silent passage above their heads, nor note the crouching figure squatted upon a low branch ahead of them beneath which the trail led them.

Tarzan let the first two pass beneath him, but as the third came swiftly on, he struck.

There was an agonized scream from the victim, and his fellows turned to see his body rise as by magic into the dense foliage of the trees above.

With frightened shrieks they wheeled once more and plunged on in their efforts to escape.

Tarzan dispatched his prisoner quickly and silently; removed the weapons and ornaments, and—oh, the greatest joy of all—a handsome doeskin breechcloth, which he quickly transferred to his own person.

Now indeed was he dressed as a man should be. None there was who could now doubt his high origin. How he should liked to have returned to the tribe to parade before their envious gaze this wondrous finery.

Taking the body across his shoulder, he moved more slowly through the trees toward the little palisaded village, for he again needed arrows.

As he approached quite close to the enclosure he saw an excited group surrounding the two fugitives, who, trembling with fright and exhaustion, were scarce able to recount the uncanny details of their adventure.

Mirando, they said, who had been ahead of them a short distance, had suddenly come screaming toward them, crying that a terrible white and naked warrior was pursuing him. The three of them had hurried toward the village as rapidly as their legs would carry them.

Again Mirando's shrill cry of mortal terror had caused them to look back, and there they had seen the most horrible sight—their companion's body flying upwards into the trees. No other sound did he utter nor was there any creature in sight about him.

The villagers were worked up into a state of fear bordering on panic, but wise old Mbonga affected to feel considerable skepticism regarding the tale, and attributed the whole fabrication to their fright in the face of some real danger.

"You tell us this great story," he said, "because you do not dare to speak the truth. You do not dare admit that when the lion sprang upon Mirando you ran away and left him. You are cowards."

Scarcely had Mbonga ceased speaking when a great crashing of branches in the trees above them caused the warriors to look up in renewed terror. The sight that met their eyes made even wise old Mbonga shudder, for there came the dead body of Mirando, to sprawl with a sickening reverberation upon the ground at their feet.

With one accord the warriors took to their heels; nor did they stop until the last of them was lost in the dense shadows of the surrounding jungle.

Again Tarzan came down into the village and renewed his supply of arrows and ate of the offering of food which the villagers had made to appease his wrath.

Before he left he carried the body of Mirando to the gate of the village, and propped it up against the palisade in such a way that the dead face seemed to be peering around the edge of the gatepost down the path which led to the jungle.

Then Tarzan returned, hunting, always hunting, to the cabin by the beach.

It took a dozen attempts on the part of the thoroughly frightened men to reenter their village, past the horrible, grinning face of their dead fellow, and when they found the food and arrows gone they knew what they had only too well feared, that Mirando had seen the evil spirit of the jungle.

That now seemed to them the logical explanation. Only those who saw this terrible god of the jungle died; for was it not true that none left alive in the village had ever seen him? Therefore, those who had died at his hands must have seen him and paid the penalty with their lives.

As long as they supplied him with arrows and food he would not harm them unless they looked upon him, so it was ordered by Mbonga that in addition to the food offering there should also be laid out an offering of arrows for this Munango-Keewati, and this was done from then on.

If you ever chance to pass that far off African village you will still see before a tiny thatched hut, built just without the village, a little iron pot in which is a quantity of food, and beside it a quiver of well-daubed arrows.

When Tarzan came in sight of the beach where stood his cabin, a strange and unusual spectacle met his vision.

On the placid waters of the landlocked harbor floated a great ship, and on the beach a small boat was drawn up.

But, most wonderful of all, a number of white men like himself were moving about between the beach and his cabin.

Tarzan saw that in many ways they were like the men of his picture books. He crept closer through the trees until he was quite close above them.

There were ten men, swarthy, suntanned, villainous looking fellows. Now they had congregated by the boat and were talking in loud, angry tones, with much gesticulating and shaking of fists.

Presently one of them, a little, mean-faced, black-bearded fellow with a countenance which reminded Tarzan of Pamba, the rat, laid his hand upon the shoulder of a giant who stood next him, and with whom all the others had been arguing and quarreling.

The little man pointed inland, so that the giant was forced to turn away from the others to look in the direction indicated. As he turned, the little, mean-faced man drew a revolver from his belt and shot the giant in the back.

The big fellow threw his hands above his head, his knees bent beneath him, and without a sound he tumbled forward upon the beach, dead.

The report of the weapon, the first that Tarzan had ever heard, filled him with wonderment, but even this unaccustomed sound could not startle his healthy nerves into even a semblance of panic.

The conduct of the white strangers it was that caused him the greatest perturbation. He puckered his brows into a frown of deep thought. It was well, thought he, that he had not given way to his first impulse to rush forward and greet these white men as brothers.

They were evidently no different from the black men—no more civilized than the apes—no less cruel than Sabor.

For a moment the others stood looking at the little, mean-faced man and the giant lying dead upon the beach.

Then one of them laughed and slapped the little man upon the back. There was much more talk and gesticulating, but less quarreling.

Presently they launched the boat and all jumped into it and rowed away toward the great ship, where Tarzan could see other figures moving about upon the deck.

When they had clambered aboard, Tarzan dropped to earth behind a great tree and crept to his cabin, keeping it always between himself and the ship.

Slipping in at the door he found that everything had been ransacked. His books and pencils strewed the floor. His weapons and shields and other little store of treasures were littered about.

As he saw what had been done a great wave of anger surged through him, and the new-made scar upon his forehead stood suddenly out, a bar of inflamed crimson against his tawny hide.

Quickly he ran to the cupboard and searched in the far recess of the lower shelf. Ah! He breathed a sigh of relief as he drew out the little tin box, and, opening it, found his greatest treasures undisturbed.

The photograph of the smiling, strong-faced young man, and the little black puzzle book were safe.

What was that?

His quick ear had caught a faint but unfamiliar sound.

Running to the window Tarzan looked toward the harbor, and there he saw that a boat was being lowered from the great ship beside the one already in the water. Soon he saw many people clambering over the sides of the larger vessel and dropping into the boats. They were coming back in full force.

For a moment longer Tarzan watched while a number of boxes and bundles were lowered into the waiting boats; then, as they shoved off from the ship's side, the ape-man snatched up a piece of paper, and with a pencil printed on it for a few moments until it bore several lines of strong, well-made, almost letter-perfect characters.

This notice he stuck upon the door with a small sharp splinter of wood. Then gathering up his precious tin box, his arrows, and as many bows and spears as he could carry, he hastened through the door and disappeared into the forest.

When the two boats were beached upon the silvery sand it was a strange assortment of humanity that clambered ashore.

Some twenty souls in all there were, if the fifteen rough and villainous appearing seamen could have been said to possess that immortal spark, since they were, forsooth, a most filthy and bloodthirsty-looking aggregation.

The others of the party were of different stamp.

One was an elderly man, with white hair and large rimmed spectacles. His slightly stooped shoulders were draped in an ill-fitting, though immaculate, frock coat; a shiny silk hat added to the incongruity of his garb in an African jungle.

The second member of the party to land was a tall young man in white ducks, while directly behind came another elderly man with a very high forehead and a fussy, excitable manner.

After these came a huge black woman clothed like Solomon as to colors. Her great eyes rolled in evident terror, first toward the jungle and then toward the cursing band of sailors who were removing the bales and boxes from the boats.

The last member of the party to disembark was a girl of about nineteen, and it was the young man who stood at the boat's bow to lift her high and dry upon land. She gave him a brave and pretty smile of thanks, but no words passed between them.

In silence the party advanced toward the cabin. It was evident that whatever their intentions, all had been decided upon before they left the ship; and so they came to the door, the sailors carrying the boxes and bales, followed by the five who were of so different a class. The men put down their burdens, and then one caught sight of the notice which Tarzan had posted.

"Ho, mates!" he cried. "What's here? This sign was not posted an hour ago or I'll eat the cook."

The others gathered about, craning their necks over the shoulders of those before them, but as few of them could read at all, and then only after the most laborious fashion, one finally turned to the little old man of the top hat and frock coat.

"Hi, perfesser," he called, "step for'rd and read the bloomin' notis."

Thus addressed, the old man came slowly to where the sailors stood, followed by the other members of his party. Adjusting his spectacles he looked for a moment at the placard and then, turning away, strolled off muttering to himself: "Most remarkable—most remarkable!"

"Hi, old fossil," cried the man who had first called on him for assistance, "did je think we wanted of you to read the bloomin' notis to yourself? Come back here and read it out loud, you old barnacle."

The old man stopped and, turning back, said: "Oh, yes, my dear sir, a thousand pardons. It was quite thoughtless of me, yes—very thoughtless. Most remarkable—most remarkable!"

Again he faced the notice and read it through, and doubtless would have turned off again to ruminate upon it had not the sailor grasped him roughly by the collar and howled into his ear.

"Read it out loud, you blithering old idiot."

"Ah, yes indeed, yes indeed," replied the professor softly, and adjusting his spectacles once more he read aloud:

THIS IS THE HOUSE OF TARZAN, THE KILLER OF BEASTS AND MANY MEN. DO NOT HARM THE THINGS WHICH ARE TARZAN'S. TARZAN WATCHES. TARZAN OF THE APES.

"Who the devil is Tarzan?" cried the sailor who had before spoken.

"He evidently speaks English," said the young man.

"But what does 'Tarzan of the Apes' mean?" cried the girl.

"I do not know, Miss Porter," replied the young man, "unless we have discovered a runaway simian from the London Zoo who has brought back a European education to his jungle home. What do you make of it, Professor Porter?" he added, turning to the old man.

Professor Archimedes Q. Porter adjusted his spectacles.

"Ah, yes, indeed; yes indeed—most remarkable, most remarkable!" said the professor; "but I can add nothing further to what I have already remarked in elucidation of this truly momentous occurrence," and the professor turned slowly in the direction of the jungle.

"But, Papa," cried the girl, "you haven't said anything about it yet."

"Tut, tut, child; tut, tut," responded Professor Porter, in a kindly and indulgent tone, "do not trouble your pretty head with such weighty and abstruse problems," and again he wandered slowly off in still another direction, his eyes bent upon the ground at his feet, his hands clasped behind him beneath the flowing tails of his coat.

"I reckon the daffy old bounder don't know no more'n we do about it," growled the rat-faced sailor.

"Keep a civil tongue in your head," cried the young man, his face paling in anger, at the insulting tone of the sailor. "You've murdered our officers and robbed us. We are absolutely in your power, but you'll treat Professor Porter and Miss Porter with respect or I'll break that vile neck of yours with my bare hands—guns or no guns," and the young fellow stepped so close to the rat-faced sailor that the latter, though he bore two revolvers and a villainous looking knife in his belt, slunk back abashed.

"You damned coward," cried the young man. "You'd never dare shoot a man until his back was turned. You don't dare shoot me even then," and he deliberately turned his back full upon the sailor and walked nonchalantly away as if to put him to the test.

The sailor's hand crept slyly to the butt of one of his revolvers; his wicked eyes glared vengefully at the retreating form of the young Englishman. The gaze of his fellows was upon him, but still he hesitated. At heart he was even a greater coward than Mr. William Cecil Clayton had imagined.

What he would have done will never be known, for there was another factor abroad which none of the party had yet guessed would enter so largely into the problems of their life on this inhospitable African shore.

Two keen eyes had watched every move of the party from the foliage of a nearby tree. Tarzan had seen the surprise caused by his notice, and while he could understand nothing of the spoken language of these strange people their gestures and facial expressions told him much.

The act of the little rat-faced sailor in killing one of his comrades had aroused a strong dislike in Tarzan, and now that he saw him quarreling with the fine-looking young man his animosity was still further stirred.

Tarzan had never seen the effects of a firearm before, though his books had taught him something of them, but when he saw the rat-faced one fingering the butt of his revolver he thought of the scene he had witnessed so short a time before, and naturally expected to see the young man murdered as had been the huge sailor earlier in the day.

So Tarzan fitted a poisoned arrow to his bow and drew a bead upon the rat-faced sailor, but the foliage was so thick that he soon saw the arrow would be deflected by the leaves or some small branch, and instead he launched a heavy spear from his lofty perch.

Clayton had taken but a dozen steps. The rat-faced sailor had half drawn his revolver; the other sailors stood watching the scene intently.

Professor Porter had already disappeared into the jungle, whither he was being followed by the fussy Samuel T. Philander, his secretary and assistant.

Esmeralda, the black woman, was busy sorting her mistress' baggage from the pile of bales and boxes beside the cabin, and Miss Porter had turned away to follow Clayton, when something caused her to turn again toward the sailor.

And then three things happened almost simultaneously. The sailor jerked out his weapon and leveled it at Clayton's back, Miss Porter screamed a warning, and a long, metal-shod spear shot like a bolt from above and passed entirely through the right shoulder of the rat-faced man.

The revolver exploded harmlessly in the air, and the seaman crumpled up with a scream of pain and terror.

Clayton turned and rushed back toward the scene. The sailors stood in a frightened group, with drawn weapons, peering into the jungle. The wounded man writhed and shrieked upon the ground.

Clayton, unseen by any, picked up the fallen revolver and slipped it inside his shirt, then he joined the sailors in gazing, mystified, into the jungle.

"Who could it have been?" whispered Jane Porter, and the young man turned to see her standing, wide-eyed and wondering, close beside him.

"I dare say Tarzan of the Apes is watching us all right," he answered, in a dubious tone. "I wonder, now, who that spear was intended for. If for Snipes, then our ape friend is a friend indeed.

"By jove, where are your father and Mr. Philander? There's someone or something in that jungle, and it's armed, whatever it is. Ho! Professor! Mr. Philander!" young Clayton shouted. There was no response.

"What's to be done, Miss Porter?" continued the young man, his face clouded by a frown of worry and indecision.

"I can't leave you here alone with these cutthroats, and you certainly can't venture into the jungle with me; yet someone must go in search of your father. He is more than apt to wandering off aimlessly, regardless of danger or direction, and Mr. Philander is only a trifle less impractical than he. You will pardon my bluntness, but our lives are all in jeopardy here, and when we get your father back something must be done to impress upon him the dangers to which he exposes you as well as himself by his absentmindedness."

"I quite agree with you," replied the girl, "and I am not offended at all. Dear old Papa would sacrifice his life for me without an instant's hesitation, provided one could keep his mind on so frivolous a matter for an entire instant. There is only one way to keep him in safety, and that is to chain him to a tree. The poor dear is *so* impractical."

"I have it!" suddenly exclaimed Clayton. "You can use a revolver, can't you?"

"Yes. Why?"

"I have one. With it you and Esmeralda will be comparatively safe in this cabin while I am searching for your father and Mr. Philander. Come, call the woman and I will hurry on. They can't have gone far."

Jane Porter did as he suggested and when he saw the door close safely behind them Clayton turned toward the jungle.

Some of the sailors were drawing the spear from their wounded comrade and, as Clayton approached, he asked if he could borrow a revolver from one of them while he searched the jungle for the professor.

The rat-faced one, finding he was not dead, had regained his composure, and with a volley of oaths directed at Clayton refused in the name of his fellows to allow the young man any firearms.

This man, Snipes, had assumed the role of chief since he had killed their former leader, and so little time had elapsed that none of his companions had as yet questioned his authority.

Clayton's only response was a shrug of the shoulders, but as he left them he picked up the spear which had transfixed Snipes, and thus primitively armed, the son of the then Lord Greystoke strode into the dense jungle.

Every few moments he called aloud the names of the wanderers. The watchers in the cabin by the beach heard the sound of his voice growing ever fainter and fainter, until at last it was swallowed up by the myriad noises of the primeval wood.

When Professor Archimedes Q. Porter and his assistant, Samuel T. Philander, after much insistence on the part of the latter, had finally turned their steps toward camp, they were as completely lost in the wild and tangled labyrinth of the matted jungle as two human beings well could be, though they did not know it.

It was by the merest caprice of fortune that they headed toward the west coast of Africa, instead of toward Zanzibar on the opposite side of the dark continent.

When in a short time they reached the beach, only to find no camp in sight, Philander was positive that they were north of their proper destination, while, as a matter of fact they were about two hundred yards south of it.

It never occurred to either of these impractical theorists to call aloud on the chance of attracting their friends' attention. Instead, with all the assurance that deductive reasoning from a wrong premise induces in one, Mr. Samuel T. Philander grasped Professor Archimedes Q. Porter firmly by the arm and hurried the weakly protesting old gentleman off in the direction of Cape Town, fifteen hundred miles to the south.

When Jane Porter and Esmeralda found themselves safely behind the cabin door, the latter's first thought was to barricade the portal from the inside. With this idea in mind she turned to search for some means of putting it into execution; but her first view of the interior of the cabin brought a shriek of terror to her lips, and like a frightened child the huge woman ran to bury her face on her mistress' shoulder.

Jane Porter, turning at the cry, saw the cause of it lying prone upon the floor before them—the whitened skeleton of a man. A further glance revealed a second skeleton upon the bed.

"What horrible place are we in?" murmured the awestruck girl. But there was no panic in her fright.

At last, disengaging herself from the frantic clutch of the still shrieking Esmeralda, Jane Porter crossed the room to look into the little cradle, knowing what she should see there before ever the tiny skeleton disclosed itself in all its pitiful and pathetic frailty.

What an awful tragedy these poor mute bones proclaimed! The girl shuddered at thought of the eventualities which might lie before herself and her friends in this ill-fated cabin, the haunt of mysterious, perhaps hostile, beings.

Quickly, with an impatient stamp of her little foot, she endeavored to shake off the gloomy forebodings, and turning to Esmeralda bade her cease her wailing.

"Stop, Esmeralda, stop it this minute!" she cried. "You are only making it worse. Why, I never saw such a big baby."

She ended lamely, a little quiver in her own voice as she thought of the three men, upon whom she depended for protection, wandering in the depth of that awful forest.

Soon the girl found that the door was equipped with a heavy wooden bar upon the inside, and after several efforts the combined strength of the two enabled them to slip it into place, the first time in twenty years.

Then they sat down upon a bench with their arms about one another, and waited.

CHAPTER FOURTEEN
AT THE MERCY OF THE JUNGLE

AFTER CLAYTON HAD PLUNGED into the jungle, the sailors—mutineers of the *Arrow*—fell into a discussion of their next step; but on one point all were agreed—that they should hasten to put off to the anchored *Arrow*, where they could at least be safe from the spears of their unseen foe. And so, while Jane Porter and Esmeralda were barricading themselves within the cabin, the cowardly crew of cutthroats were pulling rapidly for their ship in the two boats that had brought them ashore.

So much had Tarzan seen that day that his head was in a whirl of wonder. But the most wonderful sight of all, to him, was the face of the beautiful golden-haired girl.

Here at last was one of his own kind; of that he was positive. And the young man and the two old men; they, too, were much as he had pictured his own people to be.

But doubtless they were as ferocious and cruel as other men he had seen. The fact that they alone of all the party were unarmed might account for the fact that they had killed no one. They might be very different if provided with weapons.

Tarzan had seen the young man pick up the fallen revolver of the wounded Snipes and hide it away in his breast; and he had also seen him slip it cautiously to the girl as she entered the cabin door.

He did not understand anything of the motives behind all that he had seen; but, somehow, intuitively he liked the young man and the two old men, and for the girl he had a strange longing which he scarcely understood. As for the big black woman, she was evidently connected in some way to the girl, and so he liked her, also.

For the sailors, and especially Snipes, he had developed a great hatred. He knew by their threatening gestures and by the expressions upon their evil faces that they were enemies of the others of the party, and so he decided to watch them closely.

Tarzan wondered why the men had gone into the jungle, nor did it ever occur to him that one could become lost in that maze of undergrowth which to him was as simple as is the main street of your own hometown to you.

When he saw the sailors row away toward the ship, and knew that the girl and her companion were safe in his cabin, Tarzan decided to follow the young man into the jungle and learn what his errand might be. He swung off rapidly in the direction taken by Clayton, and in a short time heard faintly in the distance the now only occasional calls of the Englishman to his friends.

Presently Tarzan came up with the white man, who, almost fagged, was leaning against a tree wiping the perspiration from his forehead. The ape-man, hiding safe behind a screen of foliage, sat watching this new specimen of his own race intently.

At intervals Clayton called aloud and finally it came to Tarzan that he was searching for the old man.

Tarzan was on the point of going off to look for them himself, when he caught the yellow glint of a sleek hide moving cautiously through the jungle toward Clayton.

It was Sheeta, the leopard. Now, Tarzan heard the soft bending of grasses and wondered why the young white man was not warned. Could it be he had failed to note the loud warning? Never before had Tarzan known Sheeta to be so clumsy.

No, the white man did not hear. Sheeta was crouching for the spring, and then, shrill and horrible, there rose from the stillness of the jungle the awful cry of the challenging ape, and Sheeta turned, crashing into the underbrush.

Clayton came to his feet with a start. His blood ran cold. Never in all his life had so fearful a sound smote upon his ears. He was no coward; but if ever man felt the icy fingers of fear upon his heart, William Cecil Clayton, eldest son of Lord Greystoke of England, did that day in the fastness of the African jungle.

The noise of some great body crashing through the underbrush so close beside him, and the sound of that bloodcurdling shriek from above, tested Clayton's courage to the limit; but he could not know that it was to that very voice he owed his life, nor that the creature who hurled it forth was his own cousin—the real Lord Greystoke.

The afternoon was drawing to a close, and Clayton, disheartened and discouraged, was in a terrible quandary as to the proper course to pursue; whether to keep on in search of Professor Porter, at the almost certain risk of his own death in the jungle by night, or to return to the cabin where he might at least serve to protect Jane Porter from the perils which confronted her on all sides.

He disliked to return to camp without her father; still more, he shrank from the thought of leaving her alone and unprotected in the hands of the mutineers of the *Arrow*, or to the hundred unknown dangers of the jungle.

Possibly, too, he thought, ere this the professor and Philander might have returned to camp. Yes, that was more than likely. At least he would return and see, before he continued what bade fair to be a most fruitless quest. And so he started, stumbling back through the thick and matted underbrush in the direction that he thought the cabin lay.

To Tarzan's surprise the young man was heading further into the jungle in the general direction of Mbonga's village, and the shrewd young ape-man was convinced that he was lost.

To Tarzan this was scarcely comprehensible; but his judgment told him that no man would venture toward the village of the cruel warriors of Mbonga armed only with a spear which, from the awkward way in which he carried it, was evidently an unaccustomed weapon to this white man. Nor was he following the trail of the old men. That, they had crossed and left long since, though it had been fresh and plain before Tarzan's eyes.

Tarzan was perplexed. The fierce jungle would make easy prey of this unprotected stranger in a very short time if he were not guided quickly to the beach.

Yes, there was Numa, the lion, even now, stalking the white man a dozen paces to the right.

Clayton heard the great body paralleling his course, and now there rose upon the evening air the beast's thunderous roar. The man stopped with upraised spear and faced the brush from which issued the awful sound. The shadows were deepening, darkness was settling in.

God! To die here alone, beneath the fangs of wild beasts; to be torn and rended; to feel the hot breath of the brute on his face as the great paw crushed down upon his breast!

For a moment all was still. Clayton stood rigid, with raised spear. Presently a faint rustling of the bush apprised him of the stealthy creeping of the thing behind. It was gathering for the spring. At last he saw it, not twenty feet away—the long, lithe, muscular body and tawny head of a huge black-maned lion.

The beast was upon its belly, moving forward very slowly. As its eyes met Clayton's it stopped, and deliberately, cautiously gathered its hind quarters behind it.

In agony the man watched, fearful to launch his spear, powerless to fly.

He heard a noise in the tree above him. Some new danger, he thought, but he dared not take his eyes from the yellow-green orbs before him. There was a sharp twang as of a broken banjo string, and at the same instant an arrow appeared in the yellow hide of the crouching lion.

With a roar of pain and anger the beast sprang; but, somehow, Clayton stumbled to one side, and as he turned again to face the infuriated king of beasts, he was appalled at the sight which confronted him. Almost simultaneously with the lion's turning to renew the attack a half-naked giant dropped from the tree above squarely on the brute's back.

With lightning speed an arm that was banded layers of iron muscle encircled the huge neck, and the great beast was raised from behind, roaring and pawing the air—raised as easily as Clayton would have lifted a pet dog.

The scene he witnessed there in the twilight depths of the African jungle was burned forever into the Englishman's brain.

The man before him was the embodiment of physical perfection and giant strength; yet it was not upon these he depended in his battle with the great cat, for mighty as were his muscles, they were as nothing by comparison with Numa's. To his agility, to his brain, and to his long keen knife he owed his supremacy.

His right arm encircled the lion's neck, while the left hand plunged the knife time and again into the unprotected side behind the left shoulder.

The infuriated beast, pulled up and backwards until he stood upon his hind legs, struggled impotently in this unnatural position.

Had the battle been of a few seconds' longer duration the outcome might have been different, but it was all accomplished so quickly that the lion had scarce time to recover from the confusion of its surprise ere it sank lifeless to the ground.

Then the strange figure which had vanquished it stood erect upon the carcass, and throwing back the wild and handsome head, gave out the fearsome cry which a few moments earlier had so startled Clayton.

Before him he saw the figure of a young man, naked except for a loincloth and a few barbaric ornaments about arms and legs; on the breast a priceless diamond locket gleaming against a smooth brown skin.

The hunting knife had been returned to its homely sheath, and the man was gathering up his bow and quiver from where he had tossed them when he leaped to attack the lion.

Clayton spoke to the stranger in English, thanking him for his brave rescue and complimenting him on the wondrous strength and dexterity he had displayed, but the only answer was a steady stare and a faint shrug of the mighty shoulders, which might betoken either disparagement of the service rendered, or ignorance of Clayton's language.

When the bow and quiver had been slung to his back the wild man, for such Clayton now thought him, once more drew his knife and deftly carved a dozen large strips of meat from the lion's carcass. Then, squatting upon his haunches, he proceeded to eat, first motioning Clayton to join him.

The strong white teeth sank into the raw and dripping flesh in apparent relish of the meal, but Clayton could not bring himself to share the uncooked meat with his strange host; instead he watched him, and presently there dawned upon him the conviction that this was Tarzan of the Apes, whose notice he had seen posted upon the cabin door that morning.

If so he must speak English.

Again Clayton attempted speech with the ape-man; but the replies, now vocal, were in a strange tongue, which resembled the chattering of monkeys mingled with the growling of some wild beast.

No, this could not be Tarzan of the Apes, for it was very evident that he was an utter stranger to English.

When Tarzan had completed his repast he rose and, pointing in a very different direction from that which Clayton had been pursuing, started off through the jungle toward the point he had indicated.

Clayton, bewildered and confused, hesitated to follow him, for he thought he was but being led more deeply into the mazes of the forest; but the ape-man, seeing him disinclined to follow, returned, and, grasping him by the coat, dragged him along until he was convinced that Clayton understood what was required of him. Then he left him to follow voluntarily.

The Englishman, finally concluding that he was a prisoner, saw no alternative open but to accompany his captor, and thus they traveled slowly through the jungle while the sable mantle of the impenetrable forest night fell about them, and the stealthy footfalls of padded paws mingled with the breaking of twigs and the wild calls of the savage life that Clayton felt closing in upon him.

Suddenly Clayton heard the faint report of a firearm—a single shot, and then silence.

In the cabin by the beach two thoroughly terrified women clung to each other as they crouched upon the low bench in the gathering darkness.

Esmeralda sobbed hysterically, bemoaning the evil day that had witnessed her departure from her dear Maryland, while the girl, dry eyed and out-wardly calm, was torn by inward fears and forebodings. She feared not more for herself than for the three men whom she knew to be wandering in the abysmal depths of the savage jungle, from which she now heard issuing the almost incessant shrieks and roars, barkings and growlings of its terrifying and fearsome denizens as they sought their prey.

And now there came the sound of a heavy body brushing against the side of the cabin. She could hear the great padded paws upon the ground outside. For an instant, all was silence; even the bedlam of the forest died to a faint murmur. Then she distinctly heard the beast outside sniffing at the door, not two feet from where she crouched. Instinctively the girl shuddered, and shrank closer to the woman.

"Hush!" she whispered. "Hush, Esmeralda," for the woman's sobs and groans seemed to have attracted the thing that stalked there just beyond the thin wall.

A gentle scratching sound was heard on the door. The brute tried to force an entrance; but presently this ceased, and again she heard the great pads creeping stealthily around the cabin. Again they stopped—beneath the window on which the terrified eyes of the girl now glued themselves.

"God!" she murmured, for now, silhouetted against the moonlit sky beyond, she saw framed in the tiny square of the latticed window the head of a huge lioness. The gleaming eyes were fixed upon her in intent ferocity.

"Look, Esmeralda!" she whispered. "For God's sake, what shall we do? Look! Quick! The window!"

Esmeralda, cowering still closer to her mistress, took one frightened glance toward the little square of moonlight, just as the lioness emitted a low, savage snarl.

The sight that met the poor woman's eyes was too much for the already overstrung nerves.

"Oh, Gaberelle!" she shrieked, and slid to the floor an inert and senseless mass.

For what seemed an eternity the great brute stood with its forepaws upon the sill, glaring into the little room. Presently it tried the strength of the lattice with its great talons.

The girl had almost ceased to breathe, when, to her relief, the head disappeared and she heard the brute's footsteps leaving the window. But now they came to the door again, and once more the scratching commenced; this time with increasing force until the great beast was tearing at the massive panels in a perfect frenzy of eagerness to seize its defenseless victims.

Could Jane Porter have known the immense strength of that door, built piece by piece, she would have felt less fear of the lioness reaching her by this avenue.

Little did John Clayton imagine when he fashioned that crude but mighty portal that one day, twenty years later, it would shield a fair American girl, then unborn, from the teeth and talons of a man-eater.

For fully twenty minutes the brute alternately sniffed and tore at the door, occasionally giving voice to a wild, savage cry of baffled rage. At length, however, she gave up the attempt, and Jane Porter heard her returning toward the window, beneath which she paused for an instant, and then launched her great weight against the timeworn lattice.

The girl heard the wooden rods groan beneath the impact; but they held, and the huge body dropped back to the ground below.

Again and again the lioness repeated these tactics, until finally the horrified prisoner within saw a portion of the lattice give way, and in an instant one great paw and the head of the animal were thrust within the room.

Slowly the powerful neck and shoulders spread the bars apart, and the lithe body protruded farther and farther into the room.

As in a trance, the girl rose, her hand upon her breast, wide eyes staring horror-stricken into the snarling face of the beast scarce ten feet from her. At her feet lay the prostrate form of Esmeralda. If she could but arouse her, their combined efforts might possibly avail to beat back the fierce and bloodthirsty intruder.

Jane Porter stooped to grasp the woman by the shoulder. Roughly she shook her.

"Esmeralda! Esmeralda!" she cried. "Help me, or we are lost."

Esmeralda slowly opened her eyes. The first object they encountered was the dripping fangs of the hungry lioness.

With a horrified scream the poor woman rose to her hands and knees, and in this position scurried across the room, shrieking: "O Gaberelle! O Gaberelle!" at the top of her lungs.

Esmeralda weighed some two hundred and eighty pounds, which enhanced nothing the gazelle-like grace of her carriage when walking erect, and her extreme haste, added to her extreme corpulency, produced a most amazing result when Esmeralda elected to travel on all fours.

For a moment the lioness remained quiet with intense gaze directed upon the flitting Esmeralda, whose goal appeared to be the cupboard, into which she attempted to propel her huge bulk; but as the shelves were but nine or ten inches apart, she only succeeded in getting her head in; whereupon, with a final screech, which paled the jungle noises into insignificance, she fainted once again.

With the subsidence of Esmeralda the lioness renewed her efforts to wriggle her huge bulk through the weakening lattice.

The girl, standing pale and rigid against the farther wall, sought with ever-increasing terror for some loophole of escape. Suddenly her hand, tight-pressed against her bosom, felt the hard outline of the revolver that Clayton had left with her earlier in the day.

Quickly she snatched it from its hiding place, and, leveling it full at the lioness' face, pulled the trigger.

There was a flash of flame, the roar of the discharge, and an answering roar of pain and anger from the beast.

Jane Porter saw the great form disappear from the window, and then she, too, fainted, the revolver falling at her side.

But Sabor was not killed. The bullet had but inflicted a painful wound in one of the great shoulders. It was the surprise at the blinding flash and the deafening roar that had caused her hasty but temporary retreat.

In another instant she was back at the lattice, and with renewed fury was clawing at the aperture, but with lessened effect, since the wounded member was almost useless.

She saw her prey—the two women—lying senseless upon the floor. There was no longer any resistance to be overcome. Her meat lay before her, and Sabor had only to worm her way through the lattice to claim it.

Slowly she forced her great bulk, inch by inch, through the opening. Now her head was through, now one great forearm and shoulder.

Carefully she drew up the wounded member to insinuate it gently beyond the tight pressing bars.

A moment more and both shoulders through, the long, sinuous body and the narrow hips would glide quickly after.

It was on this sight that Jane Porter again opened her eyes.

CHAPTER FIFTEEN
THE FOREST GOD

WHEN CLAYTON HEARD THE REPORT of the firearm he fell into an agony of fear and apprehension. He knew that one of the sailors might be the author of it; but the fact that he had left the revolver with Jane, together with the overwrought condition of his nerves, made him morbidly positive that she was threatened with some great danger. Perhaps even now she was attempting to defend herself against some savage man or beast.

What were the thoughts of his strange captor or guide Clayton could only vaguely conjecture; but that he had heard the shot, and was in some manner affected by it was quite evident, for he quickened his pace so appreciably that Clayton, stumbling blindly in his wake, was down a dozen times in as many minutes in a vain effort to keep pace with him, and soon was left hopelessly behind.

Fearing that he would again be irretrievably lost, he called aloud to the wild man ahead of him, and in a moment had the satisfaction of seeing him drop lightly to his side from the branches above.

For a moment Tarzan looked at the young man closely, as though undecided as to just what was best to do; then, stooping down before Clayton, he motioned him to grasp him about the neck, and, with the man upon his back, Tarzan took to the trees.

The next few minutes were such as the young Englishman never forgot. High into bending and swaying branches he was borne with what seemed to him incredible swiftness, while Tarzan chafed at the slowness of his progress.

From one lofty branch the agile creature swung with Clayton through a dizzy arc to a neighboring tree; then for a hundred yards maybe the sure feet threaded a maze of interwoven limbs, balancing like a tightrope walker high above the black depths of verdure beneath.

From the first sensation of chilling fear Clayton passed to one of keen admiration and envy of those giant muscles and that wondrous instinct or knowledge which guided this forest god through the inky blackness of the night as easily and safely as Clayton could have strolled a London street at high noon.

Occasionally they would enter a spot where the foliage above was less dense, and the bright rays of the moon lit up before Clayton's wondering eyes the strange path they were traversing.

At such times the man fairly caught his breath at sight of the horrid depths below them, for Tarzan took the easiest way, which often led over a hundred feet above the earth.

And yet with all his seeming speed, Tarzan was in reality feeling his way with comparative slowness, searching constantly for limbs of adequate strength for the maintenance of this double weight.

Presently they came to the clearing before the beach. Tarzan's quick ears had heard the strange sounds of Sabor's efforts to force her way through the lattice, and it seemed to Clayton that they dropped a straight hundred feet to earth, so quickly did Tarzan descend. Yet when they struck the ground it was with scarce a jar; and as Clayton released his hold on the ape-man he saw him dart like a squirrel for the opposite side of the cabin.

The Englishman sprang quickly after him just in time to see the hind quarters of some huge animal about to disappear through the window of the cabin.

As Jane Porter opened her eyes to a realization of the again imminent peril which threatened her, her brave young heart gave up at last its final vestige of hope, and she turned to grope for the fallen weapon that she might mete to herself a merciful death ere the cruel fangs tore into her fair flesh.

The lioness was almost through the opening before Jane found the weapon, and she raised it quickly to her temple to shut out forever the hideous jaws gaping for their prey.

An instant she hesitated, to breathe a short and silent prayer to her Maker, and as she did so her eyes fell upon her poor Esmeralda lying inert, but alive, beside the cupboard.

How could she leave the poor, faithful thing to those merciless, yellow fangs? No, she must use one cartridge on the senseless woman ere she turned the cold muzzle toward herself again.

How she shrank from the ordeal! But it had been cruelty a thousand times less justifiable to have left the loving woman who had reared her from infancy with all a mother's care and solicitude, to regain consciousness beneath the rending claws of the great cat.

Quickly Jane Porter sprang to her feet and ran to Esmeralda's side. She pressed the muzzle of the revolver tight against that devoted heart, closed her eyes, and—

Sabor emitted a frightful shriek.

The girl, startled, pulled the trigger and turned to face the beast, and with the same movement raised the weapon against her own temple.

She did not fire a second time, for to her surprise she saw the huge animal being slowly drawn back through the window, and in the moonlight beyond she saw the heads and shoulders of two men.

As Clayton rounded the corner of the cabin to behold the animal disappearing within, it was also to see the ape-man seize the long tail in both hands, and, bracing himself with his feet against the side of the cabin, throw all his mighty strength into the effort to draw the beast out of the interior.

Clayton was quick to lend a hand, but the ape-man jabbered to him in a commanding and peremptory tone something which Clayton knew to be orders, though he could not understand them.

At last, under their combined efforts, the great body was slowly dragged farther and farther outside the window, and then there came to Clayton's mind a dawning conception of the rash bravery of his companion's act.

For a naked man to drag a shrieking, clawing man-eater forth from a window by the tail to save a strange white girl was indeed the last word in heroism.

Insofar as Clayton was concerned it was a very different matter, since the girl was not only of his own kind and race, but was the one woman in all the world whom he loved.

Though he knew that the lioness would make short work of both of them, he pulled with a will to keep it from Jane Porter. And then he recalled the battle between this man and the great, black-maned lion which he had witnessed a short time before, and he commenced to feel more assurance.

Tarzan was still issuing orders which Clayton could not understand.

He was trying to tell the stupid white man to plunge his poisoned arrows into Sabor's back and sides, and to reach the savage heart with the long, thin hunting knife that hung at Tarzan's hip; but the man would not understand, and Tarzan did not dare release his hold to do the things himself, for he knew that the puny white man never could hold mighty Sabor alone, for an instant.

Slowly the lioness was emerging from the window. At last her shoulders were out.

And then Clayton saw a thing done which not even the eternal heavens had ever seen before. Tarzan, racking his brains for some means to cope single-handed with the infuriated beast, had suddenly recalled his battle with Terkoz; and as the great shoulders came clear of the window, so that the lioness hung upon the sill only by her forepaws, Tarzan suddenly released his hold upon the brute.

With the quickness of a striking rattler he launched himself full upon Sabor's back, his strong young arms seeking and gaining a full nelson upon the beast, as he had learned it that other day during his bloody, wrestling victory over Terkoz.

With a shriek the lioness turned completely over upon her back, falling full upon her enemy; but the black-haired giant only closed tighter his hold.

Pawing and tearing at earth and air, Sabor rolled and threw herself this way and that in an effort to dislodge this strange antagonist; but ever tighter and tighter drew the iron bands that were forcing her head lower and lower upon her tawny breast.

Higher crept the steel forearms of the ape-man about the back of Sabor's neck. Weaker and weaker became the lioness' efforts.

At last Clayton saw the immense muscles of Tarzan's shoulders and biceps leap into corded knots beneath the silver moonlight. There was a long sustained and supreme effort on the ape-man's part—and the vertebrae of Sabor's neck parted with a sharp snap.

In an instant Tarzan was upon his feet, and for the second time that day Clayton heard the bull ape's savage roar of victory. Then he heard Jane's agonized cry:

"Cecil—Mr. Clayton! Oh, what is it? What is it?"

Running quickly to the cabin door, Clayton called out that all was right, and bade her to open. As quickly as she could she raised the great bar and fairly dragged Clayton within.

"What was that awful noise?" she whispered, shrinking close to him.

"It was the cry of the kill from the throat of the man who has just saved your life, Miss Porter. Wait, I will fetch him that you may thank him."

The frightened girl would not be left alone, so she accompanied Clayton to the side of the cabin where lay the dead body of the lioness.

Tarzan of the Apes was gone.

Clayton called several times, but there was no reply, and so the two returned to the greater safety of the interior.

"What a frightful sound!" cried Jane Porter, "I shudder at the mere thought of it. Do not tell me that a human throat voiced that hideous and fearsome shriek."

"But it did, Miss Porter," replied Clayton; "or at least if not a human throat that of a forest god."

And then he told her of his experiences with this strange creature— of how twice the wild man had saved his life—of the wondrous strength, and agility, and bravery—of the brown skin and the handsome face.

"I cannot make it out at all," he concluded. "At first I thought he might be Tarzan of the Apes; but he neither speaks nor understands English, so that theory is untenable."

"Well, whatever he may be," cried the girl, "we owe him our lives, and may God bless him and keep him in safety in his wild and savage jungle!"

"Amen," said Clayton, fervently.

"For the good Lord's sake, ain't I dead?"

The two turned to see Esmeralda sitting upright upon the floor, her great eyes rolling from side to side as though she could not believe their testimony as to her whereabouts.

The lioness' shriek, as Jane Porter had been about to put a bullet into poor Esmeralda, had saved the woman's life, for the little start the girl gave had turned the muzzle of the revolver to one side, and the bullet had passed harmlessly into the floor.

And now, for Jane Porter, the reaction came, and she threw herself upon the bench, sobbing with hysterical laughter.

CHAPTER SIXTEEN
"MOST REMARKABLE"

EVERAL MILES SOUTH OF THE CABIN, upon a strip of sandy beach, stood two old men, arguing.

Before them stretched the broad Atlantic; at their backs the Dark Continent; close around them loomed the impenetrable blackness of the jungle.

Savage beasts roared and growled; noises, hideous and weird, assailed their ears. They had wandered for miles in search of their camp, but always in the wrong direction. They were as hopelessly lost as though they suddenly had been transported to another world.

At such a time, indeed, every fiber of their combined intellects must have been concentrated upon the vital question of the minute—the life-and-death question to them of retracing their steps to camp.

Samuel T. Philander was speaking.

"But, my dear professor," he was saying, "I still maintain that but for the victories of Ferdinand and Isabella over the fifteenth-century Moors in Spain the world would be today a thousand years in advance of where we now find ourselves. The Moors were essentially a tolerant, broad-minded, liberal race of agriculturists, artisans, and merchants—the very type of people that has made possible such civilization as we find today in America and Europe—while the Spaniards—"

"Tut, tut, dear Mr. Philander," interrupted Professor Porter; "their religion positively precluded the possibilities you suggest. Moslemism was, is, and always will be, a blight on that scientific progress which has marked—"

"Bless me! Professor," interjected Mr. Philander, who had turned his gaze toward the jungle, "there seems to be someone approaching."

Professor Archimedes Q. Porter turned in the direction indicated by the nearsighted Mr. Philander.

"Tut, tut, Mr. Philander," he chided. "How often must I urge you to seek that absolute concentration of your mental faculties which alone may permit you to bring to bear the highest powers of intellectuality upon the momentous problems which naturally fall to the lot of great minds? And now I find you guilty of a most flagrant breach of courtesy in interrupting my learned discourse to call attention to a mere quadruped of the genus *Felis*. As I was saying, Mr.—"

"Heavens, Professor, a lion?" cried Mr. Philander, straining his weak eyes toward the dim figure outlined against the dark tropical underbrush.

"Yes, yes, Mr. Philander, if you insist upon employing slang in your discourse, 'lion.' But as I was saying—"

"Bless me, Professor," again interrupted Mr. Philander; "permit me to suggest that doubtless the Moors who were conquered in the fifteenth century will continue in that most regrettable condition for the time being at least, even though we postpone discussion of that world calamity until we may attain the enchanting view of yon *Felis carnivora* which distance proverbially is credited with lending."

In the meantime the lion had approached with quiet dignity to within ten paces of the two men, where he stood curiously watching them.

The moonlight flooded the beach, and the strange group stood out in bold relief against the yellow sand.

"Most reprehensible, most reprehensible," exclaimed Professor Porter, with a faint trace of irritation in his voice. "Never, Mr. Philander, never before in my life have I known one of these animals to be permitted to roam at large from its cage. I shall most certainly report this outrageous breach of ethics to the directors of the adjacent zoological garden."

"Quite right, Professor," agreed Mr. Philander, "and the sooner it is done the better. Let us start now."

Seizing the professor by the arm, Mr. Philander set off in the direction that would put the greatest distance between themselves and the lion.

They had proceeded but a short distance when a backward glance revealed to the horrified gaze of Mr. Philander that the lion was following them. He tightened his grip upon the protesting professor and increased his speed.

"As I was saying, Mr. Philander," repeated Professor Porter.

Mr. Philander took another hasty glance rearward. The lion also had quickened his gait, and was doggedly maintaining an unvarying distance behind them.

"He is following us!" gasped Mr. Philander, breaking into a run.

"Tut, tut, Mr. Philander," remonstrated the professor, "this unseemly haste is most unbecoming to men of letters. What will our friends think of us, who may chance to be upon the street and witness our frivolous antics? Pray let us proceed with more decorum."

Mr. Philander stole another observation astern.

Horrors! The lion was bounding along in easy leaps scarce five paces behind.

Mr. Philander dropped the professor's arm, and broke into a mad orgy of speed that would have done credit to any varsity track team.

"As I was saying, Mr. Philander—" screamed Professor Porter, as, metaphorically speaking, he himself "threw her into high." He, too, had caught a fleeting backward glimpse of cruel yellow eyes and half open mouth within startling proximity of his person.

With streaming coattails and shiny silk hat Professor Archimedes Q. Porter fled through the moonlight close upon the heels of Mr. Samuel T. Philander.

Before them a point of the jungle ran out toward a narrow promontory, and it was for the haven of the trees he saw there that Mr. Samuel T. Philander directed his prodigious leaps and bounds; while from the shadows of this same spot peered two keen eyes in interested appreciation of the race.

It was Tarzan of the Apes who watched, with face a-grin, this odd game of follow-the-leader.

He knew the two men were safe enough from attack insofar as the lion was concerned. The very fact that Numa had foregone such easy prey at all convinced the wise forest craft of Tarzan that Numa's belly already was full.

The lion might stalk them until hungry again; but the chances were that if not angered he would soon tire of the sport, and slink away to his jungle lair.

Really, the one great danger was that one of the men might stumble and fall, and then the yellow devil would be upon him in a moment and the joy of the kill would be too great a temptation to withstand.

So Tarzan swung quickly to a lower limb in line with the approaching fugitives; and as Mr. Samuel T. Philander came panting and blowing beneath him, already too spent to struggle up to the safety of the limb, Tarzan reached down and, grasping him by the collar of his coat, yanked him to the limb by his side.

Another moment brought the professor within the sphere of the friendly grip, and he, too, was drawn upward to safety just as the baffled Numa, with a roar, leaped to recover his vanishing quarry.

For a moment the two men clung panting to the great branch, while Tarzan squatted with his back to the stem of the tree, watching them with mingled curiosity and amusement.

It was the professor who first broke the silence.

"I am deeply pained, Mr. Philander, that you should have evinced such a paucity of manly courage in the presence of one of the lower orders, and by your crass timidity have caused me to exert myself to such an unaccustomed degree in order that I might resume my discourse. As I was saying, Mr. Philander, when you interrupted me, the Moors—"

"Professor Archimedes Q. Porter," broke in Mr. Philander, in icy tones, "the time has arrived when patience becomes a crime and mayhem appears garbed in the mantle of virtue. You have accused me of cowardice. You have insinuated that you ran only to overtake me, not to escape the clutches of the lion.

"Have a care, Professor Archimedes Q. Porter! I am a desperate man. Goaded by long-suffering patience the worm will turn."

"Tut, tut, Mr. Philander, tut, tut!" cautioned Professor Porter; "you forget yourself."

"I forget nothing as yet, Professor Archimedes Q. Porter; but, believe me, sir, I am tottering on the verge of forgetfulness as to your exalted position in the world of science, and your gray hairs."

The professor sat in silence for a few minutes, and the darkness hid the grim smile that wreathed his wrinkled countenance. Presently he spoke.

"Look here, Skinny Philander," he said, in belligerent tones, "if you are lookin' for a scrap, peel off your coat and come on down on the ground, and I'll punch your head just as I did sixty years ago in the alley back of Porky Evans' barn."

"Ark!" gasped the astonished Mr. Philander. "Lordy, how good that sounds! When you're human, Ark, I love you; but somehow it seems as though you had forgotten how to be human for the last twenty years."

The professor reached out a thin, trembling old hand through the darkness until it found his old friend's shoulder.

"Forgive me, Skinny," he said, softly. "It hasn't been quite twenty years, and God alone knows how hard I have tried to be 'human' for Jane's sake, and yours, too, since He took my other Jane away."

Another old hand stole up from Mr. Philander's side to clasp the one that lay upon his shoulder, and no other message could better have translated the one heart to the other.

They did not speak for some minutes. The lion below them paced nervously back and forth. The third figure in the tree was hidden by the dense shadows near the stem. He, too, was silent—motionless as a graven image.

"You certainly pulled me up into this tree just in time," said the professor at last. "I want to thank you. You saved my life."

"But I didn't pull you up here, Professor," said Mr. Philander. "Bless me! The excitement of the moment quite caused me to forget that I myself was drawn up here by some outside agency—there must be someone or something in this tree with us."

"Eh?" ejaculated Professor Porter. "Are you quite positive, Mr. Philander?"

"Most positive, Professor," replied Mr. Philander, "and," he added, "I think we should thank the party. He may be sitting right next to you now, Professor."

"Eh? What's that? Tut, tut, Mr. Philander, tut, tut!" said Professor Porter, edging cautiously nearer to Mr. Philander.

Just then it occurred to Tarzan of the Apes that Numa had loitered beneath the tree for a sufficient length of time, so he raised his young head toward the heavens, and there rang out upon the terrified ears of the two old men the awful warning challenge of the anthropoid.

The two friends, huddled trembling in their precarious position on the limb, saw the great lion halt in his restless pacing as the bloodcurdling cry smote his ears, and then slink quickly into the jungle, to be instantly lost to view.

"Even the lion trembles in fear," whispered Mr. Philander.

"Most remarkable, most remarkable," murmured Professor Porter, clutching frantically at Mr. Philander to regain the balance which the sudden fright had so perilously endangered. Unfortunately for them both,

Mr. Philander's center of equilibrium was at that very moment hanging upon the ragged edge of nothing, so that it needed but the gentle impetus supplied by the additional weight of Professor Porter's body to topple the devoted secretary from the limb.

For a moment they swayed uncertainly, and then, with mingled and most unscholarly shrieks, they pitched headlong from the tree, locked in frenzied embrace.

It was quite some moments ere either moved, for both were positive that any such attempt would reveal so many breaks and fractures as to make further progress impossible.

At length Professor Porter essayed an attempt to move one leg. To his surprise, it responded to his will as in days gone by. He now drew up its mate and stretched it forth again.

"Most remarkable, most remarkable," he murmured.

"Thank God, Professor," whispered Mr. Philander, fervently, "you are not dead, then?"

"Tut, tut, Mr. Philander, tut, tut," cautioned Professor Porter, "I do not know with accuracy as yet."

With infinite solicitude Professor Porter wiggled his right arm—joy! It was intact. Breathlessly he waved his left arm above his prostrate body—it waved!

"Most remarkable, most remarkable," he said.

"To whom are you signaling, Professor?" asked Mr. Philander, in an excited tone.

Professor Porter deigned to make no response to this puerile inquiry. Instead he raised his head gently from the ground, nodding it back and forth a half-dozen times.

"Most remarkable," he breathed. "It remains intact."

Mr. Philander had not moved from where he had fallen; he had not dared the attempt. How indeed could one move when one's arms and legs and back were broken?

One eye was buried in the soft loam; the other, rolling sidewise, was fixed in awe upon the strange gyrations of Professor Porter.

"How sad!" exclaimed Mr. Philander, half aloud. "Concussion of the brain, superinducing total mental aberration. How very sad indeed! and for one still so young!"

Professor Porter rolled over upon his stomach; gingerly he bowed his back until he resembled a huge tom cat in proximity to a yelping dog. Then he sat up and felt of various portions of his anatomy.

"They are all here," he exclaimed. "Most remarkable!"

Whereupon he arose, and, bending a scathing glance upon the still prostrate form of Mr. Samuel T. Philander, he said:

"Tut, tut, Mr. Philander; this is no time to indulge in slothful ease. We must be up and doing."

Mr. Philander lifted his other eye out of the mud and gazed in speechless rage at Professor Porter. Then he attempted to rise; nor could there have been any more surprised than he when his efforts were immediately crowned with marked success.

He was still bursting with rage, however, at the cruel injustice of Professor Porter's insinuation, and was on the point of rendering a tart rejoinder when his eyes fell upon a strange figure standing a few paces away, scrutinizing them intently.

Professor Porter had recovered his shiny silk hat, which he had brushed carefully upon the sleeve of his coat and replaced upon his head. When he saw Mr. Philander pointing to something behind him he turned to behold a giant, naked but for a loincloth and a few metal ornaments, standing motionless before him.

"Good evening, sir!" said the professor, lifting his hat.

For reply the giant motioned them to follow him, and set off up the beach in the direction from which they had recently come.

"I think it the part of discretion to follow him," said Mr. Philander.

"Tut, tut, Mr. Philander," returned the professor. "A short time since you were advancing a most logical argument in substantiation of your theory that camp lay directly south of us. I was skeptical, but you finally convinced me; so now I am positive that toward the south we must travel to reach our friends. Therefore I shall continue south."

"But, Professor Porter, this man may know better than either of us. He seems to be indigenous to this part of the world. Let us at least follow him for a short distance."

"Tut, tut, Mr. Philander," repeated the professor. "I am a difficult man to convince, but when once convinced my decision is unalterable. I shall continue in the proper direction, if I have to circumambulate the continent of Africa to reach my destination."

Further argument was interrupted by Tarzan, who, seeing that these strange men were not following him, had returned to their side.

Again he beckoned to them; but still they stood in argument.

Presently the ape-man lost patience with their stupid ignorance. He grasped the frightened Mr. Philander by the shoulder, and before that worthy gentleman knew whether he was being killed or merely maimed for life, Tarzan had tied one end of his rope securely about Mr. Philander's neck.

"Tut, tut, Mr. Philander," remonstrated Professor Porter; "it is most unbeseeming in you to submit to such indignities."

But scarcely were the words out of his mouth ere he, too, had been seized and securely bound by the neck with the same rope. Then Tarzan set off toward the north, leading the now thoroughly frightened professor and his secretary.

In deathly silence they proceeded for what seemed hours to the two tired and hopeless old men; but presently as they topped a little rise of ground they were overjoyed to see the cabin lying before them, not a hundred yards distant.

Here Tarzan released them, and, pointing toward the little building, vanished into the jungle beside them.

"Most remarkable, most remarkable!" gasped the professor. "But you see, Mr. Philander, that I was quite right, as usual; and but for your stubborn willfulness we should have escaped a series of most humiliating, not to say dangerous accidents. Pray allow yourself to be guided by a more mature and practical mind hereafter when in need of wise counsel."

Mr. Samuel T. Philander was too much relieved at the happy outcome to their adventure to take umbrage at the professor's cruel fling. Instead he grasped his friend's arm and hastened him forward in the direction of the cabin.

It was a much-relieved party of castaways that found itself once more united. Dawn discovered them still recounting their various adventures and speculating upon the identity of the strange guardian and protector they had found on this savage shore.

Esmeralda was positive that it was none other than an angel of the Lord, sent down especially to watch over them.

"Had you seen him devour the raw meat of the lion, Esmeralda," laughed Clayton, "you would have thought him a very material angel."

"There was nothing heavenly about his voice," said Jane Porter, with a little shudder at recollection of the awful roar which had followed the killing of the lioness.

"Nor did it precisely comport with my preconceived ideas of the dignity of divine messengers," remarked Professor Porter, "when the—ah—gentleman tied two highly respectable and erudite scholars neck to neck and dragged them through the jungle as though they had been cows."

CHAPTER SEVENTEEN
BURIALS

AS IT WAS NOW QUITE LIGHT, the party, none of whom had eaten or slept since the previous morning, began to bestir themselves to prepare food.

The mutineers of the *Arrow* had landed a small supply of dried meats, canned soups and vegetables, crackers, flour, tea, and coffee for the five they had marooned, and these were hurriedly drawn upon to satisfy the craving of long-famished appetites.

The next task was to make the cabin habitable, and to this end it was decided to at once remove the gruesome relics of the tragedy which had taken place there on some bygone day.

Professor Porter and Mr. Philander were deeply interested in examining the skeletons. The two larger, they stated, had belonged to a man and a woman.

The smallest skeleton was given but passing attention, as its location, in the crib, left no doubt as to its having been the infant offspring of this unhappy couple.

As they were preparing the skeleton of the man for burial, Clayton discovered a massive ring which had evidently encircled the man's finger at the time of his death, for one of the slender bones of the hand still lay within the golden bauble.

Picking it up to examine it, Clayton gave a cry of astonishment, for the ring bore the crest of the house of Greystoke.

At the same time, Jane Porter discovered the books in the cupboard, and on opening to the flyleaf of one of them saw the name, *John Clayton, London*. In a second book which she hurriedly examined was the single name, *Greystoke*.

"Why, Mr. Clayton," she cried, "what does this mean? Here are the names of some of your own people in these books."

"And here," he replied gravely, "is the great ring of the house of Greystoke which has been lost since my uncle, John Clayton, the former Lord Greystoke, disappeared, presumably lost at sea."

"But how do you account for these things being here, in this savage African jungle?" exclaimed the girl.

"There is but one way to account for it, Miss Porter," said Clayton. "The late Lord Greystoke was not drowned. He died here in this cabin and this poor thing upon the floor is all that is mortal of him."

"Then this must have been Lady Greystoke," said Jane reverently, indicating the poor mass of bones upon the bed.

"The beautiful Lady Alice," replied Clayton, "of whose many virtues and remarkable personal charms I often have heard my mother and father speak. Poor unhappy lady," he murmured sadly.

With deep reverence and solemnity the bodies of the late Lord and Lady Greystoke were buried beside their little African cabin, and between them was placed the tiny skeleton of the baby of Kala, the ape.

As Mr. Philander was placing the frail bones of the infant in a bit of sail cloth, he examined the skull minutely. Then he called Professor Porter to his side, and the two argued in low tones for several minutes.

"Most remarkable, most remarkable," said Professor Porter.

"Bless me," said Mr. Philander, "we must acquaint Mr. Clayton with our discovery at once."

"Tut, tut, Mr. Philander, tut, tut!" remonstrated Professor Archimedes Q. Porter. "Let the dead past bury its dead."

And so the white-haired old man repeated the burial service over this strange grave, while his four companions stood with bowed and uncovered heads about him.

From the trees Tarzan of the Apes watched the solemn ceremony; but most of all he watched the sweet face and graceful figure of Jane Porter.

In his savage, untutored breast new emotions were stirring. He could not fathom them. He wondered why he felt so great an interest in these people—why he had gone to such pains to save the three men. But he did not wonder why he had torn Sabor from the tender flesh of the strange girl.

Surely the men were stupid and ridiculous and cowardly. Even Manu, the monkey, was more intelligent than they. If these were creatures of his own kind he was doubtful if his past pride in blood was warranted.

But the girl, ah—that was a different matter. He did not reason here. He knew that she was created to be protected, and that he was created to protect her.

He wondered why they had dug a great hole in the ground merely to bury dry bones. Surely there was no sense in that; no one wanted to steal dry bones.

Had there been meat upon them he could have understood, for thus alone might one keep his meat from Dango, the hyena, and the other robbers of the jungle.

When the grave had been filled with earth the little party turned back toward the cabin, and Esmeralda, still weeping copiously for the two she had never heard of before today, and who had been dead twenty years, chanced to glance toward the harbor. Instantly her tears ceased.

"Look at them low-down riffraff out there!" she shrilled, pointing toward the *Arrow*. "They-all's a desecrating us, right here on this here perverted island."

And, sure enough, the *Arrow* was being worked toward the open sea, slowly, through the harbor's entrance.

"They promised to leave us firearms and ammunition," said Clayton. "The merciless beasts!"

"It is the work of that fellow they call Snipes, I am sure," said Jane Porter. "King was a scoundrel, but he had a little sense of humanity. If they had not killed him I know that he would have seen that we were properly provided for before they left us to our fate."

"I regret that they did not visit us before sailing," said Professor Porter. "I had proposed requesting them to leave the treasure with us, as I shall be a ruined man if that is lost."

Jane Porter looked at her father sadly.

"Never mind, dear," she said. "It wouldn't have done any good, because it is solely for the treasure that they killed their officers and landed us upon this awful shore."

"Tut, tut, child, tut, tut!" replied Professor Porter. "You are a good child, but inexperienced in practical matters," and Professor Porter turned and walked slowly away toward the jungle, his hands clasped beneath his long coattails and his eyes bent upon the ground.

His daughter watched him with a pathetic smile upon her lips, and then turning to Mr. Philander, she whispered:

"Please don't let him wander off again as he did yesterday. We depend upon you, you know, to keep a close watch upon him."

"He becomes more difficult to handle each day," replied Mr. Philander, with a sigh and a shake of his head. "I presume he is now off to report to the directors of the Zoo that one of their lions was at large last night. Oh, Miss Jane, you don't know what I have to contend with."

"Yes, I do, Mr. Philander; but while we all love him, you alone are best fitted to manage him; for, regardless of what he may say to you, he respects your great learning, and, therefore, has immense confidence in your judgment. The poor dear cannot differentiate between erudition and wisdom."

Mr. Philander, with a mildly puzzled expression on his face, turned to pursue Professor Porter, and in his mind he was revolving the question of whether he should feel complimented or aggrieved at Miss Porter's rather backhanded compliment.

Tarzan had seen the consternation depicted upon the faces of the little group as they witnessed the departure of the *Arrow*; so, as the ship was a wonderful novelty to him in addition, he determined to hasten out to the point of land at the north of the harbor's mouth and obtain a nearer view of the boat, as well as to learn, if possible, the direction of its flight.

Swinging through the trees with great speed, he reached the point only a moment after the ship had passed out of the harbor, so that he obtained an excellent view of the wonders of this strange, floating house.

There were some twenty men running hither and thither about the deck, pulling and hauling on ropes.

A light land breeze was blowing, and the ship had been worked through the harbor's mouth under scant sail, but now that they had cleared the point every available shred of canvas was being spread that she might stand out to sea as handily as possible.

Tarzan watched the graceful movements of the ship in rapt admiration, and longed to be aboard her. Presently his keen eyes caught the faintest suspicion of smoke on the far northern horizon, and he wondered over the cause of such a thing out on the great water.

At about the same time the lookout on the *Arrow* must have discerned it, for in a few minutes Tarzan saw the sails being shifted and shortened. The ship came about, and presently he knew that she was beating back toward land.

A man at the bows was constantly heaving into the sea a rope to the end of which a small object was fastened. Tarzan wondered what the purpose of this action might be.

At last the ship came up directly into the wind; the anchor was lowered; down came the sails. There was great scurrying about on deck.

A boat was lowered, and in it a great chest was placed. Then a dozen sailors bent to the oars and pulled rapidly toward the point where Tarzan crouched in the branches of a tree.

In the stern of the boat, as it drew nearer, Tarzan saw the rat-faced man.

It was but a few minutes later that the boat touched the beach. The men jumped out and lifted the great chest to the sand. They were on the north side of the point so that their presence was concealed from those at the cabin.

The men argued angrily for a moment. Then the rat-faced one, with several companions, ascended the low bluff on which stood the tree that concealed Tarzan. They looked about for several minutes.

"Here is a good place," said the rat-faced sailor, indicating a spot beneath Tarzan's tree.

"It is as good as any," replied one of his companions. "If they catch us with the treasure aboard it will all be confiscated anyway. We might as well bury it here on the chance that some of us will escape the gallows to come back and enjoy it later."

The rat-faced one now called to the men who had remained at the boat, and they came slowly up the bank carrying picks and shovels.

"Hurry, —— you!" cried Snipes.

"Stow it!" retorted one of the men, in a surly tone. "You're no admiral, you —— —— shrimp."

"I'm Cap'n here, though, I'll have you to understand, you swab," shrieked Snipes, with a volley of frightful oaths.

"Steady, boys," cautioned one of the men who had not spoken before. "It ain't goin' to get us nothing by fightin' amongst ourselves."

"Right enough," replied the sailor who had resented Snipes' autocratic tones; "but by the same token it ain't a-goin' to get nobody nothin' to put on airs in this bloomin' company neither."

"You fellows dig here," said Snipes, indicating a spot beneath the tree. "And while you're diggin', Peter kin be a-makin' of a map of the location, so's we kin find it again. You, Tom, and Bill, take a couple more down and fetch up the chest."

"Wot are you a-goin' to do?" asked he of the previous altercation. "Just boss?"

"Git busy there," growled Snipes. "You didn't think your Cap'n was a-goin' to dig with a shovel, did you?"

The men all looked up angrily. None of them liked Snipes, and this disagreeable show of authority since he had murdered King, the real head and ringleader of the mutineers, had only added fuel to the flames of their hatred.

"Do you mean to say that you don't intend to take a shovel, and lend a hand with this work? Your shoulder's not hurt so all-fired bad as that," said Tarrant, the sailor who had before spoken.

"Not by a —— sight," replied Snipes, fingering the butt of his revolver nervously.

"Then, by God," replied Tarrant, "if you won't take a shovel you'll take a pickax."

With the words he raised his pick above his head, and, with a mighty blow, he buried the point in Snipes' brain.

For a moment the men stood silently looking at the result of their fellow's grim humor. Then one of them spoke.

"Served the skunk jolly well right," he said.

One of the others commenced to ply his pick to the ground. The soil was soft and he threw aside the pick and grasped a shovel; then the others joined him. There was no further comment on the killing, but the men worked in a better frame of mind than they had since Snipes had assumed command.

When they had a trench of ample size to bury the chest, Tarrant suggested that they enlarge it and inter Snipes' body on top of the chest.

"It might 'elp fool any as 'appened to be diggin' 'ereabouts," he explained.

The others saw the cunning of the suggestion, and so the trench was lengthened to accommodate the corpse, and in the center a deeper hole was excavated for the box, which was first wrapped in sailcloth and then lowered to its place, which brought its top about a foot below the bottom of the grave. Earth was shoveled in and tramped down about the chest until the bottom of the grave showed level and uniform.

Two of the men rolled the rat-faced corpse unceremoniously into the grave, after first stripping it of its weapons and various other articles which the several members of the party coveted for their own.

They then filled the grave with earth and tramped upon it until it would hold no more.

The balance of the loose earth was thrown far and wide, and a mass of dead undergrowth spread in as natural a manner as possible over the new-made grave to obliterate all signs of the ground having been disturbed.

Their work done the sailors returned to the small boat, and pulled off rapidly toward the *Arrow*.

The breeze had increased considerably, and as the smoke upon the horizon was now plainly discernible in considerable volume, the mutineers lost no time in getting under full sail and bearing away toward the southwest.

Tarzan, an interested spectator of all that had taken place, sat speculating on the strange actions of these peculiar creatures.

Men were indeed more foolish and more cruel than the beasts of the jungle! How fortunate was he who lived in the peace and security of the great forest!

Tarzan wondered what the chest they had buried contained. If they did not want it why did they not merely throw it into the water? That would have been much easier.

Ah, he thought, but they do want it. They have hidden it here because they intend returning for it later.

Tarzan dropped to the ground and commenced to examine the earth about the excavation. He was looking to see if these creatures had dropped anything which he might like to own. Soon he discovered a spade hidden by the underbrush which they had laid upon the grave.

He seized it and attempted to use it as he had seen the sailors do. It was awkward work and hurt his bare feet, but he persevered until he had partially uncovered the body. This he dragged from the grave and laid to one side.

Then he continued digging until he had unearthed the chest. This also he dragged to the side of the corpse. Then he filled in the smaller hole below the grave, replaced the body and the earth around and above it, covered it over with underbrush, and returned to the chest.

Four sailors had sweated beneath the burden of its weight—Tarzan of the Apes picked it up as though it had been an empty packing case, and with the spade slung to his back by a piece of rope, carried it off into the densest part of the jungle.

He could not well negotiate the trees with his awkward burden, but he kept to the trails, and so made fairly good time.

For several hours he traveled a little north of east until he came to an impenetrable wall of matted and tangled vegetation. Then he took to the lower branches, and in another fifteen minutes he emerged into the amphitheater of the apes, where they met in council, or to celebrate the rites of the Dum-Dum.

Near the center of the clearing, and not far from the drum, or altar, he commenced to dig. This was harder work than turning up the freshly excavated earth at the grave, but Tarzan of the Apes was persevering and so he kept at his labor until he was rewarded by seeing a hole sufficiently deep to receive the chest and effectually hide it from view.

Why had he gone to all this labor without knowing the value of the contents of the chest?

Tarzan of the Apes had a man's figure and a man's brain, but he was an ape by training and environment. His brain told him that the chest contained something valuable, or the men would not have hidden it. His training had taught him to imitate whatever was new and unusual, and now the natural curiosity, which is as common to men as to apes, prompted him to open the chest and examine its contents.

But the heavy lock and massive iron bands baffled both his cunning and his immense strength, so that he was compelled to bury the chest without having his curiosity satisfied.

By the time Tarzan had hunted his way back to the vicinity of the cabin, feeding as he went, it was quite dark.

Within the little building a light was burning, for Clayton had found an unopened tin of oil which had stood intact for twenty years, a part of the supplies left with the Claytons by Black Michael. The lamps also were still usable, and thus the interior of the cabin appeared as bright as day to the astonished Tarzan.

He had often wondered at the exact purpose of the lamps. His reading and the pictures had told him what they were, but he had no idea of how they could be made to produce the wondrous sunlight that some of his pictures had portrayed them as diffusing upon all surrounding objects.

As he approached the window nearest the door he saw that the cabin had been divided into two rooms by a rough partition of boughs and sailcloth.

In the front room were the three men; the two older deep in argument, while the younger, tilted back against the wall on an improvised stool, was deeply engrossed in reading one of Tarzan's books.

Tarzan was not particularly interested in the men, however, so he sought the other window. There was the girl. How beautiful her features! How delicate her snowy skin!

She was writing at Tarzan's own table beneath the window. Upon a pile of grasses at the far side of the room lay Esmeralda, asleep.

For an hour Tarzan feasted his eyes upon the girl while she wrote. How he longed to speak to her, but he dared not attempt it, for he was convinced that, like the young man, she would not understand him, and he feared, too, that he might frighten her away.

At length she arose, leaving her manuscript upon the table. She went to the bed upon which had been spread several layers of soft grasses. These she rearranged.

Then she loosened the soft mass of golden hair which crowned her head. Like a shimmering waterfall turned to burnished metal by a dying sun it fell about her oval face; in waving lines, below her waist it tumbled.

Tarzan was spellbound. Then she extinguished the lamp and all within the cabin was wrapped in Cimmerian darkness.

Still Tarzan watched. Creeping close beneath the window he waited, listening, for half an hour. At last he was rewarded by the sounds of the regular breathing within which denotes sleep.

Cautiously he intruded his hand between the meshes of the lattice until his whole arm was within the cabin. Carefully he felt upon the desk. At last he grasped the manuscript upon which Jane Porter had been writing, and as cautiously withdrew his arm and hand, holding the precious treasure.

Tarzan folded the sheets into a small parcel which he tucked into the quiver with his arrows. Then he melted away into the jungle as softly and as noiselessly as a shadow.

CHAPTER EIGHTEEN
THE JUNGLE TOLL

EARLY THE FOLLOWING MORNING Tarzan awoke, and his first thought of the new day, as the last of yesterday, was of the wonderful writing which lay hidden in his quiver.

Hurriedly he brought it forth, hoping against hope that he could read what the beautiful girl had written there the preceding evening.

At the first glance he suffered the bitter disappointment of his whole life; never before had he so yearned for anything as now he did for the ability to interpret a message from that golden-haired divinity who had come so suddenly and so unexpectedly into his life.

What if the message were not intended for him? It was an expression of her thoughts, and that was all sufficient for Tarzan of the Apes.

And now to be baffled by strange, uncouth characters the like of which he had never seen before! Why, they even tipped in the opposite direction from all that he had ever examined either in printed books or the difficult script of the few letters he had found.

Even the little bugs of the black book were familiar friends, though their arrangement meant nothing to him; but these bugs were new and unheard of.

For twenty minutes he pored over them, when suddenly they commenced to take familiar though distorted shapes. Ah, they were his old friends, but badly crippled.

Then he began to make out a word here and a word there. His heart leaped for joy. He could read it, and he would.

In another half hour he was progressing rapidly, and, but for an exceptional word now and again, he found it very plain sailing.

Here is what he read:

WEST COAST OF AFRICA, ABOUT 10° DEGREES
SOUTH LATITUDE. (So Mr. Clayton says.)

February 3 (?), 1909.

DEAREST HAZEL:

It seems foolish to write you a letter that you may never see, but I

133

simply must tell somebody of our awful experiences since we sailed from Europe on the ill-fated *Arrow*.

If we never return to civilization, as now seems only too likely, this will at least prove a brief record of the events which led up to our final fate, whatever it may be.

As you know, we were supposed to have set out upon a scientific expedition to the Congo. Papa was presumed to entertain some wondrous theory of an unthinkably ancient civilization, the remains of which lay buried somewhere in the Congo valley. But after we were well under sail the truth came out.

It seems that an old bookworm who has a book and curio shop in Baltimore discovered between the leaves of a very old Spanish manuscript a letter written in 1550 detailing the adventures of a crew of mutineers of a Spanish galleon bound from Spain to South America with a vast treasure of "doubloons" and "pieces of eight," I suppose, for they certainly sound weird and piraty.

The writer had been one of the crew, and the letter was to his son, who was, at the very time the letter was written, master of a Spanish merchantman.

Many years had elapsed since the events the letter narrated had transpired, and the old man had become a respected citizen of an obscure Spanish town, but the love of gold was still so strong upon him that he risked all to acquaint his son with the means of attaining fabulous wealth for them both.

The writer told how when but a week out from Spain the crew had mutinied and murdered every officer and man who opposed them; but they defeated their own ends by this very act, for there was none left competent to navigate a ship at sea.

They were blown hither and thither for two months, until sick and dying of scurvy, starvation, and thirst, they had been wrecked on a small islet.

The galleon was washed high upon the beach where she went to pieces; but not before the survivors, who numbered but ten souls, had rescued one of the great chests of treasure.

This they buried well up on the island, and for three years they lived there in constant hope of being rescued.

One by one they sickened and died, until only one man was left, the writer of the letter.

The men had built a boat from the wreckage of the galleon, but having no idea where the island was located they had not dared to put to sea.

When all were dead except himself, however, the awful loneliness so weighed upon the mind of the sole survivor that he could endure it no longer, and choosing to risk death upon the open sea rather than madness on the lonely isle, he set sail in his little boat after nearly a year of solitude.

Fortunately he sailed due north, and within a week was in the track of the Spanish merchantmen plying between the West Indies and Spain, and was picked up by one of these vessels homeward bound.

The story he told was merely one of shipwreck in which all but a few had perished, the balance, except himself, dying after they reached the island. He did not mention the mutiny or the chest of buried treasure.

The master of the merchantman assured him that from the position at which they had picked him up, and the prevailing winds for the past week, he could have been on no other island than one of the Cape Verde group, which lie off the West Coast of Africa in about 16° or 17° north latitude.

His letter described the island minutely, as well as the location of the treasure, and was accompanied by the crudest, funniest little old map you ever saw; with trees and rocks all marked by scrawly X's to show the exact spot where the treasure had been buried.

When Papa explained the real nature of the expedition, my heart sank, for I know so well how visionary and impractical the poor dear has always been that I feared he had again been duped; especially when he told me that he had paid a thousand dollars for the letter and map.

To add to my distress, I learned that he had borrowed ten thousand dollars more from Robert Canler, and had given his notes for the amount.

Mr. Canler had asked for no security, and you know, dearie, what that will mean for me if Papa cannot meet them. Oh, how I detest that man!

We all tried to look on the bright side of things, but Mr. Philander, and Mr. Clayton—he joined us in London just for the adventure—both felt as skeptical as I.

Well, to make a long story short, we found the island and the treasure—a great iron-bound oak chest, wrapped in many layers of oiled sailcloth, and as strong and firm as when it had been buried nearly two hundred years ago.

It was *simply filled* with gold coin, and was so heavy that four men bent underneath its weight.

The horrid thing seems to bring nothing but murder and misfortune to those who have to do with it, for three days after we sailed from the Cape Verde Islands our own crew mutinied and killed every one of their officers.

Oh, it was the most terrifying experience one could imagine—I cannot even write of it.

They were going to kill us too, but one of them, the leader, a man named King, would not let them, and so they sailed south along the coast to a lonely spot where they found a good harbor, and here they landed and have left us.

They sailed away with the treasure today, but Mr. Clayton says they will meet with a fate similar to the mutineers of the ancient galleon, because King, the only man aboard who knew aught of navigation, was murdered on the beach by one of the men the day we landed.

I wish you could know Mr. Clayton; he is the dearest fellow imaginable, and unless I am mistaken he has fallen very much in love with me.

He is the only son of Lord Greystoke, and some day will inherit the title and estates. In addition, he is wealthy in his own right, but the fact that he is going to be an English Lord makes me very sad—you know what my sentiments have always been relative to American girls who married titled foreigners. Oh, if he were only a plain American gentleman!

But it isn't his fault, poor fellow, and in everything except birth he would do credit to my darling old country, and that is the greatest compliment I know how to pay any man.

We have had the most weird experiences since we were landed here. Papa and Mr. Philander lost in the jungle, and chased by a real lion.

Mr. Clayton lost, and attacked twice by wild beasts. Esmeralda and I cornered in an old cabin by a perfectly awful man-eating lioness. Oh, it was simply "terrifical," as Esmeralda would say.

But the strangest part of it all is the wonderful creature who rescued us. I have not seen him, but Mr. Clayton and Papa and Mr. Philander have, and they say that he is a perfectly godlike white man tanned to a dusky brown, with the strength of a wild elephant, the agility of a monkey, and the bravery of a lion.

He speaks no English and vanishes as quickly and as mysteriously after he has performed some valorous deed, as though he were a disembodied spirit.

Then we have another weird neighbor, who printed a beautiful sign in English and tacked it on the door of his cabin, which we have pre-empted, warning us to destroy none of his belongings, and signing himself "Tarzan of the Apes."

We have never seen him, though we think he is about, for one of the sailors, who was going to shoot Mr. Clayton in the back, received a spear in his shoulder from some unseen hand in the jungle.

The sailors left us but a meager supply of food, so, as we have only a single revolver with but three cartridges left in it, we do not know how we can procure meat, though Mr. Philander says that we can exist indefinitely on the wild fruit and nuts which abound in the jungle.

I am very tired now, so I shall go to my funny bed of grasses which Mr. Clayton gathered for me, but will add to this from day to day as things happen.

Lovingly,

Jane Porter.

To Hazel Strong, Baltimore, MD.

Tarzan sat in a brown study for a long time after he finished reading the letter. It was filled with so many new and wonderful things that his brain was in a whirl as he attempted to digest them all.

So they did not know that he was Tarzan of the Apes. He would tell them.

In his tree he had constructed a rude shelter of leaves and boughs, beneath which, protected from the rain, he had placed the few treasures brought from the cabin. Among these were some pencils.

He took one, and beneath Jane Porter's signature he wrote:

I am Tarzan of the Apes

He thought that would be sufficient. Later he would return the letter to the cabin.

In the matter of food, thought Tarzan, they had no need to worry—he would provide, and he did.

The next morning Jane Porter found her missing letter in the exact spot from which it had disappeared two nights before. She was mystified; but when she saw the printed words beneath her signature, she felt a cold, clammy chill run up her spine. She showed the letter, or rather the last sheet with the signature, to Clayton.

"And to think," she said, "that uncanny thing was probably watching me all the time that I was writing—oo! It makes me shudder just to think of it."

"But he must be friendly," reassured Clayton, "for he has returned your letter, nor did he offer to harm you, and unless I am mistaken he left a very substantial memento of his friendship outside the cabin door last night, for I just found the carcass of a wild boar there as I came out."

From then on scarcely a day passed that did not bring its offering of game or other food. Sometimes it was a young deer, again a quantity of strange, cooked food—cassava cakes pilfered from the village of Mbonga— or a boar, or leopard, and once a lion.

Tarzan derived the greatest pleasure of his life in hunting meat for these strangers. It seemed to him that no pleasure on earth could compare with laboring for the welfare and protection of the beautiful golden-haired girl.

Some day he would venture into the camp in daylight and talk with these people through the medium of the little bugs which were familiar to them and to Tarzan.

But he found it difficult to overcome the timidity of the wild thing of the forest, and so day followed day without seeing a fulfillment of his good intentions.

The party in the camp, emboldened by familiarity, wandered farther and yet farther into the jungle in search of nuts and fruit.

Scarcely a day passed that did not find Professor Porter straying in his preoccupied indifference toward the jaws of death. Mr. Samuel T. Philander, never what one might call robust, was worn to the shadow of a shadow through the ceaseless worry and mental distraction resultant from his Herculean efforts to safeguard the professor.

A month passed. Tarzan had finally determined to visit the camp by daylight.

It was early afternoon. Clayton had wandered to the point at the harbor's mouth to look for passing vessels. Here he kept a great mass of wood, high piled, ready to be ignited as a signal should a steamer or a sail top the far horizon.

Professor Porter was wandering along the beach south of the camp with

Mr. Philander at his elbow, urging him to turn his steps back before the two became again the sport of some savage beast.

The others gone, Jane Porter and Esmeralda had wandered into the jungle to gather fruit, and in their search were led farther and farther from the cabin.

Tarzan waited in silence before the door of the little house until they should return. His thoughts were of the beautiful girl. They were always of her now. He wondered if she would fear him, and the thought all but caused him to relinquish his plan.

He was rapidly becoming impatient for her return, that he might feast his eyes upon her and be near her, perhaps touch her. The ape-man knew no god, but he was as near to worshiping his divinity as mortal man ever comes to worship.

While he waited he passed the time printing a message to her; whether he intended giving it to her he himself could not have told, but he took infinite pleasure in seeing his thoughts expressed in print—in which he was not so uncivilized after all. He wrote:

I am Tarzan of the Apes. I want you. I am yours. You are mine. We will live here together always in my house. I will bring you the best of fruits, the tenderest deer, the finest meats that roam the jungle. I will hunt for you. I am the greatest of the jungle fighters. I will fight for you. I am the mightiest of the jungle fighters. You are Jane Porter, I saw it in your letter. When you see this you will know that it is for you and that Tarzan of the Apes loves you.

As he stood, straight as a young Indian, by the door, waiting after he had finished the message, there came to his keen ears a familiar sound. It was the passing of a great ape through the lower branches of the forest.

For an instant he listened intently, and then from the jungle came the agonized scream of a woman, and Tarzan of the Apes, dropping his first love letter upon the ground, shot like a panther into the forest.

Clayton, also, heard the scream, and Professor Porter and Mr. Philander, and in a few minutes they came panting to the cabin, calling out to each other a volley of excited questions as they approached. A glance within confirmed their worst fears.

Jane and Esmeralda were not there.

Instantly, Clayton, followed by the two old men, plunged into the jungle, calling the girl's name aloud. For half an hour they stumbled on, until Clayton, by merest chance, came upon the prostrate form of Esmeralda.

He stopped beside her, feeling for her pulse and then listening for her heartbeats. She lived. He shook her.

"Esmeralda!" he shrieked in her ear. "Esmeralda! For God's sake, where is Miss Porter? What has happened? Esmeralda!"

Slowly the woman opened her eyes. She saw Clayton. She saw the jungle about her.

"Oh, Gaberelle!" she screamed, and fainted again.

By this time Professor Porter and Mr. Philander had come up.

"What shall we do, Mr. Clayton?" asked the old professor. "Where shall we look? God could not have been so cruel as to take my little girl away from me now."

"We must arouse Esmeralda first," replied Clayton. "She can tell us what has happened. Esmeralda!" he cried again, shaking the woman roughly by the shoulder.

"O Gaberelle, I want to die!" cried the poor woman, but with eyes fast closed. "Let me die, dear Lord, don't let me see that awful face again."

"Come, come, Esmeralda," cried Clayton.

"The Lord isn't here; it's Mr. Clayton. Open your eyes."

Esmeralda did as she was bade.

"O Gaberelle! Thank the Lord," she said.

"Where's Miss Porter? What happened?" questioned Clayton.

"Ain't Miss Jane here?" cried Esmeralda, sitting up with wonderful celerity for one of her bulk. "Oh, Lord, now I remember! It must have took her away," and Esmeralda commenced to sob, and wail her lamentations.

"What took her away?" cried Professor Porter.

"A great big giant all covered with hair."

"A gorilla, Esmeralda?" questioned Mr. Philander, and the three men scarcely breathed as he voiced the horrible thought.

"I thought it was the devil; but I guess it must have been one of them gorilephants. Oh, my poor baby, my poor little honey," and again Esmeralda broke into uncontrollable sobbing.

Clayton immediately began to look about for tracks, but he could find nothing save a confusion of trampled grasses in the close vicinity, and his woodcraft was too meager for the translation of what he did see.

All the balance of the day they sought through the jungle; but as night drew on they were forced to give up in despair and hopelessness, for they did not even know in what direction the thing had borne Jane Porter.

It was long after dark ere they reached the cabin, and a sad and grief-stricken party it was that sat silently within the little structure.

Professor Porter finally broke the silence. His tones were no longer those of the erudite pedant theorizing upon the abstract and the unknowable; but those of the man of action—determined, but tinged also by a note of indescribable hopelessness and grief which wrung an answering pang from Clayton's heart.

"I shall lie down now," said the old man, "and try to sleep. Early tomorrow, as soon as it is light, I shall take what food I can carry and continue the search until I have found Jane. I will not return without her."

His companions did not reply at once. Each was immersed in his own sorrowful thoughts, and each knew, as did the old professor, what the last words meant—Professor Porter would never return from the jungle.

At length Clayton arose and laid his hand gently upon Professor Porter's bent old shoulder.

"I shall go with you, of course," he said. "Do not tell me that I need even have said so."

"I knew that you would offer—that you would wish to go, Mr. Clayton; but you must not. Jane is beyond human assistance now. I simply go that I may face my Maker with her, and know, too, that what was once my dear little girl shall not lie alone and friendless in the awful jungle.

"The same vines and leaves will cover us, the same rains beat upon us; and when the spirit of her mother is abroad, it will find us together in death, as it has always found us in life.

"No; it is I alone who may go, for she was my daughter—all that was left on earth for me to love."

"I shall go with you," said Clayton simply.

The old man looked up, regarding the strong, handsome face of William Cecil Clayton intently. Perhaps he read there the love that lay in the heart beneath—the love for his daughter.

He had been too preoccupied with his own scholarly thoughts in the past to consider the little occurrences, the chance words, which would have indicated to a more practical man that these young people were being drawn more and more closely to one another. Now they came back to him, one by one.

"As you wish," he said.

"You may count on me, also," said Mr. Philander.

"No, my dear old friend," said Professor Porter. "We may not all go. It would be cruelly wicked to leave poor Esmeralda here alone, and three of us would be no more successful than one.

"There be enough dead things in the cruel forest as it is. Come—let us try to sleep a little."

CHAPTER NINETEEN
THE CALL OF THE PRIMITIVE

FROM THE TIME TARZAN LEFT THE TRIBE of great anthropoids in which he had been raised, it was torn by continual strife and discord. Terkoz proved a cruel and capricious king, so that, one by one, many of the older and weaker apes, upon whom he was particularly prone to vent his brutish nature, took their families and sought the quiet and safety of the far interior.

But at last those who remained were driven to desperation by the continued truculence of Terkoz, and it so happened that one of them recalled the parting admonition of Tarzan:

"If you have a chief who is cruel, do not do as the other apes do, and attempt, any one of you, to pit yourself against him alone. But, instead, let two or three or four of you attack him together. Then, if you will do this, no chief will dare to be other than he should be, for four of you can kill any chief who may ever be over you."

And the ape who recalled this wise counsel repeated it to several of his fellows, so that when Terkoz returned to the tribe that day he found a warm reception awaiting him.

There were no formalities. As Terkoz reached the group, five huge, hairy beasts sprang upon him.

At heart he was an arrant coward, which is the way with bullies among apes as well as among men; so he did not remain to fight and die, but tore himself away from them as quickly as he could and fled into the sheltering boughs of the forest.

Two more attempts he made to rejoin the tribe, but on each occasion he was set upon and driven away. At last he gave it up, and turned, foaming with rage and hatred, into the jungle.

For several days he wandered aimlessly, nursing his spite and looking for some weak thing on which to vent his pent anger.

It was in this state of mind that the horrible, manlike beast, swinging from tree to tree, came suddenly upon two women in the jungle.

He was right above them when he discovered them. The first intimation Jane Porter had of his presence was when the great hairy body dropped to the earth beside her, and she saw the awful face and the snarling, hideous mouth thrust within a foot of her.

One piercing scream escaped her lips as the brute hand clutched her arm. Then she was dragged toward those awful fangs which yawned at her throat. But ere they touched that fair skin another mood claimed the anthropoid.

The tribe had kept his women. He must find others to replace them. This hairless white ape would be the first of his new household, and so he threw her roughly across his broad, hairy shoulders and leaped back into the trees, bearing Jane Porter away toward a fate a thousand times worse than death.

Esmeralda's scream of terror had mingled once with that of Jane Porter, and then, as was Esmeralda's manner under stress of emergency which required presence of mind, she swooned.

But Jane Porter did not once lose consciousness. It is true that that awful face, pressing close to hers, and the stench of the foul breath beating upon her nostrils, paralyzed her with terror; but her brain was clear, and she comprehended all that transpired.

With what seemed to her marvelous rapidity the brute bore her through the forest, but still she did not cry out or struggle. The sudden advent of the ape had confused her to such an extent that she thought now that he was bearing her toward the beach.

For this reason she conserved her energies and her voice until she could see that they had approached near enough to the camp to attract the succor she craved.

Poor child! Could she but have known it, she was being borne farther and farther into the impenetrable jungle.

The scream that had brought Clayton and the two older men stumbling through the undergrowth had led Tarzan of the Apes straight to where Esmeralda lay, but it was not Esmeralda in whom his interest centered, though pausing over her he saw that she was unhurt.

For a moment he scrutinized the ground below and the trees above, until the ape that was in him by virtue of training and environment, combined with the intelligence that was his by right of birth, told his wondrous woodcraft the whole story as plainly as though he had seen the thing happen with his own eyes.

And then he was gone again into the swaying trees, following the high-flung spoor which no other human eye could have detected, much less translated.

At boughs' ends, where the anthropoid swings from one tree to another, there is most to mark the trail, but least to point the direction of the quarry, for there the pressure is downward always, toward the small end of the branch, whether the ape be leaving or entering a tree. Nearer the center of the tree, where the signs of passage are fainter, the direction is plainly marked.

Here, on this branch, a caterpillar has been crushed by the fugitive's great foot, and Tarzan knows instinctively where that same foot would touch in the next stride. Here he looks to find a tiny particle of the demolished larva, ofttimes not more than a speck of moisture.

Again, a minute bit of bark has been upturned by the scraping hand, and the direction of the break indicates the direction of the passage. Or some great limb, or the stem of the tree itself has been brushed by the hairy body, and a tiny shred of hair tells him by the direction from which it is wedged beneath the bark that he is on the right trail.

Nor does he need to check his speed to catch these seemingly faint records of the fleeing beast.

To Tarzan they stand out boldly against all the myriad other scars and bruises and signs upon the leafy way. But strongest of all is the scent, for Tarzan is pursuing up the wind, and his trained nostrils are as sensitive as a hound's.

There are those who believe that the lower orders are specially endowed by nature with better olfactory nerves than man, but it is merely a matter of development.

Man's survival does not hinge so greatly upon the perfection of his senses. His power to reason has relieved them of many of their duties, and so they have, to some extent, atrophied, as have the muscles which move the ears and scalp, merely from disuse.

The muscles are there, about the ears and beneath your scalp, and so are the nerves which transmit sensations to the brain, but they are under-developed in you because you do not need them.

Not so with Tarzan of the Apes. From early infancy his survival had depended upon acuteness of eyesight, hearing, smell, touch, and taste far more than upon the more slowly developed organ of reason.

The least developed of all in Tarzan was the sense of taste, for he could eat luscious fruits, or raw flesh, long buried, with almost equal appreciation; but in that he differed but slightly from more civilized epicures.

Almost silently the ape-man sped on in the track of Terkoz and his prey, but the sound of his approach reached the ears of the fleeing beast and spurred it on to greater speed.

Three miles were covered before Tarzan overtook them, and then Terkoz, seeing that further flight was futile, dropped to the ground in a small open glade, that he might turn and fight for his prize or be free to escape un-hampered if he saw that the pursuer was more than a match for him.

He still grasped Jane Porter in one great arm as Tarzan bounded like a leopard into the arena which nature had provided for this primeval-like battle.

When Terkoz saw that it was Tarzan who pursued him, he jumped to the conclusion that this was Tarzan's woman, since they were of the same kind—white and hairless—and so he rejoiced at this opportunity for double revenge upon his hated enemy.

To Jane Porter the strange apparition of this godlike man was as wine to sick nerves.

From the description which Clayton and her father and Mr. Philander had given her, she knew that it must be the same wonderful creature who had saved them, and she saw in him only a protector and a friend.

But as Terkoz pushed her roughly aside to meet Tarzan's charge, and she saw the great proportions of the ape and the mighty muscles and the fierce fangs, her heart quailed. How could any animal vanquish such a mighty antagonist?

Like two charging bulls they came together, and like two wolves sought each other's throat. Against the long canines of the ape was pitted the thin blade of the man's knife.

Jane Porter—her lithe, young form flattened against the trunk of a great tree, her hands tight pressed against her rising and falling bosom, and her eyes wide with mingled horror, fascination, fear, and admiration—watched the primordial ape battle with the primeval man for possession of a woman—for her.

As the great muscles of the man's back and shoulders knotted beneath the tension of his efforts, and the huge biceps and forearm held at bay those mighty tusks, the veil of centuries of civilization and culture was swept from the blurred vision of the Baltimore girl.

When the long knife drank deep a dozen times of Terkoz's heart's blood, and the great carcass rolled lifeless upon the ground, it was a primeval woman who sprang forward with outstretched arms toward the primeval man who had fought for her and won her.

And Tarzan?

He did what no red-blooded man needs lessons in doing. He took his woman in his arms and smothered her upturned, panting lips with kisses.

For a moment Jane Porter lay there with half-closed eyes. For a moment—the first in her young life—she knew the meaning of love.

But as suddenly as the veil had been withdrawn it dropped again, and an outraged conscience suffused her face with its scarlet mantle, and a mortified woman thrust Tarzan of the Apes from her and buried her face in her hands.

Tarzan had been surprised when he had found the girl he had learned to love after a vague and abstract manner a willing prisoner in his arms. Now he was surprised that she repulsed him.

He came close to her once more and took hold of her arm. She turned upon him like a tigress, striking his great breast with her tiny hands.

Tarzan could not understand it.

A moment ago and it had been his intention to hasten Jane Porter back to her people, but that little moment was lost now in the dim and distant past of things which were but can never be again, and with it the good intention had gone to join the impossible.

Since then Tarzan of the Apes had felt a warm, lithe form close pressed to his. Hot, sweet breath against his cheek and mouth had fanned a new flame to life within his breast, and perfect lips had clung to his in burning kisses that had seared a deep brand into his soul—a brand which marked a new Tarzan.

Again he laid his hand upon her arm. Again she repulsed him. And then Tarzan of the Apes did just what his first ancestor would have done.

He took his woman in his arms and carried her into the jungle.

Early the following morning the four within the little cabin by the beach were awakened by the booming of a cannon. Clayton was the first to rush out, and there, beyond the harbor's mouth, he saw two vessels lying at anchor.

One was the *Arrow* and the other a small French cruiser. The sides of the latter were crowded with men gazing shoreward, and it was evident to Clayton, as to the others who had now joined him, that the gun which they had heard had been fired to attract their attention if they still remained at the cabin.

Both vessels lay at a considerable distance from shore, and it was doubtful if their glasses would locate the waving hats of the little party far in between the harbor's points.

Esmeralda had removed her red apron and was waving it frantically above her head; but Clayton, still fearing that even this might not be seen, hurried off toward the northern point where lay his signal pyre ready for the match.

It seemed an age to him, as to those who waited breathlessly behind, ere he reached the great pile of dry branches and underbrush.

As he broke from the dense wood and came in sight of the vessels again, he was filled with consternation to see that the *Arrow* was making sail and that the cruiser was already underway.

Quickly lighting the pyre in a dozen places, he hurried to the extreme point of the promontory, where he stripped off his shirt, and, tying it to a fallen branch, stood waving it back and forth above him.

But still the vessels continued to stand out; and he had given up all hope, when the great column of smoke, arising above the forest in one dense vertical shaft, attracted the attention of a lookout aboard the cruiser, and instantly a dozen glasses were leveled on the beach.

Presently Clayton saw the two ships come about again; and while the *Arrow* lay drifting quietly on the ocean, the cruiser steamed slowly back toward shore.

At some distance away she stopped, and a boat was lowered and dispatched toward the beach.

As it was drawn up a young officer stepped out.

"Monsieur Clayton, I presume?" he asked.

"Thank God, you have come!" was Clayton's reply. "And it may be that it is not too late even now."

"What do you mean, Monsieur?" asked the officer.

Clayton told of the abduction of Jane Porter and the need of armed men to aid in the search for her.

"*Mon Dieu!*" exclaimed the officer, sadly. "Yesterday and it would not have been too late. Today and it may be better that the poor lady were never found. It is horrible, Monsieur. It is too horrible."

Other boats had now put off from the cruiser, and Clayton, having pointed out the harbor's entrance to the officer, entered the boat with him and its nose was turned toward the little landlocked bay, into which the other craft followed.

Soon the entire party had landed where stood Professor Porter, Mr. Philander, and the weeping Esmeralda.

Among the officers in the last boats to put off from the cruiser was the commander of the vessel; and when he had heard the story of Jane's abduction, he generously called for volunteers to accompany Professor Porter and Clayton in their search.

Not an officer or a man was there of those brave and sympathetic Frenchmen who did not quickly beg leave to be one of the expedition.

The commander selected twenty men and two officers, Lieutenant d'Arnot and Lieutenant Charpentier. A boat was dispatched to the cruiser for provisions, ammunition, and carbines; the men were already armed with revolvers.

Then, to Clayton's inquiries as to how they had happened to anchor offshore and fire a signal gun, the commander, Captain Dufranne, explained that a month before they had sighted the *Arrow* bearing southwest under considerable canvas, and that when they had signaled her to come about she had but crowded on more sail.

They had kept her hull-up until sunset, firing several shots after her, but the next morning she was nowhere to be seen. They had then continued to cruise up and down the coast for several weeks, and had about forgotten the incident of the recent chase, when, early one morning a few days before, the lookout had descried a vessel laboring in the trough of a heavy sea and evidently entirely from under control.

As they steamed nearer to the derelict they were surprised to note that it was the same vessel that had run from them a few weeks earlier. Her forestaysail and mizzen spanker were set as though an effort had been made to hold her head up into the wind, but the sheets had parted, and the sails were tearing to ribbons in the half gale of wind.

In the high sea that was running it was a difficult and dangerous task to attempt to put a prize crew aboard her; and as no signs of life had been seen above deck, it was decided to stand by until the wind and sea abated; but just then a figure was seen clinging to the rail and feebly waving a mute signal of despair toward them.

Immediately a boat's crew was ordered out and an attempt was successfully made to board the *Arrow*. The sight that met the Frenchmen's eyes as they clambered over the ship's side was appalling.

A dozen dead and dying men rolled hither and thither upon the pitching deck, the living intermingled with the dead. Two of the corpses appeared to have been partially devoured as though by wolves.

The prize crew soon had the vessel under proper sail once more and the living members of the ill-starred company carried below to their hammocks.

The dead were wrapped in tarpaulins and lashed on deck to be identified by their comrades before being consigned to the deep.

None of the living was conscious when the Frenchmen reached the *Arrow*'s deck. Even the poor devil who had waved the single despairing signal of distress had lapsed into unconsciousness before he had learned whether it had availed or not.

It did not take the French officer long to learn what had caused the terrible condition aboard; for when water and brandy were sought to restore the men, it was found that not only was there not any of either, but not a vestige of food of any description.

He immediately signaled to the cruiser to send water, medicine, and provisions, and another boat made the perilous trip to the *Arrow*.

When restoratives had been applied several of the men regained consciousness, and then the whole story was told. That part of it we know up to the sailing of the *Arrow* after the murder of Snipes, and the burial of his body above the treasure chest.

It seems that the pursuit by the cruiser had so terrorized the mutineers that they had continued out across the Atlantic for several days after losing her; but on discovering the meager supply of water and provisions aboard, they had turned back toward the east.

With no one on board who understood navigation, discussions soon arose as to their whereabouts; and as three days' sailing to the east did not raise land, they bore off to the north, fearing that the high north winds that had prevailed had driven them south of the southern extremity of Africa.

They kept on a north-northeasterly course for two days, when they were overtaken by a calm which lasted for nearly a week. Their water was gone, and in another day they would be without food.

Conditions changed rapidly from bad to worse. One man went mad and leaped overboard. Soon another opened his veins and drank his own blood.

When he died they threw him overboard also, though there were those among them who wanted to keep the corpse on board. Hunger was changing them from human beasts to wild beasts.

Two days before they had been picked up by the cruiser they had become too weak to handle the vessel, and that same day three men died. On the following morning it was seen that one of the corpses had been partially devoured.

All that day the men lay glaring at each other like beasts of prey, and the following morning two of the corpses lay almost entirely stripped of flesh.

The men were but little stronger for their ghoulish repast, for the want of water was by far the greatest agony with which they had to contend. And then the cruiser had come.

When those who could had recovered, the entire story had been told to the French commander; but the men were too ignorant to be able to tell him at just what point on the coast the professor and his party had been marooned, so the cruiser had steamed slowly along within sight of land, firing occasional signal guns and scanning every inch of the beach with glasses.

They had anchored by night so as not to neglect a particle of the shoreline, and it had happened that the preceding night had brought them off the very beach where lay the little camp they sought.

The signal guns of the afternoon before had not been heard by those on shore, it was presumed, because they had doubtless been in the thick of the jungle searching for Jane Porter, where the noise of their own crashing through the underbrush would have drowned the report of a far distant gun.

By the time the two parties had narrated their several adventures, the cruiser's boat had returned with supplies and arms for the expedition.

Within a few minutes the little body of sailors and the two French officers, together with Professor Porter and Clayton, set off upon their hopeless and ill-fated quest into the untracked jungle.

CHAPTER TWENTY
HEREDITY

WHEN JANE PORTER REALIZED that she was being borne away a captive by the strange forest creature who had rescued her from the clutches of the ape she struggled desperately to escape, but the strong arms that held her as easily as though she had been but a day-old babe only pressed a little more tightly.

So presently she gave up the futile effort and lay quietly, looking through half-closed lids at the face of the man who strode easily through the tangled undergrowth with her.

The face above her was one of extraordinary beauty.

A perfect type of the strongly masculine, unmarred by dissipation, or brutal or degrading passions. For, though Tarzan of the Apes was a killer of men and of beasts, he killed as the hunter kills, dispassionately, except on those rare occasions when he had killed for hate—though not the brooding, malevolent hate which marks the features of its own with hideous lines.

When Tarzan killed he more often smiled than scowled, and smiles are the foundation of beauty.

One thing the girl had noticed particularly when she had seen Tarzan rushing upon Terkoz—the vivid scarlet band upon his forehead, from above the left eye to the scalp; but now as she scanned his features she noticed that it was gone, and only a thin white line marked the spot where it had been.

As she lay more quietly in his arms Tarzan slightly relaxed his grip upon her.

Once he looked down into her eyes and smiled, and the girl had to close her own to shut out the vision of that handsome, winning face.

Presently Tarzan took to the trees, and Jane Porter, wondering that she felt no fear, began to realize that in many respects she had never felt more secure in her whole life than now as she lay in the arms of this strong, wild creature, being borne, God alone knew where or to what fate, deeper and deeper into the savage fastness of the untamed forest.

When, with closed eyes, she commenced to speculate upon the future, and terrifying fears were conjured by a vivid imagination, she had but to raise her lids and look upon that noble face so close to hers to dissipate the last remnant of apprehension.

No, he could never harm her; of that she was convinced when she translated the fine features and the frank, brave eyes above her into the chivalry which they proclaimed.

On and on they went through what seemed to Jane Porter a solid mass of verdure, yet ever there appeared to open before this forest god a passage, as by magic, which closed behind them as they passed.

Scarce a branch scraped against her, yet above and below, before and behind, the view presented naught but a solid mass of inextricably interwoven branches and creepers.

As Tarzan moved steadily onward his mind was occupied with many strange and new thoughts. Here was a problem the like of which he had never encountered, and he felt rather than reasoned that he must meet it as a man and not as an ape.

The free movement through the middle terrace, which was the route he had followed for the most part, had helped to cool the ardor of the first fierce passion of his newfound love.

Now he discovered himself speculating upon the fate which would have fallen to the girl had he not rescued her from Terkoz.

He knew why the ape had not killed her, and he commenced to compare his intentions with those of Terkoz.

True, it was the order of the jungle for the male to take his mate by force; but could Tarzan be guided by the laws of the beasts? Was not Tarzan a Man? But what did men do? He was puzzled; for he did not know.

He wished that he might ask the girl, and then it came to him that she had already answered him in the futile struggle she had made to escape and to repulse him.

But now they had come to their destination, and Tarzan of the Apes with Jane Porter in his strong arms, swung lightly to the turf of the arena where the great apes held their councils and danced the wild orgy of the Dum-Dum.

Though they had come many miles, it was still but midafternoon, and the amphitheater was bathed in the half light which filtered through the maze of encircling foliage.

The green turf looked soft and cool and inviting. The myriad noises of the jungle seemed far distant and hushed to a mere echo of blurred sounds, rising and falling like the surf upon a remote shore.

A feeling of dreamy peacefulness stole over Jane Porter as she sank down upon the grass where Tarzan had placed her, and as she looked up at his great figure towering above her, there was added a strange sense of perfect security.

As she watched him from beneath half-closed lids, Tarzan crossed the little circular clearing toward the trees upon the further side. She noted the graceful majesty of his carriage, the perfect symmetry of his magnificent figure and the poise of his well-shaped head upon his broad shoulders.

What a perfect creature! There could be naught of cruelty or baseness beneath that godlike exterior. Never, she thought, had such a man strode the earth since God created the first in his own image.

With a bound Tarzan sprang into the trees and disappeared. Jane Porter wondered where he had gone. Had he left her there to her fate in the lonely jungle?

She glanced nervously about. Every vine and bush seemed but the lurking-place of some huge and horrible beast waiting to bury gleaming fangs into her soft flesh. Every sound she magnified into the stealthy creeping of a sinuous and malignant body.

How different now that he had left her!

For a few minutes that seemed hours to the frightened girl, she sat with tense nerves waiting for the spring of the crouching thing that was to end her misery of apprehension.

She almost prayed for the cruel teeth that would give her unconsciousness and surcease from the agony of fear.

She heard a sudden, slight sound behind her. With a cry she sprang to her feet and turned to face her end.

There stood Tarzan, his arms filled with ripe and luscious fruit.

Jane Porter reeled and would have fallen, had not Tarzan, dropping his burden, caught her in his arms. She did not lose consciousness, but she clung tightly to him, shuddering and trembling like a frightened deer.

Tarzan of the Apes stroked her soft hair and tried to comfort and quiet her as Kala had him, when, as a little ape, he had been frightened by Sabor, the lioness, or Histah, the snake.

Once he pressed his lips lightly upon her forehead, and she did not move, but closed her eyes and sighed.

She could not analyze her feelings, nor did she wish to attempt it. She was satisfied to feel the safety of those strong arms, and to leave her future to fate; for the last few hours had taught her to trust this strange wild creature of the forest as she would have trusted but few of the men of her acquaintance.

As she thought of the strangeness of it, there commenced to dawn upon her the realization that she had, possibly, learned something else which she had never really known before—love. She wondered and then she smiled.

And still smiling, she pushed Tarzan gently away; and looking at him with a half-smiling, half-quizzical expression that made her face wholly entrancing, she pointed to the fruit upon the ground, and seated herself upon the edge of the earthen drum of the anthropoids, for hunger was asserting itself.

Tarzan quickly gathered up the fruit, and, bringing it, laid it at her feet; and then he, too, sat upon the drum beside her, and with his knife opened and prepared the various fruits for her meal.

Together and in silence they ate, occasionally stealing sly glances at one another, until finally Jane Porter broke into a merry laugh in which Tarzan joined.

"I wish you spoke English," said the girl.

Tarzan shook his head, and an expression of wistful and pathetic longing sobered his laughing eyes.

Then Jane Porter tried speaking to him in French, and then in German; but she had to laugh at her own blundering attempt at the latter tongue.

"Anyway," she said to him in English, "you understand my German as well as they did in Berlin."

Tarzan had long since reached a decision as to what his future procedure should be. He had had time to recollect all that he had read of the ways of men and women in the books at the cabin. He would act as he imagined the men in the books would have acted were they in his place.

Again he rose and went into the trees, but first he tried to explain by means of signs that he would return shortly, and he did so well that Jane Porter understood and was not afraid when he had gone.

Only a feeling of loneliness came over her and she watched the point where he had disappeared, with longing eyes, awaiting his return. As before, she was appraised of his presence by a soft sound behind her, and turned to see him coming across the turf with a great armful of branches.

Then he went back again into the jungle and in a few minutes reappeared with a quantity of soft grasses and ferns. Two more trips he made until he had quite a pile of material at hand.

Then he spread the ferns and grasses upon the ground in a soft flat bed, and above it leaned many branches together so that they met a few feet over its center. Upon these he spread layers of huge leaves of the great elephant's ear, and with more branches and more leaves he closed one end of the little shelter he had built.

Then they sat down together again upon the edge of the drum and tried to talk by signs.

The magnificent diamond locket which hung about Tarzan's neck had been a source of much wonderment to Jane Porter. She pointed to it now, and Tarzan removed it and handed the pretty bauble to her.

She saw that it was the work of a skilled artisan and that the diamonds were of great brilliancy and superbly set, but the cutting of them denoted that they were of a former day.

She noticed too that the locket opened, and, pressing the hidden clasp, she saw the two halves spring apart to reveal in either section an ivory miniature.

One was of a beautiful woman and the other might have been a likeness of the man who sat beside her, except for a subtle difference of expression that was scarcely definable.

She looked up at Tarzan to find him leaning toward her gazing on the miniatures with an expression of astonishment. He reached out his hand for the locket and took it away from her, examining the likenesses within with unmistakable signs of surprise and new interest. His manner clearly denoted that he had never before seen them, nor imagined that the locket opened.

This fact caused Jane Porter to indulge in further speculation, and it taxed her imagination to picture how this beautiful ornament came into the possession of a wild and savage creature of the unexplored jungles of Africa.

Still more wonderful was how it contained the likeness of one who might be a brother, or, more likely, the father of this woodland demigod who was even ignorant of the fact that the locket opened.

Tarzan was still gazing with fixity at the two faces. Presently he removed the quiver from his shoulder, and emptying the arrows upon the ground reached into the bottom of the bag-like receptacle and drew forth a flat object wrapped in many soft leaves and tied with bits of long grass.

Carefully he unwrapped it, removing layer after layer of leaves until at length he held a photograph in his hand.

Pointing to the miniature of the man within the locket he handed the photograph to Jane Porter, holding the open locket beside it.

The photograph only served to puzzle the girl still more, for it was evidently another likeness of the same man whose picture rested in the locket beside that of the beautiful young woman.

Tarzan was looking at her with an expression of puzzled bewilderment in his eyes as she glanced up at him. He seemed to be framing a question with his lips.

The girl pointed to the photograph and then to the miniature and then to him, as though to indicate that she thought the likenesses were of him, but he only shook his head, and then shrugging his great shoulders, he took the photograph from her and having carefully rewrapped it, placed it again in the bottom of his quiver.

For a few moments he sat in silence, his eyes bent upon the ground, while Jane Porter held the little locket in her hand, turning it over and over in an endeavor to find some further clue that might lead to the identity of its original owner.

At length a simple explanation occurred to her.

The locket had belonged to Lord Greystoke, and the likenesses were of himself and Lady Alice.

This wild creature had simply found it in the cabin by the beach. How stupid of her not to have thought of that solution before.

But to account for the strange likeness between Lord Greystoke and this forest god—that was quite beyond her, and it is not strange that she could not imagine that this naked savage was indeed an English nobleman.

At length Tarzan looked up to watch the girl as she examined the locket. He could not fathom the meaning of the faces within, but he could read the interest and fascination upon the face of the live young creature by his side.

She noticed that he was watching her and thinking that he wished his ornament again she held it out to him. He took it from her and taking the chain in his two hands he placed it about her neck, smiling at her expression of surprise at his unexpected gift.

Jane Porter shook her head vehemently and would have removed the golden links from about her throat, but Tarzan would not let her. Taking her hands in his, when she insisted upon it, he held them tightly to prevent her.

At last she desisted and with a little laugh raised the locket to her lips, and, rising, dropped him a little curtsy.

Tarzan did not know precisely what she meant, but he guessed correctly that it was her way of acknowledging the gift, and so he rose, and taking the locket in his hand, stooped gravely like some courtier of old, and pressed his lips upon it where hers had rested.

It was a stately and gallant little compliment performed with the grace and dignity of utter unconsciousness of self. It was the hallmark of his aristocratic birth, the natural outcropping of many generations of fine breeding, an hereditary instinct of graciousness which a lifetime of uncouth and savage training and environment could not eradicate.

It was growing dark now, and so they ate again of the fruit which was both food and drink for them; then Tarzan rose, and leading Jane Porter to the little bower he had erected, motioned her to go within.

For the first time in hours a feeling of fear swept over her, and Tarzan felt her draw away as though shrinking from him.

Contact with this girl for half a day had left a very different Tarzan from the one on whom the morning's sun had risen.

Now, in every fiber of his being, heredity spoke louder than training.

He had not in one swift transition become a polished gentleman from a savage ape-man, but at last the instincts of the former predominated, and over all was the desire to please the woman he loved, and to appear well in her eyes.

So Tarzan of the Apes did the only thing he knew to assure Jane Porter of her safety. He removed his hunting knife from its sheath and handed it to her hilt first, again motioning her into the bower.

The girl understood, and taking the long knife she entered and lay down upon the soft grasses while Tarzan of the Apes stretched himself upon the ground across the entrance.

And thus the rising sun found them in the morning.

When Jane Porter awoke, she did not at first recall the strange events of the preceding day, and so she wondered at her odd surroundings—the little leafy bower, the soft grasses of her bed, the unfamiliar prospect from the opening at her feet.

Slowly the circumstances of her position crept one by one into her mind. And then a great wonderment arose in her heart—a mighty wave of thankfulness and gratitude that though she had been in such terrible danger, yet she was unharmed.

She moved to the entrance of the shelter to look for Tarzan. He was gone; but this time no fear assailed her for she knew that he would return.

In the grass at the entrance to her bower she saw the imprint of his body where he had lain all night to guard her. She knew that the fact that he had been there was all that had permitted her to sleep in such peaceful security.

With him near, who could entertain fear? She wondered if there was another man on earth with whom a girl could feel so safe in the heart of this savage African jungle. Why even the lions and panthers had no fears for her now.

She looked up to see his lithe form drop softly from a nearby tree. As he caught her eyes upon him his face lighted with that frank and radiant smile that had won her confidence the day before.

As he approached her Jane Porter's heart beat faster and her eyes brightened as they had never done before at the approach of any man.

He had again been gathering fruit and this he laid at the entrance of her bower. Once more they sat down together to eat.

Jane Porter commenced to wonder what his plans were. Would he take her back to the beach or would he keep her here? Suddenly she realized that the matter did not seem to give her much concern. Could it be that she did not care!

She began to comprehend, also, that she was entirely contented sitting here by the side of this smiling giant eating delicious fruit in a sylvan paradise far within the remote depths of an African jungle—that she was contented and very happy.

She could not understand it. Her reason told her that she should be torn by wild anxieties, weighted by dread fears, cast down by gloomy forebodings; but instead, her heart was singing and she was smiling into the answering face of the man beside her.

When they had finished their breakfast Tarzan went to her bower and recovered his knife. The girl had entirely forgotten it. She realized that it was because she had forgotten the fear that prompted her to accept it.

Motioning her to follow, Tarzan walked toward the trees at the edge of the arena, and taking her in one strong arm swung to the branches above.

The girl knew that he was taking her back to her people, and she could not understand the sudden feeling of loneliness and sorrow which crept over her.

For hours they swung slowly along.

Tarzan of the Apes did not hurry. He tried to draw out the sweet pleasure of that journey with those dear arms about his neck as long as possible, and so he went far south of the direct route to the beach.

Several times they halted for brief rests, which Tarzan did not need, and at noon they stopped for an hour at a little brook, where they quenched their thirst, and ate.

So it was nearly sunset when they came to the clearing, and Tarzan, dropping to the ground beside a great tree, parted the tall jungle grass and pointed out the little cabin to her.

She took him by the hand to lead him to it, that she might tell her father that this man had saved her from death and worse than death, that he had watched over her as carefully as a mother might have done.

But again the timidity of the wild thing in the face of human habitation swept over Tarzan of the Apes. He drew back, shaking his head.

The girl came close to him, looking up with pleading eyes. Somehow she could not bear the thought of his going back into the terrible jungle alone.

Still he shook his head, and finally he drew her to him very gently and stooped to kiss her, but first he looked into her eyes and waited to learn if she were pleased, or if she would repulse him.

Just an instant the girl hesitated, and then she realized the truth, and throwing her arms about his neck she drew his face to hers and kissed him—unashamed.

"I love you—I love you," she murmured.

From far in the distance came the faint sound of many guns. Tarzan and Jane Porter raised their heads.

From the cabin came Mr. Philander and Esmeralda.

From where Tarzan and the girl stood they could not see the two vessels lying at anchor in the harbor.

Tarzan pointed toward the sounds, touched his breast and pointed again. She understood. He was going, and something told her that it was because he thought her people were in danger.

Again he kissed her.

"Come back to me," she whispered. "I shall wait for you—always."

He was gone—and Jane Porter turned to walk across the clearing to the cabin.

Mr. Philander was the first to see her. It was dusk and Mr. Philander was very nearsighted.

"Quickly, Esmeralda!" he cried. "Let us seek safety within; it is a lioness. Bless me!"

Esmeralda did not bother to verify Mr. Philander's vision. His tone was enough. She was within the cabin and had slammed and bolted the door before he had finished pronouncing her name. The "Bless me" was startled out of Mr. Philander by the discovery that Esmeralda, in the exuberance of her haste, had fastened him upon the same side of the door as was the close-approaching lioness.

He beat furiously upon the heavy portal.

"Esmeralda! Esmeralda!" he shrieked. "Let me in. I am being devoured by a lion."

Esmeralda thought that the noise upon the door was made by the lioness in her attempts to pursue her, so, after her custom, she fainted.

Mr. Philander cast a frightened glance behind him.

Horrors! The thing was quite close now. He tried to scramble up the side of the cabin, and succeeded in catching a fleeting hold upon the thatched roof.

For a moment he hung there, clawing with his feet like a cat on a clothesline, but presently a piece of the thatch came away, and Mr. Philander, preceding it, was precipitated upon his back.

At the instant he fell a remarkable item of natural history leaped to his mind. If one feigns death lions and lionesses are supposed to ignore one, according to Mr. Philander's faulty memory.

So Mr. Philander lay as he had fallen, frozen into the horrid semblance of death. As his arms and legs had been extended stiffly upward as he came to earth upon his back, the attitude of death was anything but impressive.

Jane Porter had been watching his antics in mild-eyed surprise. Now she laughed—a little choking gurgle of a laugh; but it was enough. Mr. Philander rolled over upon his side and peered about. At length he discovered her.

"Jane!" he cried. "Jane Porter. Bless me!"

He scrambled to his feet and rushed toward her. He could not believe that it was she, and alive.

"Bless me! Where did you come from? Where in the world have you been? How——"

"Mercy, Mr. Philander," interrupted the girl, "I can never remember so many questions."

"Well, well," said Mr. Philander. "Bless me! I am so filled with surprise and exuberant delight at seeing you safe and well again that I scarcely know what I am saying, really. But come, tell me all that has happened to you."

CHAPTER TWENTY-ONE
THE VILLAGE OF TORTURE

AS THE LITTLE EXPEDITION OF SAILORS toiled through the dense jungle searching for signs of Jane Porter, the futility of their venture became more and more apparent, but the grief of the old man and the hopeless eyes of the young Englishman prevented the kindhearted d'Arnot from turning back.

He thought that there might be a bare possibility of finding her body, or the remains of it, for he was positive that she had been devoured by some beast of prey. He deployed his men into a skirmish line from the point where Esmeralda had been found, and in this extended formation they pushed their way, sweating and panting, through the tangled vines and creepers.

It was slow work. Noon found them but a few miles inland. They halted for a brief rest then, and after pushing on for a short distance further one of the men discovered a well-marked trail.

It was an old elephant track, and d'Arnot, after consulting with Professor Porter and Clayton, decided to follow it.

The path wound through the jungle in a northeasterly direction, and along it the column moved in single file.

Lieutenant d'Arnot was in the lead and moving at a quick pace, for the trail was comparatively open. Immediately behind him came Professor Porter, but as he could not keep pace with the younger man d'Arnot was a hundred yards in advance when suddenly a half-dozen black warriors arose about him.

D'Arnot gave a warning shout to his column as the warriors closed on him, but before he could draw his revolver he had been pinioned and dragged into the jungle.

His cry had alarmed the sailors and a dozen of them sprang forward past Professor Porter, running up the trail to their officer's aid.

They did not know the cause of his outcry, only that it was a warning of danger ahead. They had rushed past the spot where d'Arnot had been seized when a spear hurled from the jungle transfixed one of the men, and then a volley of arrows fell among them.

Raising their rifles they fired into the underbrush in the direction from which the missiles had come.

By this time the balance of the party had come up, and volley after volley was fired toward the concealed foe. It was these shots that Tarzan and Jane Porter had heard.

Lieutenant Charpentier, who had been bringing up the rear of the column, now came running to the scene, and on hearing the details of the ambush ordered the men to follow him, and plunged into the tangled vegetation.

In an instant they were in a hand-to-hand fight with some fifty warriors of Mbonga's village. Arrows and bullets flew thick and fast.

Queer African knives and French gun butts mingled for a moment in savage and bloody duels, but soon the natives fled into the jungle, leaving the Frenchmen to count their losses.

Four of the twenty were dead, a dozen others were wounded, and Lieutenant d'Arnot was missing. Night was falling rapidly, and their predicament was rendered doubly worse through the fact that they could not even find the elephant trail which they had been following.

There was but one thing to do, make camp where they were until daylight. Lieutenant Charpentier ordered a clearing made and a circular abatis of underbrush constructed about the camp.

This work was not completed until long after dark, the men building a huge fire in the center of the clearing to give them light to work by.

When all was safe as could be made from the attack of wild beasts and savage men, Lieutenant Charpentier placed sentries about the little camp and the tired and hungry men threw themselves upon the ground to sleep.

The groans of the wounded, mingled with the roaring and growling of the great beasts which the noise and firelight had attracted, kept sleep, except in its most fitful form, from the tired eyes. It was a sad and hungry party that lay through the long night praying for dawn.

The men who had seized d'Arnot had not waited to participate in the fight which followed, but instead had dragged their prisoner a little way through the jungle and then struck the trail further on beyond the scene of the fighting in which their fellows were engaged.

They hurried him along, the sounds of battle growing fainter and fainter as they drew away from the contestants until there suddenly broke upon d'Arnot's vision a good-sized clearing at one end of which stood a thatched and palisaded village.

It was now dusk, but the watchers at the gate saw the approaching trio and distinguished one as a prisoner ere they reached the portals.

A cry went up within the palisade. A great throng of women and children rushed out to meet the party.

And then began for the French officer the most terrifying experience which man can encounter upon earth—the reception of a prisoner into a village of African cannibals.

To add to the fiendishness of their cruel savagery was the poignant memory of still crueler barbarities practiced upon them and theirs by the white officers of that arch hypocrite, Leopold II of Belgium, because of whose atrocities they had fled the Congo Free State—a pitiful remnant of what once had been a mighty tribe.

They fell upon d'Arnot tooth and nail, beating him with sticks and stones and tearing at him with clawlike hands. Every vestige of clothing was torn from him, and the merciless blows fell upon his bare and quivering flesh. But not once did the Frenchman cry out in pain. He breathed a silent prayer that he be quickly delivered from his torture.

But the death he prayed for was not to be so easily had. Soon the warriors beat the women away from their prisoner. He was to be saved for nobler sport than this, and the first wave of their passion having subsided they contented themselves with crying out taunts and insults and spitting upon him.

Presently they reached the center of the village. There d'Arnot was bound securely to the great post from which no live man had ever been released.

A number of the women scattered to their several huts to fetch pots and water, while others built a row of fires on which portions of the feast were to be boiled while the balance would be slowly dried in strips for future use, as they expected the other warriors to return with many prisoners.

The festivities were delayed awaiting the return of the warriors who had remained to engage in the skirmish with the white men, so that it was quite late when all were in the village, and the dance of death commenced to circle around the doomed officer.

Half fainting from pain and exhaustion, d'Arnot watched from beneath half-closed lids what seemed but the vagary of delirium, or some horrid nightmare from which he must soon awake.

The frightful faces, daubed with color—the gaping mouths and drawn-back lips—the yellow teeth, sharp filed—the rolling, demon eyes—the shining naked bodies—the cruel spears. Surely no such creatures really existed upon earth—he must indeed be dreaming.

The savage, whirling bodies circled nearer. Now a spear sprang forth and touched his arm. The sharp pain and the feel of hot, trickling blood assured him of the awful reality of his hopeless position.

Another spear and then another touched him. He closed his eyes and held his teeth firm set—he would not cry out.

He was a soldier of France, and he would teach these beasts how an officer and a gentleman died.

Tarzan of the Apes needed no interpreter to translate the story of those distant shots. With Jane Porter's kisses still warm upon his lips he was swinging with incredible rapidity through the forest trees straight toward the village of Mbonga.

He was not interested in the location of the encounter, for he judged that that would soon be over. Those who were killed he could not aid, those who escaped would not need his assistance.

It was to those who had neither been killed or escaped that he hastened. And he knew that he would find them by the great post in the center of Mbonga's village.

Many times had Tarzan seen Mbonga's raiding parties return from the northward with prisoners, and always were the same scenes enacted about that grim stake, beneath the flaring light of many fires.

He knew, too, that they seldom lost much time before consummating the fiendish purpose of their captures. He doubted that he would arrive in time to do more than avenge.

On he sped. Night had fallen and he traveled high along the upper terrace where the gorgeous tropic moon lighted the dizzy pathway through the gently undulating branches of the treetops.

Presently he caught the reflection of a distant blaze. It lay to the right of his path. It must be the light from the campfire the two men had built before they were attacked—Tarzan knew nothing of the presence of the sailors.

So sure was Tarzan of his jungle knowledge that he did not turn from his course, but passed the glare at a distance of a half mile. It was the campfire of the Frenchmen.

In a few minutes more Tarzan swung into the trees above Mbonga's village. Ah, he was not quite too late! Or, was he? He could not tell. The figure at the stake was very still, yet the warriors were but pricking it.

Tarzan knew their customs. The death blow had not been struck. He could tell almost to a minute how far the dance had gone.

In another instant Mbonga's knife would sever one of the victim's ears—that would mark the beginning of the end, for very shortly after only a writhing mass of mutilated flesh would remain.

There would still be life in it, but death then would be the only charity it craved.

The stake stood forty feet from the nearest tree. Tarzan coiled his rope. Then there rose suddenly above the fiendish cries of the dancing demons the awful challenge of the ape-man.

The dancers halted as though turned to stone.

The rope sped with singing whir high above their heads. It was quite invisible in the flaring lights of the campfires.

D'Arnot opened his eyes. A huge warrior, standing directly before him, lunged backward as though felled by an invisible hand.

Struggling and shrieking, his body, rolling from side to side, moved quickly toward the shadows beneath the trees.

The natives, their eyes protruding in horror, watched spellbound.

Once beneath the trees, the body rose straight into the air, and as it disappeared into the foliage above, the terrified natives, screaming with fright, broke into a mad race for the village gate.

D'Arnot was left alone.

He was a brave man, but he had felt the short hairs bristle upon the nape of his neck when that uncanny cry rose upon the air.

As the writhing body of the warrior soared, as though by unearthly power, into the dense foliage of the forest, d'Arnot felt an icy shiver run along his spine, as though death had risen from a dark grave and laid a cold and clammy finger on his flesh.

As d'Arnot watched the spot where the body had entered the tree he heard the sounds of movement there.

The branches swayed as though under the weight of a man's body—there was a crash and the warrior came sprawling to earth again—to lie very quietly where he had fallen.

Immediately after him came another body, but this one alighted erect.

D'Arnot saw a clean-limbed young giant emerge from the shadows into the firelight and come quickly toward him.

What could it mean? Who could it be? Some new creature of torture and destruction, doubtless.

D'Arnot waited. His eyes never left the face of the advancing man. Nor did those frank, clear eyes waver beneath his fixed gaze.

D'Arnot was reassured, but still without much hope, though he felt that that face could not mask a cruel heart.

Without a word Tarzan of the Apes cut the bonds which held the Frenchman. Weak from suffering and loss of blood, he would have fallen but for the strong arm that caught him.

He felt himself lifted from the ground. There was a sensation as of flying, and then he lost consciousness.

CHAPTER TWENTY-TWO
THE SEARCH PARTY

WHEN DAWN BROKE upon the little camp of Frenchmen in the heart of the jungle it found a sad and disheartened group.

As soon as it was light enough to see their surroundings Lieutenant Charpentier sent men in groups of three in several directions to locate the trail, and in ten minutes it was found and the expedition was hurrying back toward the beach.

It was slow work, for they bore the bodies of six dead men, two more having succumbed during the night, and several of those who were wounded required support to move even very slowly.

Charpentier had decided to return to camp for reinforcements, and then make an attempt to track down the natives and rescue d'Arnot.

It was late in the afternoon when the exhausted men reached the clearing by the beach, but for two of them the return brought so great a happiness that all their suffering and heartbreaking grief was forgotten on the instant.

As the little party emerged from the jungle the first person that Professor Porter and Cecil Clayton saw was Jane Porter, standing by the cabin door.

With a little cry of joy and relief she ran forward to greet them, throwing her arms about her father's neck and bursting into tears for the first time since they had been cast upon this hideous and adventurous shore.

Professor Porter strove manfully to suppress his own emotions, but the strain upon his nerves and weakened vitality were too much for him, and at length, burying his old face in the girl's shoulder, he sobbed quietly like a tired child.

Jane Porter led him toward the cabin, and the Frenchmen turned toward the beach from which several of their fellows were advancing to meet them.

Clayton, wishing to leave father and daughter alone, joined the sailors and remained talking with the officers until their boat pulled away toward the cruiser whither Lieutenant Charpentier was bound to report the unhappy outcome of his adventure.

Then Clayton turned back slowly toward the cabin. His heart was filled with happiness. The woman he loved was safe.

He wondered by what manner of miracle she had been spared. To see her alive seemed almost unbelievable.

As he approached the cabin he saw Jane Porter coming out. When she saw him she hurried forward to meet him.

"Jane!" he cried, "God has been good to us, indeed. Tell me how you escaped—what form Providence took to save you for—us."

He had never before called her by her given name. Forty-eight hours before it would have suffused Jane Porter with a soft glow of pleasure to have heard that name from Clayton's lips—now it frightened her.

"Mr. Clayton," she said quietly, extending her hand, "first let me thank you for your chivalrous loyalty to my dear father. He has told me how noble and self-sacrificing you have been. How can we ever repay you!"

Clayton noticed that she did not return his familiar salutation, but he felt no misgivings on that score. She had been through so much. This was no time to force his love upon her, he quickly realized.

"I am already repaid," he said. "Just to see you and Professor Porter both safe, well, and together again. I do not think that I could much longer have endured the pathos of his quiet and uncomplaining grief.

"It was the saddest experience of my life, Miss Porter; and then, added to it, there was my own grief—the greatest I have ever known. But his was so hopeless—it was pitiful. It taught me that no love, not even that of a man for his wife, may be so deep and terrible and self-sacrificing as the love of a father for his daughter."

The girl bowed her head. There was a question she wanted to ask, but it seemed almost sacrilegious in the face of the love of these two men and the terrible suffering they had endured while she sat laughing and happy beside a godlike creature of the forest, eating delicious fruits and looking with eyes of love into answering eyes.

But love is a strange master, and human nature is still stranger, so she asked her question, though she was not coward enough to attempt to justify herself to her own conscience. She felt self-hate, but she asked her question nevertheless.

"Where is the forest man who went to rescue you? Why did he not return?"

"I do not understand," said Clayton. "Whom do you mean?"

"He who has saved each of us—who saved me from the gorilla."

"Oh," cried Clayton, in surprise. "It was he who rescued you? You have not told me anything of your adventure, don't you know; tell me, do."

"But the wood man," she urged. "Have you not seen him? When we heard the shots in the jungle, very faint and far away, he left me. We had just reached the clearing, and he hurried off in the direction of the fighting. I know he went to aid you."

Her tone was almost pleading—her manner tense with suppressed emotion. Clayton could not but notice it, and he wondered, vaguely, why she was so deeply moved—so anxious to know the whereabouts of this strange creature. He did not suspect the truth, for how could he?

Yet a feeling of apprehension of some impending sorrow haunted him, and in his breast, unknown to himself, was implanted the first germ of jealousy and suspicion of the ape-man, to whom he owed his life.

"We did not see him," he replied quietly. "He did not join us." And then after a moment of thoughtful pause: "Possibly he joined his own tribe—the men who attacked us." He did not know why he had said it, for he did not believe it; but love is a strange master.

The girl looked at him wide-eyed for a moment.

"No!" she exclaimed vehemently, much too vehemently he thought. "It could not be. He is a gentleman."

Clayton looked puzzled. The little green-eyed devil taunted him.

"He is a strange, half-savage creature of the jungle, Miss Porter. We know nothing of him. He neither speaks nor understands any European tongue— and his ornaments and weapons are those of the West Coast savages."

Clayton was speaking rapidly.

"There are no other human beings than savages within hundreds of miles, Miss Porter. He must belong to the tribes which attacked us, or to some other equally savage—he may even be a cannibal."

Jane blanched.

"I will not believe it," she half whispered. "It is not true. You shall see," she said, addressing Clayton, "that he will come back and that he will prove that you are wrong. You do not know him as I do. I tell you that he is a gentleman."

Clayton was a generous and chivalrous man, but something in the girl's breathless defense of the forest man stirred him to unreasoning jealousy, so that for the instant he forgot all that they owed to this wild demigod, and he answered her with a half sneer upon his lip.

"Possibly you are right, Miss Porter," he said, "but I do not think that any of us need worry about our carrion-eating acquaintance. The chances are that he is some half-demented castaway who will forget us more quickly, but no more surely, than we shall forget him. He is only a beast of the jungle, Miss Porter."

The girl did not answer, but she felt her heart shrivel within her. Anger and hate against one we love steels our hearts, but contempt or pity leaves us silent and ashamed.

She knew that Clayton spoke merely what he thought, and for the first time she began to analyze the structure which supported her newfound love, and to subject its object to a critical examination.

Slowly she turned and walked back to the cabin. She tried to imagine her wood-god by her side in the saloon of an ocean liner. She saw him eating with his hands, tearing his food like a beast of prey, and wiping his greasy fingers upon his thighs. She shuddered.

She saw him as she introduced him to her friends—uncouth, illiterate—a boor; and the girl winced.

She had reached her room now, and as she sat upon the edge of her bed of ferns and grasses, with one hand resting upon her rising and falling bosom, she felt the hard outlines of the man's locket beneath her waist.

She drew it out, holding it in the palm of her hand for a moment with tear-blurred eyes bent upon it. Then she raised it to her lips, and crushing it there buried her face in the soft ferns, sobbing.

"Beast?" she murmured. "Then God make me a beast; for, man or beast, I am yours."

She did not see Clayton again that day. Esmeralda brought her supper to her, and she sent word to her father that she was suffering from the reaction following her adventure.

The next morning Clayton left early with the relief expedition in search of Lieutenant d'Arnot. There were two hundred armed men this time, with ten officers and two surgeons, and provisions for a week.

They carried bedding and hammocks, the latter for transporting their sick and wounded.

It was a determined and angry company—a punitive expedition as well as one of relief. They reached the sight of the skirmish of the previous expedition shortly after noon, for they were now traveling a known trail and no time was lost in exploring.

From there on the elephant-track led straight to Mbonga's village. It was but two o'clock when the head of the column halted upon the edge of the clearing.

Lieutenant Charpentier, who was in command, immediately sent a portion of his force through the jungle to the opposite side of the village. Another detachment was dispatched to a point before the village gate, while he remained with the balance upon the south side of the clearing.

It was arranged that the party which was to take its position to the north, and which would be the last to gain its station, should commence the assault, and that their opening volley should be the signal for a concerted rush from all sides in an attempt to carry the village by storm at the first charge.

For half an hour the men with Lieutenant Charpentier crouched in the dense foliage of the jungle, waiting the signal. To them it seemed like hours. They could see natives in the fields, and others moving in and out of the village gate.

At length the signal came—a sharp rattle of musketry, and like one man, an answering volley tore from the jungle to the west and to the south.

The natives in the field dropped their implements and broke madly for the palisade. The French bullets mowed them down, and the French sailors bounded over their prostrate bodies straight for the village gate.

So sudden and unexpected the assault had been that the sailors reached the gates before the frightened natives could bar them, and in another minute the village street was filled with armed men fighting hand to hand in an inextricable tangle.

For a few moments the natives held their ground within the entrance to the street, but the revolvers, rifles, and cutlasses of the Frenchmen crumpled the native spearmen and struck down the archers with their bows half-drawn.

Soon the battle turned to a wild rout, and then to a grim massacre; for the French sailors had seen bits of d'Arnot's uniform upon several of the warriors who opposed them.

They spared the children and those of the women whom they were not forced to kill in self-defense, but when at length they stopped, panting, blood covered, and sweating, it was because there lived to oppose them no single warrior in all the village of Mbonga.

Carefully they ransacked every hut and corner of the village, but no sign of d'Arnot could they find. They questioned the prisoners by signs, and finally one of the sailors who had served in the French Congo found that he could make them understand the bastard tongue that passes for language between the whites and the native tribes of the coast, but even then they could learn nothing definite regarding the fate of d'Arnot.

Only excited gestures and expressions of fear could they obtain in response to their inquiries concerning their fellow; and at last they became convinced that these were but evidences of the guilt of these demons who had slaughtered and eaten their comrade two nights before.

At length all hope left them, and they prepared to camp for the night within the village. The prisoners were herded into three huts where they were heavily guarded. Sentries were posted at the barred gates, and finally the village was wrapped in the silence of slumber, except for the wailing of the native women for their dead.

The next morning they set out upon the return march. Their original intention had been to burn the village, but this idea was abandoned and the prisoners were left behind, weeping and moaning, but with roofs to cover them and a palisade for refuge from the beasts of the jungle.

Slowly the expedition retraced its steps of the preceding day. Ten loaded hammocks retarded its pace. In eight of them lay the more seriously wounded, while two swung beneath the weight of the dead.

Clayton and Lieutenant Charpentier brought up the rear of the column; the Englishman silent in respect for the other's grief, for d'Arnot and Charpentier had been inseparable friends since boyhood.

Clayton could not but realize that the Frenchman felt his grief the more keenly because d'Arnot's sacrifice had been so futile, since Jane Porter had been rescued before d'Arnot had fallen into the hands of the cannibals, and again because the service in which he had lost his life had been outside his duty and for strangers and aliens; but when he spoke of it to Lieutenant Charpentier, the latter shook his head.

"No, Monsieur," he said, "d'Arnot would have chosen to die thus. I only grieve that I could not have died for him, or at least with him. I wish that you could have known him better, Monsieur. He was indeed an officer and a gentleman—a title conferred on many, but deserved by so few.

"He did not die futilely, for his death in the cause of a strange American girl will make us, his comrades, face our ends the more bravely, however they may come to us."

Clayton did not reply, but within him rose a new respect for Frenchmen which remained undimmed ever after.

It was quite late when they reached the cabin by the beach. A single shot before they emerged from the jungle had announced to those in camp as well as on the ship that the expedition had been too late—for it had been prearranged that when they came within a mile or two of camp one shot was to be fired to denote failure, or three for success, while two would have indicated that they had found no sign of either d'Arnot or his captors.

So it was a solemn party that awaited their coming, and few words were spoken as the dead and wounded men were tenderly placed in boats and rowed silently toward the cruiser.

Clayton, exhausted from his five days of laborious marching through the jungle and from the effects of his two battles with the natives, turned toward the cabin to seek a mouthful of food and then the comparative ease of his bed of grasses after two nights in the jungle.

By the cabin door stood Jane Porter.

"The poor lieutenant?" she asked. "Did you find no trace of him?"

"We were too late, Miss Porter," he replied sadly.

"Tell me. What had happened?" she asked.

"I cannot, Miss Porter, it is too horrible."

"You do not mean that they had tortured him?" she whispered.

"We do not know what they did to him *before* they killed him," he answered, his face drawn with fatigue and the sorrow he felt for poor d'Arnot and he emphasized the word before.

"*Before* they killed him! What do you mean? They are not—? They are not—?"

She was thinking of what Clayton had said of the forest man's probable relationship to this tribe and she could not frame the awful word.

"Yes, Miss Porter, they were—cannibals," he said, almost bitterly, for to him too had suddenly come the thought of the forest man, and the strange, unaccountable jealousy he had felt two days before swept over him once more.

And then in sudden brutality that was as unlike Clayton as courteous consideration is unlike an ape, he blurted out:

"When your forest god left you he was doubtless hurrying to the feast."

He was sorry ere the words were spoken though he did not know how cruelly they had cut the girl. His regret was for his baseless disloyalty to one who had saved the lives of every member of his party, nor ever offered harm to one.

The girl's head went high.

"There could be but one suitable reply to your assertion, Mr. Clayton," she said icily, "and I regret that I am not a man, that I might make it." She turned quickly and entered the cabin.

Clayton was an Englishman, so the girl had passed quite out of sight before he deduced what reply a man would have made.

"Upon my word," he said ruefully, "she called me a liar. And I fancy I jolly well deserved it," he added thoughtfully. "Clayton, my boy, I know you are tired out and unstrung, but that's no reason why you should make an ass of yourself. You'd better go to bed."

But before he did so he called gently to Jane Porter upon the opposite side of the sailcloth partition, for he wished to apologize, but he might as well have addressed the Sphinx. Then he wrote upon a piece of paper and shoved it beneath the partition.

Jane Porter saw the little note and ignored it, for she was very angry and hurt and mortified, but—she was a woman, and so eventually she picked it up and read it.

My Dear Miss Porter:

I had no reason to insinuate what I did. My only excuse is that my nerves must be unstrung—which is no excuse at all.

Please try and think that I did not say it. I am very sorry. I would not have hurt *you*, above all others in the world. Say that you forgive me.

Wm. Cecil Clayton.

"He did think it or he never would have said it," reasoned the girl, "but it cannot be true—oh, I know it is not true!"

One sentence in the letter frightened her: "I would not have hurt *you,* above all others in the world."

A week ago that sentence would have filled her with delight, now it depressed her.

She wished she had never met Clayton. She was sorry that she had ever seen the forest god. No, she was glad. And there was that other note she had found in the grass before the cabin the day after her return from the jungle, the love note signed by Tarzan of the Apes.

Who could be this new suitor? If he were another of the wild denizens of this terrible forest what might he not do to claim her?

"Esmeralda! Wake up," she cried. "You make me so irritable, sleeping there peacefully when you know perfectly well that the world is filled with sorrow."

"Gaberelle!" screamed Esmeralda, sitting up. "What is it now? A hip-ponocerous? Where is he, Miss Jane?"

"Nonsense, Esmeralda, there is nothing. Go back to sleep. You are bad enough asleep, but you are infinitely worse awake."

"Yes, honey, but what's the matter with you, precious? You act sort of disgranulated this evening."

"Oh, Esmeralda, I'm just plain ugly tonight," said the girl. "Don't pay any attention to me—that's a dear."

"Yes, honey; now you go right to sleep. Your nerves are all on edge. What with all these ripotamuses and man-eating geniuses that Mr. Philander been telling about—Lord, it ain't no wonder we all get nervous prosecution."

Jane Porter crossed the little room, laughing, and kissing the woman's faithful old cheek, bid Esmeralda good night.

CHAPTER TWENTY-THREE
BROTHER MEN

WHEN D'ARNOT REGAINED CONSCIOUSNESS, he found himself lying upon a bed of soft ferns and grasses beneath a little "A"-shaped shelter of boughs.

At his feet an opening looked out upon a green sward, and at a little distance beyond was the dense wall of jungle and forest.

He was very lame and sore and weak, and as full consciousness returned he felt the sharp torture of many cruel wounds and the dull aching of every bone and muscle in his body as a result of the hideous beating he had received.

Even the turning of his head caused him such excruciating agony that he lay still with closed eyes for a long time.

He tried to piece out the details of his adventure prior to the time he lost consciousness to see if they would explain his present whereabouts—he wondered if he were among friends or foes.

At length he recollected the whole hideous scene at the stake, and finally recalled the strange white figure in whose arms he had sunk into oblivion.

D'Arnot wondered what fate lay in store for him now. He could neither see nor hear any signs of life about him.

The incessant hum of the jungle—the rustling of millions of leaves—the buzz of insects—the voices of the birds and monkeys seemed blended into a strangely soothing purr, as though he lay apart, far from the myriad life whose sounds came to him only as a blurred echo.

At length he fell into a quiet slumber, nor did he awake again until afternoon.

Once more he experienced the strange sense of utter bewilderment that had marked his earlier awakening, but soon he recalled the recent past, and looking through the opening at his feet he saw the figure of a man squatting on his haunches.

The broad, muscular back was turned toward him, but, tanned though it was, d'Arnot saw that it was the back of a white man, and he thanked God.

The Frenchman called faintly. The man turned, and rising, came toward the shelter. His face was very handsome—the handsomest, thought d'Arnot, that he had ever seen.

Stooping, he crawled into the shelter beside the wounded officer, and placed a cool hand upon his forehead.

D'Arnot spoke to him in French, but the man only shook his head—sadly, it seemed to the Frenchman.

Then d'Arnot tried English, but still the man shook his head. Italian, Spanish, and German brought similar discouragement.

D'Arnot knew a few words of Norwegian, Russian, Greek, and also had a smattering of the language of one of the West Coast tribes—the man denied them all.

After examining d'Arnot's wounds the man left the shelter and disappeared. In half an hour he was back with fruit and a hollow gourd-like vegetable filled with water.

D'Arnot drank and ate a little. He was surprised that he had no fever. Again he tried to converse with his strange nurse, but the attempt was useless.

Suddenly the man hastened from the shelter only to return a few minutes later with several pieces of bark and—wonder of wonders—a lead pencil.

Squatting beside d'Arnot he wrote for a minute on the smooth inner surface of the bark; then he handed it to the Frenchman.

D'Arnot was astonished to see, in plain print-like characters, a message in English:

I am Tarzan of the Apes. Who are you? Can you read this language?

D'Arnot seized the pencil—then he stopped. This strange man wrote English—evidently he was an Englishman.

"Yes," said d'Arnot, "I read English. I speak it also. Now we may talk. First let me thank you for all that you have done for me."

The man only shook his head and pointed to the pencil and the bark.

"Mon Dieu!" cried d'Arnot. "If you are English why is it then that you cannot speak English?"

And then in a flash it came to him—the man was a mute, possibly a deaf mute.

So d'Arnot wrote a message on the bark, in English.

I am Paul d'Arnot, Lieutenant in the navy of France. I thank you for what you have done for me. You have saved my life, and all that I have is yours. May I ask how it is that one who writes English does not speak it?

Tarzan's reply filled d'Arnot with still greater wonder:

I speak only the language of my tribe—the great apes who were Kerchak's;

and a little of the languages of Tantor, the elephant, and Numa, the lion, and of
the other folks of the jungle I understand. With a human being I have never
spoken, except once with Jane Porter, by signs. This is the first time I have spoken
with another of my kind through written words.

D'Arnot was mystified. It seemed incredible that there lived upon earth
a full-grown man who had never spoken with a fellow man, and still more
preposterous that such a one could read and write.

He looked again at Tarzan's message—"except once, with Jane Porter."
That was the American girl who had been carried into the jungle by
a gorilla.

A sudden light commenced to dawn on d'Arnot—this then was the
"gorilla." He seized the pencil and wrote:

Where is Jane Porter?

And Tarzan replied, below:

Back with her people in the cabin of Tarzan of the Apes.

She is not dead then? Where was she? What happened to her?

She is not dead. She was taken by Terkoz to be his wife; but Tarzan of the
Apes took her away from Terkoz and killed him before he could harm her.

None in all the jungle may face Tarzan of the Apes in battle, and live. I am
Tarzan of the Apes—mighty fighter.

D'Arnot wrote:

I am glad she is safe. It pains me to write, I will rest a while.

And then Tarzan:

Yes, rest. When you are well I shall take you back to your people.

For many days d'Arnot lay upon his bed of soft ferns. The second day a fever had come and d'Arnot thought that it meant infection and he knew that he would die.

An idea came to him. He wondered why he had not thought of it before.

He called Tarzan and indicated by signs that he would write, and when Tarzan had fetched the bark and pencil, d'Arnot wrote:

Can you go to my people and lead them here? I will write a message that you may take to them, and they will follow you.

Tarzan shook his head and taking the bark, wrote:

I had thought of that—the first day; but I dared not. The great apes come often to this spot, and if they found you here, wounded and alone, they would kill you.

D'Arnot turned on his side and closed his eyes. He did not wish to die; but he felt that he was going, for the fever was mounting higher and higher. That night he lost consciousness.

For three days he was in delirium, and Tarzan sat beside him and bathed his head and hands and washed his wounds.

On the fourth day the fever broke as suddenly as it had come, but it left d'Arnot a shadow of his former self, and very weak. Tarzan had to lift him that he might drink from the gourd.

The fever had not been the result of infection, as d'Arnot had thought, but one of those that commonly attack travelers in the jungles of Africa, and either kill or leave them as suddenly as d'Arnot's had left him.

Two days after, d'Arnot was tottering about the amphitheater, Tarzan's strong arm about him to keep him from falling.

They sat beneath the shade of a great tree, and Tarzan found some smooth bark that they might converse.

D'Arnot wrote the first message:

What can I do to repay you for all that you have done for me?

And Tarzan, in reply:

Teach me to speak the language of men.

And so d'Arnot commenced at once, pointing out familiar objects and repeating their names in French, for he thought that it would be easier to teach this man his own language, since he understood it himself best of all.

It meant nothing to Tarzan, of course, for he could not tell one language from another, so when he pointed to the word man which he had printed upon a piece of bark he learned from d'Arnot that it was pronounced *homme*, and in the same way he was taught to pronounce ape, *singe* and tree, *arbre*.

He was a most eager student, and in two more days had mastered so much French that he could speak little sentences such as: "That is a tree," "this is grass," "I am hungry," and the like, but d'Arnot found that it was difficult to teach him the French construction upon a foundation of English.

The Frenchman wrote little lessons for him in English and had Tarzan repeat them in French, but as a literal translation was usually very poor French Tarzan was often confused.

D'Arnot realized now that he had made a mistake, but it seemed too late to go back and do it all over again and force Tarzan to unlearn all that he had learned, especially as they were rapidly approaching a point where they would be able to converse.

On the third day after the fever broke Tarzan wrote a message asking d'Arnot if he felt strong enough to be carried back to the cabin. Tarzan was as anxious to go as d'Arnot, for he longed to see Jane Porter again.

It had been hard for him to remain with the Frenchman all these days for that very reason, and that he had unselfishly done so spoke more glowingly for his nobility of character than even did his rescuing the French officer from Mbonga's clutches.

D'Arnot, only too willing to attempt the journey, wrote:

But you cannot carry me all the distance through this tangled forest.

Tarzan laughed.

"*Mais oui*," he said, and d'Arnot laughed aloud to hear the phrase that he used so often glide from Tarzan's tongue.

So they set out, d'Arnot marveling as had Clayton and Jane Porter at the wondrous strength and agility of the ape-man.

Midafternoon brought them to the clearing, and as Tarzan dropped to earth from the branches of the last tree his heart leaped and bounded against his ribs in anticipation of seeing Jane Porter so soon again.

No one was in sight outside the cabin, and d'Arnot was perplexed to note that neither the cruiser nor the *Arrow* was at anchor in the bay.

An atmosphere of loneliness pervaded the spot, which caught suddenly at both men as they strode toward the cabin.

Neither spoke, yet both knew before they opened the closed door what they would find beyond.

Tarzan lifted the latch and pushed the great door in upon its wooden hinges. It was as they had feared. The cabin was deserted.

The men turned and looked at one another. D'Arnot knew that his people thought him dead; but Tarzan thought only of the woman who had kissed him in love and now had fled from him while he was serving one of her people.

A great bitterness rose in his heart. He would go away, far into the jungle and join his tribe. Never would he see one of his own kind again, nor could he bear the thought of returning to the cabin. He would leave that forever behind him with the great hopes he had nursed there of finding his own race and becoming a man among men.

And the Frenchman? D'Arnot? What of him? He could get along as Tarzan had. Tarzan did not want to see him more. He wanted to get away from everything that might remind him of Jane Porter.

As Tarzan stood upon the threshold brooding, d'Arnot had entered the cabin. Many comforts he saw that had been left behind. He recognized numerous articles from the cruiser—a camp oven, some kitchen utensils, a rifle and many rounds of ammunition, canned foods, blankets, two chairs and a cot—and several books and periodicals, mostly American.

"They must intend returning," thought d'Arnot.

He walked over to the table that John Clayton had built so many years before to serve as a desk, and on it he saw two notes addressed to Tarzan of the Apes.

One was in a strong masculine hand and was unsealed. The other, in a woman's hand, was sealed.

"Here are two messages for you, Tarzan of the Apes," cried d'Arnot, turning toward the door; but his companion was not there.

D'Arnot walked to the door and looked out. Tarzan was nowhere in sight. He called aloud but there was no response.

"Mon Dieu!" exclaimed d'Arnot, "he has left me. I feel it. He has gone back into his jungle and left me here alone."

And then he remembered the look on Tarzan's face when they had discovered that the cabin was empty—such a look as the hunter sees in the eyes of the wounded deer he has wantonly brought down.

The man had been hard hit—d'Arnot realized it now—but why? He could not understand.

The Frenchman looked about him. The loneliness and the horror of the place commenced to get on his nerves—already weakened by the ordeal of suffering and sickness he had passed through.

To be left here alone beside this awful jungle—never to hear a human voice or see a human face—in constant dread of savage beasts and more terribly savage men—a prey to solitude and hopelessness. It was awful.

And far to the east Tarzan of the Apes was speeding through the middle terrace back to his tribe. Never had he traveled with such reckless speed. He felt that he was running away from himself—that by hurtling through the forest like a frightened squirrel he was escaping from his own thoughts. But no matter how fast he went he found them always with him.

He passed above the sinuous body of Sabor, the lioness, going in the opposite direction—toward the cabin, thought Tarzan.

What could d'Arnot do against Sabor—or if Bolgani, the gorilla, should come upon him—or Numa, the lion, or cruel Sheeta?

Tarzan paused in his flight.

"What are you, Tarzan?" he asked aloud. "An ape or a man?

"If you are an ape you will do as the apes would do—leave one of your kind to die in the jungle if it suited your whim to go elsewhere.

"If you are a man, you will return to protect your kind. You will not run away from one of your own people, because one of them has run away from you."

D'Arnot closed the cabin door. He was very nervous. Even brave men, and d'Arnot was a brave man, are sometimes frightened by solitude.

He loaded one of the rifles and placed it within easy reach. Then he went to the desk and took up the unsealed letter addressed to Tarzan.

Possibly it contained word that his people had but left the beach temporarily. He felt that it would be no breach of ethics to read this letter, so he took the enclosure from the envelope and read:

To Tarzan of the Apes:

We thank you for the use of your cabin, and are sorry that you did not permit us the pleasure of seeing and thanking you in person.

We have harmed nothing, but have left many things for you which may add to your comfort and safety here in your lonely home.

If you know the strange white man who saved our lives so many times, and brought us food, and if you can converse with him, thank him, also, for his kindness.

We sail within the hour, never to return; but we wish you and that other jungle friend to know that we shall always thank you for what you did for strangers on your shore, and that we should have done infinitely more to reward you both had you given us the opportunity.

Very respectfully,

Wm. Cecil Clayton.

"Never to return," muttered d'Arnot, and threw himself face downward upon the cot.

An hour later he started up listening. Something was at the door trying to enter.

D'Arnot reached for the loaded rifle and placed it to his shoulder.

Dusk was falling, and the interior of the cabin was very dark; but the man could see the latch moving from its place.

He felt his hair rising upon his scalp.

Gently the door opened until a thin crack showed something standing just beyond.

D'Arnot sighted along the blue barrel at the crack of the door—and then he pulled the trigger.

CHAPTER TWENTY-FOUR
LOST TREASURE

WHEN THE EXPEDITION RETURNED, following their fruitless endeavor to succor d'Arnot, Captain Dufranne was anxious to steam away as quickly as possible, and all save Jane Porter had acquiesced.

"No," she said, determinedly, "I shall not go, nor should you, for there are two friends in that jungle who will come out of it some day expecting to find us awaiting them.

"Your officer, Captain Dufranne, is one of them, and the forest man who has saved the lives of every member of my father's party is the other.

"He left me at the edge of the jungle two days ago to hasten to the aid of my father and Mr. Clayton, as he thought, and he has stayed to rescue Lieutenant d'Arnot; of that you may be sure.

"Had he been too late to be of service to the lieutenant he would have been back before now—the fact that he is not back is sufficient proof to me that he is delayed because Lieutenant d'Arnot is wounded, or he has had to follow his captors further than the village which your sailors attacked."

"But poor d'Arnot's uniform and all his belongings were found in that village, Miss Porter," argued the captain, "and the natives showed great excitement when questioned as to the white man's fate."

"Yes, Captain, but they did not admit that he was dead and as for his clothes and accouterments being in their possession—why more civilized peoples than these poor natives strip their prisoners of every article of value whether they intend killing them or not.

"Even the soldiers of my own dear South looted not only the living but the dead. It is strong circumstantial evidence, I will admit, but it is not positive proof."

"Possibly your forest man, himself, was captured or killed by the cannibals," suggested Captain Dufranne.

The girl laughed.

"You do not know him," she replied, a little thrill of pride setting her nerves a-tingle at the thought that she spoke of her own.

"I admit that he would be worth waiting for, this superman of yours," laughed the captain. "I most certainly should like to see him."

"Then wait for him, my dear captain," urged the girl, "for I intend doing so."

The Frenchman would have been a very much surprised man could he have interpreted the true meaning of the girl's words.

They had been walking from the beach toward the cabin as they talked, and now they joined a little group sitting on camp stools in the shade of a great tree beside the cabin.

Professor Porter was there, and Mr. Philander and Clayton, with

Lieutenant Charpentier and two of his brother officers, while Esmeralda hovered in the background, ever and anon venturing opinions and comments with the freedom of an old and much-indulged family servant.

The officers arose and saluted as their superior approached, and Clayton surrendered his camp stool to Jane Porter.

"We were just discussing poor Paul's fate," said Captain Dufranne. "Miss Porter insists that we have no absolute proof of his death—nor have we. And on the other hand she maintains that the continued absence of your omnipotent jungle friend indicates that d'Arnot is still in need of his services, either because he is wounded, or still is a prisoner in a more distant native village."

"It has been suggested," ventured Lieutenant Charpentier, "that the wild man may have been a member of the native tribe that attacked our party—that he was hastening to aid *them*—his own people."

Jane Porter shot a quick glance at Clayton.

"It seems vastly more reasonable," said Professor Porter.

"I do not agree with you," objected Mr. Philander. "He had ample opportunity to harm us himself, or to lead his people against us. Instead, during our long residence here, he has been uniformly consistent in his role of protector and provider."

"That is true," interjected Clayton, "yet we must not overlook the fact that except for himself the only human beings within hundreds of miles are savage cannibals. He was armed precisely as are they, which indicates that he has maintained relations of some nature with them, and the fact that he is but one against possibly thousands suggests that these relations could scarcely have been other than friendly."

"It seems improbable then that he is not connected with them," remarked the captain; "possibly a member of this tribe."

"Or," added another of the officers, "that otherwise he could even have lived a sufficient length of time among the savage denizens of the jungle, brute and human, to have become proficient in woodcraft, or in the use of African weapons."

"You are judging him according to your own standards, gentlemen," said Jane Porter. "An ordinary white man such as any of you—pardon me, I did not mean just that—rather, a white man above the ordinary in physique and intelligence could never, I grant you, have lived a year alone and naked in this tropical jungle; but this man not only surpasses the average white man in strength and agility, but as far transcends our trained athletes and 'strong men' as they surpass a day-old babe; and his courage and ferocity in battle are those of the wild beast."

"He has certainly won a loyal champion, Miss Porter," said Captain Dufranne, laughing. "I am sure that there be none of us here but would willingly face death a hundred times in its most terrifying forms to deserve the tributes of one even half so loyal—or so beautiful."

"You would not wonder that I defend him," said the girl, "could you have seen him as I saw him, battling in my behalf with that huge hairy brute.

"Could you have seen him charge the monster as a bull might charge a grizzly—absolutely without sign of fear or hesitation—you would have believed him more than human.

"Could you have seen those mighty muscles knotting under the brown skin—could you have seen them force back those awful fangs—you too would have thought him invincible.

"And could you have seen the chivalrous treatment which he accorded a strange girl of a strange race, you would feel the same absolute confidence in him that I feel."

"You have won your suit, my fair pleader," cried the captain. "This court finds the defendant not guilty, and the cruiser shall wait a few days longer that he may have an opportunity to come and thank the divine Portia."

"For the Lord's sake honey," cried Esmeralda. "You all don't mean to tell *me* that you're going to stay right here in this here land of carnivable animals when you all got the opportunity to escapade on that boat? Don't you tell me *that*, honey."

"Why, Esmeralda! You should be ashamed of yourself," cried Jane. "Is this any way to show your gratitude to the man who saved your life twice?"

"Well, Miss Jane, that's all jest as you say; but that there forest man never did save us to stay here. He done save us so we all could get *away* from here. I expect he be mighty peevish when he find we ain't got no more sense than to stay right here after he done give us the chance to get away.

"I hoped I'd never have to sleep in this here geological garden another night and listen to all them lonesome noises that come out of that jumble after dark."

"I don't blame you a bit, Esmeralda," said Clayton, "and you certainly did hit it off right when you called them 'lonesome' noises. I never have been able to find the right word for them but that's it, don't you know, lonesome noises."

"You and Esmeralda had better go and live on the cruiser," said Jane Porter, in fine scorn. "What would you think if you *had* to live all of your life in that jungle as our forest man has done?"

"I'm afraid I'd be a blooming bounder as a wild man," laughed Clayton, ruefully. "Those noises at night make the hair on my head bristle. I suppose that I should be ashamed to admit it, but it's the truth."

"I don't know about that," said Lieutenant Charpentier. "I never thought much about fear and that sort of thing—never tried to determine whether I was a coward or brave man; but the other night as we lay in the jungle there after poor d'Arnot was taken, and those jungle noises rose and fell around us I began to think that I was a coward indeed. It was not the roaring and growling of the big beasts that affected me so much as it was the stealthy noises—the ones that you heard suddenly close by and then listened vainly for a repetition of—the unaccountable sounds as of a great body moving almost noiselessly, and the knowledge that you didn't *know* how close it was, or whether it were creeping closer after you ceased to hear it? It was those noises—and the eyes.

"*Mon Dieu!* I shall see them in the dark forever—the eyes that you see, and those that you don't see, but feel—ah, they are the worst."

All were silent for a moment, and then Jane Porter spoke.

"And he is out there," she said, in an awe-hushed whisper. "Those eyes will be glaring at him tonight, and at your comrade Lieutenant d'Arnot. Can you leave them, gentlemen, without at least rendering them the passive succor which remaining here a few days longer might insure them?"

"Tut, tut, child," said Professor Porter. "Captain Dufranne is willing to remain, and for my part I am perfectly willing, perfectly willing—as I always have been to humor your childish whims."

"We can utilize the morrow in recovering the chest, Professor," suggested Mr. Philander.

"Quite so, quite so, Mr. Philander, I had almost forgotten the treasure," exclaimed Professor Porter. "Possibly we can borrow some men from Captain Dufranne to assist us, and one of the prisoners to point out the location of the chest."

"Most assuredly, my dear professor, we are all yours to command," said the captain.

And so it was arranged that on the next day Lieutenant Charpentier was to take a detail of ten men, and one of the mutineers of the *Arrow* as a guide, and unearth the treasure; and that the cruiser would remain for a full week in the little harbor. At the end of that time it was to be assumed that d'Arnot was truly dead, and that the forest man would not return while they remained. Then the two vessels were to leave with all the party.

Professor Porter did not accompany the treasure-seekers on the following day, but when he saw them returning empty-handed toward noon, he hastened forward to meet them—his usual preoccupied indifference entirely vanished, and in its place a nervous and excited manner.

"Where is the treasure?" he cried to Clayton, while yet a hundred feet separated them.

Clayton shook his head.

"Gone," he said, as he neared the professor.

"Gone! It cannot be. Who could have taken it?" cried Professor Porter.

"God only knows, Professor," replied Clayton. "We might have thought the fellow who guided us was lying about the location, but his surprise and consternation on finding no chest beneath the body of the murdered Snipes were too real to be feigned.

"And then our spades showed us that *something* had been buried beneath the corpse, for a hole had been there and it had been filled with loose earth."

"But who could have taken it?" repeated Professor Porter.

"Suspicion might naturally fall on the men of the cruiser," said Lieutenant Charpentier, "but for the fact that Sublieutenant Janviers here assures me that no men have had shore leave—that none has been on shore since we anchored here except under command of an officer.

"I do not know that you would suspect our men, but I am glad that there is now no chance for suspicion to fall on them," he concluded.

"It would never have occurred to me to suspect the men to whom we owe so much," replied Professor Porter, graciously. "I would as soon suspect my dear Clayton here, or Mr. Philander."

The Frenchmen smiled, both officers and sailors. It was plain to see that a burden had been lifted from their minds.

"The treasure has been gone for some time," continued Clayton. "In fact the body fell apart as we lifted it, which indicates that whoever removed the treasure did so while the corpse was still fresh, for it was intact when we first uncovered it."

"There must have been several in the party," said Jane, who had joined them. "You remember that it took four men to carry it."

"By jove!" cried Clayton. "That's right. It must have been done by a party of natives. Probably one of them saw the men bury the chest and then returned immediately after with a party of his friends, and carried it off."

"Speculation is futile," said Professor Porter, sadly. "The chest is gone. We shall never see it again, nor the treasure that was in it."

Only Jane Porter knew what the loss meant to her father, and none there knew what it meant to her.

Six days later Captain Dufranne announced that they would sail early on the morrow.

Jane Porter would have begged for a further reprieve, had it not been that she too had begun to believe that her forest lover would return no more.

In spite of herself she began to entertain doubts and fears. The reasonableness of the arguments of these disinterested French officers commenced to convince her against her will.

That he was a cannibal she would not believe, but that he was an adopted member of some native tribe at length seemed possible to her.

She would not admit that he could be dead. It was impossible to believe that that perfect body, so filled with triumphant life, could ever cease to harbor the vital spark—as soon believe that immortality were dust.

As Jane Porter permitted herself to harbor these thoughts, others equally unwelcome forced themselves upon her.

If he belonged to some native tribe he had a native wife—a dozen of them perhaps—and wild, unruly children. The girl shuddered, and when they told her that the cruiser would sail on the morrow she was almost glad.

It was she, though, who suggested that arms, ammunition, supplies, and comforts be left behind in the cabin, ostensibly for that intangible personality who had signed himself Tarzan of the Apes, and for d'Arnot should he still be living, but really, she hoped, for her forest god—even though his feet should prove of clay.

And at the last minute she left a message for him, to be transmitted by Tarzan of the Apes.

Jane Porter was the last to leave the cabin, returning on some trivial pretext after the others had started for the boat.

She kneeled down beside the bed in which she had spent so many nights, and offered up a prayer for the safety of her primeval man, and crushing his locket to her lips she murmured:

"I love you, and because I love you I believe in you. But if I did not believe, still should I love. May God have pity on my soul that I would acknowledge it. Had you come back for me, and there had been no other way, I would have gone into the jungle with you—forever."

CHAPTER TWENTY-FIVE
THE OUTPOST OF THE WORLD

WITH THE REPORT OF HIS GUN d'Arnot saw the door fly open and the figure of a man pitch headlong within onto the cabin floor.

The Frenchman in his panic raised his gun to fire again into the prostrate form, but suddenly in the half dusk of the open door he saw that the man was white and in another instant realized that he had shot his friend and protector, Tarzan of the Apes.

With a cry of anguish d'Arnot sprang to the ape-man's side, and kneeling, lifted the latter's head in his arms—calling Tarzan's name aloud.

There was no response, and then d'Arnot placed his ear above the man's heart. To his joy he heard its steady beating beneath.

Carefully he lifted Tarzan to the cot, and then, after closing and bolting the door, he lighted one of the lamps and examined the wound.

The bullet had struck a glancing blow upon the skull. There was an ugly flesh wound, but no signs of a fracture of the skull.

D'Arnot breathed a sigh of relief, and went about bathing the blood from Tarzan's face.

Soon the cool water revived him, and presently he opened his eyes to look in questioning surprise at d'Arnot.

The latter had bound the wound with pieces of cloth, and as he saw that Tarzan had regained consciousness he arose and going to the table wrote a message, which he handed to the ape-man, explaining the terrible mistake he had made and how thankful he was that the wound was not more serious.

Tarzan, after reading the message, sat on the edge of the couch and laughed.

"It is nothing," he said in French, and then, his vocabulary failing him, he wrote:

You should have seen what Bolgani did to me, and Kerchak, and Terkoz, before I killed them—then you would laugh at such a little scratch.

D'Arnot handed Tarzan the two messages that had been left for him.

Tarzan read the first one through with a look of sorrow on his face. The second one he turned over and over, searching for an opening—he had never seen a sealed envelope before. At length he handed it to d'Arnot.

The Frenchman had been watching him, and knew that Tarzan was puzzled over the envelope. How strange it seemed that to a full-grown white man an envelope was a mystery. D'Arnot opened it and handed the letter back to Tarzan.

Sitting on a camp stool the ape-man spread the written sheet before him and read:

To Tarzan of the Apes:

Before I leave let me add my thanks to those of Mr. Clayton for the kindness you have shown in permitting us the use of your cabin.

That you never came to make friends with us has been a great regret to us. We should have liked so much to have seen and thanked our host.

There is another I should like to thank also, but he did not come back, though I cannot believe that he is dead.

I do not know his name. He is the great white giant who wore the diamond locket upon his breast.

If you know him and can speak his language carry my thanks to him, and tell him that I waited seven days for him to return.

Tell him, also, that in my home in America, in the city of Baltimore, there will always be a welcome for him if he cares to come.

I found a note you wrote me lying among the leaves beneath a tree near the cabin. I do not know how you learned to love me, who have never spoken to me, and I am very sorry if it is true, for I have already given my heart to another.

But know that I am always your friend,

Jane Porter.

Tarzan sat with gaze fixed upon the floor for nearly an hour. It was evident to him from the notes that they did not know that he and Tarzan of the Apes were one and the same.

"I have given my heart to another," he repeated over and over again to himself.

Then she did not love him! How could she have pretended love, and raised him to such a pinnacle of hope only to cast him down to such utter depths of despair!

Maybe her kisses were only signs of friendship. How did he know, who knew nothing of the customs of human beings?

Suddenly he arose, and, bidding d'Arnot good night as he had learned to do, threw himself upon the couch of ferns that had been Jane Porter's.

D'Arnot extinguished the lamp, and lay down upon the cot.

For a week they did little but rest, d'Arnot coaching Tarzan in French. At the end of that time the two men could converse quite easily.

One night, as they were sitting within the cabin before retiring, Tarzan turned to d'Arnot.

"Where is America?" he said.

D'Arnot pointed toward the northwest.

"Many thousands of miles across the ocean," he replied. "Why?"

"I am going there."

D'Arnot shook his head.

"It is impossible, my friend," he said.

Tarzan rose, and, going to one of the cupboards, returned with a well-thumbed geography.

Turning to a map of the world, he said:

"I have never quite understood all this; explain it to me, please."

When d'Arnot had done so, showing him that the blue represented all the water on the earth, and the bits of other colors the continents and islands, Tarzan asked him to point out the spot where they now were.

D'Arnot did so.

"Now point out America," said Tarzan.

And as d'Arnot placed his finger upon North America, Tarzan smiled and laid his palm upon the page, spanning the great ocean that lay between the two continents.

"You see it is not so very far," he said; "scarce the width of my hand."

D'Arnot laughed. How could he make the man understand?

Then he took a pencil and made a tiny point upon the shore of Africa.

"This little mark," he said, "is many times larger upon this map than your cabin is upon the earth. Do you see now how very far it is?"

Tarzan thought for a long time.

"Do any white men live in Africa?" he asked.

"Yes."

"Where are the nearest?"

D'Arnot pointed out a spot on the shore just north of them.

"So close?" asked Tarzan, in surprise.

"Yes," said d'Arnot; "but it is not close."

"Have they big boats to cross the ocean?"

"Yes."

"We shall go there tomorrow," announced Tarzan.

Again d'Arnot smiled and shook his head.

"It is too far. We should die long before we reached them."

"Do you wish to stay here then forever?" asked Tarzan.

"No," said d'Arnot.

"Then we shall start tomorrow. I do not like it here longer. I should rather die than remain here."

"Well," answered d'Arnot, with a shrug, "I do not know, my friend, but that I also would rather die than remain here. If you go, I shall go with you."

"It is settled then," said Tarzan. "I shall start for America tomorrow."

"How will you get to America without money?" asked d'Arnot.

"What is money?" inquired Tarzan.

It took a long time to make him understand even imperfectly.

"How do men get money?" he asked at last.

"They work for it."

"Very well. I will work for it, then."

"No, my friend," returned d'Arnot, "you need not worry about money, nor need you work for it. I have enough for two—enough for twenty. Much more than is good for one man and you shall have all you need if ever we reach civilization."

So on the following day they started north along the shore. Each man carrying a rifle and ammunition, beside bedding and some food and cooking utensils.

The latter seemed to Tarzan a most useless encumbrance, so he threw his away.

"But you must learn to eat cooked food, my friend," remonstrated d'Arnot. "No civilized men eat raw flesh."

"There will be time enough when I reach civilization," said Tarzan. "I do not like the things and they only spoil the taste of good meat."

For a month they traveled north. Sometimes finding food in plenty and again going hungry for days.

They saw no signs of natives nor were they molested by wild beasts. Their journey was a miracle of ease.

Tarzan asked questions and learned rapidly. D'Arnot taught him many of the refinements of civilization—even to the use of knife and fork; but sometimes Tarzan would drop them in disgust and grasp his food in his strong brown hands, tearing it with his molars like a wild beast.

Then d'Arnot would expostulate with him, saying:

"You must not eat like a brute, Tarzan, while I am trying to make a gentleman of you. *Mon Dieu!* Gentlemen do not thus—it is terrible."

Tarzan would grin sheepishly and pick up his knife and fork again, but at heart he hated them.

On the journey he told d'Arnot about the great chest he had seen the sailors bury; of how he had dug it up and carried it to the gathering place of the apes and buried it there.

"It must be the treasure chest of Professor Porter," said d'Arnot. "It is too bad, but of course you did not know."

Then Tarzan recalled the letter written by Jane Porter to her friend—the one he had stolen when they first came to his cabin, and now he knew what was in the chest and what it meant to Jane Porter.

"Tomorrow we shall go back after it," he announced to d'Arnot.

"Go back?" exclaimed d'Arnot. "But, my dear fellow, we have now been three weeks upon the march. It would require three more to return to the treasure, and then, with that enormous weight which required, you say, four sailors to carry, it would be months before we had again reached this spot."

"It must be done, my friend," insisted Tarzan. "You may go on toward civilization, and I will return for the treasure. I can go very much faster alone."

"I have a better plan, Tarzan," exclaimed d'Arnot. "We shall go on together to the nearest settlement, and there we will charter a boat and sail back down the coast for the treasure and so transport it easily. That will be safer and quicker and also not require us to be separated. What do you think of that plan?"

"Very well," said Tarzan. "The treasure will be there whenever we go for it; and while I could fetch it now, and catch up with you in a moon or two, I shall feel safer for you to know that you are not alone on the trail. When I see how helpless you are, d'Arnot, I often wonder how the human race has escaped annihilation all these ages which you tell me about. Why, Sabor, single handed, could exterminate a thousand of you."

D'Arnot laughed.

"You will think more highly of your genus when you have seen its armies and navies, its great cities, and its mighty engineering works. Then you will realize that it is mind, and not muscle, that makes the human animal greater than the mighty beasts of your jungle.

"Alone and unarmed, a single man is no match for any of the larger beasts; but if ten men were together, they would combine their wits and their muscles against their savage enemies, while the beasts, being unable to reason, would never think of combining against the men. Otherwise, Tarzan of the Apes, how long would you have lasted in the savage wilderness?"

"You are right, d'Arnot," replied Tarzan, "for if Kerchak had come to Tublat's aid that night at the Dum-Dum, there would have been an end of me. But Kerchak could never think far enough ahead to take advantage of any such opportunity. Even Kala, my mother, could never plan ahead. She simply ate what she needed when she needed it, and if the supply was very scarce, even though she found plenty for several meals, she would never gather any ahead.

"I remember that she used to think it very silly of me to burden myself with extra food upon the march, though she was quite glad to eat it with me, if the way chanced to be barren of sustenance."

"Then you knew your mother, Tarzan?" asked d'Arnot, in surprise.

"Yes. She was a great, fine ape, larger than I, and weighing twice as much."

"And your father?" asked d'Arnot.

"I did not know him. Kala told me he was a white ape, and hairless like myself. I know now that he must have been a white man."

D'Arnot looked long and earnestly at his companion.

"Tarzan," he said at length, "it is impossible that the ape, Kala, was your mother. If such a thing can be, which I doubt, you would have inherited some of the characteristics of the ape, but you have not—you are pure man, and, I should say, the offspring of highly bred and intelligent parents. Have you not the slightest clue to your past?"

"Not the slightest," replied Tarzan.

"No writings in the cabin that might have told something of the lives of its original inmates?"

"I have read everything that was in the cabin with the exception of one book which I know now to be written in a language other than English. Possibly you can read it."

Tarzan fished the little black diary from the bottom of his quiver, and handed it to his companion.

D'Arnot glanced at the title page.

"It is the diary of John Clayton, Lord Greystoke, an English nobleman, and it is written in French," he said.

Then he proceeded to read the diary that had been written over twenty years before, and which recorded the details of the story which we already know—the story of adventure, hardships and sorrow of John Clayton and his wife Alice, from the day they left England until an hour before he was struck down by Kerchak.

D'Arnot read aloud. At times his voice broke, and he was forced to stop reading for the pitiful hopelessness that spoke between the lines.

Occasionally he glanced at Tarzan; but the ape-man sat upon his haunches, like a carven image, his eyes fixed upon the ground.

Only when the little babe was mentioned did the tone of the diary alter from the habitual note of despair which had crept into it by degrees after the first two months upon the shore.

Then the passages were tinged with a subdued happiness that was even sadder than the rest.

One entry showed an almost hopeful spirit.

Today our little boy is six months old. He is sitting in Alice's lap beside the table where I am writing—a happy, healthy, perfect child.

Somehow, even against all reason, I seem to see him a grown man, taking his father's place in the world—the second John Clayton—and bringing added honors to the house of Greystoke.

There—as though to give my prophecy the weight of his endorsement—he has grabbed my pen in his chubby fists and with his ink-begrimed little fingers has placed the seal of his tiny fingerprints upon the page.

And there, on the margin of the page, were the partially blurred imprints of four wee fingers and the outer half of the thumb.

When d'Arnot had finished the diary the two men sat in silence for some minutes.

"Well! Tarzan of the Apes, what think you?" asked d'Arnot. "Does not this little book clear up the mystery of your parentage?

"Why man, you are Lord Greystoke."

Tarzan shook his head.

"The book speaks of but one child," he replied. "Its little skeleton lay in the crib, where it died crying for nourishment, from the first time I entered the cabin until Professor Porter's party buried it, with its father and mother, beside the cabin.

"No, that was the babe the book speaks of—and the mystery of my origin is deeper than before, for I have thought much of late of the possibility of that cabin having been my birthplace.

"I am afraid that Kala spoke the truth," he concluded sadly.

D'Arnot shook his head. He was unconvinced, and in his mind had sprung the determination to prove the correctness of his theory, for he had discovered the key which alone could unlock the mystery, or consign it forever to the realms of the unfathomable.

A week later the two men came suddenly upon a clearing in the forest.

In the distance were several buildings surrounded by a strong palisade. Between them and the enclosure stretched a cultivated field in which a number of villagers were working.

The two halted at the edge of the jungle.

Tarzan fitted his bow with a poisoned arrow, but d'Arnot placed a hand upon his arm.

"What would you do, Tarzan?" he asked.

"They will try to kill us if they see us," replied Tarzan. "I prefer to be the killer."

"Maybe they are friends," suggested d'Arnot.

"They are strangers," was Tarzan's only reply.

And again he drew back his shaft.

"You must not, Tarzan!" cried d'Arnot. "Men do not kill wantonly. *Mon Dieu!* but you have much to learn.

"I pity the ruffler who crosses you, my wild man, when I take you to Paris. I will have my hands full keeping your neck from beneath the guillotine."

Tarzan lowered his bow and smiled.

"I do not know why I should kill the warriors back there in my jungle, yet not kill them here. Suppose Numa, the lion, should spring out upon us, I should say, then, I presume: Good morning, Monsieur Numa, how is Madame Numa, eh?"

"Wait until the men spring upon you," replied d'Arnot, "then you may kill them. Do not assume that men are your enemies until they prove it."

"Come," said Tarzan, "let us go and present ourselves to be killed," and he started straight across the field, his head high held and the tropical sun beating upon his smooth, brown skin.

Behind him came d'Arnot, clothed in some garments which had been discarded at the cabin by Clayton when the officers of the French cruiser had fitted him out in more presentable fashion.

Presently one of the villagers looked up, and beholding Tarzan, turned, shrieking, toward the palisade.

In an instant the air was filled with cries of terror from the fleeing gardeners, but before any had reached the palisade a white man emerged from the enclosure, rifle in hand, to discover the cause of the commotion.

What he saw brought his rifle to his shoulder, and Tarzan of the Apes would have felt cold lead once again had not d'Arnot cried loudly to the man with the leveled gun:

"Do not fire! We are friends!"

"Halt, then!" was the reply.

"Stop, Tarzan!" cried d'Arnot. "He thinks we are enemies."

Tarzan dropped into a walk, and together he and d'Arnot advanced toward the white man by the gate.

The latter eyed them in puzzled bewilderment.

"What manner of men are you?" he asked, in French.

"White men," replied d'Arnot. "We have been lost in the jungle for a long time."

The man had lowered his rifle and now advanced with outstretched hand.

"I am Father Constantine of the French Mission here," he said, "and I am glad to welcome you."

"This is Monsieur Tarzan, Father Constantine," replied d'Arnot, indicating the ape-man; and as the priest extended his hand to Tarzan, d'Arnot added: "and I am Paul d'Arnot, of the French Navy."

Father Constantine took the hand which Tarzan extended in imitation of the priest's act, while the latter took in the superb physique and handsome face in one quick, keen glance.

And thus came Tarzan of the Apes to the first outpost of civilization.

For a week they remained there, and the ape-man, keenly observant, learned much of the ways of men; while native women sewed upon white duck garments for himself and d'Arnot so that they might continue their journey properly clothed.

CHAPTER TWENTY-SIX
THE HEIGHT OF CIVILIZATION

ANOTHER MONTH BROUGHT THEM to a little group of buildings at the mouth of a wide river, and there Tarzan saw many boats, and was filled with the old timidity of the wild thing by the sight of many men.

Gradually he became accustomed to the strange noises and the odd ways of civilization, so that presently none might know that two short months before, this handsome Frenchman in immaculate white ducks, who laughed and chatted with the gayest of them, had been swinging naked through primeval forests to pounce upon some unwary victim, which, raw, was to fill his savage belly.

The knife and fork, so contemptuously flung aside a month before, Tarzan now manipulated as exquisitely as did the polished d'Arnot.

So apt a pupil had he been that the young Frenchman had labored assiduously to make of Tarzan of the Apes a polished gentleman insofar as nicety of manners and speech were concerned.

"God made you a gentleman at heart, my friend," d'Arnot had said; "but we want His works to show upon the exterior also."

As soon as they had reached the little port, d'Arnot had cabled his government of his safety, and requested a three-months' leave, which had been granted.

He had also cabled his bankers for funds, and the enforced wait of a month, under which both chafed, was due to their inability to charter a vessel for the return to Tarzan's jungle after the treasure.

During their stay at the coast town "Monsieur Tarzan" became the wonder of the townspeople because of several occurrences which to Tarzan seemed the merest of nothings.

Once a huge black man, crazed by drink, had run amuck and terrorized the town, until his evil star had led him to where the black-haired French giant lolled upon the veranda of the hotel.

Mounting the broad steps, with brandished knife, the drunkard made straight for a party of four men sitting at a table sipping the inevitable absinth.

Shouting in alarm, the four took to their heels, and then the man spied Tarzan.

With a roar he charged the ape-man, while half a hundred heads peered from sheltering windows and doorways to witness the butchering of the poor Frenchman by the giant ruffian.

Tarzan met the rush with the fighting smile that the joy of battle always brought to his lips.

As the man closed upon him, steel muscles gripped the wrist of the uplifted knife-hand, and a single swift wrench left the hand dangling below a broken bone.

With the pain and surprise, the madness left the huge man, and as Tarzan dropped back into his chair the fellow turned, crying with agony, and dashed wildly toward the native village.

On another occasion as Tarzan and d'Arnot sat at dinner with a number of others, the talk fell upon lions and lion hunting.

Opinion was divided as to the bravery of the king of beasts—some maintaining that he was an arrant coward, but all agreeing that it was with a feeling of greater security that they gripped their express rifles when the monarch of the jungle roared about a camp at night.

D'Arnot and Tarzan had agreed that his past be kept secret, and so none other than the French officer knew of the ape-man's familiarity with the beasts of the jungle.

"Monsieur Tarzan has not expressed himself," said one of the party. "A man of his prowess who has spent some time in Africa, as I understand Monsieur Tarzan has, must have had experiences with lions—yes?"

"Some," replied Tarzan, dryly. "Enough to know that each of you are right in your judgment of the characteristics of the lions—you have met. But one might as well judge all men by the fellow who ran amuck last week, or decide that all men are cowards because one has met a cowardly man.

"There is as much individuality among the lower orders, gentlemen, as there is among ourselves. Today we may go out and stumble upon a lion which is over-timid—he runs away from us. Tomorrow we may meet his uncle or his twin brother, and our friends wonder why we do not return from the jungle. For myself, I always assume that a lion is ferocious, and so I am never caught off my guard."

"There would be little pleasure in hunting," retorted the first speaker, "if one is afraid of the thing he hunts."

D'Arnot smiled. Tarzan afraid!

"I do not exactly understand what you mean by fear," said Tarzan. "Like lions, fear is a different thing in different men, but to me the only pleasure in the hunt is the knowledge that the hunted thing has power to harm me as much as I have to harm him. If I went out with a couple of rifles and a gun bearer, and twenty or thirty beaters, to hunt a lion, I should not feel that the lion had much chance, and so the pleasure of the hunt would be lessened in proportion to the increased safety which I felt."

"Then I am to take it that Monsieur Tarzan would prefer to go naked into the jungle, armed only with a jackknife, to kill the king of beasts," laughed the other, good-naturedly, but with the merest touch of sarcasm in his tone.

"And a piece of rope," added Tarzan.

Just then the deep roar of a lion sounded from the distant jungle, as though to challenge whoever dared enter the lists with him.

"There is your opportunity, Monsieur Tarzan," bantered the Frenchman.

"I am not hungry," said Tarzan simply.

The men laughed, all but d'Arnot. He alone knew that a savage beast had spoken its simple reason through the lips of the ape-man.

"But you are afraid, just as any of us would be, to go out there naked, armed only with a knife and a piece of rope," said the banterer. "Is it not so?"

"No," replied Tarzan. "Only a fool performs any act without reason."

"Five thousands francs is a reason," said the other. "I wager you that amount you cannot bring back a lion from the jungle under the conditions we have named—naked and armed only with a knife and a piece of rope."

Tarzan glanced toward d'Arnot and nodded his head.

"Make it ten thousand," said d'Arnot.

"Done," replied the other.

Tarzan arose.

"I shall have to leave my clothes at the edge of the settlement, so that if I do not return before daylight I shall have something to wear through the streets."

"You are not going now," exclaimed the wagerer—"at night?"

"Why not?" asked Tarzan. "Numa walks abroad at night—it will be easier to find him."

"No," said the other, "I do not want your blood upon my hands. It will be foolhardy enough if you go forth by day."

"I shall go now," replied Tarzan, and went to his room for his knife and rope.

The men accompanied him to the edge of the jungle, where he left his clothes in a small storehouse.

But when he would have entered the blackness of the undergrowth they tried to dissuade him; and the wagerer was most insistent of all that he abandon his foolhardy venture.

"I will accede that you have won," he said, "and the ten thousand francs are yours if you will but give up this foolish attempt, which can only end in your death."

Tarzan laughed, and in another moment the jungle had swallowed him.

The men stood silent for some moments and then slowly turned and walked back to the hotel veranda.

Tarzan had no sooner entered the jungle than he took to the trees, and it was with a feeling of exultant freedom that he swung once more through the forest branches.

This was life! Ah, how he loved it! Civilization held nothing like this in its narrow and circumscribed sphere, hemmed in by restrictions and conventionalities. Even clothes were a hindrance and a nuisance.

At last he was free. He had not realized what a prisoner he had been.

How easy it would be to circle back to the coast, and then make toward the south and his own jungle and cabin.

Now he caught the scent of Numa, for he was traveling upwind. Presently his quick ears detected the familiar sound of padded feet and the brushing of a huge, fur-clad body through the undergrowth.

Tarzan came quietly above the unsuspecting beast and silently stalked him until he came into a little patch of moonlight.

Then the quick noose settled and tightened about the tawny throat, and, as he had done it a hundred times in the past, Tarzan made fast the end to a strong branch and, while the beast fought and clawed for freedom, dropped to the ground behind him, and leaping upon the great back, plunged his long thin blade a dozen times into the fierce heart.

Then with his foot upon the carcass of Numa, he raised his voice in the awesome victory cry of his savage tribe.

For a moment Tarzan stood irresolute, swayed by conflicting emotions of loyalty to d'Arnot and a mighty lust for the freedom of his own jungle. At last the vision of a beautiful face, and the memory of warm lips crushed to his dissolved the fascinating picture he had been drawing of his old life.

The ape-man threw the warm carcass of Numa across his shoulders and took to the trees once more.

The men upon the veranda had sat for an hour, almost in silence.

They had tried ineffectually to converse on various subjects, and always the thing uppermost in the mind of each had caused the conversation to lapse.

"Mon Dieu," said the wagerer at length, "I can endure it no longer. I am going into the jungle with my express and bring back that madman."

"I will go with you," said one.

"And I"—"And I"—"And I," chorused the others.

As though the suggestion had broken the spell of some horrid nightmare they hastened to their various quarters, and presently were headed toward the jungle—each man heavily armed.

"God! What was that?" suddenly cried one of the party, an Englishman, as Tarzan's savage cry came faintly to their ears.

"I heard the same thing once before," said a Belgian, "when I was in the gorilla country. My carriers said it was the cry of a great bull ape who has made a kill."

D'Arnot remembered Clayton's description of the awful roar with which Tarzan had announced his kills, and he half smiled in spite of the horror which filled him to think that the uncanny sound could have issued from a human throat—from the lips of his friend.

As the party stood finally near the edge of the jungle, debating as to the best distribution of their forces, they were startled by a low laugh near them, and turning, beheld advancing toward them a giant figure bearing a dead lion upon its broad shoulders.

Even d'Arnot was thunderstruck, for it seemed impossible that the man could have so quickly dispatched a lion with the pitiful weapons he had taken, or that alone he could have borne the huge carcass through the tangled jungle.

The men crowded about Tarzan with many questions, but his only answer was a laughing depreciation of his feat.

To Tarzan it was as though one should eulogize a butcher for his heroism in killing a cow, for Tarzan had killed so often for food and for self-preservation that the act seemed anything but remarkable to him. But he was indeed a hero in the eyes of these men—men accustomed to hunting big game.

Incidentally, he had won ten thousand francs, for d'Arnot insisted that he keep it all.

This was a very important item to Tarzan, who was just commencing to realize the power which lay behind the little pieces of metal and paper which always changed hands when human beings rode, or ate, or slept, or clothed themselves, or drank, or worked, or played, or sheltered themselves from the rain or cold or sun.

It had become evident to Tarzan that without money one must die. D'Arnot had told him not to worry, since he had more than enough for both, but the ape-man was learning many things and one of them was that people looked down upon one who accepted money from another without giving something of equal value in exchange.

Shortly after the episode of the lion hunt, d'Arnot succeeded in chartering an ancient tub for the coastwise trip to Tarzan's landlocked harbor.

It was a happy morning for them both when the little vessel weighed anchor and made for the open sea.

The trip to the beach was uneventful, and the morning after they dropped anchor before the cabin, Tarzan, garbed once more in his jungle regalia and carrying a spade, set out alone for the amphitheater of the apes where lay the treasure.

Late the next day he returned, bearing the great chest upon his shoulder, and at sunrise the little vessel was worked through the harbor's mouth and took up her northward journey.

Three weeks later Tarzan and d'Arnot were passengers on board a French steamer bound for Lyons, and after a few days in that city d'Arnot took Tarzan to Paris.

The ape-man was anxious to proceed to America, but d'Arnot insisted that he must accompany him to Paris first, nor would he divulge the nature of the urgent necessity upon which he based his demand.

One of the first things which d'Arnot accomplished after their arrival was to arrange to visit a high official of the police department, an old friend; and to take Tarzan with him.

Adroitly d'Arnot led the conversation from point to point until the policeman had explained to the interested Tarzan many of the methods in vogue for apprehending and identifying criminals.

Not the least interesting to Tarzan was the part played by fingerprints in this fascinating science.

"But of what value are these imprints," asked Tarzan, "when, after a few years the lines upon the fingers are entirely changed by the wearing out of the old tissue and the growth of new?"

"The lines never change," replied the official. "From infancy to senility the fingerprints of an individual change only in size, except as injuries alter the loops and whorls. But if imprints have been taken of the thumb and four fingers of both hands one must needs lose all entirely to escape identification."

"It is marvelous," exclaimed d'Arnot. "I wonder what the lines upon my own fingers may resemble."

"We can soon see," replied the police officer, and ringing a bell he summoned an assistant to whom he issued a few directions.

The man left the room, but presently returned with a little hardwood box which he placed on his superior's desk.

"Now," said the officer, "you shall have your fingerprints in a second."

He drew from the little case a square of plate glass, a little tube of thick ink, a rubber roller, and a few snowy white cards.

Squeezing a drop of ink onto the glass, he spread it back and forth with the rubber roller until the entire surface of the glass was covered to his satisfaction with a very thin and uniform layer of ink.

"Place the four fingers of your right hand upon the glass, thus," he said to d'Arnot. "Now the thumb. That is right. Now place them in just the same position upon this card, here, no—a little to the right. We must leave room for the thumb and the fingers of the left hand. There, that's it. Now the same with the left."

"Come, Tarzan," cried d'Arnot, "let's see what your whorls look like."

Tarzan complied readily, asking many questions of the officer during the operation.

"Do fingerprints show racial characteristics?" he asked.

"I think not," replied the officer.

"Could the fingerprints of an ape be detected from those of a man?"

"Probably, because the ape's would be far simpler than those of the higher organism."

"But a cross between an ape and a man might show the characteristics of either progenitor?" continued Tarzan.

"Yes, I should think likely," responded the official; "but the science has not progressed sufficiently to render it exact enough in such matters. I should hate to trust its findings further than to differentiate between individuals. There it is absolute. No two people born into the world probably have ever had identical lines upon all their digits. It is very doubtful if any single fingerprint will ever be exactly duplicated by any finger other than the one which originally made it."

"Does the comparison require much time or labor?" asked d'Arnot.

"Ordinarily but a few moments, if the impressions are distinct."

D'Arnot drew a little black book from his pocket and commenced turning the pages.

Tarzan looked at the book in surprise. How did d'Arnot come to have his book?

Presently d'Arnot stopped at a page on which were five tiny little smudges.

He handed the open book to the policeman.

"Are these imprints similar to mine or Monsieur Tarzan's or can you say that they are identical with either?"

The officer drew a powerful glass from his desk and examined all three specimens carefully, making notations meanwhile upon a pad of paper.

Tarzan realized now what was the meaning of their visit to the police officer.

The answer to his life's riddle lay in these tiny marks.

With tense nerves he sat leaning forward in his chair, but suddenly he relaxed and dropped back, smiling.

D'Arnot looked at him in surprise.

"You forget that for twenty years the dead body of the child who made those fingerprints lay in the cabin of his father, and that all my life I have seen it lying there," said Tarzan bitterly.

The policeman looked up in astonishment.

"Go ahead, Captain, with your examination," said d'Arnot, "we will tell you the story later—provided Monsieur Tarzan is agreeable."

Tarzan nodded his head.

"But you are mad, my dear d'Arnot," he insisted. "Those little fingers are buried on the west coast of Africa."

"I do not know as to that, Tarzan," replied d'Arnot. "It is possible, but if you are not the son of John Clayton then how in heaven's name did you come into that God forsaken jungle where no white man other than John Clayton had ever set foot?"

"You forget—Kala," said Tarzan.

"I do not even consider her," replied d'Arnot.

The friends had walked to the broad window overlooking the boulevard as they talked. For some time they stood there gazing out upon the busy throng beneath, each wrapped in his own thoughts.

"It takes some time to compare fingerprints," thought d'Arnot, turning to look at the police officer.

To his astonishment he saw the official leaning back in his chair hastily scanning the contents of the little black diary.

D'Arnot coughed. The policeman looked up, and, catching his eye, raised his finger to admonish silence.

D'Arnot turned back to the window, and presently the police officer spoke.

"Gentlemen," he said.

Both turned toward him.

"There is evidently a great deal at stake which must hinge to a greater or lesser extent upon the absolute correctness of this comparison. I therefore ask that you leave the entire matter in my hands until Monsieur Desquerc, our expert, returns. It will be but a matter of a few days."

"I had hoped to know at once," said d'Arnot. "Monsieur Tarzan sails for America tomorrow."

"I will promise that you can cable him a report within two weeks," replied the officer; "but what it will be I dare not say. There are resemblances, yet—well, we had better leave it for Monsieur Desquerc to solve."

CHAPTER TWENTY-SEVEN
The Giant Again

A TAXI CAB DREW UP before an old-fashioned residence upon the outskirts of Baltimore.

A man of about forty, well built and with strong, regular features, stepped out, and paying the chauffeur dismissed him.

A moment later the passenger was entering the library of the old home.

"Ah, Mr. Canler!" exclaimed an old man, rising to greet him.

"Good evening, my dear Professor," cried the man, extending a cordial hand.

"Who admitted you?" asked the professor.

"Esmeralda."

"Then she will acquaint Jane with the fact that you are here," said the old man.

"No, Professor," replied Canler, "for I came primarily to see you."

"Ah, I am honored," said Professor Porter.

"Professor," continued Robert Canler, with great deliberation, as though carefully weighing his words, "I have come this evening to speak with you about Jane.

"You know my aspirations, and you have been generous enough to approve my suit."

Professor Archimedes Q. Porter fidgeted in his armchair. The subject always made him uncomfortable. He could not understand why. Canler was a splendid match.

"But Jane," continued Canler, "I cannot understand her. She puts me off first on one ground and then another. I have always the feeling that she breathes a sigh of relief every time I bid her good-bye."

"Tut, tut," said Professor Porter. "Tut, tut, Mr. Canler. Jane is a most obedient daughter. She will do precisely as I tell her."

"Then I can still count on your support?" asked Canler, a tone of relief marking his voice.

"Certainly, sir; certainly, sir," exclaimed Professor Porter. "How could you doubt it?"

"There is young Clayton, you know," suggested Canler. "He has been hanging about for months. I don't know that Jane cares for him; but beside his title they say he has inherited a very considerable estate from his father, and it might not be strange, if he finally won her, unless—" and Canler paused.

"Tut—tut, Mr. Canler; unless—what?"

"Unless, you see fit to request that Jane and I be married at once," said Canler, slowly and distinctly.

"I have already suggested to Jane that it would be desirable," said Professor Porter sadly, "for we can no longer afford to keep up this house, and live as her associations demand."

"What was her reply?" asked Canler.

"She said she was not ready to marry anyone yet," replied Professor Porter, "and that we could go and live upon the farm in northern Wisconsin which her mother left her.

"It is a little more than self-supporting. The tenants have always made a living from it, and been able to send Jane a trifle beside, each year. She is planning on our going up there the first of the week. Philander and Mr. Clayton have already gone to get things in readiness for us."

"Clayton has gone there?" exclaimed Canler, visibly chagrined. "Why was I not told? I would gladly have gone and seen that every comfort was provided."

"Jane feels that we are already too much in your debt, Mr. Canler," said Professor Porter.

Canler was about to reply, when the sound of footsteps came from the hall without, and Jane Porter entered the room.

"Oh, I beg your pardon!" she exclaimed, pausing on the threshold. "I thought you were alone, Papa."

"It is only I, Jane," said Canler, who had risen, "won't you come in and join the family group? We were just speaking of you."

"Thank you," said Jane Porter, entering and taking the chair Canler placed for her. "I only wanted to tell Papa that Tobey is coming down from the college tomorrow to pack his books. I want you to be sure, Papa, to indicate all that you can do without until fall. Please don't carry this entire library to Wisconsin, as you would have carried it to Africa, if I had not put my foot down."

"Was Tobey here?" asked Professor Porter.

"Yes, I just left him. He and Esmeralda are exchanging religious experiences on the back porch now."

"Tut, tut, I must see him at once!" cried the professor. "Excuse me just a moment, children," and the old man hastened from the room.

As soon as he was out of earshot Canler turned to Jane Porter.

"See here, Jane," he said bluntly. "How long is this thing going on like this? You haven't refused to marry me, but you haven't promised either. I want to get the license tomorrow, so that we can be married quietly before you leave for Wisconsin. I don't care for any fuss or feathers, and I'm sure you don't either."

The girl turned cold, but she held her head bravely.

"Your father wishes it, you know," added Canler.

"Yes, I know."

She spoke scarcely above a whisper.

"Do you realize that you are buying me, Mr. Canler?" she said finally, and in a cold, level voice. "Buying me for a few paltry dollars? Of course you do, Robert Canler, and the hope of just such a contingency was in your mind when you loaned Papa the money for that hair-brained escapade, which but for a most mysterious circumstance would have been surprisingly successful.

"But you, Mr. Canler, would have been the most surprised. You had no idea that the venture would succeed. You are too good a businessman for that. And you are too good a businessman to loan money for buried-treasure seeking, or to loan money without security—unless you had some special object in view.

"You knew that without security you had a greater hold on the honor of the Porters than with it. You knew the one best way to force me to marry you, without seeming to force me.

"You have never mentioned the loan. In any other man I should have thought that the prompting of a magnanimous and noble character. But you are deep, Mr. Robert Canler. I know you better than you think I know you.

"I shall certainly marry you if there is no other way, but let us understand each other once and for all."

While she spoke Robert Canler had alternately flushed and paled, and when she ceased speaking he arose, and with a cynical smile upon his strong face, said:

"You surprise me, Jane. I thought you had more self-control—more pride. Of course you are right. I am buying you and I knew that you knew it, but I thought you would prefer to pretend that it was otherwise. I should have thought your self-respect and your Porter pride would have shrunk from admitting, even to yourself, that you were a bought woman.

"But have it your own way, dear girl," he added lightly. "I am going to have you, and that is all that interests me."

Without a word the girl turned and left the room.

Jane Porter was not married before she left with her father and Esmeralda for her little Wisconsin farm, and as she coldly bid Robert Canler good-bye as her train pulled out, he called to her that he would join them in a week or two.

At their destination they were met by Clayton and Mr. Philander in a huge touring car belonging to the former, and quickly whirled away through the dense northern woods toward the little farm which the girl had not visited before since childhood.

The farmhouse, which stood on a little elevation some hundred yards from the tenant house, had undergone a complete transformation during the three weeks that Clayton and Mr. Philander had been there.

The former had imported a small army of carpenters and plasterers, plumbers and painters from a distant city, and what had been but a dilapidated shell when they reached it was now a cozy little two-story house filled with every modern convenience procurable in so short a time.

"Why, Mr. Clayton, what have you done?" cried Jane Porter, her heart sinking within her as she realized the probable size of the expenditure that had been made.

"S-sh," cautioned Clayton. "Don't let your father guess. If you don't tell him he will never notice, and I simply couldn't think of him living in the terrible squalor and sordidness which Mr. Philander and I found. It was so little when I would like to do so much, Jane. For his sake, please, never mention it."

"But you know that we can't repay you," cried the girl. "Why do you want to put me under such terrible obligations?"

"Don't, Jane," said Clayton sadly. "If it had been just you, believe me, I wouldn't have done it, for I knew from the start that it would only hurt me in your eyes, but I couldn't think of that dear old man living in the hole we found here.

"Won't you please believe that I did it just for him and give me that little crumb of pleasure at least?"

"I do believe you, Mr. Clayton," said the girl, "because I know you are big enough and generous enough to have done it just for him—and, oh Cecil, I wish I might repay you as you deserve—as you would wish."

"Why can't you, Jane?"

"Because I love another."

"Canler?"

"No."

"But you are going to marry him. He told me as much before I left Baltimore."

The girl winced.

"I do not love him," she said, almost proudly.

"It is because of the money, Jane?"

She nodded.

"Then am I so much less desirable than Canler? I have money enough, and far more, for every need," he said bitterly.

"I do not love you, Cecil," she said, "but I respect you. If I must disgrace myself by such a bargain with any man, I prefer that it be one I already despise. I should loathe the man to whom I sold myself without love, whomsoever he might be.

"You will be happier," she concluded, "alone—with my respect and friendship, than with me and my contempt."

He did not press the matter further, but if ever a man had murder in his heart it was William Cecil Clayton, Lord Greystoke, when, a week later, Robert Canler drew up before the farmhouse in his purring six cylinder.

A week passed; a tense, uneventful, but uncomfortable week for all the inmates of the little Wisconsin farmhouse.

Canler was insistent that Jane marry him at once.

At length she gave in from sheer loathing of the continued and hateful importuning.

It was agreed that on the morrow Canler was to drive to town and bring back the license and a minister.

Clayton had wanted to leave as soon as the plan was announced, but the girl's tired, hopeless look kept him. He could not desert her.

Something might happen yet, he tried to console himself by thinking. And in his heart, he knew that it would require but a tiny spark to turn his hatred for Canler into the bloodlust of the killer.

Early the next morning Canler set out for town.

In the east smoke could be seen lying low over the forest, for a fire had been raging for a week not far from them, but the wind still lay in the west and no danger threatened them.

About noon Jane Porter started off for a walk. She would not let Clayton accompany her. She wanted to be alone, she said, and he respected her wishes.

In the house Professor Porter and Mr. Philander were immersed in an absorbing discussion of some weighty scientific problem. Esmeralda dozed in the kitchen, and Clayton, heavy-eyed after a sleepless night, threw himself down upon the couch in the living room and soon dropped into a fitful slumber.

To the east the black smoke clouds rose higher into the heavens, suddenly they eddied, and then commenced to drift rapidly toward the west.

On and on they came. The inmates of the tenant house were gone, for it was market day, and none was there to see the rapid approach of the fiery demon.

Soon the flames had spanned the road to the south and cut off Canler's return. A little fluctuation of the wind now carried the path of the forest fire to the north, then blew back and the flames nearly stood still as though held in leash by some master hand.

Suddenly, out of the northeast, a great black car came careening down the road.

With a jolt it stopped before the cottage, and a black-haired giant leaped out to run up onto the porch. Without a pause he rushed into the house. On the couch lay Clayton. The man started in surprise, but with a bound was at the side of the sleeping man.

Shaking him roughly by the shoulder, he cried:

"My God, Clayton, are you all mad here? Don't you know you are nearly surrounded by fire? Where is Miss Porter?"

Clayton sprang to his feet. He did not recognize the man, but he understood the words and was upon the veranda in a bound.

"Scott!" he cried, and then, dashing back into the house, "Jane! Jane! where are you?"

In an instant Esmeralda, Professor Porter, and Mr. Philander had joined the two men.

"Where is Miss Jane?" cried Clayton, seizing Esmeralda by the shoulders and shaking her roughly.

"Oh, Gaberelle, Mister Clayton, she done gone for a walk."

"Hasn't she come back yet?" and, without waiting for a reply, Clayton dashed out into the yard, followed by the others.

"Which way did she go?" cried the black-haired giant of Esmeralda.

"Down that road," cried the frightened woman, pointing toward the south where a mighty wall of roaring flames shut out the view.

"Put these people in the other car," shouted the stranger to Clayton. "I saw one as I drove up—and get them out of here by the north road.

"Leave my car here. If I find Miss Porter we shall need it. If I don't, no one will need it. Do as I say," as Clayton hesitated, and then they saw the lithe figure bound away cross the clearing toward the northwest where the forest still stood, untouched by flame.

In each rose the unaccountable feeling that a great responsibility had been raised from their shoulders; a kind of implicit confidence in the power of the stranger to save Jane Porter if she could be saved.

"Who was that?" asked Professor Porter.

"I do not know," replied Clayton. "He called me by name and he knew Jane, for he asked for her. And he called Esmeralda by name."

"There was something most startling familiar about him," exclaimed Mr. Philander, "And yet, bless me, I know I never saw him before."

"Tut, tut!" cried Professor Porter. "Most remarkable! Who could it have been, and why do I feel that Jane is safe, now that he has set out in search of her?"

"I can't tell you, Professor," said Clayton soberly, "but I know I have the same uncanny feeling."

"But come," he cried, "we must get out of here ourselves, or we shall be shut off," and the party hastened toward Clayton's car.

When Jane Porter turned to retrace her steps homeward, she was alarmed to note how near the smoke of the forest fire seemed, and as she hastened onward her alarm became almost a panic when she perceived that the rushing flames were rapidly forcing their way between herself and the cottage.

At length she was compelled to turn into the dense thicket and attempt to force her way to the west in an effort to circle around the flames and regain her home.

In a short time the futility of her attempt became apparent and then her one hope lay in retracing her steps to the road and flying for her life to the south toward the town.

The twenty minutes that it took her to regain the road was all that had been needed to cut off her retreat as effectually as her advance had been cut off before.

A short run down the road brought her to a horrified stand, for there before her was another wall of flame. An arm of the parent conflagration had shot out a half mile south of its mate to embrace this tiny strip of road in its implacable clutches.

Jane Porter knew that it was useless again to attempt to force her way through the undergrowth.

She had tried it once, and failed. Now she realized that it would be but a matter of minutes ere the whole space between the enemy on the north and the enemy on the south would be a seething mass of billowing flames.

Calmly the girl kneeled down in the dust of the roadway and prayed to her Maker to give her strength to meet her fate bravely, and to deliver her father and her friends from death.

She did not think to pray for deliverance for herself; for she knew there was no hope—not even God could save her now.

Suddenly she heard her name being called aloud through the forest:

"Jane! Jane Porter!" It rang strong and clear, but in a strange voice.

"Here!" she called in reply. "Here! In the roadway!"

Then through the branches of the trees she saw a figure swinging with the speed of a squirrel.

A veering of the wind blew a cloud of smoke about them and she could no longer see the man who was speeding toward her, but suddenly she felt a great arm about her. Then she was lifted up, and she felt the rushing of the wind and the occasional brush of a branch as she was borne along.

She opened her eyes.

Far below her lay the undergrowth and the hard earth.

About her was the waving foliage of the forest.

From tree to tree swung the giant figure which bore her, and it seemed to Jane that she was living over in a dream the experience that had been hers in that far African jungle.

Oh, if it were but the same man who had borne her so swiftly through the tangled verdure on that other day; but that were impossible. Yet who else in all the world was there with the strength and agility to do what this man was now doing?

She stole a sudden glance at the face close to hers, and then she gave a little frightened gasp—it was he!

"My man!" she murmured, "No, it is the delirium which precedes death."

She must have spoken aloud, for the eyes that bent occasionally to hers lighted with a smile.

"Yes, your man, Jane Porter. Your savage, primeval man come out of the jungle to claim his mate—the woman who ran away from him," he added almost fiercely.

"I did not run away," she whispered. "I would only consent to leave when they had waited a week for you to return."

They had come to a point beyond the fire now, and he had turned back to the clearing.

Side by side they were walking toward the cottage. The wind had changed once more and the fire was burning back upon itself—another hour like that and it would be burned out.

"Why did you not return?" she asked.

"I was nursing d'Arnot. He was badly wounded."

"Ah, I knew it!" she exclaimed.

"They said you had gone to join the local villagers—that they were your people."

He laughed.

"But you did not believe them, Jane?"

"No—what shall I call you?" she asked. "What is your name?"

"I was Tarzan of the Apes when you first knew me," he said.

"Tarzan of the Apes!" she cried—"and that was your note I answered when I left?"

"Yes, whose did you think it was?"

"I did not know; only that it could not be yours, for Tarzan of the Apes had written in English, and you could not understand a word of any language."

Again he laughed.

"It is a long story, but it was I who wrote what I could not speak—and now d'Arnot has made matters worse by teaching me to speak French instead of English.

"Come," he added, "jump into my car, we must overtake your father, they are only a little way ahead."

As they drove along, he said:

"Then when you said in your note to Tarzan of the Apes that you loved another—you might have meant me?"

"I might have," she answered, simply.

"But in Baltimore—oh, how I have searched for you—they told me you would possibly be married by now. That a man named Canler had come up here to wed you. Is that true?"

"Yes."

"Do you love him?"

"No."

"Do you love me?"

She buried her face in her hands.

"I am promised to another. I cannot answer you, Tarzan of the Apes," she cried.

"You have answered. Now, tell me why you would marry one you do not love."

"My father owes him money."

Suddenly there came back to Tarzan the memory of the letter he had read—and the name Robert Canler and the hinted trouble which he had been unable to understand then.

He smiled.

"If your father had not lost the treasure you would not feel forced to keep your promise to this man Canler?"

"I could ask him to release me."

"And if he refused?"

"I have given my promise."

He was silent for a moment. The car was plunging along the uneven road at a reckless pace, for the fire showed threateningly at their right, and another change of the wind might sweep it on with raging fury across this one avenue of escape.

Finally they passed the danger point, and Tarzan reduced their speed.

"Suppose I should ask him?" ventured Tarzan.

"He would scarcely accede to the demand of a stranger," said the girl. "Especially one who wanted me himself."

"Terkoz did," said Tarzan, grimly.

Jane Porter shuddered and looked fearfully up at the giant figure beside her, for she knew that he meant the great anthropoid he had killed in her defense.

"This is not an African jungle," she said. "You are no longer a savage beast. You are a gentleman, and gentlemen do not kill in cold blood."

"I am still a wild beast at heart," he said, in a low voice, as though to himself.

Again they were silent for a time.

"Jane Porter," said the man, at length, "if you were free, would you marry me?"

She did not reply at once, but he waited patiently.

The girl was trying to collect her thoughts.

What did she know of this strange creature at her side? What did he know of himself? Who was he? Who, his parents?

Why, his very name echoed his mysterious origin and his savage life.

He had no name. Could she be happy with this jungle waif? Could she find anything in common with a husband whose life had been spent in the treetops of an African wilderness, frolicking and fighting with fierce anthropoids; tearing his food from the quivering flank of fresh-killed prey, sinking his strong teeth into raw flesh, and tearing away his portion while his mates growled and fought about him for their share?

Could he ever rise to her social sphere? Could she bear to think of sinking to his? Would either be happy in such a horrible misalliance?

"You do not answer," he said. "Do you shrink from wounding me?"

"I do not know what answer to make," said Jane Porter sadly. "I do not know my own mind."

"You do not love me, then?" he asked, in a level tone.

"Do not ask me. You will be happier without me. You were never meant for the formal restrictions and conventionalities of society—civilization would become irksome to you, and in a little while you would long for the freedom of your old life—a life to which I am as totally unfitted as you to mine."

"I think I understand you," he replied quietly. "I shall not urge you, for I would rather see you happy than to be happy myself. I see now that you could not be happy with—an ape."

There was just the faintest tinge of bitterness in his voice.

"Don't," she remonstrated. "Don't say that. You do not understand."

But before she could go on a sudden turn in the road brought them into the midst of a little hamlet.

Before them stood Clayton's car surrounded by the party he had brought from the cottage.

CHAPTER TWENTY-EIGHT
CONCLUSION

AT THE SIGHT OF JANE PORTER, cries of relief and delight broke from every lip, and as Tarzan's car stopped beside the other, Professor Porter caught his daughter in his arms.

For a moment no one noticed Tarzan, sitting silently in his seat.

Clayton was the first to remember, and, turning, held out his hand.

"How can we ever thank you?" he exclaimed. "You have saved us all. You called me by name at the cottage, but I do not seem to recall yours, though there is something very familiar about you. It is as though I had known you well under very different conditions a long time ago."

Tarzan smiled as he took the proffered hand.

"You are quite right, Monsieur Clayton," he said, in French. "You will pardon me if I do not speak to you in English. I am just learning it, and while I understand it fairly well I speak it very poorly."

"But who are you?" insisted Clayton, speaking in French this time himself.

"Tarzan of the Apes."

Clayton started back in surprise.

"By jove!" he exclaimed. "It is true."

And Professor Porter and Mr. Philander pressed forward to add their thanks to Clayton's, and to voice their surprise and pleasure at seeing their jungle friend so far from his savage home.

The party now entered the modest little hostelry, where Clayton soon made arrangements for their entertainment.

They were sitting in the little, stuffy parlor when the distant chugging of an approaching automobile caught their attention.

Mr. Philander, who was sitting near the window, looked out as the car drew in sight, finally stopping beside the other automobiles.

"Bless me!" said Mr. Philander, a shade of annoyance in his tone. "It is Mr. Canler. I had hoped, er—I had thought or—er—how very happy we should be that he was not caught in the fire," he ended lamely.

"Tut, tut! Mr. Philander," said Professor Porter. "Tut, tut! I have often admonished my pupils to count ten before speaking. Were I you, Mr. Philander, I should count at least a thousand, and then maintain a discreet silence."

"Bless me, yes!" acquiesced Mr. Philander. "But who is the clerical-appearing gentleman with him?"

Jane Porter blanched.

Clayton moved uneasily in his chair.

Professor Porter removed his spectacles nervously, and breathed upon them, but replaced them on his nose without wiping.

The ubiquitous Esmeralda grunted.

Only Tarzan did not comprehend.

Presently Robert Canler burst into the room.

"Thank God!" he cried. "I feared the worst, until I saw your car, Clayton. I was cut off on the south road and had to go away back to town, and then strike east to this road. I thought we'd never reach the cottage."

No one seemed to enthuse much. Tarzan eyed Robert Canler as Sabor eyes her prey.

Jane Porter glanced at him and coughed nervously.

"Mr. Canler," she said, "this is Monsieur Tarzan, an old friend."

Canler turned and extended his hand. Tarzan rose and bowed as only d'Arnot could have taught a gentleman to do it, but he did not seem to see Canler's hand.

Nor did Canler appear to notice the oversight.

"This is the Reverend Mr. Tousley, Jane," said Canler, turning to the clerical party behind him. "Mr. Tousley, Miss Porter."

Mr. Tousley bowed and beamed.

Canler introduced him to the others.

"We can have the ceremony at once, Jane," said Canler. "Then you and I can catch the midnight train in town."

Tarzan understood the plan instantly. He glanced out of half-closed eyes at Jane Porter but he did not move.

The girl hesitated. The room was tense with the silence of taut nerves.

All eyes turned toward Jane Porter, awaiting her reply.

"Can't we wait a few days?" she asked. "I am all unstrung. I have been through so much today."

Canler felt the hostility that emanated from each member of the party. It made him angry.

"We have waited as long as I intend to wait," he said roughly. "You have promised to marry me. I shall be played with no longer. I have the license and here is the preacher. Come, Mr. Tousley; come, Jane. There are witnesses aplenty—more than enough," he added with a disagreeable inflection; and taking Jane Porter by the arm, he started to lead her toward the waiting minister.

But scarcely had he taken a single step ere a heavy hand closed upon his arm with a grip of steel.

Another hand shot to his throat and in a moment he was being shaken high above the floor, as a cat might shake a mouse.

Jane Porter turned in horrified surprise toward Tarzan.

And, as she looked into his face, she saw the crimson band upon his forehead that she had seen that other day in far distant Africa, when Tarzan of the Apes had closed in mortal combat with the great anthropoid—Terkoz.

She knew that murder lay in that savage heart, and with a little cry of horror she sprang forward to plead with the ape-man. But her fears were more for Tarzan than for Canler. She realized the stern retribution which justice metes to the murderer.

Before she could reach them, however, Clayton had jumped to Tarzan's side and attempted to drag Canler from his grasp.

With a single sweep of one mighty arm the Englishman was hurled across the room, and then Jane laid a firm white hand upon Tarzan's wrist, and looked up into his eyes.

"For my sake," she said.

The grasp upon Canler's throat relaxed.

Tarzan looked down into the beautiful face before him.

"Do you wish this to live?" he asked in surprise.

"I do not wish him to die at your hands, my friend," she replied. "I do not wish you to become a murderer."

Tarzan removed his hand from Canler's throat.

"Do you release her from her promise?" he asked. "It is the price of your life."

Canler, gasping for breath, nodded.

"Will you go away and never molest her further?"

Again the man nodded his head, his face distorted by fear of the death that had been so close.

Tarzan released him, and Canler staggered toward the door. In another moment he was gone, and the terror-stricken preacher with him.

Tarzan turned toward Jane.

"May I speak with you for a moment, alone," he asked.

The girl nodded and started toward the door leading to the narrow veranda of the little hotel. She passed out to await Tarzan and so did not hear the conversation which followed.

"Wait," cried Professor Porter, as Tarzan was about to follow.

The professor had been stricken dumb with surprise by the rapid developments of the past few minutes.

"Before we go further, sir, I should like an explanation of the events which have just transpired. By what right, sir, did you interfere between my daughter and Mr. Canler? I had promised him her hand, sir, and regardless of our personal likes or dislikes, sir, that promise must be kept."

"I interfered, Professor Porter," replied Tarzan, "because your daughter does not love Mr. Canler—she does not wish to marry him. That is enough for me to know."

"You do not know what you have done," said Professor Porter. "Now he will doubtless refuse to marry her."

"He most certainly will," said Tarzan, emphatically.

"And further," added Tarzan, "you need not fear that your pride will suffer, Professor Porter, for you will be able to pay the Canler person what you owe him the moment you reach home."

"Tut, tut, sir!" exclaimed Professor Porter. "What do you mean, sir?"

"Your treasure has been found," said Tarzan.

"What—what is that you are saying?" cried the professor. "You are mad, man. It cannot be."

"It is, though. It was I who stole it, not knowing either its value or to whom it belonged. I saw the sailors bury it, and, apelike, I had to dig it up and bury it again elsewhere. When d'Arnot told me what it was and what it meant to you I returned to the jungle and recovered it. It had caused so much crime and suffering and sorrow that d'Arnot thought it best not to attempt to bring the treasure itself on here, as had been my intention, so I have brought a letter of credit instead.

"Here it is, Professor Porter," and Tarzan drew an envelope from his pocket and handed it to the astonished professor, "two hundred and forty-one thousand dollars. The treasure was most carefully appraised by experts, but lest there should be any question in your mind, d'Arnot himself bought it and is holding it for you, should you prefer the treasure to the credit."

"To the already great burden of the obligations we owe you, sir," said Professor Porter, with trembling voice, "is now added this greatest of all services. You have given me the means to save my honor."

Clayton, who had left the room a moment after Canler, now returned.

"Pardon me," he said. "I think we had better try to reach town before dark and take the first train out of this forest. A native just rode by from the north, who reports that the fire is moving slowly in this direction."

This announcement broke up further conversation, and the entire party went out to the waiting automobiles.

Clayton, with Jane Porter, the professor and Esmeralda occupied Clayton's car, while Tarzan took Mr. Philander in with him.

"Bless me!" exclaimed Mr. Philander, as the car moved off after Clayton's machine. "Who would ever have thought it possible! The last time I saw you you were a veritable wild man, skipping about among the branches of a tropical African forest, and now you are driving me along a Wisconsin road in a French automobile. Bless me! But it is most remarkable."

"Yes," assented Tarzan, and then, after a pause, "Mr. Philander, do you recall any of the details of the finding and burying of three skeletons found in my cabin beside that African jungle?"

"Very distinctly, sir, very distinctly," replied Mr. Philander.

"Was there anything peculiar about any of those skeletons?"

Mr. Philander eyed Tarzan narrowly.

"Why do you ask?"

"It means a great deal to me to know," replied Tarzan. "Your answer may clear up a mystery. It can do no worse, at any rate, than to leave it still a mystery. I have been entertaining a theory concerning those skeletons for the past two months, and I want you to answer my question to the best of your knowledge—were the three skeletons you buried all human skeletons?"

"No," said Mr. Philander, "the smallest one, the one found in the crib, was the skeleton of an anthropoid ape."

"Thank you," said Tarzan.

In the car ahead, Jane Porter was thinking fast and furiously. She had felt the purpose for which Tarzan had asked a few words with her, and she knew that she must be prepared to give him an answer in the very near future.

He was not the sort of person one could put off, and somehow that very thought made her wonder if she did not really fear him.

And could she love where she feared?

She realized the spell that had been upon her in the depths of that far-off jungle, but there was no spell of enchantment now in prosaic Wisconsin.

Nor did the immaculate young Frenchman appeal to the primal woman in her, as had the stalwart forest god.

Did she love him? She did not know—now.

She glanced at Clayton out of the corner of her eye. Was not here a man trained in the same school of environment in which she had been trained—a man with social position and culture such as she had been taught to consider as the prime essentials to congenial association?

Did not her best judgment point to this young English nobleman, whose love she knew to be of the sort a civilized woman should crave, as the logical mate for such as herself?

Could she love Clayton? She could see no reason why she could not. Jane was not coldly calculating by nature, but training, environment, and heredity had all combined to teach her to reason even in matters of the heart.

That she had been carried off her feet by the strength of the young giant when his great arms were about her in the distant African forest, and again today, in the Wisconsin woods, seemed to her only attributable to a temporary mental reversion to type on her part—to the psychological appeal of the primeval man to the primeval woman in her nature.

If he should never touch her again, she reasoned, she would never feel attracted toward him. She had not loved him, then. It had been nothing more than a passing hallucination, super-induced by excitement and by personal contact.

Excitement would not always mark their future relations, should she marry him, and the power of personal contact eventually would be dulled by familiarity.

Again she glanced at Clayton. He was very handsome and every inch a gentleman. She should be very proud of such a husband.

And then he spoke—a minute sooner or a minute later might have made all the difference in the world to three lives—but chance stepped in and pointed out to Clayton the psychological moment.

"You are free now, Jane," he said. "Won't you say yes—I will devote my life to making you very happy."

"Yes," she whispered.

That evening in the little waiting room at the station Tarzan caught Jane Porter alone for a moment.

"You are free now, Jane," he said, "and I have come across the ages out of the dim and distant past from the lair of the primeval man to claim you—for your sake I have become a civilized man—for your sake I have crossed oceans and continents—for your sake I will be whatever you will me to be. I can make you happy, Jane, in the life you know and love best. Will you marry me?"

For the first time she realized the depths of the man's love—all that he had accomplished in so short a time solely for love of her. Turning her head she buried her face in her arms.

What had she done? Because she had been afraid she might succumb to the pleas of this giant, she had burned her bridges behind her—in her groundless apprehension that she might make a terrible mistake, she had made a worse one.

And then she told him all—told him the truth word by word, without attempting to shield herself or condone her error.

"What can we do?" he asked. "You have admitted that you love me. You know that I love you; but I do not know the ethics of society by which you are governed. I shall leave the decision to you, for you know best what will be for your eventual welfare."

"I cannot tell him, Tarzan," she said. "He too, loves me, and he is a good man. I could never face you nor any other honest person if I repudiated my promise to Mr. Clayton. I shall have to keep it—and you must help me bear the burden, though we may not see each other again after tonight."

The others were entering the room now and Tarzan turned toward the little window.

But he saw nothing outside—within he saw a patch of greensward surrounded by a matted mass of gorgeous tropical plants and flowers, and, above, the waving foliage of mighty trees, and, over all, the blue of an equatorial sky.

In the center of the greensward a young woman sat upon a little mound of earth, and beside her sat a young giant. They ate pleasant fruit and looked into each other's eyes and smiled. They were very happy, and they were all alone.

His thoughts were broken in upon by the station agent who entered asking if there was a gentleman by the name of Tarzan in the party.

"I am Monsieur Tarzan," said the ape-man.

"Here is a message for you, forwarded from Baltimore; it is a cablegram from Paris."

Tarzan took the envelope and tore it open. The message was from d'Arnot.

It read:

Fingerprints prove you Greystoke. Congratulations.

D'Arnot.

As Tarzan finished reading, Clayton entered and came toward him with extended hand.

Here was the man who had Tarzan's title, and Tarzan's estates, and was going to marry the woman whom Tarzan loved—the woman who loved Tarzan. A single word from Tarzan would make a great difference in this man's life.

It would take away his title and his lands and his castles, and—it would take them away from Jane Porter also.

"I say, old man," cried Clayton, "I haven't had a chance to thank you for all you've done for us. It seems as though you had your hands full saving our lives in Africa and here.

"I'm awfully glad you came on here. We must get better acquainted. I often thought about you, you know, and the remarkable circumstances of your environment.

"If it's any of my business, how the devil did you ever get into that bally jungle?"

"I was born there," said Tarzan, quietly. "My mother was an Ape, and of course she couldn't tell me much about it. I never knew who my father was."*

---

*The further adventures of Tarzan, and what came of his noble act of self-renunciation, are told in *The Return of Tarzan*, now available in the Edgar Rice Burroughs Authorized Library.

AT THE
EARTH'S CORE
JUSKO

I had selected my longest arrow, and with all my strength had bent the bow until the very tip of the shaft rested upon the thumb of my left hand, and then as the great creature darted toward us I let drive straight for that tough breast...

Contents

PROLOGUE

IN THE FIRST PLACE PLEASE BEAR IN MIND that I do not expect you to believe this story. Nor could you wonder had you witnessed a recent experience of mine when, in the armor of blissful and stupendous ignorance, I gaily narrated the gist of it to a Fellow of the Royal Geological Society on the occasion of my last trip to London.

You would surely have thought that I had been detected in no less a heinous crime than the purloining of the Crown Jewels from the Tower, or putting poison in the coffee of His Majesty the King.

The erudite gentleman in whom I confided congealed before I was half through—it is all that saved him from exploding—and my dreams of an Honorary Fellowship, gold medals, and a niche in the Hall of Fame faded into the thin, cold air of his arctic atmosphere.

But I believe the story, and so would you, and so would the learned Fellow of the Royal Geological Society, had you and he heard it from the lips of the man who told it to me. Had you seen, as I did, the fire of truth in those gray eyes; had you felt the ring of sincerity in that quiet voice; had you realized the pathos of it all—you, too, would believe. You would not have needed the final ocular proof that I had—the weird rhamphorhynchus-like creature which he had brought back with him from the inner world.

I came upon him quite suddenly, and no less unexpectedly, upon the rim of the great Sahara Desert. He was standing before a goatskin tent amidst a clump of date palms within a tiny oasis. Close by was an Arab douar of some eight or ten tents.

I had come down from the north to hunt lion. My party consisted of a dozen children of the desert. As we approached the little clump of verdure I saw the man come from his tent and with hand-shaded eyes peer intently at us. At sight of me he advanced rapidly to meet us.

"May the good Lord be praised!" he cried. "I have been watching you for hours, hoping against hope. Tell me the date. What year is it?"

And when I had told him he staggered as though he had been struck full in the face, so that he was compelled to grasp my stirrup leather for support.

"It cannot be!" he cried after a moment. "It cannot be! Tell me that you are mistaken, or that you are but joking."

"I am telling you the truth, my friend," I replied. "Why should I deceive a stranger, or attempt to, in so simple a matter as the date?"

For some time he stood in silence, with bowed head.

"Ten years!" he murmured, at last, "Ten years, and I thought that at the most it could be scarce more than one!"

That night he told me his story—the story that I give you here as nearly in his own words as I can recall them.

CHAPTER ONE
TOWARD THE ETERNAL FIRES

I WAS BORN IN CONNECTICUT about thirty years ago. My name is David Innes. My father was a wealthy mine owner. When I was nineteen he died. All his property was to be mine when I had attained my majority—provided that I had devoted the two years intervening in close application to the great business I was to inherit.

I did my best to fulfil the last wishes of my parent—not because of the inheritance, but because I loved and honored my father. For six months I toiled in the mines and in the counting rooms, for I wished to know every minute detail of the business.

Then Perry interested me in his invention. He was an old fellow who had devoted the better part of a long life to the perfection of a mechanical subterranean prospector. As relaxation he studied paleontology. I looked over his plans, listened to his arguments, inspected his working model—and then, convinced, I advanced the funds necessary to construct a full-sized, practical prospector.

I shall not go into the details of its construction—it lies out there in the desert now—about two miles from here. Tomorrow you may care to ride out and see it. Roughly, it is a steel cylinder a hundred feet long, and jointed so that it may turn and twist through solid rock if need be. At one end is a mighty revolving drill operated by an engine which Perry said generated more power to the cubic inch than any other engine did to the cubic foot. I remember that he used to claim that that invention alone would make us fabulously wealthy—we were going to make the whole thing public after the successful issue of our first secret trial—but Perry never returned from that trial trip, and I only after ten years.

I recall as it were but yesterday the night of that momentous occasion upon which we were to test the practicality of that wondrous invention. It was near midnight when we repaired to the lofty tower in which Perry had constructed his "iron mole" as he was wont to call the thing. The great nose rested upon the bare earth of the floor. We passed through the doors into the outer jacket, secured them, and then passing on into the cabin, which contained the controlling mechanism within the inner tube, switched on the electric lights.

Perry looked to his generator; to the great tanks that held the life-giving chemicals with which he was to manufacture fresh air to replace that which we consumed in breathing; to his instruments for recording temperatures, speed, distance, and for examining the materials through which we were to pass.

He tested the steering device, and overlooked the mighty cogs which transmitted its marvelous velocity to the giant drill at the nose of his strange craft.

Our seats, into which we strapped ourselves, were so arranged upon transverse bars that we would be upright whether the craft were ploughing her way downward into the bowels of the earth, or running horizontally along some great seam of coal, or rising vertically toward the surface again.

At length all was ready. Perry bowed his head in prayer. For a moment we were silent, and then the old man's hand grasped the starting lever. There was a frightful roaring beneath us—the giant frame trembled and vibrated—there was a rush of sound as the loose earth passed up through the hollow space between the inner and outer jackets to be deposited in our wake. We were off!

The noise was deafening. The sensation was frightful. For a full minute neither of us could do aught but cling with the proverbial desperation of the drowning man to the handrails of our swinging seats. Then Perry glanced at the thermometer.

"Gad!" he cried, "it cannot be possible—quick! What does the distance meter read?"

That and the speedometer were both on my side of the cabin, and as I turned to take a reading from the former I could see Perry muttering.

"Ten degrees rise—it cannot be possible!" and then I saw him tug frantically upon the steering wheel.

As I finally found the tiny needle in the dim light I translated Perry's evident excitement, and my heart sank within me. But when I spoke I hid the fear which haunted me.

"It will be seven hundred feet, Perry," I said, "by the time you can turn her into the horizontal."

"You'd better lend me a hand then, my boy," he replied, "for I cannot budge her out of the vertical alone. God give that our combined strength may be equal to the task, for else we are lost."

I wormed my way to the old man's side with never a doubt but that the great wheel would yield on the instant to the power of my young and vigorous muscles. Nor was my belief mere vanity, for always had my physique been the envy and despair of my fellows. And for that very reason it had waxed even greater than nature had intended, since my natural pride in my great strength had led me to care for and develop my body and my muscles by every means within my power. What with boxing, football, and baseball, I had been in training since childhood.

And so it was with the utmost confidence that I laid hold of the huge iron rim; but though I threw every ounce of my strength into it, my best effort was as unavailing as Perry's had been—the thing would not budge—the grim, insensate, horrible thing that was holding us upon the straight road to death!

At length I gave up the useless struggle, and without a word returned to my seat. There was no need for words—at least none that I could imagine, unless Perry desired to pray. And I was quite sure that he would, for he never left an opportunity neglected where he might sandwich in a prayer. He prayed when he arose in the morning, he prayed before he ate, he prayed when he had finished eating, and before he went to bed at night he prayed again. In between he often found excuses to pray even when the provocation seemed rather far-fetched to my worldly eyes—now that he was about to die I felt positive that I should witness a perfect orgy of prayer—if one may allude with such a simile to so solemn an act.

But to my astonishment I discovered that with death staring him in the face Abner Perry was transformed into a new being. From his lips there flowed—not prayer—but a clear and limpid stream of undiluted profanity, and it was all directed at that quietly stubborn piece of unyielding mechanism.

"I should think, Perry," I chided, "that a man of your professed religiousness would rather be at his prayers than cursing in the presence of imminent death."

"Death!" he cried. "Death is it that appalls you? That is nothing by comparison with the loss the world must suffer. Why, David, within this iron cylinder we have demonstrated possibilities that science has scarce dreamed. We have harnessed a new principle, and with it animated a piece of steel with the power of ten thousand men. That two lives will be snuffed out is nothing to the world calamity that entombs in the bowels of the earth the discoveries that I have made and proved in the successful construction of the thing that is now carrying us farther and farther toward the eternal central fires."

I am frank to admit that for myself I was much more concerned with our own immediate future than with any problematical loss which the world might be about to suffer. The world was at least ignorant of its bereavement, while to me it was a real and terrible actuality.

"What can we do?" I asked, hiding my perturbation beneath the mask of a low and level voice.

"We may stop here, and die of asphyxiation when our atmosphere tanks are empty," replied Perry, "or we may continue on with the slight hope that we may later sufficiently deflect the prospector from the vertical to carry us along the arc of a great circle which must eventually return us to the surface. If we succeed in so doing before we reach the higher internal temperature we may even yet survive. There would seem to me to be about one chance in several million that we shall succeed—otherwise we shall die more quickly but no more surely than as though we sat supinely waiting for the torture of a slow and horrible death."

I glanced at the thermometer. It registered 110 degrees. While we were talking the mighty iron mole had bored its way over a mile into the rock of the earth's crust.

"Let us continue on, then," I replied. "It should soon be over at this rate. You never intimated that the speed of this thing would be so high, Perry. Didn't you know it?"

"No," he answered. "I could not figure the speed exactly, for I had no instrument for measuring the mighty power of my generator. I reasoned, however, that we should make about five hundred yards an hour."

"And we are making seven miles an hour," I concluded for him, as I sat with my eyes upon the distance meter. "How thick is the earth's crust, Perry?" I asked.

"There are almost as many conjectures as to that as there are geologists," was his answer. "One estimates it thirty miles, because the internal heat, increasing at the rate of about one degree to each sixty to seventy feet depth, would be sufficient to fuse the most refractory substances at that distance beneath the surface. Another finds that the phenomena of precession and nutation require that the earth, if not entirely solid, must at least have a shell not less than eight hundred to a thousand miles in thickness. So there you are. You may take your choice."

"And if it should prove solid?" I asked.

"It will be all the same to us in the end, David," replied Perry. "At the best our oil fuel will suffice to carry us but three or four days, while our atmosphere cannot last to exceed three. Neither, then, is sufficient to bear us in safety through eight thousand miles of rock to the antipodes."

"If the crust is of sufficient thickness we shall come to a final stop between six and seven hundred miles beneath the earth's surface; but during the last hundred and fifty miles of our journey we shall be corpses. Am I correct?" I asked.

"Quite correct, David. Are you frightened?"

"I do not know. It all has come so suddenly that I scarce believe that either of us realizes the real terrors of our position. I feel that I should be reduced to panic; but yet I am not. I imagine that the shock has been so great as to partially stun our sensibilities."

Again I turned to the thermometer. The mercury was rising with less rapidity. It was now but 140 degrees, although we had penetrated to a depth of nearly four miles. I told Perry, and he smiled.

"We have shattered one theory at least," was his only comment, and then he returned to his self-assumed occupation of fluently cursing the steering wheel. I once heard a pirate swear, but his best efforts would have seemed like those of a tyro alongside of Perry's masterful and scientific imprecations.

Once more I tried my hand at the wheel, but I might as well have essayed to swing the earth itself. At my suggestion Perry stopped the generator, and as we came to rest I again threw all my strength into a supreme effort to move the thing even a hair's breadth—but the results were as barren as when we had been traveling at top speed.

I shook my head sadly, and motioned to the starting lever. Perry pulled it toward him, and once again we were plunging downward toward eternity at the rate of seven miles an hour. I sat with my eyes glued to the thermometer and the distance meter. The mercury was rising very slowly now, though even at 145 degrees it was almost unbearable within the narrow confines of our metal prison.

About noon, or twelve hours after our start upon this unfortunate journey, we had bored to a depth of eighty-four miles, at which point the mercury registered 153 degrees F.

Perry was becoming more hopeful, although upon what meager food he sustained his optimism I could not conjecture. From cursing he had turned to singing—I felt that the strain had at last affected his mind. For several hours we had not spoken except as he asked me for the readings of the instruments from time to time, and I announced them. My thoughts were filled with vain regrets. I recalled numerous acts of my past life which I should have been glad to have had a few more years to live down. There was the affair in the Latin Commons at Andover when Calhoun and I had put gunpowder in the stove—and nearly killed one of the masters. And then—but what was the use, I was about to die and atone for all these things and several more. Already the heat was sufficient to give me a foretaste of the hereafter. A few more degrees and I felt that I should lose consciousness.

"What are the readings now, David?" Perry's voice broke in upon my somber reflections.

"Ninety miles and 153 degrees," I replied.

"Gad, but we've knocked that thirty-mile-crust theory into a cocked hat!" he cried gleefully.

"Precious lot of good it will do us," I growled back.

"But, my boy," he continued, "doesn't that temperature reading mean anything to you? Why it hasn't gone up in six miles. Think of it, son!"

"Yes, I'm thinking of it," I answered; "but what difference will it make when our air supply is exhausted whether the temperature is 153 degrees or 153,000? We'll be just as dead, and no one will know the difference, anyhow." But I must admit that for some unaccountable reason the stationary temperature did renew my waning hope. What I hoped for I could not have explained, nor did I try. The very fact, as Perry took pains to explain, of the blasting of several very exact and learned scientific hypotheses made it apparent that we could not know what lay before us within the bowels of the earth, and so we might continue to hope for the best, at least until we were dead—when hope would no longer be essential to our happiness. It was very good, and logical reasoning, and so I embraced it.

At one hundred miles the temperature had *dropped to 152½ degrees*! When I announced it Perry reached over and hugged me.

From then on until noon of the second day it continued to drop until it became as uncomfortably cold as it had been unbearably hot before. At a depth of two hundred and forty miles our nostrils were assailed by almost overpowering ammonia fumes, and the temperature had dropped to *ten below zero*! We suffered nearly two hours of this intense and bitter cold, until at about two hundred and forty-five miles from the surface of the earth we entered a stratum of solid ice, when the mercury quickly rose to 32 degrees. During the next three hours we passed through ten miles of ice, eventually emerging into another series of ammonia-impregnated strata, where the mercury again fell to ten degrees below zero.

Slowly it rose once more until we were convinced that at last we were nearing the molten interior of the earth. At four hundred miles the temperature had reached 152 degrees. Feverishly I watched the thermometer. Slowly it rose. Perry had ceased singing and was at last praying.

Our hopes had received such a deathblow that the gradually increasing heat seemed to our distorted imaginations much greater than it really was. For another hour I saw that pitiless column of mercury rise and rise until at four hundred and ten miles it stood at 153 degrees. Now it was that we began to hang upon those readings in almost breathless anxiety.

One hundred and fifty-three degrees had been the maximum temperature above the ice stratum. Would it stop at this point again, or would it continue its merciless climb? We knew that there was no hope, and yet with the persistence of life itself we continued to hope against practical certainty.

Already the air tanks were at low ebb—there was barely enough of the precious gases to sustain us for another twelve hours. But would we be alive to know or care? It seemed incredible.

At four hundred and twenty miles I took another reading.

"Perry!" I shouted. "Perry, man! She's going down! She's going down! She's 152 degrees again."

"Gad!" he cried. "What can it mean? Can the earth be cold at the center?"

"I do not know, Perry," I answered; "but thank God, if I am to die it shall not be by fire—that is all that I have feared. I can face the thought of any death but that." Down, down went the mercury until it stood as low as it had seven miles from the surface of the earth, and then of a sudden the realization broke upon us that death was very near. Perry was the first to discover it. I saw him fussing with the valves that regulate the air supply. And at the same time I experienced difficulty in breathing. My head felt dizzy—my limbs heavy.

I saw Perry crumple in his seat. He gave himself a shake and sat erect again. Then he turned toward me.

"Good-bye, David," he said, "I guess this is the end," and then he smiled and closed his eyes.

"Good-bye, Perry, and good luck to you," I answered, smiling back at him. But I fought off that awful lethargy. I was very young—I did not want to die.

For an hour I battled against the cruelly enveloping death that surrounded me upon all sides. At first I found that by climbing high into the framework above me I could find more of the precious life-giving elements, and for a while these sustained me. It must have been an hour after Perry had succumbed that I at last came to the realization that I could no longer carry on this unequal struggle against the inevitable.

With my last flickering ray of consciousness I turned mechanically toward the distance meter. It stood at exactly five hundred miles from the earth's surface—and then of a sudden the huge thing that bore us came to a stop. The rattle of hurtling rock through the hollow jacket ceased. The wild racing of the giant drill betokened that it was running loose in *air*—and then another truth flashed upon me. The point of the prospector was *above* us. Slowly it dawned on me that since passing through the ice strata it had been above. We had turned in the ice and sped upward toward the earth's crust. Thank God! We were safe!

I put my nose to the intake pipe through which samples were to have been taken during the passage of the prospector through the earth, and my fondest hopes were realized—a flood of fresh air was pouring into the iron cabin. The reaction left me in a state of collapse, and I lost consciousness.

CHAPTER TWO
A STRANGE WORLD

I WAS UNCONSCIOUS LITTLE MORE THAN AN INSTANT, for as I lunged forward from the crossbeam to which I had been clinging, and fell with a crash to the floor of the cabin, the shock brought me to myself.

My first concern was with Perry. I was horrified at the thought that upon the very threshold of salvation he might be dead. Tearing open his shirt I placed my ear to his breast. I could have cried with relief—his heart was beating quite regularly.

At the water tank I wetted my handkerchief, slapping it smartly across his forehead and face several times. In a moment I was rewarded by the raising of his lids. For a time he lay wide-eyed and quite uncomprehending. Then his scattered wits slowly foregathered, and he sat up sniffing the air with an expression of wonderment upon his face.

"Why, David," he cried at last, "it's air, as sure as I live. Why—why what does it mean? Where in the world are we? What has happened?"

"It means that we're back at the surface all right, Perry," I cried; "but where, I don't know. I haven't opened her up yet. Been too busy reviving you. Lord, man, but you had a close squeak!"

"You say we're back at the surface, David? How can that be? How long have I been unconscious?"

"Not long. We turned in the ice stratum. Don't you recall the sudden whirling of our seats? After that the drill was above us instead of below. We didn't notice it at the time; but I recall it now."

"You mean to say that we turned back in the ice stratum, David? That is not possible. The prospector cannot turn unless its nose is deflected. If the nose were deflected from the outside—by some external force or resistance—the steering wheel within would have moved in response. The steering wheel has not budged, David, since we started. You know that."

I did know it; but here we were with our drill racing in pure air, and copious volumes of it pouring into the cabin.

"We couldn't have turned in the ice stratum, Perry, I know as well as you," I replied; "but the fact remains that we did, for here we are this minute at the surface of the earth again, and I am going out to see just where."

"Better wait till morning, David—it must be midnight now."

I glanced at the chronometer.

"Half after twelve. We have been out seventy-two hours, so it must be midnight. Nevertheless I'm going to have a look at the blessed sky that I had given up all hope of ever seeing again," and so saying I lifted the bars from the inner door, and swung it open. There was quite a quantity of loose material in the jacket, and this I had to remove with a shovel to get at the opposite door in the outer shell.

In a short time I had removed enough of the earth and rock to the floor of the cabin to expose the door beyond. Perry was directly behind me as I threw it open. The upper half was above the surface of the ground. With an expression of surprise I turned and looked at Perry—it was broad daylight without!

"Something seems to have gone wrong either with our calculations or the chronometer," I said. Perry shook his head—there was a strange expression in his eyes.

"Let's have a look beyond that door, David," he cried.

Together we stepped out to stand in silent contemplation of a landscape at once weird and beautiful. Before us a low and level shore stretched down to a silent sea. As far as the eye could reach the surface of the water was dotted with countless tiny isles—some of towering, barren, granitic rock—others resplendent in gorgeous trappings of tropical vegetation, myriad starred with the magnificent splendor of vivid blooms.

Behind us rose a dark and forbidding wood of giant arborescent ferns intermingled with the commoner types of a primeval tropical forest. Huge creepers depended in great loops from tree to tree, dense underbrush overgrew a tangled mass of fallen trunks and branches. Upon the outer verge we could see the same splendid coloring of countless blossoms that glorified the islands, but within the dense shadows all seemed dark and gloomy as the grave.

And upon all the noonday sun poured its torrid rays out of a cloudless sky.

"Where on earth can we be?" I asked, turning to Perry.

For some moments the old man did not reply. He stood with bowed head, buried in deep thought. But at last he spoke.

"David," he said, "I am not so sure that we are *on* earth."

"What do you mean, Perry?" I cried. "Do you think that we are dead, and that this is heaven?"

He smiled, and turning, pointed to the nose of the prospector protruding from the ground at our backs.

"But for that, David, I might believe that we were indeed come to the country beyond the Styx. The prospector renders that theory untenable—it, certainly, could never have gone to heaven. However I am willing to concede that we actually may be in another world from that which we have always known. If we are not *on* earth, there is every reason to believe that we may be *in* it."

"We may have quartered through the earth's crust and come out upon some tropical island of the West Indies," I suggested.

Again Perry shook his head.

"Let us wait and see, David," he replied, "and in the meantime suppose we do a bit of exploring up and down the coast—we may find a native who can enlighten us."

As we walked along the beach Perry gazed long and earnestly across the water. Evidently he was wrestling with a mighty problem.

"David," he said abruptly, "do you perceive anything unusual about the horizon?"

As I looked I began to appreciate the reason for the strangeness of the landscape that had haunted me from the first with an illusive suggestion of the bizarre and unnatural—*there was no horizon*! As far as the eye could reach out the sea continued and upon its bosom floated tiny islands, those in the distance reduced to mere specks; but ever beyond them was the sea, until the impression became quite real that one was *looking up* at the most distant point that the eye could fathom—the distance was lost in the distance. That was all—there was no clear-cut horizontal line marking the dip of the globe below the line of vision.

"A great light is commencing to break on me," continued Perry, taking out his watch. "I believe that I have partially solved the riddle. It is now two o'clock. When we emerged from the prospector the sun was directly above us. Where is it now?"

I glanced up to find the great orb still motionless in the center of the heavens. And such a sun! I had scarcely noticed it before. Fully thrice the size of the sun I had known throughout my life, and apparently so near that the sight of it carried the conviction that one might almost reach up and touch it.

"My God, Perry, where are we?" I exclaimed. "This thing is beginning to get on my nerves."

"I think that I may state quite positively, David," he commenced, "that we are—" but he got no further. From behind us in the vicinity of the prospector there came the most thunderous, awe-inspiring roar that ever had fallen upon my ears. With one accord we turned to discover the author of that fearsome noise.

Had I still retained the suspicion that we were on earth the sight that met my eyes would quite entirely have banished it. Emerging from the forest was a colossal beast which closely resembled a bear. It was fully as large as the largest elephant, and with great forepaws armed with huge claws. Its nose, or snout, depended nearly a foot below its lower jaw, much after the manner of a rudimentary trunk. The giant body was covered by a coat of thick, shaggy hair.

Roaring horribly it came toward us at a ponderous, shuffling trot. I turned toward Perry to suggest that it might be wise to seek other surroundings—the idea had evidently occurred to Perry previously, for he was already a hundred paces away, and with each second his prodigious bounds increased the distance. I had never guessed what latent speed possibilities the old gentleman possessed.

I saw that he was headed toward a little point of the forest which ran out toward the sea not far from where we had been standing, and as the mighty creature, the sight of which had galvanized him into such remarkable action, was forging steadily toward me I set off after Perry, though at a somewhat more decorous pace. It was evident that the massive beast pursuing us was not built for speed, so all that I considered necessary was to gain the trees sufficiently ahead of it to enable me to climb to the safety of some great branch before it came up.

Notwithstanding our danger I could not help but laugh at Perry's frantic capers as he essayed to gain the safety of the lower branches of the trees he now had reached. The stems were bare for a distance of some fifteen feet—at least on those trees which Perry attempted to ascend, for the suggestion of safety carried by the larger of the forest giants had evidently attracted him to them. A dozen times he scrambled up the trunks like a huge cat only to fall back to the ground once more, and with each failure he cast a horrified glance over his shoulder at the oncoming brute, simultaneously emitting terror-stricken shrieks that awoke the echoes of the grim forest.

At length he spied a dangling creeper about the bigness of one's wrist, and when I reached the trees he was racing madly up it, hand over hand. He had almost reached the lowest branch of the tree from which the creeper depended when the thing parted beneath his weight and he fell sprawling at my feet.

The misfortune now was no longer amusing, for the beast was already too close to us for comfort. Seizing Perry by the shoulder I dragged him to his feet, and rushing to a smaller tree—one that he could easily encircle with his arms and legs—I boosted him as far up as I could, and then left him to his fate, for a glance over my shoulder revealed the awful beast almost upon me.

It was the great size of the thing alone that saved me. Its enormous bulk rendered it too slow upon its feet to cope with the agility of my young muscles, and so I was enabled to dodge out of its way and run completely behind it before its slow wits could direct it in pursuit.

The few seconds of grace that this gave me found me safely lodged in the branches of a tree a few paces from that in which Perry had at last found a haven.

Did I say safely lodged? At the time I thought we were quite safe, and so did Perry. He was praying—raising his voice in thanksgiving at our deliverance—and had just completed a sort of paeon of gratitude that the thing couldn't climb a tree when without warning it reared up beneath him on its enormous tail and hind feet, and reached those fearfully armed paws quite to the branch upon which he crouched.

The accompanying roar was all but drowned in Perry's scream of fright, and he came near tumbling headlong into the gaping jaws beneath him, so precipitate was his impetuous haste to vacate the dangerous limb. It was with a deep sigh of relief that I saw him gain a higher branch in safety.

And then the brute did that which froze us both anew with horror. Grasping the tree's stem with his powerful paws he dragged down with all the great weight of his huge bulk and all the irresistible force of those mighty muscles. Slowly, but surely, the stem began to bend toward him.

Inch by inch he worked his paws upward as the tree leaned more and more from the perpendicular. Perry clung chattering in a panic of terror. Higher and higher into the bending and swaying tree he clambered. More and more rapidly was the treetop inclining toward the ground.

I saw now why the great brute was armed with such enormous paws. The use that he was putting them to was precisely that for which nature had intended them. The slothlike creature was herbivorous, and to feed that mighty carcass entire trees must be stripped of their foliage. The reason for its attacking us might easily be accounted for on the supposition of an ugly disposition such as that which the fierce and stupid rhinoceros of Africa possesses. But these were later reflections. At the moment I was too frantic with apprehension on Perry's behalf to consider aught other than a means to save him from the death that loomed so close.

Realizing that I could outdistance the clumsy brute in the open, I dropped from my leafy sanctuary intent only on distracting the thing's attention from Perry long enough to enable the old man to gain the safety of a larger tree. There were many close by which not even the terrific strength of that titanic monster could bend.

As I touched the ground I snatched a broken limb from the tangled mass that matted the junglelike floor of the forest and, leaping unnoticed behind the shaggy back, dealt the brute a terrific blow. My plan worked like magic. From the previous slowness of the beast I had been led to look for no such marvelous agility as he now displayed. Releasing his hold upon the tree he dropped on all fours and at the same time swung his great, wicked tail with a force that would have broken every bone in my body had it struck me; but, fortunately, I had turned to flee at the very instant that I felt my blow land upon the towering back.

As it started in pursuit of me I made the mistake of running along the edge of the forest rather than making for the open beach. In a moment I was knee-deep in rotting vegetation, and the awful thing behind me was gaining rapidly as I floundered and fell in my efforts to extricate myself.

A fallen log gave me an instant's advantage, for climbing upon it I leaped to another a few paces farther on, and in this way was able to keep clear of the mush that carpeted the surrounding ground. But the zigzag course that this necessitated was placing such a heavy handicap upon me that my pursuer was steadily gaining upon me.

Suddenly from behind I heard a tumult of howls, and sharp, piercing barks—much the sound that a pack of wolves raises when in full cry. Involuntarily I glanced backward to discover the origin of this new and menacing note with the result that I missed my footing and went sprawling once more upon my face in the deep muck.

My mammoth enemy was so close by this time that I knew I must feel the weight of one of his terrible paws before I could rise, but to my surprise the blow did not fall upon me. The howling and snapping and barking of the new element which had been infused into the melee now seemed centered quite close behind me, and as I raised myself upon my hands and glanced around I saw what it was that had distracted the *dyryth*, as I afterward learned the thing is called, from my trail.

It was surrounded by a pack of some hundred wolflike creatures—wild dogs they seemed—that rushed growling and snapping in upon it from all sides, so that they sank their white fangs into the slow brute and were away again before it could reach them with its huge paws or sweeping tail.

But these were not all that my startled eyes perceived. Chattering and gibbering through the lower branches of the trees came a company of manlike creatures evidently urging on the dog pack. Their skins were very black, and their features pronounced. The head receded rapidly above the eyes, leaving little or no forehead. Their arms were rather longer and their legs shorter in proportion to the torso than in man, and later I noticed that their great toes protruded at right angles from their feet—because of their arboreal habits, I presume. Behind them trailed long, slender tails which they used in climbing quite as much as they did either their hands or feet.

I had stumbled to my feet the moment that I discovered that the wolf-dogs were holding the dyryth at bay. At sight of me several of the savage creatures left off worrying the great brute to come slinking with bared fangs toward me, and as I turned to run toward the trees again to seek safety among the lower branches, I saw a number of the man-apes leaping and chattering in the foliage of the nearest tree.

Between them and the beasts behind me there was little choice, but at least there was a doubt as to the reception these grotesque parodies on humanity would accord me, while there was none as to the fate which awaited me beneath the grinning fangs of my fierce pursuers.

And so I raced on toward the trees intending to pass beneath that which held the man-things and take refuge in another farther on; but the wolf-dogs were very close behind me—so close that I had despaired of escaping them, when one of the creatures in the tree above swung down headforemost, his tail looped about a great limb, and grasping me beneath my armpits swung me in safety up among his fellows.

There they fell to examining me with the utmost excitement and curiosity. They picked at my clothing, my hair, and my flesh. They turned me about to see if I had a tail, and when they discovered that I was not so equipped they fell into roars of laughter. Their teeth were very large and white and even, except for the upper canines which were a trifle longer than the others—protruding just a bit when the mouth was closed.

When they had examined me for a few moments one of them discovered that my clothing was not a part of me, with the result that garment by garment they tore it from me amidst peals of the wildest laughter. Apelike, they essayed to don the apparel themselves, but their ingenuity was not sufficient to the task and so they gave it up.

In the meantime I had been straining my eyes to catch a glimpse of Perry, but nowhere about could I see him, although the clump of trees in which he had first taken refuge was in full view. I was much exercised by fear that something had befallen him, and though I called his name aloud several times there was no response.

Tired at last of playing with my clothing the creatures threw it to the ground, and catching me, one on either side, by an arm, started off at a most terrifying pace through the treetops. Never have I experienced such a journey before or since—even now I oftentimes awake from a deep sleep haunted by the horrid remembrance of that awful experience.

From tree to tree the agile creatures sprang like flying squirrels, while the cold sweat stood upon my brow as I glimpsed the depths beneath, into which a single misstep on the part of either of my bearers would hurl me. As they bore me along, my mind was occupied with a thousand bewildering thoughts. What had become of Perry? Would I ever see him again? What were the intentions of these half-human things into whose hands I had fallen? Were they inhabitants of the same world into which I had been born? No! It could not be. But yet where else? I had not left that earth—of that I was sure. Still neither could I reconcile the things which I had seen to a belief that I was still in the world of my birth. With a sigh I gave it up.

CHAPTER THREE
A CHANGE OF MASTERS

WE MUST HAVE TRAVELED SEVERAL MILES through the dark and dismal wood when we came suddenly upon a dense village built high among the branches of the trees. As we approached it my escort broke into wild shouting which was immediately answered from within, and a moment later a swarm of creatures of the same strange race as those who had captured me poured out to meet us. Again I was the center of a wildly chattering horde. I was pulled this way and that. Pinched, pounded, and thumped until I was black and blue, yet I do not think that their treatment was dictated by either cruelty or malice—I was a curiosity, a freak, a new plaything, arid their childish minds required the added evidence of all their senses to back up the testimony of their eyes.

Presently they dragged me within the village, which consisted of several hundred rude shelters of boughs and leaves supported upon the branches of the trees. Between the huts, which sometimes formed crooked streets, were dead branches and the trunks of small trees which connected the huts upon one tree to those within adjoining trees; the whole network of huts and pathways forming an almost solid flooring a good fifty feet above the ground.

I wondered why these agile creatures required connecting bridges between the trees, but later when I saw the motley aggregation of half-savage beasts which they kept within their village I realized the necessity for the pathways. There were a number of the same vicious wolf-dogs which we had left worrying the dyryth, and many goatlike animals whose distended udders explained the reason for their presence.

My guard halted before one of the huts into which I was pushed; then two of the creatures squatted down before the entrance—to prevent my escape, doubtless. Though where I should have escaped to I certainly had not the remotest conception.

I had no more than entered the dark shadows of the interior than there fell upon my ears the tones of a familiar voice, in prayer.

"Perry!" I cried. "Dear old Perry! Thank the Lord you are safe."

"David! Can it be possible that you escaped?" And the old man stumbled toward me and threw his arms about me.

He had seen me fall before the dyryth, and then he had been seized by a number of the ape-creatures and borne through the treetops to their village. His captors had been as inquisitive as to his strange clothing as had mine, with the same result. As we looked at each other we could not help but laugh.

"With a tail, David," remarked Perry, "you would make a very handsome ape."

"Maybe we can borrow a couple," I rejoined. "They seem to be quite the thing this season. I wonder what the creatures intend doing with us, Perry. They don't seem really savage. What do you suppose they can be? You were about to tell me where we are when that great hairy frigate bore down upon us—have you really any idea at all?"

"Yes, David," he replied, "I know precisely where we are. We have made a magnificent discovery, my boy! We have proved that the earth is hollow. We have passed entirely through its crust to the inner world." ·

"Perry, you are mad!"

"Not at all, David. For two hundred and fifty miles our prospector bore us through the crust beneath our outer world. At that point it reached the center of gravity of the five-hundred-mile-thick crust. Up to that point we had been descending—direction is, of course, merely relative. Then at the moment that our seats revolved—the thing that made you believe that we had turned about and were speeding upward—we passed the center of gravity and, though we did not alter the direction of our progress, yet we were in reality moving upward—toward the surface of the inner world. Does not the strange fauna and flora which we have seen convince you that you are not in the world of your birth? And the horizon—could it present the strange aspect which we both noted unless we were indeed standing upon the inside surface of a sphere?"

"But the sun, Perry!" I urged. "How in the world can the sun shine through five hundred miles of solid crust?"

"It is not the sun of the outer world that we see here. It is another sun—an entirely different sun—that casts its eternal noonday effulgence upon the face of the inner world. Look at it now, David—if you can see it from the doorway of this hut—and you will see that it is still in the exact center of the heavens. We have been here for many hours—yet it is still noon.

"And withal it is very simple, David. The earth was once a nebulous mass. It cooled, and as it cooled it shrank. At length a thin crust of solid matter formed upon its outer surface—a sort of shell; but within it was partially molten matter and highly expanded gases. As it continued to cool, what happened? Centrifugal force hurled the particles of the nebulous center toward the crust as rapidly as they approached a solid state. You have seen the same principle practically applied in the modern cream separator. Presently there was only a small superheated core of gaseous matter remaining within a huge vacant interior left by the contraction of the cooling gases. The equal attraction of the solid crust from all directions maintained this luminous core in the exact center of the hollow globe. What remains of it is the sun you saw today—a relatively tiny thing at the exact center of the earth. Equally to every part of this inner world it diffuses its perpetual noonday light and torrid heat.

"This inner world must have cooled sufficiently to support animal life long ages after life appeared upon the outer crust, but that the same agencies were at work here is evident from the similar forms of both animal and vegetable creation which we have already seen. Take the great beast which attacked us, for example. Unquestionably a counterpart of the Megatherium of the post-Pliocene period of the outer crust, whose fossilized skeleton has been found in South America."

"But the grotesque inhabitants of this forest?" I urged. "Surely they have no counterpart in the earth's history."

"Who can tell?" he rejoined. "They may constitute the link between ape and man, all traces of which have been swallowed by the countless convulsions which have racked the outer crust, or they may be merely the result of evolution along slightly different lines—either is quite possible."

Further speculation was interrupted by the appearance of several of our captors before the entrance of the hut. Two of them entered and dragged us forth. The perilous pathways and the surrounding trees were filled with the black ape-men, their females, and their young. There was not an ornament, a weapon, or a garment among the lot.

"Quite low in the scale of creation," commented Perry.

"Quite high enough to play the deuce with us, though," I replied. "Now what do you suppose they intend doing with us?"

We were not long in learning. As on the occasion of our trip to the village we were seized by a couple of the powerful creatures and whirled away through the treetops, while about us and in our wake raced a chattering, jibbering, grinning horde of sleek, black ape-things.

Twice my bearers missed their footing, and my heart ceased beating as we plunged toward instant death among the tangled deadwood beneath. But on both occasions those lithe, powerful, tails reached out and found sustaining branches, nor did either of the creatures loosen their grasp upon me. In fact, it seemed that the incidents were of no greater moment to them than would be the stubbing of one's toe at a street crossing in the outer world—they but laughed uproariously and sped on with me.

For some time they continued through the forest—how long I could not guess for I was learning, what was later borne very forcefully to my mind, that time ceases to be a factor the moment means for measuring it cease to exist. Our watches were gone, and we were living beneath a stationary sun. Already I was puzzled to compute the period of time which had elapsed, since we broke through the crust of the inner world. It might be hours, or it might be days—who in the world could tell where it was always noon! By the sun, no time had elapsed—but my judgment told me that we must have been several hours in this strange world.

Presently the forest terminated, and we came out upon a level plain. A short distance before us rose a few low, rocky hills. Toward these our captors urged us, and after a short time led us through a narrow pass into a tiny, circular valley. Here they got down to work, and we were soon convinced that if we were not to die to make a Roman holiday, we were to die for some other purpose. The attitude of our captors altered immediately they entered the natural arena within the rocky hills. Their laughter ceased. Grim ferocity marked their bestial faces—bared fangs menaced us.

We were placed in the center of the amphitheater—the thousand creatures forming a great ring about us. Then a wolf-dog was brought— *hyaenodon* Perry called it—and turned loose with us inside the circle. The thing's body was as large as that of a full-grown mastiff, its legs were short and powerful, and its jaws broad and strong. Dark, shaggy hair covered its back and sides, while its breast and belly were quite white. As it slunk toward us it presented a most formidable aspect with its upcurled lips baring its mighty fangs.

Perry was on his knees, praying. I stooped and picked up a small stone. At my movement the beast veered off a bit and commenced circling us. Evidently it had been a target for stones before. The ape-things were dancing up and down urging the brute on with savage cries, until at last, seeing that I did not throw, he charged us.

At Andover, and later at Yale, I had pitched on winning ball teams. My speed and control must both have been above the ordinary, for I made such a record during my senior year at college that overtures were made to me in behalf of one of the great major-league teams; but in the tightest pinch that ever had confronted me in the past I had never been in such need for control as now.

As I wound up for the delivery, I held my nerves and muscles under absolute command, though the grinning jaws were hurtling toward me at terrific speed. And then I let go, with every ounce of my weight and muscle and science back of that throw. The stone caught the hyaenodon full upon the end of the nose, and sent him bowling over upon his back.

At the same instant a chorus of shrieks and howls arose from the circle of spectators, so that for a moment I thought that the upsetting of their champion was the cause; but in this I soon saw that I was mistaken. As I looked, the ape-things broke in all directions toward the surrounding hills, and then I distinguished the real cause of their perturbation. Behind them, streaming through the pass which leads into the valley, came a swarm of hairy men—gorilla-like creatures armed with spears and hatchets, and bearing long, oval shields.

Like demons they set upon the ape-things, and before them the hy-aenodon, which had now regained its senses and its feet, fled howling with fright. Past us swept the pursued and the pursuers, nor did the hairy ones accord us more than a passing glance until the arena had been emptied of its former occupants. Then they returned to us, and one who seemed to have authority among them directed that we be brought with them.

When we had passed out of the amphitheater onto the great plain we saw a caravan of men and women—human beings like ourselves—and for the first time hope and relief filled my heart, until I could have cried out in the exuberance of my happiness. It is true that they were a half-naked, wild-appearing aggregation; but they at least were fashioned along the same lines as ourselves—there was nothing grotesque or horrible about them as about the other creatures in this strange, weird world.

But as we came closer, our hearts sank once more, for we discovered that the poor wretches were chained neck to neck in a long line, and that the gorilla-men were their guards. With little ceremony Perry and I were chained at the end of the line, and without further ado the interrupted march was resumed.

Up to this time the excitement had kept us both up; but now the tiresome monotony of the long march across the sunbaked plain brought on all the agonies consequent to long-denied sleep. On and on we stumbled beneath that hateful noonday sun. If we fell we were prodded with a sharp spear point. Our companions in chains did not stumble. They strode along proudly erect. Occasionally they would exchange words with one another in a monosyllabic language. They were a noble-appearing race with well-formed heads and perfect physiques. The men were heavily bearded, tall and muscular; the women, smaller and more gracefully molded, with great masses of raven hair caught into loose knots upon their heads. The features of both sexes were well proportioned—there was not a face among them that would have been called even plain if judged by earthly standards. They wore no ornaments; but this I later learned was due to the fact that their captors had stripped them of everything of value. As garmenture the women possessed a single robe of some light-colored, spotted hide, rather similar in appearance to a leopard's skin. This they wore either supported entirely about the waist by a leathern thong, so that it hung partially below the knee on one side, or possibly looped gracefully across one shoulder. Their feet were shod with skin sandals. The men wore loincloths of the hide of some shaggy beast, long ends of which depended before and behind nearly to the ground. In some instances these ends were finished with the strong talons of the beast from which the hides had been taken.

Our guards, whom I already have described as gorilla-like men, were rather lighter in build than a gorilla, but even so they were indeed mighty creatures. Their arms and legs were proportioned more in conformity with human standards, but their entire bodies were covered with shaggy, brown hair, and their faces were quite as brutal as those of the few stuffed specimens of the gorilla which I had seen in the museums at home.

Their only redeeming feature lay in the development of the head above and back of the ears. In this respect they were not one whit less human than we. They were clothed in a sort of tunic of light cloth which reached to the knees. Beneath this they wore only a loincloth of the same material, while their feet were shod with rather heavy sandals apparently made of the thick hide of some mammoth creature of this inner world.

Their arms and necks were encircled by many ornaments of metal—silver predominating—and on their tunics were sewn the heads of tiny reptiles in odd and rather artistic designs. They talked among themselves as they marched along on either side of us, but in a language which I perceived differed from that employed by our fellow prisoners. When they addressed the latter they used what appeared to be a third language, and which I later learned is a mongrel tongue rather analogous to the Pidgin-English of the Chinese coolie.

How far we marched I have no conception, nor has Perry. Both of us were asleep much of the time for hours before a halt was called—then we dropped in our tracks. I say "for hours;" but how may one measure time where time does not exist! When our march commenced the sun stood at zenith, when we halted our shadows still pointed toward nadir. Whether an instant or an eternity of earthly time elapsed who may say! That march may have occupied nine years and eleven months of the ten years that I spent in the inner world, or it may have been accomplished in the fraction of a second—I cannot tell. But this I do know, that since you have told me that ten years have elapsed since I departed from this earth I have lost all respect for time—I am commencing to doubt that such a thing exists other than in the weak, finite mind of man.

CHAPTER FOUR
DIAN THE BEAUTIFUL

WHEN OUR GUARDS AROUSED US FROM SLEEP we were much refreshed. They gave us food. Strips of dried meat it was, but it put new life and strength into us, so that now we too marched with high-held heads, and took noble strides. At least I did, for I was young and proud; but poor Perry hated walking. On earth I had often seen him call a cab to travel a square—he was paying for it now, and his old legs wobbled so that I put my arm about him and half carried him through the balance of those frightful marches.

The country began to change at last, and we wound up out of the level plain through mighty mountains of virgin granite. The tropical verdure of the lowlands was replaced by hardier vegetation, but even here the effects of constant heat and light were apparent in the immensity of the trees and the profusion of foliage and blooms. Crystal streams roared through their rocky channels, fed by the perpetual snows which we could see far above us. Above the snowcapped heights hung masses of heavy clouds. It was these, Perry explained, which evidently served the double purpose of replenishing the melting snows and protecting them from the direct rays of the sun.

By this time we had picked up a smattering of the bastard language in which our guards addressed us, as well as making good headway in the rather charming tongue of our co-captives. Directly ahead of me in the chain gang was a young woman. Three feet of chain linked us together in a forced companionship which I, at least, soon rejoiced in. For I found her a willing teacher, and from her I learned the language of her tribe, and much of the life and customs of the inner world—at least that part of it with which she was familiar.

She told me that she was called Dian the Beautiful, and that she belonged to the tribe of Amoz, which dwells in the cliffs above the Darel Az, or shallow sea.

"How came you here?" I asked her.

"I was running away from Jubal the Ugly One," she answered, as though that was explanation quite sufficient.

"Who is Jubal the Ugly One?" I asked. "And why did you run away from him?"

She looked at me in surprise.

"Why *does* a woman run away from a man?" She answered my question with another.

"They do not, where I come from," I replied. "Sometimes they run after them."

But she could not understand. Nor could I get her to grasp the fact that I was of another world. She was quite as positive that creation was originated solely to produce her own kind and the world she lived in as are many of the outer world.

"But Jubal," I insisted. "Tell me about him, and why you ran away to be chained by the neck and scourged across the face of a world."

"Jubal the Ugly One placed his trophy before my father's house. It was the head of a mighty *tandor*. It remained there and no greater trophy was placed beside it. So I knew that Jubal the Ugly One would come and take me as his mate. None other so powerful wished me, or they would have slain a mightier beast and thus have won me from Jubal. My father is not a mighty hunter. Once he was, but a *sadok* tossed him, and never again had he the full use of his right arm. My brother, Dacor the Strong One, had gone to the land of Sari to steal a mate for himself. Thus there was none, father, brother, or lover, to save me from Jubal the Ugly One, and I ran away and hid among the hills that skirt the land of Amoz. And there these Sagoths found me and made me captive."

"What will they do with you?" I asked. "Where are they taking us?"

Again she looked her incredulity.

"I can almost believe that you are of another world," she said, "for otherwise such ignorance were inexplicable. Do you really mean that you do not know that the Sagoths are the creatures of the Mahars—the mighty Mahars who think that they own Pellucidar and all that walks or grows upon its surface, or creeps or burrows beneath, or swims within its lakes and oceans, or flies through its air? Next you will be telling me that you never before heard of the Mahars!"

I was loath to do it, and further incur her scorn; but there was no alternative if I were to absorb knowledge, so I made a clean breast of my pitiful ignorance as to the mighty Mahars. She was shocked. But she did her very best to enlighten me, though much that she said was as Greek would have been to her. She described the Mahars largely by comparisons. In this way they were like unto *thipdars*, in that to the hairless *lidi*.

About all I gleaned of them was that they were quite hideous, had wings, and. webbed feet; lived in cities built beneath the ground; could swim under water for great distances, and were very, very wise. The Sagoths were their weapon of offense and defense, and the races like herself were their hands and feet—they were the slaves and servants who did all the manual labor. The Mahars were the heads—the brains—of the inner world. I longed to see this wondrous race of supermen.

Perry learned the language with me. When we halted, as we occasionally did, though sometimes the halts seemed ages apart, he would join in the conversation, as would Ghak the Hairy One, he who was chained just ahead of Dian the Beautiful. Ahead of Ghak was Hooja the Sly One. He too entered the conversation occasionally. Most of his remarks were directed toward Dian the Beautiful. It didn't take half an eye to see that he had developed a bad case; but the girl appeared totally oblivious to his thinly veiled advances. Did I say thinly veiled? There is a race of men in New Zealand, or Australia, I have forgotten which, who indicate their preference for the lady of their affections by banging her over the head with a bludgeon. By comparison with this method Hooja's lovemaking might be called thinly veiled. At first it caused me to blush violently although I have seen several Old Years out at Rectors, and in other less fashionable places off Broadway, and in Vienna, and Hamburg.

But the girl! She was magnificent. It was easy to see that she considered herself as entirely above and apart from her present surroundings and company. She talked with me, and with Perry, and with the taciturn Ghak because we were respectful; but she couldn't even see Hooja the Sly One, much less hear him, and that made him furious. He tried to get one of the Sagoths to move the girl up ahead of him in the slave gang, but the fellow only poked him with his spear and told him that he had selected the girl for his own property—that he would buy her from the Mahars as soon as they reached Phutra. Phutra, it seemed, was the city of our destination.

After passing over the first chain of mountains we skirted a salt sea, upon whose bosom swam countless horrid things. Seal-like creatures there were with long necks stretching ten and more feet above their enormous bodies, and whose snake heads were split with gaping mouths bristling with countless fangs. There were huge tortoises too, paddling about among these other reptiles, which Perry said were Plesiosaurs of the Lias. I didn't question his veracity—they might have been most anything.

Dian told me they were *tandorazes*, or tandors of the sea, and that the other, and more fearsome reptiles, which occasionally rose from the deep to do battle with them, were *azdyryths*, or sea-dyryths—Perry called them Ichthyosaurs. They resembled a whale with the head of an alligator.

I had forgotten what little geology I had studied at school—about all that remained was an impression of horror that the illustrations of restored prehistoric monsters had made upon me, and a well-defined belief that any man with a pig's shank and a vivid imagination could "restore" most any sort of paleolithic monster he saw fit, and take rank as a first-class paleontologist. But when I saw these sleek, shiny carcasses shimmering in the sunlight as they emerged from the ocean, shaking their giant heads; when I saw the waters roll from their sinuous bodies in miniature waterfalls as they glided hither and thither, now upon the surface, now half submerged; as I saw them meet, open-mouthed, hissing and snorting, in their titanic and interminable warring I realized how futile is man's poor, weak imagination by comparison with Nature's incredible genius.

And Perry! He was absolutely flabbergasted. He said so himself.

"David," he remarked, after we had marched for a long time beside that awful sea. "David, I used to teach geology, and I thought that I believed what I taught; but now I see that I did not believe it—that it is impossible for man to believe such things as these unless he sees them with his own eyes. We take things for granted, perhaps, because we are told them over and over again, and have no way of disproving them—like religions, for example; but we don't believe them, we only think we do. If you ever get back to the outer world you will find that the geologists and paleontologists will be the first to set you down a liar, for they know that no such creatures as they restore ever existed. It is all right to *imagine* them as existing in an equally imaginary epoch—but now? poof!"

At the next halt Hooja the Sly One managed to find enough slack chain to permit him to worm himself back quite close to Dian. We were all standing, and as he edged near the girl she turned her back upon him in such a truly earthly feminine manner that I could scarce repress a smile; but it was a short-lived smile for on the instant the Sly One's hand fell upon the girl's bare arm, jerking her roughly toward him.

I was not then familiar with the customs or social ethics which prevailed within Pellucidar; but even so I did not need the appealing look which the girl shot at me from her magnificent eyes to influence my subsequent act. What the Sly One's intention was I paused not to inquire; but instead, before he could lay hold of her with his other hand, I placed a right to the point of his jaw that felled him in his tracks.

A roar of approval went up from those of the other prisoners and the Sagoths who had witnessed the brief drama; not, as I later learned, because I had championed the girl, but for the neat and, to them, astounding method by which I had bested Hooja.

And the girl? At first she looked at me with wide, wondering eyes, and then she dropped her head, her face half averted, and a delicate flush suffused her cheek. For a moment she stood thus in silence, and then her head went high, and she turned her back upon me as she had upon Hooja. Some of the prisoners laughed, and I saw the face of Ghak the Hairy One go very black as he looked at me searchingly. And what I could see of Dian's cheek went suddenly from red to white.

Immediately after we resumed the march, and though I realized that in some way I had offended Dian the Beautiful I could not prevail upon her to talk with me that I might learn wherein I had erred—in fact I might quite as well have been addressing a sphinx for all the attention I got. At last my own foolish pride stepped in and prevented my making any further attempts, and thus a companionship that without my realizing it had come to mean a great deal to me was cut off. Thereafter I confined my conversation to Perry. Hooja did not renew his advances toward the girl, nor did he again venture near me.

Again the weary and apparently interminable marching became a perfect nightmare of horrors to me. The more firmly fixed became the realization that the girl's friendship had meant so much to me, the more I came to miss it; and the more impregnable the barrier of silly pride. But I was very young and would not ask Ghak for the explanation which I was sure he could give, and that might have made everything all right again.

On the march, or during halts, Dian refused consistently to notice me—when her eyes wandered in my direction she looked either over my head or directly through me. At last I became desperate, and determined to swallow my self-esteem, and again beg her to tell me how I had offended, and how I might make reparation. I made up my mind that I should do this at the next halt. We were approaching another range of mountains at the time, and when we reached them, instead of winding across them through some high-flung pass we entered a mighty natural tunnel—a series of labyrinthine grottoes, dark as Erebus.

The guards had no torches or light of any description. In fact we had seen no artificial light or sign of fire since we had entered Pellucidar. In a land of perpetual noon there is no need of light above ground, yet I marveled that they had no means of lighting their way through these dark, subterranean passages. So we crept along at a snail's pace, with much stumbling and falling—the guards keeping up a singsong chant ahead of us, interspersed with certain high notes which I found always indicated rough places and turns.

Halts were now more frequent, but I did not wish to speak to Dian until I could see from the expression of her face how she was receiving my apologies. At last a faint glow ahead forewarned us of the end of the tunnel, for which I for one was devoutly thankful. Then at a sudden turn we emerged into the full light of the noonday sun.

But with it came a sudden realization of what meant to me a real catastrophe—Dian was gone, and with her a half-dozen other prisoners. The guards saw it too, and the ferocity of their rage was terrible to behold. Their awesome, bestial faces were contorted in the most diabolical expressions, as they accused each other of responsibility for the loss. Finally they fell upon us, beating us with their spear shafts, and hatchets. They had already killed two near the head of the line, and were like to have finished the balance of us when their leader finally put a stop to the brutal slaughter. Never in all my life had I witnessed a more horrible exhibition of bestial rage—I thanked God that Dian had not been one of those left to endure it.

Of the twelve prisoners who had been chained ahead of me each alternate one had been freed commencing with Dian. Hooja was gone. Ghak remained. What could it mean? How had it been accomplished? The commander of the guards was investigating. Soon he discovered that the rude locks which had held the neckbands in place had been deftly picked.

"Hooja the Sly One," murmured Ghak, who was now next to me in line. "He has taken the girl that you would not have," he continued, glancing at me.

"That I would not have!" I cried. "What do you mean?"

He looked at me closely for a moment.

"I have doubted your story that you are from another world," he said at last, "but yet upon no other grounds could your ignorance of the ways of Pellucidar be explained. Do you really mean that you do not know that you offended the Beautiful One, and how?"

"I do not know, Ghak," I replied.

"Then shall I tell you. When a man of Pellucidar intervenes between another man and the woman the other man would have, the woman belongs to the victor. Dian the Beautiful belongs to you. You should have claimed her or released her. Had you taken her hand, it would have indicated your desire to make her your mate, and had you raised her hand above her head and then dropped it, it would have meant that you did not wish her for a mate and that you released her from all obligation to you. By doing neither you have put upon her the greatest affront that a man may put upon a woman. Now she is your slave. No man will take her as mate, or may take her honorably, until he shall have overcome you in combat, and men do not choose slave women as their mates—at least not the men of Pellucidar."

"I did not know, Ghak," I cried. "I did not know. Not for all Pellucidar would I have harmed Dian the Beautiful by word, or look, or act of mine. I do not want her as my slave. I do not want her as my—" but here I stopped. The vision of that sweet and innocent face floated before me amidst the soft mists of imagination, and where I had on the second believed that I clung only to the memory of a gentle friendship I had lost, yet now it seemed that it would have been disloyalty to her to have said that I did not want Dian the Beautiful as my mate. I had not thought of her except as a welcome friend in a strange, cruel world. Even now I did not think that I loved her.

I believe Ghak must have read the truth more in my expression than in my words, for presently he laid his hand upon my shoulder.

"Man of another world," he said, "I believe you. Lips may lie, but when the heart speaks through the eyes it tells only the truth. Your heart has spoken to me. I know now that you meant no affront to Dian the Beautiful. She is not of my tribe; but her mother is my sister. She does not know it—her mother was stolen by Dian's father who came with many others of the tribe of Amoz to battle with us for our women—the most beautiful women of Pellucidar. Then was her father king of Amoz, and her mother was daughter of the king of Sari—to whose power I, his son, have succeeded. Dian is the daughter of kings, though her father is no longer king since the sadok tossed him and Jubal the Ugly One wrested his kingship from him. Because of her lineage the wrong you did her was greatly magnified in the eyes of all who saw it. She will never forgive you."

I asked Ghak if there was not some way in which I could release the girl from the bondage and ignominy I had unwittingly placed upon her.

"If ever you find her, yes," he answered. "Merely to raise her hand above her head and drop it in the presence of others is sufficient to release her; but how may you ever find her, you who are doomed to a life of slavery yourself in the buried city of Phutra?"

"Is there no escape?" I asked.

"Hooja the Sly One escaped and took the others with him," replied Ghak.

"But there are no more dark places on the way to Phutra, and once there it is not so easy—the Mahars are very wise. Even if one escaped from Phutra there are the thipdars—they would find you, and then—" the Hairy One shuddered. "No, you will never escape the Mahars."

It was a cheerful prospect. I asked Perry what he thought about it; but he only shrugged his shoulders and continued a long-winded prayer he had been at for some time. He was wont to say that the only redeeming feature of our captivity was the ample time it gave him for the improvisation of prayers—it was becoming an obsession with him. The Sagoths had begun to take notice of his habit of declaiming throughout entire marches. One of them asked him what he was saying—to whom he was talking. The question gave me an idea, so I answered quickly before Perry could say anything.

"Do not interrupt him," I said. "He is a very holy man in the world from which we come. He is speaking to spirits which you cannot see—do not interrupt him or they will spring out of the air upon you and rend you limb from limb—like that," and I jumped toward the great brute with a loud "Boo!" that sent him stumbling backward.

I took a long chance, I realized, but if we could make any capital out of Perry's harmless mania I wanted to make it while the making was prime. It worked splendidly. The Sagoths treated us both with marked respect during the balance of the journey, and then passed the word along to their masters, the Mahars.

Two marches after this episode we came to the city of Phutra. The entrance to it was marked by two lofty towers of granite, which guarded a flight of steps leading to the buried city. Sagoths were on guard here as well as at a hundred or more other towers scattered about over a large plain.

CHAPTER FIVE
SLAVES

A S WE DESCENDED THE BROAD STAIRCASE which led to the main avenue of Phutra I caught my first sight of the dominant race of the inner world. Involuntarily I shrank back as one of the creatures approached to inspect us. A more hideous thing it would be impossible to imagine. The all-powerful Mahars of Pellucidar are great reptiles, some six or eight feet in length, with long narrow heads and great round eyes. Their beaklike mouths are lined with sharp, white fangs, and the backs of their huge, lizard bodies are serrated into bony ridges from their necks to the end of their long tails. Their feet are equipped with three webbed toes, while from the forefeet membranous wings, which are attached to their bodies just in front of the hind legs, protrude at an angle of forty-five degrees toward the rear, ending in sharp points several feet above their bodies.

I glanced at Perry as the thing passed me to inspect him. The old man was gazing at the horrid creature with wide astonished eyes. When it passed on, he turned to me.

"A rhamphorhynchus of the Middle Olitic, David," he said, "but, gad, how enormous! The largest remains we ever have discovered have never indicated a size greater than that attained by an ordinary crow."

As we continued on through the main avenue of Phutra we saw many thousand of the creatures coming and going upon their daily duties. They paid but little attention to us. Phutra is laid out underground with a regularity that indicates remarkable engineering skill. It is hewn from solid limestone strata. The streets are broad and of a uniform height of twenty feet. At intervals tubes pierce the roof of this underground city, and by means of lenses and reflectors transmit the sunlight, softened and diffused, to dispel what would otherwise be Cimmerian darkness. In like manner air is introduced.

Perry and I were taken, with Ghak, to a large public building, where one of the Sagoths who had formed our guard explained to a Maharan official the circumstances surrounding our capture. The method of communication between these two was remarkable in that no spoken words were exchanged. They employed a species of sign language. As I was to learn later, the Mahars have no ears, nor any spoken language. Among themselves they communicate by means of what Perry says must be a sixth sense which is cognizant of a fourth dimension.

I never did quite grasp him, though he endeavored to explain it to me upon numerous occasions. I suggested telepathy, but he said no, that it was not telepathy since they could only communicate when in each other's presence, nor could they talk with the Sagoths or the other inhabitants of Pellucidar by the same method they used to converse with one another.

"What they do," said Perry, "is to project their thoughts into the fourth dimension, when they become appreciable to the sixth sense of their listener. Do I make myself quite clear?"

"You do not. Perry," I replied. He shook his head in despair, and returned to his work. They had set us to carrying a great accumulation of Maharan literature from one apartment to another, and there arranging it upon shelves. I suggested to Perry that we were in the public library of Phutra, but later, as he commenced to discover the key to their written language, he assured me that we were handling the ancient archives of the race.

During this period my thoughts were continually upon Dian the Beautiful. I was, of course, glad that she had escaped the Mahars, and the fate that had been suggested by the Sagoth who had threatened to purchase her upon our arrival at Phutra. I often wondered if the little party of fugitives had been overtaken by the guards who had returned to search for them. Sometimes I was not so sure but that I should have been more contented to know that Dian was here in Phutra, than to think of her at the mercy of Hooja the Sly One.

Ghak, Perry, and I often talked together of possible escape, but the Sarian was so steeped in his lifelong belief that no one could escape from the Mahars except by a miracle, that he was not much aid to us—his attitude was of one who waits for the miracle to come to him.

At my suggestion Perry and I fashioned some swords of scraps of iron which we discovered among some rubbish in the cells where we slept, for we were permitted almost unrestrained freedom of action within the limits of the building to which we had been assigned. So great were the number of slaves who waited upon the inhabitants of Phutra that none of us was apt to be overburdened with work, nor were our masters unkind to us.

We hid our new weapons beneath the skins which formed our beds, and then Perry conceived the idea of making bows and arrows—weapons apparently unknown within Pellucidar. Next came shields; but these I found it easier to steal from the walls of the outer guardroom of the building.

We had completed these arrangements for our protection after leaving Phutra when the Sagoths who had been sent to recapture the escaped prisoners returned with four of them, of whom Hooja was one. Dian and two others had eluded them. It so happened that Hooja was confined in the same building with us. He told Ghak that he had not seen Dian or the others after releasing them within the dark grotto. What had become of them he had not the faintest conception—they might be wandering yet, lost within the labyrinthine tunnel, if not dead from starvation.

I was now still further apprehensive as to the fate of Dian, and at this time, I imagine, came the first realization that my affection for the girl might be prompted by more than friendship. During my waking hours she was constantly the subject of my thoughts, and when I slept her dear face haunted my dreams. More than ever was I determined to escape the Mahars.

"Perry," I confided to the old man, "if I have to search every inch of this diminutive world I am going to find Dian the Beautiful and right the wrong I unintentionally did her." That was the excuse I made for Perry's benefit.

"Diminutive world!" he scoffed. "You don't know what you are talking about, my boy," and then he showed me a map of Pellucidar which he had recently discovered among the manuscript he was arranging.

"Look," he cried, pointing to it, "this is evidently water, and all this land. Do you notice the general configuration of the two areas? Where the oceans are upon the outer crust, is land here. These relatively small areas of ocean follow the general lines of the continents of the outer world.

"We know that the crust of the globe is 500 miles in thickness; then the inside diameter of Pellucidar must be 7,000 miles, and the superficial area 165,480,000 square miles. Three-fourths of this is land. Think of it! A land area of 124,110,000 square miles! Our own world contains but 53,000,000 square miles of land, the balance of its surface being covered by water. Just as we often compare nations by their relative land areas, so if we compare these two worlds in the same way we have the strange anomaly of a larger world within a smaller one!

"Where within vast Pellucidar would you search for your Dian? Without stars, or moon, or changing sun how could you find her even though you knew where she might be found?"

The proposition was a corker. It quite took my breath away; but I found that it left me all the more determined to attempt it.

"If Ghak will accompany us we may be able to do it," I suggested.

Perry and I sought him out and put the question straight to him.

"Ghak," I said, "we are determined to escape from this bondage. Will you accompany us?"

"They will set the thipdars upon us," he said, "and then we shall be killed; but—" he hesitated—"I would take the chance if I thought that I might possibly escape and return to my own people."

"Could you find your way back to your own land?" asked Perry. "And could you aid David in his search for Dian?"

"Yes."

"But how," persisted Perry, "could you travel a strange country without heavenly bodies or a compass to guide you?"

Ghak didn't know what Perry meant by heavenly bodies or a compass, but he assured us that you might blindfold any man of Pellucidar and carry him to the farthermost corner of the world, yet he would be able to come directly to his own home again by the shortest route. He seemed surprised to think that we found anything wonderful in it. Perry said it must be some sort of homing instinct such as is possessed by certain breeds of earthly pigeons. I didn't know, of course, but it gave me an idea.

"Then Dian could have found her way directly to her own people?" I asked.

"Surely," replied Ghak, "unless some mighty beast of prey killed her."

I was for making the attempted escape at once, but both Perry and Ghak counseled waiting for some propitious accident which would insure us some small degree of success. I didn't see what accident could befall a whole community in a land of perpetual daylight where the inhabitants had no fixed habits of sleep. Why, I am sure that some of the Mahars never sleep, while others may, at long intervals, crawl into the dark recesses beneath their dwellings and curl up in protracted slumber. Perry says that if a Mahar stays awake for three years he will make up all his lost sleep in a long year's snooze. That may be all true, but I never saw but three of them asleep, and it was the sight of these three that gave me a suggestion for our means of escape.

I had been searching about far below the levels that we slaves were supposed to frequent—possibly fifty feet beneath the main floor of the building—among a network of corridors and apartments, when I came suddenly upon three Mahars curled up upon a bed of skins. At first I thought they were dead, but later their regular breathing convinced me of my error. Like a flash the thought came to me of the marvelous opportunity these sleeping reptiles offered as a means of eluding the watchfulness of our captors and the Sagoth guards.

Hastening back to Perry where he pored over a musty pile of, to me, meaningless hieroglyphics, I explained my plan to him. To my surprise he was horrified.

"It would be murder, David," he cried.

"Murder to kill a reptilian monster?" I asked in astonishment.

"Here they are not monsters, David," he replied. "Here they are the dominant race—we are the 'monsters'—the lower orders. In Pellucidar evolution has progressed along different lines than upon the outer earth. There terrible convulsions of nature time and time again wiped out the existing species—but for this fact some monster of the Saurozoic epoch might rule today upon our own world. We see here what might well have occurred in our own history had conditions been what they have been here.

"Life within Pellucidar is far younger than upon the outer crust. Here man has but reached a stage analogous to the Stone Age of our own world's history, but for countless millions of years these reptiles have been progressing. Possibly it is the sixth sense which I am sure they possess that has given them an advantage over the other and more frightfully armed of their fellows; but this we may never know. They look upon us as we look upon the beasts of our fields, and I learn from their written records that other races of Mahars feed upon men—they keep them in great droves, as we keep cattle. They breed them most carefully, and when they are quite fat, they kill and eat them."

I shuddered.

"What is there horrible about it, David?" the old man asked. "They understand us no better than we understand the lower animals of our own world. Why, I have come across here very learned discussions of the question as to whether *gilaks*, that is men, have any means of communication. One writer claims that we do not even reason—that our every act is mechanical, or instinctive. The dominant race of Pellucidar, David, have not yet learned that men converse among themselves, or reason. Because we do not converse as they do it is beyond them to imagine that we converse at all. It is thus that we reason in relation to the brutes of our own world. They know that the Sagoths have a spoken language, but yet they cannot comprehend it, or how it manifests itself, since they have no auditory apparatus. They believe that the motions of the lips alone convey the meaning. That the Sagoths can communicate with us is incomprehensible to them.

"Yes, David," he concluded, "it would entail murder to carry out your plan."

"Very well then, Perry," I replied. "I shall become a murderer."

He got me to go over the plan again most carefully, and for some reason which was not at the time clear to me insisted upon a very careful description of the apartments and corridors I had just explored.

"I wonder, David," he said at length, "as you are determined to carry out your wild scheme, if we could not accomplish something of very real and lasting benefit for the human race of Pellucidar at the same time. Listen. I have learned much of a most surprising nature from these archives of the Mahars. That you may appreciate my plan I shall briefly outline the history of the race.

"Once the males were all-powerful, but ages ago the females, little by little, assumed the mastery. For other ages no noticeable change took place in the race of Mahars. It continued to progress under the intelligent and beneficent rule of the ladies. Science took vast strides. This was especially true of the sciences which we know as biology and eugenics. Finally a certain female scientist announced the fact that she had discovered a method whereby eggs might be fertilized by chemical means after they were laid—all true reptiles, you know, are hatched from eggs.

"What happened? Immediately the necessity for males ceased to exist—the race was no longer dependent upon them. More ages elapsed until at the present time we find a race consisting exclusively of females. But here is the point. The secret of this chemical formula is kept by a single race of Mahars. It is in the city of Phutra, and unless I am greatly in error I judge from your description of the vaults through which you passed today that it lies hidden in the cellar of this building.

"For two reasons they hide it away and guard it jealously. First, because upon it depends the very life of the race of Mahars, and second, owing to the fact that when it was public property as at first so many were experimenting with it that the danger of overpopulation became very grave.

"David, if we can escape, and at the same time take with us this great secret what will we not have accomplished for the human race within Pellucidar!"

The very thought of it fairly overpowered me. Why, we two would be the means of placing the men of the inner world in their rightful place among created things. Only the Sagoths would then stand between them and absolute supremacy, and I was not quite sure but that the Sagoths owed all their power to the greater intelligence of the Mahars—I could not believe that these gorilla-like beasts were the mental superiors of the human race of Pellucidar.

"Why, Perry," I exclaimed, "you and I may reclaim a whole world! Together we can lead the races of men out of the darkness of ignorance into the light of advancement and civilization. At one step we may carry them from the Age of Stone to the twentieth century. It's marvelous—absolutely marvelous just to think about it."

"David," said the old man, "I believe that God sent us here for just that purpose—it shall be my life work to teach them His word—to lead them into the light of His mercy while we are training their hearts and hands in the ways of culture and civilization."

"You are right, Perry," I said, "and while you are teaching them to pray I'll be teaching them to fight, and between us we'll make a race of men that will be an honor to us both."

Ghak had entered the apartment some time before we concluded our conversation, and now he wanted to know what we were so excited about. Perry thought we had best not tell him too much, and so I only explained that I had a plan for escape. When I had outlined it to him, he seemed about as horror-struck as Perry had been; but for a different reason. The Hairy One only considered the horrible fate that would be ours were we discovered; but at last I prevailed upon him to accept my plan as the only feasible one, and when I had assured him that I would take all the responsibility for it were we captured, he accorded a reluctant assent.

CHAPTER SIX
THE BEGINNING OF HORROR

WITHIN PELLUCIDAR one time is as good as another. There were no nights to mask our attempted escape. All must be done in broad daylight—all but the work I had to do in the apartment beneath the building. So we determined to put our plan to an immediate test lest the Mahars who made it possible should awake before I reached them; but we were doomed to disappointment, for no sooner had we reached the main floor of the building on our way to the pits beneath, than we encountered hurrying bands of slaves being hastened under strong Sagoth guard out of the edifice to the avenue beyond.

Other Sagoths were darting hither and thither in search of other slaves, and the moment that we appeared we were pounced upon and hustled into the line of marching humans.

What the purpose or nature of the general exodus we did not know, but presently through the line of captives ran the rumor that two escaped slaves had been recaptured—a man and a woman—and that we were marching to witness their punishment, for the man had killed a Sagoth of the detachment that had pursued and overtaken them.

At the intelligence my heart sprang to my throat, for I was sure that the two were of those who escaped in the dark grotto with Hooja the Sly One, and that Dian must be the woman. Ghak thought so too, as did Perry.

"Is there naught that we may do to save her?" I asked Ghak.

"Naught," he replied.

Along the crowded avenue we marched, the guards showing unusual cruelty toward us, as though we, too, had been implicated in the murder of their fellow. The occasion was to serve as an object lesson to all other slaves of the danger and futility of attempted escape, and the fatal consequences of taking the life of a superior being, and so I imagine the Sagoths felt amply justified in making the entire proceeding as uncomfortable and painful to us as possible.

They jabbed us with their spears and struck at us with their hatchets at the least provocation, and at no provocation at all. It was a most uncomfortable half hour that we spent before we were finally herded through a low entrance into a huge building the center of which was given up to a good-sized arena. Benches surrounded this open space upon three sides, and along the fourth were heaped huge boulders which rose in receding tiers toward the roof.

At first I couldn't make out the purpose of this mighty pile of rock, unless it were intended as a rough and picturesque background for the scenes which were enacted in the arena before it, but presently, after the wooden benches had been pretty well filled by slaves and Sagoths, I discovered the purpose of the boulders, for then the Mahars began to file into the enclosure.

They marched directly across the arena toward the rocks upon the opposite side, where, spreading their batlike wings, they rose above the high wall of the pit, settling down upon the boulders above. These were the reserved seats, the boxes of the elect.

Reptiles that they are, the rough surface of a great stone is to them as plush as upholstery to us. Here they lolled, blinking their hideous eyes, and doubtless conversing with one another in their sixth-sense-fourth-dimension language.

For the first time I beheld their queen. She differed from the others in no feature that was appreciable to my earthly eyes, in fact all Mahars look alike to me; but when she crossed the arena after the balance of her female subjects had found their boulders, she was preceded by a score of huge Sagoths, the largest I ever had seen, and on either side of her waddled a huge thipdar, while behind came another score of Sagoth guardsmen.

At the barrier the Sagoths clambered up the steep side with truly apelike agility, while behind them the haughty queen rose upon her wings with her two frightful dragons close beside her, and settled down upon the largest boulder of them all in the exact center of that side of the amphitheater which is reserved for the dominant race. Here she squatted, a most repulsive and uninteresting queen; though doubtless quite as well assured of her beauty and divine right to rule as the proudest monarch of the outer world.

And then the music started—music without sound! The Mahars cannot hear, so the drums and fifes and horns of earthly bands are unknown among them. The "band" consists of a score or more Mahars. It filed out in the center of the arena where the creatures upon the rocks might see it, and there it performed for fifteen or twenty minutes.

Their technique consisted in waving their tails and moving their heads in a regular succession of measured movements resulting in a cadence which evidently pleased the eye of the Mahar as the cadence of our own instrumental music pleases our ears. Sometimes the band took measured steps in unison to one side or the other, or backward and again forward—it all seemed very silly and meaningless to me, but at the end of the first piece the Mahars upon the rocks showed the first indications of enthusiasm that I had seen displayed by the dominant race of Pellucidar. They beat their great wings up and down, and smote their rocky perches with their mighty tails until the ground shook. Then the band started another piece, and all was again as silent as the grave. That was one great beauty about

Mahar music—if you didn't happen to like a piece that was being played all you had to do was shut your eyes.

When the band had exhausted its repertory it took wing and settled upon rocks above and behind the queen. Then the business of the day was on. A man and woman were pushed into the arena by a couple of Sagoth guardsmen. I leaned far forward in my seat to scrutinize the female—hoping against hope that she might prove to be another than Dian the Beautiful. Her back was toward me for a while, and the sight of the great mass of raven hair piled high upon her head filled me with alarm.

Presently a door in one side of the arena wall was opened to admit a huge, shaggy, bull-like creature.

"A Bos," whispered Perry, excitedly. "His kind roamed the outer crust with the cave bear and the mammoth ages and ages ago. We have been carried back a million years, David, to the childhood of a planet—is it not wondrous?"

But I saw only the raven hair of a half-naked girl, and my heart stood still in dumb misery at the sight of her, nor had I any eyes for the wonders of natural history. But for Perry and Ghak I should have leaped to the floor of the arena and shared whatever fate lay in store for this priceless treasure of the Stone Age.

With the advent of the Bos—they call the thing a *thag* within Pellucidar—two spears were tossed into the arena at the feet of the prisoners. It seemed to me that a bean shooter would have been as effective against the mighty monster as these pitiful weapons.

As the animal approached the two, bellowing and pawing the ground with the strength of many earthly bulls, another door directly beneath us was opened, and from it issued the most terrific roar that ever had fallen upon my outraged ears. I could not at first see the beast from which emanated this fearsome challenge, but the sound had the effect of bringing the two victims around with a sudden start, and then I saw the girl's face—she was not Dian! I could have wept for relief.

And now, as the two stood frozen in terror, I saw the author of that fearsome sound creeping stealthily into view. It was a huge tiger—such as hunted the great Bos through the jungles primeval when the world was young. In contour and markings it was not unlike the noblest of the Bengals of our own world, but as its dimensions were exaggerated to colossal proportions so too were its colorings exaggerated. Its vivid yellows fairly screamed aloud; its whites were as eider down; its blacks glossy as the finest anthracite coal, and its coat long and shaggy as a mountain goat. That it is a beautiful animal there is no gainsaying, but if its size and colors are magnified here within Pellucidar, so is the ferocity of its disposition. It is not the occasional member of its species that is a man hunter—all are man hunters; but they do not confine their foraging to man alone, for there is no flesh or fish within Pellucidar that they will not eat with relish in the constant efforts which they make to furnish their huge carcasses with sufficient sustenance to maintain their mighty thews.

Upon one side of the doomed pair the thag bellowed and advanced, and upon the other *tarag*, the frightful, crept toward them with gaping mouth and dripping fangs.

The man seized the spears, handing one of them to the woman. At the sound of the roaring of the tiger the bull's bellowing became a veritable frenzy of rageful noise. Never in my life had I heard such an infernal din as the two brutes made, and to think that it was all lost upon the hideous reptiles for whom the show was staged!

The thag was charging now from one side, and the tarag from the other. The two puny things standing between them seemed already lost, but at the very moment that the beasts were upon them the man grasped his companion by the arm and together they leaped to one side, while the frenzied creatures came together like locomotives in collision.

There ensued a battle royal which for sustained and frightful ferocity transcends the power of imagination or description. Time and again the colossal bull tossed the enormous tiger high into the air, but each time that the huge cat touched the ground he returned to the encounter with apparently undiminished strength, and seemingly increased ire.

For a while the man and woman busied themselves only with keeping out of the way of the two creatures, but finally I saw them separate and each creep stealthily toward one of the combatants. The tiger was now upon the bull's broad back, clinging to the huge neck with powerful fangs while its long, strong talons ripped the heavy hide into shreds and ribbons.

For a moment the bull stood bellowing and quivering with pain and rage, its cloven hoofs widespread, its tail lashing viciously from side to side, and then, in a mad orgy of bucking, it went careening about the arena in frenzied attempt to unseat its rending rider. It was with difficulty that the girl avoided the first mad rush of the wounded animal.

All its efforts to rid itself of the tiger seemed futile, until in desperation it threw itself upon the ground, rolling over and over. A little of this so disconcerted the tiger, knocking its breath from it I imagine, that it lost its hold, and then, quick as a cat, the great thag was up again and had buried those mighty horns deep in the tarag's abdomen, pinning him to the floor of the arena.

The great cat clawed at the shaggy head until eyes and ears were gone, and naught but a few strips of ragged, bloody flesh remained upon the skull. Yet through all the agony of that fearful punishment the thag still stood motionless pinning down his adversary, and then the man leaped in, seeing that the blind bull would be the least formidable enemy, and ran his spear through the tarag's heart.

As the animal's fierce clawing ceased, the bull raised his gory, sightless head, and with a horrid roar ran headlong across the arena. With great leaps and bounds he came, straight toward the arena wall directly beneath where we sat, and then accident carried him, in one of his mighty springs, completely over the barrier into the midst of the slaves and Sagoths just in front of us.

Swinging his bloody horns from side to side the beast cut a wide swath before him straight upward toward our seats. Before him slaves and gorilla-men fought in mad stampede to escape the menace of the creature's death agonies, for such only could that frightful charge have been.

Forgetful of us, our guards joined in the general rush for the exits, many of which pierced the wall of the amphitheater behind us. Perry, Ghak, and I became separated in the chaos which reigned for a few moments after the beast cleared the wall of the arena, each intent upon saving his own hide.

I ran to the right, passing several exits choked with the fear-mad mob that were battling to escape. One would have thought that an entire herd of thags was loose behind them, rather than a single blinded, dying beast; but such is the effect of panic upon a crowd.

CHAPTER SEVEN
FREEDOM

ONCE OUT OF THE DIRECT PATH of the animal, fear of it left me, but another emotion as quickly gripped me—hope of escape that the demoralized condition of the guards made possible for the instant.

I thought of Perry, and but for the hope that I might better encompass his release if myself free I should have put the thought of freedom from me at once. As it was I hastened on toward the right searching for an exit toward which no Sagoths were fleeing, and at last I found it—a low, narrow aperture leading into a dark corridor.

Without thought of the possible consequences, I darted into the shadows of the tunnel, feeling my way along through the gloom for some distance. The noises of the amphitheater had grown fainter and fainter until now all was as silent as the tomb about me. Faint light filtered from above through occasional ventilating and lighting tubes, but it was scarce sufficient to enable my human eyes to cope with the darkness, and so I was forced to move with extreme care, feeling my way along step by step with a hand upon the wall beside me.

Presently the light increased and a moment later, to my delight, I came upon a flight of steps leading upward, at the top of which the brilliant light of the noonday sun shone through an opening in the ground.

Cautiously I crept up the stairway to the tunnel's end, and peering out saw the broad plain of Phutra before me. The numerous lofty, granite towers which mark the several entrances to the subterranean city were all in front of me—behind, the plain stretched level and unbroken to the nearby foothills. I had come to the surface, then, beyond the city, and my chances for escape seemed much enhanced.

My first impulse was to await darkness before attempting to cross the plain, so deeply implanted are habits of thought; but of a sudden I recollected the perpetual noonday brilliance which envelops Pellucidar, and with a smile I stepped forth into the daylight.

Rank grass, waist high, grows upon the plain of Phutra—the gorgeous flowering grass of the inner world, each particular blade of which is tipped with a tiny, five-pointed blossom—brilliant little stars of varying colors that twinkle in the green foliage to add still another charm to the weird, yet lovely, landscape.

But then the only aspect which attracted me was the distant hills in which I hoped to find sanctuary, and so I hastened on, trampling the myriad beauties beneath my hurrying feet. Perry says that the force of gravity is less upon the surface of the inner world than upon that of the outer. He explained it all to me once, but I was never particularly brilliant in such matters and so most of it has escaped me. As I recall it the difference is due in some part to the counter-attraction of that portion of the earth's crust directly opposite the spot upon the face of Pellucidar at which one's calculations are being made. Be that as it may, it always seemed to me that I moved with greater speed and agility within Pellucidar than upon the outer surface—there was a certain airy lightness of step that was most pleasing, and a feeling of bodily detachment which I can only compare with that occasionally experienced in dreams.

And as I crossed Phutra's flower-bespangled plain that time I seemed almost to fly, though how much of the sensation was due to Perry's suggestion and how much to actuality I am sure I do not know. The more I thought of Perry the less pleasure I took in my newfound freedom. There could be no liberty for me within Pellucidar unless the old man shared it with me, and only the hope that I might find some way to encompass his release kept me from turning back to Phutra.

Just how I was to help Perry I could scarce imagine, but I hoped that some fortuitous circumstances might solve the problem for me. It was quite evident however that little less than a miracle could aid me, for what could I accomplish in this strange world, naked and unarmed? It was even doubtful that I could retrace my steps to Phutra should I once pass beyond view of the plain, and even were that possible, what aid could I bring to Perry no matter how far I wandered?

The case looked more and more hopeless the longer I viewed it, yet with a stubborn persistency I forged ahead toward the foothills. Behind me no sign of pursuit developed, before me I saw no living thing. It was as though I moved through a dead and forgotten world.

I have no idea, of course, how long it took me to reach the limit of the plain, but at last I entered the foothills, following a pretty little canyon upward toward the mountains. Beside me frolicked a laughing brooklet, hurrying upon its noisy way down to the silent sea. In its quieter pools I discovered many small fish, of four- or five-pound weight I should imagine. In appearance, except as to size and color, they were not unlike the whale of our own seas. As I watched them playing about I discovered, not only that they suckled their young, but that at intervals they rose to the surface to breathe as well as to feed upon certain grasses and a strange, scarlet lichen which grew upon the rocks just above the water line.

It was this last habit that gave me the opportunity I craved to capture one of these herbivorous cetaceans—that is what Perry calls them—and make as good a meal as one can on raw, warm-blooded fish; but I had become rather used, by this time, to the eating of food in its natural state, though I still balked on the eyes and entrails, much to the amusement of Ghak, to whom I always passed these delicacies.

Crouching beside the brook, I waited until one of the diminutive, purple whales rose to nibble at the long grasses which overhung the water, and then, like the beast of prey that man really is, I sprang upon my victim, appeasing my hunger while he yet wriggled to escape.

Then I drank from the clear pool, and after washing my hands and face continued my flight. Above the source of the brook I encountered a rugged climb to the summit of a long ridge. Beyond was a steep declivity to the shore of a placid, inland sea, upon the quiet surface of which lay several beautiful islands.

The view was charming in the extreme, and as no man or beast was to be seen that might threaten my newfound liberty, I slid over the edge of the bluff, and half sliding, half falling, dropped into the delightful valley, the very aspect of which seemed to offer a haven of peace and security.

The gently sloping beach along which I walked was thickly strewn with strangely shaped, colored shells; some empty, others still housing as varied a multitude of mollusks as ever might have drawn out their sluggish lives along the silent shores of the antediluvian seas of the outer crust. As I walked I could not but compare myself with the first man of that other world, so complete the solitude which surrounded me, so primal and untouched the virgin wonders and beauties of adolescent nature. I felt myself a second Adam wending my lonely way through the childhood of a world, searching for my Eve, and at the thought there rose before my mind's eye the exquisite outlines of a perfect face surmounted by a loose pile of wondrous, raven hair.

As I walked, my eyes were bent upon the beach so that it was not until

I had come quite upon it that I discovered that which shattered all my beautiful dream of solitude and safety and peace and primal overlordship. The thing was a hollowed log drawn up upon the sands, and in the bottom of it lay a crude paddle.

The rude shock of awakening to what doubtless might prove some new form of danger was still upon me when I heard a rattling of loose stones from the direction of the bluff, and turning my eyes in that direction I beheld the author of the disturbance, a great copper-colored man, running rapidly toward me.

There was that in the haste with which he came which seemed quite sufficiently menacing, so that I did not need the added evidence of brandishing spear and scowling face to warn me that I was in no safe position, but whither to flee was indeed a momentous question.

The speed of the fellow seemed to preclude the possibility of escaping him upon the open beach. There was but a single alternative—the rude skiff—and with a celerity which equaled his, I pushed the thing into the sea and as it floated gave a final shove and clambered in over the end.

A cry of rage rose from the owner of the primitive craft, and an instant later his heavy, stone-tipped spear grazed my shoulder and buried itself in the bow of the boat beyond. Then I grasped the paddle, and with feverish haste urged the awkward, wobbly thing out upon the surface of the sea.

A glance over my shoulder showed me that the copper-colored one had plunged in after me and was swimming rapidly in pursuit. His mighty strokes bade fair to close up the distance between us in short order, for at best I could make but slow progress with my unfamiliar craft, which nosed stubbornly in every direction but that which I desired to follow, so that fully half my energy was expended in turning its blunt prow back into the course.

I had covered some hundred yards from shore when it became evident that my pursuer must grasp the stern of the skiff within the next half-dozen strokes. In a frenzy of despair, I bent to that grandfather of all paddles in a hopeless effort to escape, and still the copper giant behind me gained and gained.

His hand was reaching upward for the stern when I saw a sleek, sinuous body shoot from the depths below. The man saw it too, and the look of terror that overspread his face assured me that I need have no further concern as to him, for the fear of certain death was in his look.

And then about him coiled the great, slimy folds of a hideous monster of that prehistoric deep—a mighty serpent of the sea, with fanged jaws, and darting forked tongue, with bulging eyes, and bony protuberances upon head and snout that formed short, stout horns.

As I looked at that hopeless struggle my eyes met those of the doomed man, and I could have sworn that in his I saw an expression of hopeless appeal. But whether I did or no there swept through me a sudden compassion for the fellow. He was indeed a brother-man, and that he might have killed me with pleasure had he caught me was forgotten in the extremity of his danger.

Unconsciously I had ceased paddling as the serpent rose to engage my pursuer, so now the skiff still drifted close beside the two. The monster seemed to be but playing with his victim before he closed his awful jaws upon him and dragged him down to his dark den beneath the surface to devour him. The huge, snakelike body coiled and uncoiled about its prey. The hideous, gaping jaws snapped in the victim's face. The forked tongue, lightning-like, ran in and out upon the copper skin.

Nobly the giant battled for his life, beating with his stone hatchet against the bony armor that covered that frightful carcass; but for all the damage he inflicted he might as well have struck with his open palm.

At last I could endure no longer to sit supinely by while a fellow man was dragged down to a horrible death by that repulsive reptile. Embedded in the prow of the skiff lay the spear that had been cast after me by him whom I suddenly desired to save. With a wrench I tore it loose, and standing upright in the wobbly log drove it with all the strength of my two arms straight into the gaping jaws of the hydrophidian.

With a loud hiss the creature abandoned its prey to turn upon me, but the spear, imbedded in its throat, prevented it from seizing me though it came near to overturning the skiff in its mad efforts to reach me.

CHAPTER EIGHT
THE MAHAR TEMPLE

THE ABORIGINE, APPARENTLY UNINJURED, climbed quickly into the skiff, and seizing the spear with me helped to hold off the infuriated creature. Blood from the wounded reptile was now crimsoning the waters about us and soon from the weakening struggles it became evident that I had inflicted a death wound upon it. Presently its efforts to reach us ceased entirely, and with a few convulsive movements it turned upon its back quite dead.

And then there came to me a sudden realization of the predicament in which I had placed myself. I was entirely within the power of the savage man whose skiff I had stolen. Still clinging to the spear I looked into his face to find him scrutinizing me intently, and there we stood for some several minutes, each clinging tenaciously to the weapon the while we gazed in stupid wonderment at each other.

What was in his mind I do not know, but in my own was merely the question as to how soon the fellow would recommence hostilities.

Presently he spoke to me, but in a tongue which I was unable to translate. I shook my head in an effort to indicate my ignorance of his language, at the same time addressing him in the bastard tongue that the Sagoths use to converse with the human slaves of the Mahars.

To my delight he understood and answered me in the same jargon.

"What do you want of my spear?" he asked.

"Only to keep you from running it through me," I replied.

"I would not do that," he said, "for you have just saved my life," and with that he released his hold upon it and squatted down in the bottom of the skiff.

"Who are you," he continued, "and from what country do you come?"

I too sat down, laying the spear between us, and tried to explain how I came to Pellucidar, and wherefrom, but it was as impossible for him to grasp or believe the strange tale I told him as I fear it is for you upon the outer crust to believe in the existence of the inner world.

To him it seemed quite ridiculous to imagine that there was another world far beneath his feet peopled by beings similar to himself, and he laughed uproariously the more he thought upon it. But it was ever thus. That which has never come within the scope of our really pitifully meager world experience cannot be—our finite minds cannot grasp that which may not exist in accordance with the conditions which obtain about us upon the outside of the insignificant grain of dust which wends its tiny way among the boulders of the universe—the speck of moist dirt we so proudly call the World.

So I gave it up and asked him about himself. He said he was a Mezop, and that his name was Ja.

"Who are the Mezops?" I asked. "Where do they live?"

He looked at me in surprise.

"I might indeed believe that you were from another world," he said, "for who of Pellucidar could be so ignorant! The Mezops live upon the islands of the seas. Insofar as I ever have heard no Mezop lives elsewhere, and no others than Mezops dwell upon islands, but of course it may be different in other far-distant lands. I do not know. At any rate in this sea and those nearby it is true that only people of my race inhabit the islands.

"We are fishermen, though we be great hunters as well, often going to the mainland in search of the game that is scarce upon all but the larger islands. And we are warriors also," he added proudly. "Even the Sagoths of the Mahars fear us. Once, when Pellucidar was young, the Sagoths were wont to capture us for slaves as they do the other men of Pellucidar, it is handed down from father to son among us that this is so; but we fought so desperately and slew so many Sagoths, and those of us that were captured killed so many Mahars in their own cities that at last they learned that it were better to leave us alone, and later came the time that the Mahars became too indolent even to catch their own fish, except for amusement, and then they needed us to supply their wants, and so a truce was made between the races. Now they give us certain things which we are unable to produce in return for the fish that we catch, and the Mezops and the Mahars live in peace.

"The great ones even come to our islands. It is there, far from the prying eyes of their own Sagoths, that they practice their religious rites in the temples they have budded there with our assistance. If you live among us you will doubtless see the manner of their worship, which is strange indeed, and most unpleasant for the poor slaves they bring to take part in it."

As Ja talked I had an excellent opportunity to inspect him more closely. He was a huge fellow, standing I should say six feet six or seven inches, well developed and of a coppery red not unlike that of our own North American Indian, nor were his features dissimilar to theirs. He had the aquiline nose found among many tribes, the prominent cheek bones, and black hair and eyes. All in all, Ja was an impressive and handsome creature, and he talked well too, even in the miserable makeshift language we were compelled to use.

During our conversation Ja had taken the paddle and was propelling the skiff with vigorous strokes toward a large island that lay some half mile from the mainland. The skill with which he handled his crude and awkward craft elicited my deepest admiration, since it had been so short a time before that I had made such pitiful work of it.

As we touched the pretty, level beach Ja leaped out and I followed him. Together we dragged the skiff far up into the bushes that grew beyond the sand.

"We must hide our canoes," explained Ja, "for the Mezops of Luana are always at war with us and would steal them if they found them," he nodded toward an island farther out at sea, and at so great a distance that it seemed but a blur hanging in the distant sky. The upward curve of the surface of Pellucidar was constantly revealing the impossible to the surprised eyes of the outer-earthly. To see land and water curving upward in the distance until it seemed to stand on edge where it melted into the distant sky, and to feel that seas and mountains hung suspended directly above one's head required such a complete reversal of the perceptive and reasoning faculties as almost to stupefy one.

No sooner had we hidden the canoe than Ja plunged into the jungle, presently emerging into a narrow but well-defined trail which wound hither and thither much after the manner of the highways of all primitive folk, but there was one peculiarity about this Mezop trail which I was later to find distinguished them from all other trails that I ever have seen within or without the earth.

It would run on, plain and clear and well defined to end suddenly in the midst of a tangle of matted jungle, then Ja would turn directly back in his tracks for a little distance, spring into a tree, climb through it to the other side, drop onto a fallen log, leap over a low bush and alight once more upon a distinct trail which he would follow back for a short distance only to turn directly about and retrace his steps until after a mile or less this new pathway ended as suddenly and mysteriously as the former section. Then he would pass again across some media which would reveal no spoor, to take up the broken thread of the trail beyond.

As the purpose of this remarkable avenue dawned upon me I could not but admire the native shrewdness of the ancient progenitor of the

Mezops who hit upon this novel plan to throw his enemies from his track and delay or thwart them in their attempts to follow him to his deep-buried cities.

To you of the outer earth it might seem a slow and tortuous method of traveling through the jungle, but were you of Pellucidar you would realize that time is no factor where time does not exist. So labyrinthine are the windings of these trails, so varied the connecting links and the distances which one must retrace one's steps from the paths' ends to find them that a Mezop often reaches man's estate before he is familiar even with those which lead from his own city to the sea.

In fact three-fourths of the education of the young male Mezop consists in familiarizing himself with these jungle avenues, and the status of an adult is largely determined by the number of trails which he can follow upon his own island. The females never learn them, since from birth to death they never leave the clearing in which the village of their nativity is situated except they be taken to mate by a male from another village, or captured in war by the enemies of their tribe.

After proceeding through the jungle for what must have been upward of five miles we emerged suddenly into a large clearing in the exact center of which stood as strange an appearing village as one might well imagine.

Large trees had been chopped down fifteen or twenty feet above the ground, and upon the tops of them spherical habitations of woven twigs, mud covered, had been built. Each ball-like house was surmounted by some manner of carven image, which Ja told me indicated the identity of the owner.

Horizontal slits, six inches high and two or three feet wide, served to admit light and ventilation. The entrances to the houses were through small apertures in the bases of the trees and thence upward by rude ladders through the hollow trunks to the rooms above. The houses varied in size from two to several rooms. The largest that I entered was divided into two floors and eight apartments.

All about the village, between it and the jungle, lay beautifully cultivated fields in which the Mezops raised such cereals, fruits, and vegetables as they required. Women and children were working in these gardens as we crossed toward the village. At sight of Ja they saluted deferentially, but to me they paid not the slightest attention. Among them and about the outer verge of the cultivated area were many warriors. These too saluted Ja, by touching the points of their spears to the ground directly before them.

Ja conducted me to a large house in the center of the village—the house with eight rooms—and taking me up into it gave me food and drink. There I met his mate, a comely girl with a nursing baby in her arms. Ja told her of how I had saved his life, and she was thereafter most kind and hospitable toward me, even permitting me to hold and amuse the tiny bundle of humanity whom Ja told me would one day rule the tribe, for Ja, it seemed, was the chief of the community.

We had eaten and rested, and I had slept, much to Ja's amusement, for it seemed that he seldom if ever did so, and then the red man proposed that I accompany him to the temple of the Mahars which lay not far from his village.

"We are not supposed to visit it," he said; "but the great ones cannot hear and if we keep well out of sight they need never know that we have been there. For my part I hate them and always have, but the other chieftains of the island think it best that we continue to maintain the amicable relations which exist between the two races; otherwise I should like nothing better than to lead my warriors amongst the hideous creatures and exterminate them—Pellucidar would be a better place to live were there none of them."

I wholly concurred in Ja's belief, but it seemed that it might be a difficult matter to exterminate the dominant race of Pellucidar. Thus conversing we followed the intricate trail toward the temple, which we came upon in a small clearing surrounded by enormous trees similar to those which must have flourished upon the outer crust during the carboniferous age.

Here was a mighty temple of hewn rock built in the shape of a rough oval with rounded roof in which were several large openings. No doors or windows were visible in the sides of the structure, nor was there need of any, except one entrance for the slaves, since, as Ja explained, the Mahars flew to and from their place of ceremonial, entering and leaving the building by means of the apertures in the roof.

"But," added Ja, "there is an entrance near the base of which even the Mahars know nothing. Come," and he led me across the clearing and about the end to a pile of loose rock which lay against the foot of the wall. Here he removed a couple of large boulders, revealing a small opening which led straight within the building, or so it seemed, though as I entered after Ja I discovered myself in a narrow place of extreme darkness.

"We are within the outer wall," said Ja. "It is hollow. Follow me closely."

The red man groped ahead a few paces and then began to ascend a primitive ladder similar to that which leads from the ground to the upper stories of his house. We ascended for some forty feet when the interior of the space between the walls commenced to grow lighter and presently we came opposite an opening in the inner wall which gave us an unobstructed view of the entire interior of the temple.

The lower floor was an enormous tank of clear water in which numerous hideous Mahars swam lazily up and down. Artificial islands of granite rock dotted this artificial sea, and upon several of them I saw men and women like myself.

"What are the human beings doing here?" I asked.

"Wait and you shall see," replied Ja. "They are to take a leading part in the ceremonies which will follow the advent of the queen. You may be thankful that you are not upon the same side of the wall as they."

Scarcely had he spoken than we heard a great fluttering of wings above and a moment later a long procession of the frightful reptiles of Pellucidar winged slowly and majestically through the large central opening in the roof and circled in stately manner about the temple.

There were several Mahars first, and then at least twenty awe-inspiring pterodactyls—thipdars, they are called within Pellucidar. Behind these came the queen, flanked by other thipdars as she had been when she entered the amphitheater at Phutra.

Three times they wheeled about the interior of the oval chamber, to settle finally upon the damp, cold boulders that fringe the outer edge of the pool. In the center of one side the largest rock was reserved for the queen, and here she took her place surrounded by her terrible guard.

All lay quiet for several minutes after settling to their places. One might have imagined them in silent prayer. The poor slaves upon the diminutive islands watched the horrid creatures with wide eyes. The men, for the most part, stood erect and stately with folded arms, awaiting their doom; but the women and children clung to one another, hiding behind the males. They are a noble-looking race, these cavemen of Pellucidar, and if our progenitors were as they, the human race of the outer crust has deteriorated rather than improved with the march of the ages. All they lack is opportunity. We have opportunity, and little else.

Now the queen moved. She raised her ugly head, looking about; then very slowly she crawled to the edge of her throne and slid noiselessly into the water. Up and down the long tank she swam, turning at the ends as you have seen captive seals turn in their tiny tanks, turning upon their backs and diving below the surface.

Nearer and nearer to the island she came until at last she remained at rest before the largest, which was directly opposite her throne. Raising her hideous head from the water she fixed her great, round eyes upon the slaves. They were fat and sleek, for they had been brought from a distant Mahar city where human beings are kept in droves, and bred and fattened, as we breed and fatten beef cattle.

The queen fixed her gaze upon a plump young maiden. Her victim tried to turn away, hiding her face in her hands and kneeling behind a woman; but the reptile, with unblinking eyes, stared on with such fixity that I could have sworn her vision penetrated the woman, and the girl's arms to reach at last the very center of her brain.

Slowly the reptile's head commenced to move to and fro, but the eyes never ceased to bore toward the frightened girl, and then the victim responded. She turned wide, fear-haunted eyes toward the Mahar queen, slowly she rose to her feet, and then as though dragged by some unseen power she moved as one in a trance straight toward the reptile, her glassy eyes fixed upon those of her captor.

To the water's edge she came, nor did she even pause, but stepped into the shallows beside the little island. On she moved toward the Mahar, who now slowly retreated as though leading her victim on. The water rose to the girl's knees, and still she advanced, chained by that clammy eye. Now the water was at her waist; now her armpits. Her fellows upon the island looked on in horror, helpless to avert her doom in which they saw a forecast of their own.

The Mahar sank now till only the long upper bill and eyes were exposed above the surface of the water, and the girl had advanced until the end of that repulsive beak was but an inch or two from her face, her horror-filled eyes riveted upon those of the reptile.

Now the water passed above the girl's mouth and nose—her eyes and forehead all that showed—yet still she walked on after the retreating Mahar.

The queen's head slowly disappeared beneath the surface and after it went the eyes of her victim—only a slow ripple widened toward the shores to mark where the two vanished.

For a time all was silence within the temple. The slaves were motionless in terror. The Mahars watched the surface of the water for the reappearance of their queen, and presently at one end of the tank her head rose slowly into view. She was backing toward the surface, her eyes fixed before her as they had been when she dragged the helpless girl to her doom.

And then to my utter amazement I saw the forehead and eyes of the maiden come slowly out of the depths, following the gaze of the reptile just as when she had disappeared beneath the surface. On and on came the girl until she stood in water that reached barely to her knees, and though she had been beneath the surface sufficient time to have drowned her thrice over there was no indication, other than her dripping hair and glistening body, that she had been submerged at all.

Again and again the queen led the girl into the depths and out again, until the uncanny weirdness of the thing got on my nerves so that I could have leaped into the tank to the child's rescue had I not taken a firm hold of myself.

Once they were below much longer than usual, and when they came to the surface I was horrified to see that one of the girl's arms was gone—gnawed completely off at the shoulder—but the poor thing gave no indication of realizing pain, only the horror in her set eyes seemed intensified.

The next time they appeared the other arm was gone, and then the breasts, and then a part of the face—it was awful. The poor creatures on the islands awaiting their fate tried to cover their eyes with their hands to hide the fearful sight, but now I saw that they too were under the hypnotic spell of the reptiles, so that they could only crouch in terror with their eyes fixed upon the terrible thing that was transpiring before them.

Finally the queen was under much longer than ever before, and when she rose she came alone and swam sleepily toward her boulder. The moment she mounted it seemed to be the signal for the other Mahars to enter the tank, and then commenced, upon a larger scale, a repetition of the uncanny performance through which the queen had led her victim.

Only the women and children fell prey to the Mahars—they being the weakest and most tender—and when they had satisfied their appetite for human flesh, some of them devouring two and three of the slaves, there were only a score of full-grown men left, and I thought that for some reason these were to be spared, but such was far from the case, for as the last Mahar crawled to her rock the queen's thipdars darted into the air, circled the temple once and then, hissing like steam engines, swooped down upon the remaining slaves.

There was no hypnotism here—just the plain, brutal ferocity of the beast of prey, tearing, rending, and gulping its meat, but at that it was less horrible than the uncanny method of the Mahars. By the time the thipdars had disposed of the last of the slaves the Mahars were all asleep upon their rocks, and a moment later the great pterodactyls swung back to their posts beside the queen, and themselves dropped into slumber.

"I thought the Mahars seldom, if ever, slept," I said to Ja.

"They do many things in this temple which they do not do elsewhere," he replied. "The Mahars of Phutra are not supposed to eat human flesh, yet slaves are brought here by thousands and almost always you will find Mahars on hand to consume them. I imagine that they do not bring their Sagoths here, because they are ashamed of the practice, which is supposed to obtain only among the least advanced of their race; but I would wager my canoe against a broken paddle that there is no Mahar but eats human flesh whenever she can get it."

"Why should they object to eating human flesh," I asked, "if it is true that they look upon us as lower animals?"

"It is not because they consider us their equals that they are supposed to look with abhorrence upon those who eat our flesh," replied Ja; "it is merely that we are warm-blooded animals. They would not think of eating the meat of a thag, which we consider such a delicacy, any more than I would think of eating a snake. As a matter of fact it is difficult to explain just why this sentiment should exist among them."

"I wonder if they left a single victim," I remarked, leaning far out of the opening in the rocky wall to inspect the temple better. Directly below me the water lapped the very side of the wall, there being a break in the boulders at this point as there was at several other places about the side of the temple.

My hands were resting upon a small piece of granite which formed a part of the wall, and all my weight upon it proved too much for it. It slipped and I lunged forward. There was nothing to grasp to save myself and I plunged headforemost into the water below.

Fortunately the tank was deep at this point, and I suffered no injury from the fall, but as I was rising to the surface my mind filled with the horrors of my position as I thought of the terrible doom which awaited me the moment the eyes of the reptiles fell upon the creature that had disturbed their slumber.

As long as I could I remained beneath the surface, swimming rapidly in the direction of the islands that I might prolong my life to the utmost. At last I was forced to rise for air, and as I cast a terrified glance in the direction of the Mahars and the thipdars I was almost stunned to see that not a single one remained upon the rocks where I had last seen them, nor as I searched the temple with my eyes could I discern any within it.

For a moment I was puzzled to account for the thing, until I realized that the reptiles, being deaf, could not have been disturbed by the noise my body made when it hit the water, and that as there is no such thing as time within Pellucidar there was no telling how long I had been beneath the surface. It was a difficult thing to attempt to figure out by earthly standards—this matter of elapsed time—but when I set myself to it I began to realize that I might have been submerged a second or a month or not at all. You have no conception of the strange contradictions and impossibilities which arise when all methods of measuring time, as we know them upon earth, are nonexistent.

I was about to congratulate myself upon the miracle which had saved me for the moment, when the memory of the hypnotic powers of the Mahars filled me with apprehension lest they be practicing their uncanny art upon me to the end that I merely imagined that I was alone in the temple. At the thought cold sweat broke out upon me from every pore, and as I crawled from the water onto one of the tiny islands I was trembling like a leaf—you cannot imagine the awful horror which even the simple thought of the repulsive Mahars of Pellucidar induces in the human mind, and to feel that you are in their power—that they are crawling, slimy, and abhorrent, to drag you down beneath the waters and devour you! It is frightful.

But they did not come, and at last I came to the conclusion that I was indeed alone within the temple. How long I should be alone was the next question to assail me as I swam frantically about once more in search of a means to escape.

Several times I called to Ja, but he must have left after I tumbled into the tank, for I received no response to my cries. Doubtless he had felt as certain of my doom when he saw me topple from our hiding place as I had, and lest he too should be discovered, had hastened from the temple and back to his village.

I knew that there must be some entrance to the building beside the doorways in the roof, for it did not seem reasonable to believe that the thousands of slaves which were brought here to feed the Mahars the human flesh they craved would all be carried through the air, and so I continued my search until at last it was rewarded by the discovery of several loose granite blocks in the masonry at one end of the temple.

A little effort proved sufficient to dislodge enough of these stones to permit me to crawl through into the clearing, and a moment later I had scurried across the intervening space to the dense jungle beyond.

Here I sank panting and trembling upon the matted grasses beneath the giant trees, for I felt that I had escaped from the grinning fangs of death, out of the depths of my own grave. Whatever dangers lay hidden in this island jungle, there could be none so fearsome as those which I had just escaped. I knew that I could meet death bravely enough if it but came in the form of some familiar beast or man—anything other than the hideous and uncanny Mahars.

CHAPTER NINE
THE FACE OF DEATH

I MUST HAVE FALLEN ASLEEP from exhaustion. When I awoke I was very hungry, and after busying myself searching for fruit for a while, I set off through the jungle to find the beach. I knew that the island was not so large but that I could easily find the sea if I did but move in a straight line, but there came the difficulty as there was no way in which I could direct my course and hold it, the sun, of course, being always directly above my head, and the trees so thickly set that I could see no distant object which might serve to guide me in a straight line.

As it was I must have walked for a great distance since I ate four times and slept twice before I reached the sea, but at last I did so, and my pleasure at the sight of it was greatly enhanced by the chance discovery of a hidden canoe among the bushes through which I had stumbled just prior to coming upon the beach.

I can tell you that it did not take me long to pull that awkward craft down to the water and shove it far out from shore. My experience with Ja had taught me that if I were to steal another canoe I must be quick about it and get far beyond the owner's reach as soon as possible.

I must have come out upon the opposite side of the island from that at which Ja and I had entered it, for the mainland was nowhere in sight. For a long time I paddled around the shore, though well out, before I saw the mainland in the distance. At the sight of it I lost no time in directing my course toward it, for I had long since made up my mind to return to Phutra and give myself up that I might be once more with Perry and Ghak the Hairy One.

I felt that I was a fool ever to have attempted to escape alone, especially in view of the fact that our plans were already well formulated to make a break for freedom together. Of course I realized that the chances of the success of our proposed venture were slim indeed, but I knew that I never could enjoy freedom without Perry so long as the old man lived, and I had learned that the probability that I might find means from without to rescue him was less than slight.

Had Perry been dead, I should gladly have pitted my strength and wit against the savage and primordial world in which I found myself. I could have lived in seclusion within some rocky cave until I had found the means to outfit myself with the crude weapons of the Stone Age, and then set out in search of her whose image had now become the constant companion of my waking hours, and the central and beloved figure of my dreams.

But, to the best of my knowledge, Perry still lived and it was my duty and wish to be again with him, that we might share the dangers and vicissitudes of the strange world we had discovered. And Ghak, too; the great, shaggy man had found a place in the hearts of us both, for he was indeed every inch a man and king. Uncouth, perhaps, and brutal, too, if judged too harshly by the standards of effete twentieth-century civilization, but withal noble, dignified, chivalrous, and lovable.

Chance carried me to the very beach upon which I had discovered Ja's canoe, and a short time later I was scrambling up the steep bank to retrace my steps from the plain of Phutra. But my troubles came when I entered the canyon beyond the summit, for here I found that several of them centered at the point where I crossed the divide, and which one I had traversed to reach the pass I could not for the life of me remember.

It was all a matter of chance and so I set off down that which seemed the easiest going, and in this I made the same mistake that many of us do in selecting the path along which we shall follow out the course of our lives, and again learned that it is not always best to follow the line of least resistance.

By the time I had eaten eight meals and slept twice I was convinced that I was upon the wrong trail, for between Phutra and the inland sea I had not slept at all, and had eaten but once. To retrace my steps to the summit of the divide and explore another canyon seemed the only solution of my problem, but a sudden widening and levelness of the canyon just before me seemed to suggest that it was about to open into a level country, and with the lure of discovery strong upon me I decided to proceed but a short distance farther before I turned back.

The next turn of the canyon brought me to its mouth, and before me I saw a narrow plain leading down to an ocean. At my right the side of the canyon continued to the water's edge, the valley lying to my left, and the foot of it running gradually into the sea, where it formed a broad level beach.

Clumps of strange trees dotted the landscape here and there almost to the water, and rank grass and ferns grew between. From the nature of the vegetation I was convinced that the land between the ocean and the foothills was swampy, though directly before me it seemed dry enough all the way to the sandy strip along which the restless waters advanced and retreated.

Curiosity prompted me to walk down to the beach, for the scene was very beautiful. As I passed along beside the deep and tangled vegetation of the swamp I thought that I saw a movement of the ferns at my left, but though I stopped a moment to look it was not repeated, and if anything lay hid there my eyes could not penetrate the dense foliage to discern it.

Presently I stood upon the beach looking out over the wide and lonely sea across whose forbidding bosom no human being had yet ventured, to discover what strange and mysterious lands lay beyond, or what its invisible islands held of riches, wonders, or adventure. What savage races, what fierce and formidable beasts were this very instant watching the lapping of the waves upon its farther shore! How far did it extend? Perry had told me that the seas of Pellucidar were small in comparison with those of the outer crust, but even so this great ocean might stretch its broad expanse for thousands of miles. For countless ages it had rolled up and down its countless miles of shore, and yet today it remained all unknown beyond the tiny strip that was visible from its beaches.

The fascination of speculation was strong upon me. It was as though I had been carried back to the birth time of our own outer world to look upon its lands and seas ages before man had traversed either. Here was a new world, all untouched. It called to me to explore it. I was dreaming of the excitement and adventure which lay before us could Perry and I but escape the Mahars, when something, a slight noise I imagine, drew my attention behind me.

As I turned, romance, adventure, and discovery in the abstract took wing before the terrible embodiment of all three in concrete form that I beheld advancing upon me.

A huge, slimy amphibian it was, with toad-like body and the mighty jaws of an alligator. Its immense carcass must have weighed tons, and yet it moved swiftly and silently toward me. Upon one hand was the bluff that ran from the canyon to the sea, on the other the fearsome swamp from which the creature had sneaked upon me, behind lay the mighty untracked sea, and before me in the center of the narrow way that led to safety stood this huge mountain of terrible and menacing flesh.

A single glance at the thing was sufficient to assure me that I was facing one of those long-extinct, prehistoric creatures whose fossilized remains are found within the outer crust as far back as the Triassic formation, a gigantic labyrinthodon. And there I was, unarmed, and, with the exception of a loincloth, as naked as I had come into the world. I could imagine how my first ancestor felt that distant, prehistoric morn that he encountered for the first time the terrifying progenitor of the thing that had me cornered now beside the restless, mysterious sea.

Unquestionably he had escaped, or I should not have been within Pellucidar or elsewhere, and I wished at that moment that he had handed down to me with the various attributes that I presume I have inherited from him, the specific application of the instinct of self-preservation which saved him from the fate which loomed so close before me today.

To seek escape in the swamp or in the ocean would have been similar to jumping into a den of lions to escape one upon the outside. The sea and swamp both were doubtless alive with these mighty, carnivorous amphibians, and if not, the individual that menaced me would pursue me into either the sea or the swamp with equal facility.

There seemed nothing to do but stand supinely and await my end. I thought of Perry—how he would wonder what had become of me. I thought of my friends of the outer world, and of how they all would go on living their lives in total ignorance of the strange and terrible fate that had overtaken me, or unguessing the weird surroundings which had witnessed the last frightful agony of my extinction. And with these thoughts came a realization of how unimportant to the life and happiness of the world is the existence of any one of us. We may be snuffed out without an instant's warning, and for a brief day our friends speak of us with subdued voices. The following morning, while the first worm is busily engaged in testing the construction of our coffin, they are teeing up for the first hole to suffer more acute sorrow over a sliced ball than they did over our, to us, untimely demise.

The labyrinthodon was coming more slowly now. He seemed to realize that escape for me was impossible, and I could have sworn that his huge, fanged jaws grinned in pleasurable appreciation of my predicament, or was it in anticipation of the juicy morsel which would so soon be pulp between those formidable teeth?

He was about fifty feet from me when I heard a voice calling to me from the direction of the bluff at my left. I looked and could have shouted in delight at the sight that met my eyes, for there stood Ja, waving frantically to me, and urging me to run for it to the cliff's base.

I had no idea that I should escape the monster that had marked me for his breakfast, but at least I should not die alone. Human eyes would watch my end. It was cold comfort I presume, but yet I derived some slight peace of mind from the contemplation of it.

To run seemed ridiculous, especially toward that steep and unscalable cliff, and yet I did so, and as I ran I saw Ja, agile as a monkey, crawl down the precipitous face of the rocks, clinging to small projections, and the tough creepers that had found roothold here and there.

The labyrinthodon evidently thought that Ja was coming to double his portion of human flesh, so he was in no haste to pursue me to the cliff and frighten away this other titbit. Instead he merely trotted along behind me.

As I approached the foot of the cliff I saw what Ja intended doing, but I doubted if the thing would prove successful. He had come down to within twenty feet of the bottom, and there, clinging with one hand to a small ledge, and with his feet resting precariously upon tiny bushes that grew from the solid face of the rock, he lowered the point of his long spear until it hung some six feet above the ground.

To clamber up that slim shaft without dragging Ja down and precipitating both to the same doom from which the copper-colored one was attempting to save me seemed utterly impossible, and as I came near the spear I told Ja so, and that I could not risk him to try to save myself.

But he insisted that he knew what he was doing and was in no danger himself.

"The danger is still yours," he called, "for unless you move much more rapidly than you are now, the *sithic* will be upon you and drag you back before ever you are halfway up the spear—he can rear up and reach you with ease anywhere below where I stand."

Well, Ja should know his own business, I thought, and so I grasped the spear and clambered up toward the red man as rapidly as I could—being so far removed from my simian ancestors as I am. I imagine the slow-witted sithic, as Ja called him, suddenly realized our intentions and that he was quite likely to lose all his meal instead of having it doubled as he had hoped.

When he saw me clambering up that spear he let out a hiss that fairly shook the ground, and came charging after me at a terrific rate. I had reached the top of the spear by this time, or almost; another six inches would give me a hold on Ja's hand, when I felt a sudden wrench from below and glancing fearfully downward saw the mighty jaws of the monster close on the sharp point of the weapon.

I made a frantic effort to reach Ja's hand, the sithic gave a tremendous tug that came near to jerking Ja from his frail hold on the surface of the rock, the spear slipped from his fingers, and still clinging to it I plunged feet foremost toward my executioner.

At the instant that he felt the spear come away from Ja's hand the creature must have opened his huge jaws to catch me, for when I came down, still clinging to the butt end of the weapon, the point yet rested in his mouth and the result was that the sharpened end transfixed his lower jaw.

With the pain he snapped his mouth closed. I fell upon his snout, lost my hold upon the spear, rolled the length of his face and head, across his short neck onto his broad back and from there to the ground.

Scarce had I touched the earth than I was upon my feet, dashing madly for the path by which I had entered this horrible valley. A glance over my shoulder showed me the sithic engaged in pawing at the spear stuck through his lower jaw, and so busily engaged did he remain in this occupation that I had gained the safety of the cliff top before he was ready to take up the pursuit. When he did not discover me in sight within the valley he dashed, hissing, into the rank vegetation of the swamp and that was the last that I saw of him.

CHAPTER TEN
PHUTRA AGAIN

I HASTENED TO THE CLIFF EDGE above Ja and helped him to a secure footing. He would not listen to any thanks for his attempt to save me, which had come so near miscarrying.

"I had given you up for lost when you tumbled into the Mahar temple," he said, "for not even I could save you from their clutches, and you may imagine my surprise when on seeing a canoe dragged up upon the beach of the mainland I discovered your own footprints in the sand beside it.

"I immediately set out in search of you, knowing as I did that you must be entirely unarmed and defenseless against the many dangers which lurk upon the mainland both in the form of savage beasts and reptiles, and men as well. I had no difficulty in tracking you to this point. It is well that I arrived when I did."

"But why did you do it?" I asked, puzzled at this show of friendship on the part of a man of another world and a different race and color.

"You saved my life," he replied; "from that moment it became my duty to protect and befriend you. I would have been no true Mezop had I evaded my plain duty; but it was a pleasure in this instance for I like you. I wish that you would come and live with me. You shall become a member of my tribe. Among us there is the best of hunting and fishing, and you shall have, to choose a mate from, the most beautiful girls of Pellucidar. Will you come?"

I told him about Perry then, and Dian the Beautiful, and how my duty was to them first. Afterward I should return and visit him—if I could ever find his island.

"Oh, that is easy, my friend," he said. "You need merely to come to the foot of the highest peak of the Mountains of the Clouds. There you will find a river which flows into the Lural Az. Directly opposite the mouth of the river you will see three large islands far out, so far that they are barely discernible, the one to the extreme left as you face them from the mouth of the river is Anoroc, where I rule the tribe of Anoroc."

"But how am I to find the Mountains of the Clouds?" I asked.

"Men say that they are visible from half Pellucidar," he replied.

"How large is Pellucidar?" I asked, wondering what sort of theory these primitive men had concerning the form and substance of their world.

"The Mahars say it is round, like the inside of a tola shell," he answered, "but that is ridiculous, since, were it true, we should fall back were we to travel far in any direction, and all the waters of Pellucidar would run to one spot and drown us. No, Pellucidar is quite flat and extends no man knows how far in all directions. At the edges, so my ancestors have reported and handed down to me, is a great wall that prevents the earth and waters from escaping over into the burning sea whereon Pellucidar floats; but I never have been so far from Anoroc as to have seen this wall with my own eyes. However, it is quite reasonable to believe that this is true, whereas there is no reason at all in the foolish belief of the Mahars. According to them Pellucidarians who live upon the opposite side walk always with their heads pointed downward!" and Ja laughed uproariously at the very thought.

If was plain to see that the human folk of this inner world had not advanced far in learning, and the thought that the ugly Mahars had so outstripped them was a very pathetic one indeed. I wondered how many ages it would take to lift these people out of their ignorance even were it given to Perry and me to attempt it. Possibly we would be killed for our pains as were those men of the outer world who dared challenge the dense ignorance and superstitions of the earth's younger days. But it was worth the effort if the opportunity ever presented itself.

And then it occurred to me that here was an opportunity—that I might make a small beginning upon Ja, who was my friend, and thus note the effect of my teaching upon a Pellucidarian.

"Ja," I said, "what would you say were I to tell you that insofar as the Mahars' theory of the shape of Pellucidar is concerned it is correct?"

"I would say," he replied, "that either you are a fool, or took me for one."

"But, Ja," I insisted, "if their theory is incorrect how do you account for the fact that I was able to pass through the earth from the outer crust to Pellucidar. If your theory is correct all is a sea of flame beneath us, wherein no peoples could exist, and yet I come from a great world that is covered with human beings, and beasts, and birds, and fishes in mighty oceans."

"You live upon the underside of Pellucidar, and walk always with your head pointed downward?" he scoffed. "And were I to believe that, my friend, I should indeed be mad."

I attempted to explain the force of gravity to him, and by the means of the dropped fruit to illustrate how impossible it would be for a body to fall off the earth under any circumstances. He listened so intently that I thought I had made an impression, and started the train of thought that would lead him to a partial understanding of the truth. But I was mistaken.

"Your own illustration," he said finally, "proves the falsity of your theory." He dropped a fruit from his hand to the ground. "See," he said, "without support even this tiny fruit falls until it strikes something that stops it. If Pellucidar were not supported upon the flaming sea it too would fall as the fruit falls—you have proven it yourself!" He had me, that time—you could see it in his eye.

It seemed a hopeless job and I gave it up, temporarily at least, for when I contemplated the necessary explanation of our solar system and the universe I realized how futile it would be to attempt to picture to Ja or any other Pellucidarian the sun, the moon, the planets, and the countless stars. Those born within the inner world could no more conceive of such things than can we of the outer crust reduce to factors appreciable to our finite minds such terms as space and eternity.

"Well, Ja," I laughed, "whether we be walking with our feet up or down, here we are, and the question of greatest importance is not so much where we came from as where we are going now. For my part I wish that you could guide me to Phutra where I may give myself up to the Mahars once more that my friends and I may work out the plan of escape which the Sagoths interrupted when they gathered us together and drove us to the arena to witness the punishment of the slaves who killed the guardsman. I wish now that I had not left the arena for by this time my friends and I might have made good our escape, whereas this delay may mean the wrecking of all our plans, which depended for their consummation upon the continued sleep of the three Mahars who lay in the pit beneath the building in which we were confined."

"You would return to captivity?" cried Ja.

"My friends are there," I replied, "the only friends I have in Pellucidar, except yourself. What else may I do under the circumstances?"

He thought for a moment in silence. Then he shook his head sorrowfully.

"It is what a brave man and a good friend should do," he said; "yet it seems most foolish, for the Mahars will most certainly condemn you to death for running away, and so you will be accomplishing nothing for your friends by returning. Never in all my life have I heard of a prisoner returning to the Mahars of his own free will. There are but few who escape them, though some do, and these would rather die than be recaptured."

"I see no other way, Ja," I said, "though I can assure you that I would rather go to Sheol after Perry than to Phutra. However, Perry is much too pious to make the probability at all great that I should ever be called upon to rescue him from the former locality."

Ja asked me what Sheol was, and when I explained, as best I could, he said, "You are speaking of Molop Az, the flaming sea upon which Pellucidar floats. All the dead who are buried in the ground go there. Piece by piece they are carried down to Molop Az by the little demons who dwell there. We know this because when graves are opened we find that the bodies have been partially or entirely borne off. That is why we of Anoroc place our dead in high trees where the birds may find them and bear them bit by bit to the Dead World above the Land of Awful Shadow. If we kill an enemy we place his body in the ground that it may go to Molop Az."

As we talked we had been walking up the canyon down which I had come to the great ocean and the sithic. Ja did his best to dissuade me from returning to Phutra, but when he saw that I was determined to do so, he consented to guide me to a point from which I could see the plain where lay the city. To my surprise the distance was but short from the beach where I had again met Ja. It was evident that I had spent much time following the windings of a tortuous canyon, while just beyond the ridge lay the city of Phutra near to which I must have come several times.

As we topped the ridge and saw the granite gate towers dotting the flowered plain at our feet Ja made a final effort to persuade me to abandon my mad purpose and return with him to Anoroc, but I was firm in my resolve, and at last he bid me good-bye, assured in his own mind that he was looking upon me for the last time.

I was sorry to part with Ja, for I had come to like him very much indeed. With his hidden city upon the island of Anoroc as a base, and his savage warriors as escort Perry and I could have accomplished much in the line of exploration, and I hoped that were we successful in our effort to escape we might return to Anoroc later.

There was, however, one great thing to be accomplished first—at least it was the great thing to me—the finding of Dian the Beautiful. I wanted to make amends for the affront I had put upon her in my ignorance, and I wanted to—well, I wanted to see her again, and to be with her.

Down the hillside I made my way into the gorgeous field of flowers, and then across the rolling land toward the shadowless columns that guard the ways to buried Phutra. At a quarter mile from the nearest entrance I was discovered by the Sagoth guard, and in an instant four of the gorilla-men were dashing toward me.

Though they brandished their long spears and yelled wildly at me I paid not the slightest attention to them, walking quietly toward them as though unaware of their existence. My manner had the effect upon them that I had hoped, and as we came quite near together they ceased their savage shouting. It was evident that they had expected me to turn and flee at sight of them, thus presenting that which they most enjoyed, a moving human target at which to cast their spears.

"What do you here?" shouted one, and then as he recognized me, "Ho! It is the slave who claims to be from another world—he who escaped when the thag ran amuck within the amphitheater. But why do you return, having once made good your escape?"

"I did not 'escape'," I replied. "I but ran away to avoid the thag, as did others, and coming into a long passage I became confused and lost my way in the foothills beyond Phutra. Only now have I found my way back."

"And you come of your free will back to Phutra!" exclaimed one of the guardsmen.

"Where else might I go?" I asked. "I am a stranger within Pellucidar and know no other where than Phutra. Why should I not desire to be in Phutra? Am I not well fed and well treated? Am I not happy? What better lot could man desire?"

The Sagoths scratched their heads. This was a new one on them, and so being stupid brutes they took me to their masters whom they felt would be better fitted to solve the riddle of my return, for riddle they still considered it.

I had spoken to the Sagoths as I had for the purpose of throwing them off the scent of my purposed attempt at escape. If they thought that I was so satisfied with my lot within Phutra that I would voluntarily return when I had once had so excellent an opportunity to escape, they would never for an instant imagine that I could be occupied in arranging another escape immediately upon my return to the city.

So they led me before a slimy Mahar who clung to a slimy rock within the large room that was the thing's office. With cold, reptilian eyes the creature seemed to bore through the thin veneer of my deceit and read my inmost thoughts. It heeded the story which the Sagoths told of my return to Phutra, watching the gorilla-men's lips and fingers during the recital. Then it questioned me through one of the Sagoths.

"You say that you returned to Phutra of your own free will, because you think yourself better off here than elsewhere—do you not know that you may be the next chosen to give up your life in the interests of the wonderful scientific investigations that our learned ones are continually occupied with?"

I hadn't heard of anything of that nature, but I thought best not to admit it.

"I could be in no more danger here," I said, "than naked and unarmed in the savage jungles or upon the lonely plains of Pellucidar. I was fortunate, I think, to return to Phutra at all. As it was I barely escaped death within the jaws of a huge sithic. No, I am sure that I am safer in the hands of intelligent creatures such as rule Phutra. At least such would be the case in my own world, where human beings like myself rule supreme. There the higher races of man extend protection and hospitality to the stranger within their gates, and being a stranger here I naturally assumed that a like courtesy would be accorded me."

The Mahar looked at me in silence for some time after I ceased speaking and the Sagoth had translated my words to his master. The creature seemed deep in thought. Presently she communicated some message to the Sagoth. The latter turned, and motioning me to follow him, left the presence of the reptile. Behind and on either side of me marched the balance of the guard.

"What are they going to do with me?" I asked the fellow at my right.

"You are to appear before the learned ones who will question you regarding this strange world from which you say you come."

After a moment's silence he turned to me again.

"Do you happen to know," he asked, "what the Mahars do to slaves who lie to them?"

"No," I replied, "nor does it interest me, as I have no intention of lying to the Mahars."

"Then be careful that you don't repeat the impossible tale you told Sol-to-to just now—another world, indeed, where human beings rule!" he concluded in fine scorn.

"But it is the truth," I insisted. "From where else then did I come? I am not of Pellucidar. Anyone with half an eye could see that."

"It is your misfortune then," he remarked drily, "that you may not be judged by one with but half an eye."

"What will they do with me," I asked, "if they do not have a mind to believe me?"

"You may be sentenced to the arena, or go to the pits to be used in research work by the learned ones," he replied.

"And what will they do with me there?" I persisted.

"No one knows except the Mahars and those who go to the pits with them, but as the latter never return, their knowledge does them but little good. It is said that the learned ones cut up their subjects while they are yet alive, thus learning many useful things. However I should not imagine that it would prove very useful to him who was being cut up; but of course this is all but conjecture. The chances are that ere long you will know much more about it than I," and he grinned as he spoke. The Sagoths have a well-developed sense of humor.

"And suppose it is the arena," I continued; "what then?"

"You saw the two who met the tarag and the thag the time that you escaped?" he said.

"Yes."

"Your end in the arena would be similar to what was intended for them," he explained, "though of course the same kinds of animals might not be employed."

"It is sure death in either event?" I asked.

"What becomes of those who go below with the learned ones I do not know, nor does any other," he replied; "but those who go to the arena may come out alive and thus regain their liberty, as did the two whom you saw."

"They gained their liberty? And how?"

"It is the custom of the Mahars to liberate those who remain alive within the arena after the beasts depart or are killed. Thus it has happened that several mighty warriors from far distant lands, whom we have captured on our slave raids, have battled the brutes turned in upon them and slain them, thereby winning their freedom. In the instance which you witnessed the beasts killed each other, but the result was the same—the man and woman were liberated, furnished with weapons, and started on their homeward journey. Upon the left shoulder of each a mark was burned—the mark of the Mahars—which will forever protect these two from slaving parties."

"There is a slender chance for me then if I be sent to the arena, and none at all if the learned ones drag me to the pits?"

"You are quite right," he replied; "but do not felicitate yourself too quickly should you be sent to the arena, for there is scarce one in a thousand who comes out alive."

To my surprise they returned me to the same building in which I had been confined with Perry and Ghak before my escape. At the doorway I was turned over to the guards there.

"He will doubtless be called before the investigators shortly," said he who had brought me back, "so have him in readiness."

The guards in whose hands I now found myself, upon hearing that I had returned of my own volition to Phutra evidently felt that it would be safe to give me liberty within the building as had been the custom before I had escaped, and so I was told to return to whatever duty had been mine formerly.

My first act was to hunt up Perry, whom I found poring as usual over the great tomes that he was supposed to be merely dusting and rearranging upon new shelves.

As I entered the room he glanced up and nodded pleasantly to me, only to resume his work as though I had never been away at all. I was both astonished and hurt at his indifference. And to think that I was risking death to return to him purely from a sense of duty and affection!

"Why, Perry!" I exclaimed, "haven't you a word for me after my long absence?"

"Long absence!" he repeated in evident astonishment. "What do you mean?"

"Are you crazy, Perry? Do you mean to say that you have not missed me since that time we were separated by the charging thag within the arena?"

"'That time'," he repeated. "Why man, I have but just returned from the arena! You reached here almost as soon as I. Had you been much later I should indeed have been worried, and as it is I had intended asking you about how you escaped the beast as soon as I had completed the translation of this most interesting passage."

"Perry, you *are* mad," I exclaimed. "Why, the Lord only knows how long I have been away. I have been to other lands, discovered a new race of humans within Pellucidar, seen the Mahars at their worship in their hidden temple, and barely escaped with my life from them and from a great labyrinthodon that I met afterward, following my long and tedious wanderings across an unknown world. I must have been away for months, Perry, and now you barely look up from your work when I return and insist that we have been separated but a moment. Is that any way to treat a friend? I'm surprised at you. Perry, and if I'd thought for a moment that you cared no more for me than this I should not have returned to chance death at the hands of the Mahars for your sake."

The old man looked at me for a long time before he spoke. There was a puzzled expression upon his wrinkled face, and a look of hurt sorrow in his eyes.

"David, my boy," he said, "how could you for a moment doubt my love for you? There is something strange here that I cannot understand. I know that I am not mad, and I am equally sure that you are not; but how in the world are we to account for the strange hallucinations that each of us seems to harbor relative to the passage of time since last we saw each other. You are positive that months have gone by, while to me it seems equally certain that not more than an hour ago I sat beside you in the amphitheater. Can it be that both of us are right and at the same time both are wrong? First tell me what time is, and then maybe I can solve our problem. Do you catch my meaning?"

I did, and said so.

"Yes," continued the old man, "we are both right. To me, bent over my book here, there has been no lapse of time. I have done little or nothing to waste my energies and so have required neither food nor sleep, but you, on the contrary, have walked and fought and wasted strength and tissue which must needs be rebuilt by nutriment and food, and so, having eaten and slept many times since last you saw me you naturally measure the lapse of time largely by these acts. As a matter of fact, David, I am rapidly coming to the conviction that there is no such thing as time—surely there can be no time here within Pellucidar, where there are no means for measuring or recording time. Why, the Mahars themselves take no account of such a thing as time. I find here in all their literary works but a single tense, the present. There seems to be neither past nor future with them. Of course it is impossible for our outer-earthly minds to grasp such a condition, but our recent experiences seem to demonstrate its existence."

It was too big a subject for me, and I said so, but Perry seemed to enjoy nothing better than speculating upon it, and after listening with interest to my account of the adventures through which I had passed he returned once more to the subject, which he was enlarging upon with considerable fluency when he was interrupted by the entrance of a Sagoth.

"Come!" commanded the intruder, beckoning to me. "The investigators would speak with you."

"Good-bye, Perry!" I said, clasping the old man's hand. "There may be nothing but the present and no such thing as time, but I feel that I am about to take a trip into the hereafter from which I shall never return. If you and Ghak should manage to escape I want you to promise me that you will find Dian the Beautiful and tell her that with my last words I asked her forgiveness for the unintentional affront I put upon her, and that my one wish was to be spared long enough to right the wrong that I had done her."

Tears came to Perry's eyes.

"I cannot believe but that you will return, David," he said. "It would be awful to think of living out the balance of my life without you among these hateful and repulsive creatures. If you are taken away I shall never escape, for I feel that I am as well off here as I should be anywhere within this buried world. Good-bye, my boy, good-bye!" and then his old voice faltered and broke, and as he hid his face in his hands the Sagoth guardsman grasped me roughly by the shoulder and hustled me from the chamber.

CHAPTER ELEVEN
FOUR DEAD MAHARS

A MOMENT LATER I WAS STANDING before a dozen Mahars—the official investigators of Phutra. They asked me many questions, through a Sagoth interpreter. I answered them all truthfully. They seemed particularly interested in my account of the outer earth and the strange vehicle which had brought Perry and me to Pellucidar. I thought that I had convinced them, and after they had sat in silence for a long time following my examination, I expected to be ordered returned to my quarters.

During this apparent silence they were debating through the medium of strange, unspoken language the merits of my tale. At last the head of the tribunal communicated the result of their conference to the officer in charge of the Sagoth guard.

"Come," he said to me, "you are sentenced to the experimental pits for having dared to insult the intelligence of the mighty ones with the ridiculous tale you have had the temerity to unfold to them."

"Do you mean that they do not believe me?" I asked, totally astonished.

"Believe you!" he laughed. "Do you mean to say that you expected any one to believe so impossible a lie?"

It was hopeless, and so I walked in silence beside my guard down through dark corridors and runways toward my awful doom. At a low level we came upon a number of lighted chambers in which we saw many Mahars engaged in various occupations. To one of these chambers my guard escorted me, and before leaving they chained me to a side wall. There were other humans similarly chained. Upon a long table lay a victim even as I was ushered into the room. Several Mahars stood about the poor creature holding him down so that he could not move. Another, grasping a sharp knife with her three-toed forefoot, was laying open the victim's chest and abdomen. No anesthetic had been administered and the shrieks and groans of the tortured man were terrible to hear. This, indeed, was vivisection with a vengeance. Cold sweat broke out upon me as I realized that soon my turn would come. And to think that where there was no such thing as time I might easily imagine that my suffering was enduring for months before death finally released me!

The Mahars had paid not the slightest attention to me as I had been brought into the room. So deeply immersed were they in their work that I am sure they did not even know that the Sagoths had entered with me. The door was close by. Would that I could reach it! But those heavy chains precluded any such possibility. I looked about for some means of escape from my bonds. Upon the floor between me and the Mahars lay a tiny surgical instrument which one of them must have dropped. It looked not unlike a buttonhook, but was much smaller, and its point was sharpened. A hundred times in my boyhood days had I picked locks with a buttonhook. Could I but reach that little bit of polished steel I might yet effect at least a temporary escape.

Crawling to the limit of my chain, I found that by reaching one hand as far out as I could my fingers still fell an inch short of the coveted instrument. It was tantalizing! Stretch every fiber of my being as I would, I could not quite make it.

At last I turned about and extended one foot toward the object. My heart came to my throat! I could just touch the thing! But suppose that in my effort to drag it toward me I should accidentally shove it still farther away and thus entirely out of reach! Cold sweat broke out upon me from every pore. Slowly and cautiously I made the effort. My toes dropped upon the cold metal. Gradually I worked it toward me until I felt that it was within reach of my hand and a moment later I had turned about and the precious thing was in my grasp.

Assiduously I fell to work upon the Mahar lock that held my chain. It was pitifully simple. A child might have picked it, and a moment later I was free. The Mahars were now evidently completing their work at the table. One already turned away and was examining other victims, evidently with the intention of selecting the next subject.

Those at the table had their backs toward me. But for the creature walking toward us I might have escaped that moment. Slowly the thing approached me, when its attention was attracted by a huge slave chained a few yards to my right. Here the reptile stopped and commenced to go over the poor devil carefully, and as it did so its back turned toward me for an instant, and in that instant I gave two mighty leaps that carried me out of the chamber into the corridor beyond, down which I raced with all the speed I could command.

Where I was, or whither I was going, I knew not. My only thought was to place as much distance as possible between me and that frightful chamber of torture.

Presently I reduced my speed to a brisk walk, and later realizing the danger of running into some new predicament, were I not careful, I moved still more slowly and cautiously. After a time I came to a passage that seemed in some mysterious way familiar to me, and presently, chancing to glance within a chamber which led from the corridor I saw three Mahars curled up in slumber upon a bed of skins. I could have shouted aloud in joy and relief. It was the same corridor and the same Mahars that I had intended to have lead so important a role in our escape from Phutra. Providence had indeed been kind to me, for the reptiles still slept.

My one great danger now lay in returning to the upper levels in search of Perry and Ghak, but there was nothing else to be done, and so I hastened upward. When I came to the frequented portions of the building I found a large burden of skins in a corner and these I lifted to my head, carrying them in such a way that ends and corners fell down about my shoulders completely hiding my face. Thus disguised I found Perry and Ghak together in the chamber where we had been wont to eat and sleep.

Both were glad to see me, it is needless to say, though of course they had known nothing of the fate that had been meted out to me by my judges. It was decided that no time should now be lost before attempting to put our plan of escape to the test, as I could not hope to remain hidden from the Sagoths long, nor could I forever carry that bale of skins about upon my head without arousing suspicion. However it seemed likely that it would carry me once more safely through the crowded passages and chambers of the upper levels, and so I set out with Perry and Ghak—the stench of the illy cured pelts fairly choking me.

Together we repaired to the first tier of corridors beneath the main floor of the building, and here Perry and Ghak halted to await me. The buildings are cut out of the solid limestone formation. There is nothing at all remarkable about their architecture. The rooms are sometimes rectangular, sometimes circular, and again oval in shape. The corridors which connect them are narrow and not always straight. The chambers are lighted by diffused sunlight reflected through tubes similar to those by which the avenues are lighted. The lower the tiers of chambers, the darker. Most of the corridors are entirely unlighted. The Mahars can see quite well in semidarkness.

Down to the main floor we encountered many Mahars, Sagoths, and slaves; but no attention was paid to us as we had become a part of the domestic life of the building. There was but a single entrance leading from the place into the avenue and this was well guarded by Sagoths—this doorway alone were we forbidden to pass. It is true that we were not supposed to enter the deeper corridors and apartments except on special occasions when we were instructed to do so; but as we were considered a lower order without intelligence there was little reason to fear that we could accomplish any harm by so doing, and so we were not hindered as we entered the corridor which led below.

Wrapped in a skin I carried three swords, and the two bows, and the arrows which Perry and I had fashioned. As many slaves bore skin-wrapped burdens to and fro my load attracted no comment. Where I left Ghak and Perry there were no other creatures in sight, and so I withdrew one sword from the package, and leaving the balance of the weapons with Perry, started on alone toward the lower levels.

Having come to the apartment in which the three Mahars slept I entered silently on tiptoe, forgetting that the creatures were without the sense of hearing. With a quick thrust through the heart I disposed of the first but my second thrust was not so fortunate, so that before I could kill the next of my victims it had hurled itself against the third, who sprang quickly up, facing me with wide-distended jaws. But fighting is not the occupation which the race of Mahars loves, and when the thing saw that I already had dispatched two of its companions, and that my sword was red with their blood, it made a dash to escape me. But I was too quick for it, and so, half hopping, half flying, it scurried down another corridor with me close upon its heels.

Its escape meant the utter ruin of our plan, and in all probability my instant death. This thought lent wings to my feet; but even at my best I could do no more than hold my own with the leaping thing before me.

Of a sudden it turned into an apartment on the right of the corridor, and an instant later as I rushed in I found myself facing two of the Mahars. The one who had been there when we entered had been occupied with a number of metal vessels, into which had been put powders and liquids as I judged from the array of flasks standing about upon the bench where it had been working. In an instant I realized what I had stumbled upon. It was the very room for the finding of which Perry had given me minute directions. It was the buried chamber in which was hidden the Great Secret of the race of Mahars. And on the bench beside the flasks lay the skin-bound book which held the only copy of the thing I was to have sought, after dispatching the three Mahars in their sleep.

There was no exit from the room other than the doorway in which I now stood facing the two frightful reptiles. Cornered, I knew that they would fight like demons, and they were well equipped to fight if fight they must. Together they launched themselves upon me, and though I ran one of them through the heart on the instant, the other fastened its gleaming fangs about my sword arm above the elbow, and then with her sharp talons commenced to rake me about the body, evidently intent upon disemboweling me. I saw that it was useless to hope that I might release my arm from that powerful, viselike grip which seemed to be severing my arm from my body. The pain I suffered was intense, but it only served to spur me to greater efforts to overcome my antagonist.

Back and forth across the floor we struggled—the Mahar dealing me terrific, cutting blows with her forefeet, while I attempted to protect my body with my left hand, at the same time watching for an opportunity to transfer my blade from my now useless sword hand to its rapidly weakening mate. At last I was successful, and with what seemed to me my last ounce of strength I ran the blade through the ugly body of my foe.

Soundless, as it had fought, it died, and though weak from pain and loss of blood, it was with an emotion of triumphant pride that I stepped across its convulsively stiffening corpse to snatch up the most potent secret of a world. A single glance assured me it was the very thing that Perry had described to me.

And as I grasped it did I think of what it meant to the human race of Pellucidar—did there flash through my mind the thought that countless generations of my own kind yet unborn would have reason to worship me for the thing that I had accomplished for them? Did I? I did not. I thought of a beautiful oval face, gazing out of limpid eyes, through a waving mass of jet-black hair. I thought of red, red lips, God-made for kissing. And of a sudden, apropos of nothing, standing there alone in the secret chamber of the Mahars of Pellucidar, I realized that I loved Dian the Beautiful.

CHAPTER TWELVE
PURSUIT

FOR AN INSTANT I STOOD THERE thinking of her, and then, with a sigh, I tucked the book in the thong that supported my loincloth, and turned to leave the apartment. At the bottom of the corridor which leads aloft from the lower chambers I whistled in accordance with the prearranged signal which was to announce to Perry and Ghak that I had been successful. A moment later they stood beside me, and to my surprise I saw that Hooja the Sly One accompanied them.

"He joined us," explained Perry, "and would not be denied. The fellow is a fox. He scents escape, and rather than be thwarted of our chance now I told him that I would bring him to you, and let you decide whether he might accompany us."

I had no love for Hooja, and no confidence in him. I was sure that if he thought it would profit him he would betray us; but I saw no way out of it now, and the fact that I had killed four Mahars instead of only the three I had expected to, made it possible to include the fellow in our scheme of escape.

"Very well," I said, "you may come with us, Hooja; but at the first intimation of treachery I shall run my sword through you. Do you understand?"

He said that he did.

Sometime later we had removed the skins from the four Mahars, and so succeeded in crawling inside of them ourselves that there seemed an excellent chance for us to pass unnoticed from Phutra. It was not an easy thing to fasten the hides together where we had split them along the belly to remove them from their carcasses, but by remaining out until the others had all been sewed in with my help, and then leaving an aperture in the breast of Perry's skin through which he could pass his hands to sew me up, we were enabled to accomplish our design to really much better purpose than I had hoped. We managed to keep the heads erect by passing our swords up through the necks, and by the same means were enabled to move them about in a lifelike manner. We had our greatest difficulty with the webbed feet, but even that problem was finally solved, so that when we moved about we did so quite naturally. Tiny holes punctured in the baggy throats into which our heads were thrust permitted us to see well enough to guide our progress.

Thus we started up toward the main floor of the building. Ghak headed the strange procession, then came Perry, followed by Hooja, while I brought up the rear, after admonishing Hooja that I had so arranged my sword that I could thrust it through the head of my disguise into his vitals were he to show any indication of faltering.

As the noise of hurrying feet warned me that we were entering the busy corridors of the main level, my heart came up into my mouth. It is with no sense of shame that I admit that I was frightened—never before in my life, nor since, did I experience any such agony of soul-searing fear and suspense as enveloped me. If it be possible to sweat blood, I sweat it then.

Slowly, after the manner of locomotion habitual to the Mahars, when they are not using their wings, we crept through throngs of busy slaves, Sagoths, and Mahars. After what seemed an eternity we reached the outer door which leads into the main avenue of Phutra. Many Sagoths loitered near the opening. They glanced at Ghak as he padded between them. Then Perry passed, and then Hooja. Now it was my turn, and then in a sudden fit of freezing terror I realized that the warm blood from my wounded arm was trickling down through the dead foot of the Mahar skin I wore and leaving its telltale mark upon the pavement, for I saw a Sagoth call a companion's attention to it.

The guard stepped before me and pointing to my bleeding foot spoke to me in the sign language which these two races employ as a means of communication. Even had I known what he was saying I could not have replied with the dead thing that covered me. I once had seen a great Mahar freeze a presumptuous Sagoth with a look. It seemed my only hope, and so I tried it. Stopping in my tracks I moved my sword so that it made the dead head appear to turn inquiring eyes upon the gorilla-man. For a long moment I stood perfectly still eyeing the fellow with those dead eyes. Then I lowered the head and started slowly on. For a moment all hung in the balance, but before I touched him the guard stepped to one side, and I passed on out into the avenue.

On we went up the broad street, but now we were safe for the very numbers of our enemies that surrounded us on all sides. Fortunately, there was a great concourse of Mahars repairing to the shallow lake which lies a mile or more from the city. They go there to indulge their amphibian proclivities in diving for small fish, and enjoying the cool depths of the water. It is a freshwater lake, shallow, and free from the larger reptiles which make the use of the great seas of Pellucidar impossible for any but their own kind.

In the thick of the crowd we passed up the steps and out onto the plain. For some distance Ghak remained with the stream that was traveling toward the lake, but finally, at the bottom of a little gully he halted, and there we remained until all had passed and we were alone. Then, still in our disguises, we set off directly away from Phutra.

The heat of the vertical rays of the sun was fast making our horrible prisons unbearable, so that after passing a low divide, and entering a sheltering forest, we finally discarded the Mahar skins that had brought us thus far in safety.

I shall not weary you with the details of that bitter and galling flight. How we traveled at a dogged run until we dropped in our tracks. How we were beset by strange and terrible beasts. How we barely escaped the cruel fangs of lions and tigers the size of which would dwarf into pitiful insignificance the greatest felines of the outer world.

On and on we raced, our one thought to put as much distance between ourselves and Phutra as possible. Ghak was leading us to his own land—the land of Sari. No sign of pursuit had developed, and yet we were sure that somewhere behind us relentless Sagoths were dogging our tracks. Ghak said they never failed to hunt down their quarry until they had captured it or themselves been turned back by a superior force.

Our only hope, he said, lay in reaching his tribe which was quite strong enough in their mountain fastness to beat off any number of Sagoths.

And at last, after what seemed months, and may, I now realize, have been years, we came in sight of the dun escarpment which buttressed the foothills of Sari. At almost the same instant, Hooja, who looked ever quite as much behind as before, announced that he could see a body of men far behind us topping a low ridge in our wake. It was the long-expected pursuit.

I asked Ghak if we could make Sari in time to escape them.

"We may," he replied; "but you will find that the Sagoths can move with incredible swiftness, and as they are almost tireless they are doubtless much fresher than we. Then—" he paused, glancing at Perry.

I knew what he meant. The old man was nearly exhausted. For much of the period of our flight either Ghak or I had half supported him on the march. With such a handicap, less fleet pursuers than the Sagoths might easily overtake us before we could scale the rugged heights which confronted us.

"You and Hooja go on ahead," I said. "Perry and I will make it if we are able. We cannot travel as rapidly as you two, and there is no reason why all should be lost because of that. It can't be helped—we have simply to face it."

"I will not desert a companion," was Ghak's simple reply. I hadn't known that this great, hairy, primeval man had any such nobility of character stowed away inside him. I had always liked him, but now to my liking was added honor and respect. Yes, and love.

But still I urged him to go on ahead, insisting that if he could reach his people he might be able to bring out a sufficient force to drive off the Sagoths and rescue Perry and myself.

No, he wouldn't leave us, and that was all there was to it, but he suggested that Hooja might hurry on and warn the Sarians of the king's danger. It didn't require much urging to start Hooja—the naked idea was enough to send him leaping on ahead of us into the foothills which we now had reached.

Perry realized that he was jeopardizing Ghak's life and mine and the old fellow fairly begged us to go on without him, although I knew that he was suffering a perfect anguish of terror at the thought of falling into the hands of the Sagoths. Ghak finally solved the problem, in part, by lifting Perry in his powerful arms and carrying him. While the act cut down Ghak's speed he still could travel faster thus than when half supporting the stumbling old man.

CHAPTER THIRTEEN
THE SLY ONE

THE SAGOTHS WERE GAINING ON US RAPIDLY, for once they had sighted us they had greatly increased their speed. On and on we stumbled up the narrow canyon that Ghak had chosen to approach the heights of Sari. On either side rose precipitous cliffs of gorgeous, parti-colored rock, while beneath our feet a thick mountain grass formed a soft and noiseless carpet. Since we had entered the canyon we had had no glimpse of our pursuers, and I was commencing to hope that they had lost our trail and that we would reach the now rapidly nearing cliffs in time to scale them before we should be overtaken.

Ahead we neither saw nor heard any sign which might betoken the success of Hooja's mission. By now he should have reached the outposts of the Sarians, and we should at least hear the savage cries of the tribesmen as they swarmed to arms in answer to their king's appeal for succor. In another moment the frowning cliffs ahead should be black with primeval warriors. But nothing of the kind happened—as a matter of fact the Sly One had betrayed us. At the moment that we expected to see Sarian spearmen charging to our relief at Hooja's back, the craven traitor was sneaking around the outskirts of the nearest Sarian village, that he might come up from the other side when it was too late to save us, claiming that he had become lost among the mountains.

Hooja still harbored ill will against me because of the blow I had struck in Dian's protection, and his malevolent spirit was equal to sacrificing us all that he might be revenged upon me.

As we drew nearer the barrier cliffs and no sign of rescuing Sarians appeared Ghak became both angry and alarmed, and presently as the sounds of rapidly approaching pursuit fell upon our ears, he called to me over his shoulder that we were lost.

A backward glance gave me a glimpse of the first of the Sagoths at the far end of a considerable straight stretch of canyon through which we had just passed, and then a sudden turning shut the ugly creature from my view; but the loud howl of triumphant rage which rose behind us was evidence that the gorilla-man had sighted us.

Again the canyon veered sharply to the left, but to the right another branch ran on at a lesser deviation from the general direction, so that it appeared more like the main canyon than the left-hand branch. The Sagoths were now not over two hundred and fifty yards behind us, and I saw that it was hopeless for us to expect to escape other than by a ruse. There was a bare chance of saving Ghak and Perry, and as I reached the branching of the canyon I took the chance.

Pausing there I waited until the foremost Sagoth hove into sight. Ghak and Perry had disappeared around a bend in the left-hand canyon, and as the Sagoth's savage yell announced that he had seen me I turned and fled up the right-hand branch. My ruse was successful, and the entire party of man hunters raced headlong after me up one canyon while Ghak bore Perry to safety up the other.

Running had never been my particular athletic forte, and now when my very life depended upon fleetness of foot I cannot say that I ran any better than on the occasions when my pitiful base running had called down upon my head the rooters' raucous and reproachful cries of "Ice wagon," and "Call a cab."

The Sagoths were gaining on me rapidly. There was one in particular, fleeter than his fellows, who was perilously close. The canyon had become but a rocky slit, rising roughly at a steep angle toward what seemed a pass between two abutting peaks. What lay beyond I could not even guess— possibly a sheer drop of hundreds of feet into the corresponding valley upon the other side. Could it be that I had plunged into a cul-de-sac.

Realizing that I could not hope to outdistance the Sagoths to the top of the canyon I had determined to risk all in an attempt to check them temporarily, and to this end had unslung my rudely made bow and plucked an arrow from the skin quiver which hung behind my shoulder. As I fitted the shaft with my right hand I stopped and wheeled toward the gorilla-man.

In the world of my birth I never had drawn a shaft, but since our escape from Phutra I had kept the party supplied with small game by means of my arrows, and so, through necessity, had developed a fair degree of accuracy. During our flight from Phutra I had restrung my bow with a piece of heavy gut taken from a huge tiger which Ghak and I had worried and finally dispatched with arrows, spear, and sword. The hard wood of the bow was extremely tough and this, with the strength and elasticity of my new string, gave me unwonted confidence in my weapon.

Never had I greater need of steady nerves than then—never were my nerves and muscles under better control. I sighted as carefully and deliberately as though at a straw target. The Sagoth had never before seen a bow and arrow, but of a sudden it must have swept over his dull intellect that the thing I held toward him was some sort of engine of destruction, for he too came to a halt, simultaneously swinging his hatchet for a throw. It is one of the many methods in which they employ this weapon, and the accuracy of aim which they achieve, even under the most unfavorable circumstances, is little short of miraculous.

My shaft was drawn back its full length—my eye had centered its sharp point upon the left breast of my adversary; and then he launched his hatchet and I released my arrow. At the instant that our missiles flew I leaped to one side, but the Sagoth sprang forward to follow up his attack with a spear thrust. I felt the swish of the hatchet as it grazed my head, and at the same instant my shaft pierced the Sagoth's savage heart, and with a single groan he lunged almost at my feet—stone dead.

Close behind him were two more—fifty yards perhaps—but the distance gave me time to snatch up the dead guardsman's shield, for the close call his hatchet had just given me had borne in upon me the urgent need I had for one. Those which I had purloined at Phutra we had not been able to bring along because their size precluded our concealing them within the skins of the Mahars which had brought us safely from the city.

With the shield slipped well up on my left arm I let fly another arrow, which brought down a second Sagoth, and then as his fellow's hatchet sped toward me I caught it upon the shield, and fitted another shaft for him; but he did not wait to receive it. Instead, he turned and retreated toward the main body of gorilla-men. Evidently he had seen enough of me for the moment.

Once more I took up my flight, nor were the Sagoths apparently overanxious to press their pursuit so closely as before. Unmolested I reached the top of the canyon where I found a sheer drop of two or three hundred feet to the bottom of a rocky chasm; but on the left a narrow ledge rounded the shoulder of the overhanging cliff. Along this I advanced, and at a sudden turning, a few yards beyond the canyon's end, the path widened, and at my left I saw the opening to a large cave. Before, the ledge continued until it passed from sight about another projecting buttress of the mountain.

Here, I felt, I could defy an army, for but a single foeman could advance upon me at a time, nor could he know that I was awaiting him until he came full upon me around the corner of the turn. About me lay scattered stones crumbled from the cliff above. They were of various sizes and shapes, but enough were of handy dimensions for use as ammunition in lieu of my precious arrows. Gathering a number of stones into a little pile beside the mouth of the cave I waited the advance of the Sagoths.

As I stood there, tense and silent, listening for the first faint sound that should announce the approach of my enemies, a slight noise from within the cave's black depths attracted my attention. It might have been produced by the moving of the great body of some huge beast rising from the rocky floor of its lair. At almost the same instant I thought that I caught the scraping of hide sandals upon the ledge beyond the turn. For the next few seconds my attention was considerably divided.

And then from the inky blackness at my right I saw two flaming eyes glaring into mine. They were on a level that was over two feet above my head. It is true that the beast who owned them might be standing upon a ledge within the cave, or that it might be rearing up upon its hind legs; but I had seen enough of the monsters of Pellucidar to know that I might be facing some new and frightful Titan whose dimensions and ferocity eclipsed those of any I had seen before.

Whatever it was, it was coming slowly toward the entrance of the cave, and now, deep and forbidding, it uttered a low and ominous growl. I waited no longer to dispute possession of the ledge with the thing which owned that voice. The noise had not been loud—I doubt if the Sagoths heard it at all—but the suggestion of latent possibilities behind it was such that I knew it could only emanate from a gigantic and ferocious beast.

As I backed along the ledge I soon was past the mouth of the cave, where I no longer could see those fearful flaming eyes, but an instant later I caught sight of the fiendish face of a Sagoth as it was warily advanced beyond the cliff's turn on the far side of the cave's mouth. As the fellow saw me he leaped along the ledge in pursuit, and after him came as many of his companions as could crowd upon each other's heels. At the same time the beast emerged from the cave, so that he and the Sagoths came face to face upon that narrow ledge.

The thing was an enormous cave bear, rearing its colossal bulk fully eight feet at the shoulder, while from the tip of its nose to the end of its stubby tail it was fully twelve feet in length. As it sighted the Sagoths it emitted a most frightful roar, and with open mouth charged full upon them. With a cry of terror the foremost gorilla-man turned to escape, but behind him he ran full upon his onrushing companions.

The horror of the following seconds is indescribable. The Sagoth nearest the cave bear, finding his escape blocked, turned and leaped deliberately to an awful death upon the jagged rocks three hundred feet below. Then those giant jaws reached out and gathered in the next—there was a sickening sound of crunching bones, and the mangled corpse was dropped over the cliff's edge. Nor did the mighty beast even pause in his steady advance along the ledge.

Shrieking Sagoths were now leaping madly over the precipice to escape him, and the last I saw he rounded the turn still pursuing the demoralized remnant of the man hunters. For a long time I could hear the horrid roaring of the brute intermingled with the screams and shrieks of his victims, until finally the awful sounds dwindled and disappeared in the distance.

Later I learned from Ghak, who had finally come to his tribesmen and returned with a party to rescue me, that the *ryth*, as it is called, pursued the Sagoths until it had exterminated the entire band. Ghak was, of course, positive that I had fallen prey to the terrible creature, which, within Pellucidar, is truly the king of beasts.

Not caring to venture back into the canyon, where I might fall prey either to the cave bear or the Sagoths I continued on along the ledge, believing that by following around the mountain I could reach the land of Sari from another direction. But I evidently became confused by the twisting and turning of the canyons and gullies, for I did not come to the land of Sari then, nor for a long time thereafter.

CHAPTER FOURTEEN
THE GARDEN OF EDEN

WITH NO HEAVENLY GUIDE, it is little wonder that I became confused and lost in the labyrinthine maze of those mighty hills. What, in reality, I did was to pass entirely through them and come out above the valley upon the farther side. I know that I wandered for a long time, until tired and hungry I came upon a small cave in the face of the limestone formation which had taken the place of the granite farther back.

The cave which took my fancy lay halfway up the precipitous side of a lofty cliff. The way to it was such that I knew no extremely formidable beast could frequent it, nor was it large enough to make a comfortable habitat for any but the smaller mammals or reptiles. Yet it was with the utmost caution that I crawled within its dark interior.

Here I found a rather large chamber, lighted by a narrow cleft in the rock above which let the sunlight filter in in sufficient quantities partially to dispel the utter darkness which I had expected. The cave was entirely empty, nor were there any signs of its having been recently occupied. The opening was comparatively small, so that after considerable effort I was able to lug up a boulder from the valley below which entirely blocked it.

Then I returned again to the valley for an armful of grasses and on this trip was fortunate enough to knock over an *orthopi*, the diminutive horse of Pellucidar, a little animal about the size of a fox terrier, which abounds in all parts of the inner world. Thus, with food and bedding I returned to my lair, where after a meal of raw meat, to which I had now become quite accustomed, I dragged the boulder before the entrance and curled myself upon a bed of grasses—a naked, primeval, caveman, as savagely primitive as my prehistoric progenitors.

I awoke rested but hungry, and pushing the boulder aside crawled out upon the little rocky shelf which was my front porch. Before me spread a small but beautiful valley, through the center of which a clear and sparkling river wound its way down to an inland sea, the blue waters of which were just visible between the two mountain ranges which embraced this little paradise. The sides of the opposite hills were green with verdure, for a great forest clothed them to the foot of the red and yellow and copper-green of the towering crags which formed their summit. The valley itself was carpeted with a luxuriant grass, while here and there patches of wild flowers made great splashes of vivid color against the prevailing green.

Dotted over the face of the valley were little clusters of palmlike trees—three or four together as a rule. Beneath these stood antelope, while others grazed in the open, or wandered gracefully to a nearby ford to drink. There were several species of this beautiful animal, the most magnificent somewhat resembling the giant eland of Africa, except that their spiral horns form a complete curve backward over their ears and then forward again beneath them, ending in sharp and formidable points some two feet before the face and above the eyes. In size they remind one of a purebred Hereford bull, yet they are very agile and fast. The broad yellow bands that stripe the dark roan of their coats made me take them for zebra when I first saw them. All in all they are handsome animals, and added the finishing touch to the strange and lovely landscape that spread before my new home.

I had determined to make the cave my headquarters, and with it as a base make a systematic exploration of the surrounding country in search of the land of Sari. First I devoured the remainder of the carcass of the orthopi I had killed before my last sleep. Then I hid the Great Secret in a deep niche at the back of my cave, rolled the boulder before my front door, and with bow, arrows, sword, and shield scrambled down into the peaceful valley.

The grazing herds moved to one side as I passed through them, the little orthopi evincing the greatest wariness and galloping to safest distances. All the animals stopped feeding as I approached, and after moving to what they considered a safe distance stood contemplating me with serious eyes and upcocked ears. Once one of the old bull antelopes of the striped species lowered his head and bellowed angrily—even taking a few steps in my direction, so that I thought he meant to charge; but after I had passed, he resumed feeding as though nothing had disturbed him.

Near the lower end of the valley I passed a number of tapirs, and across the river saw a great sadok, the enormous double-horned progenitor of the modern rhinoceros. At the valley's end the cliffs upon the left run out into the sea, so that to pass around them as I desired to do it was necessary to scale them in search of a ledge along which I might continue my journey. Some fifty feet from the base I came upon a projection which formed a natural path along the face of the cliff, and this I followed out over the sea toward the cliff's end.

Here the ledge inclined rapidly upward toward the top of the cliffs—the stratum which formed it evidently having been forced up at this steep angle when the mountains behind it were born. As I climbed carefully up the ascent my attention suddenly was attracted aloft by the sound of strange hissing, and what resembled the flapping of wings.

And at the first glance there broke upon my horrified vision the most frightful thing I had seen even within Pellucidar. It was a giant dragon such as is pictured in the legends and fairy tales of earth folk. Its huge body must have measured forty feet in length, while the batlike wings that supported it in midair had a spread of fully thirty. Its gaping jaws were armed with long, sharp teeth, and its claws equipped with horrible talons.

The hissing noise which had first attracted my attention was issuing from its throat, and seemed to be directed at something beyond and below me which I could not see. The ledge upon which I stood terminated abruptly a few paces farther on, and as I reached the end I saw the cause of the reptile's agitation.

Sometime in past ages an earthquake had produced a fault at this point, so that beyond the spot where I stood the strata had slipped down a matter of twenty feet. The result was that the continuation of my ledge lay twenty feet below me, where it ended as abruptly as did the end upon which I stood.

And here, evidently halted in flight by this insurmountable break in the ledge, stood the object of the creature's attack—a girl cowering upon the narrow platform, her face buried in her arms, as though to shut out the sight of the frightful death which hovered just above her.

The dragon was circling lower, and seemed about to dart in upon its prey. There was no time to be lost, scarce an instant in which to weigh the possible chances that I had against the awfully armed creature; but the sight of that frightened girl below me called out to all that was best in me, and the instinct for protection of the other sex, which nearly must have equaled the instinct of self-preservation in primeval man, drew me to the girl's side like an irresistible magnet.

Almost thoughtless of the consequences, I leaped from the end of the ledge upon which I stood, for the tiny shelf twenty feet below. At the same instant the dragon darted in toward the girl, but my sudden advent upon the scene must have startled him for he veered to one side, and then rose above us once more.

The noise I made as I landed beside her convinced the girl that her end had come, for she thought that I was the dragon; but finally when no cruel fangs closed upon her she raised her eyes in astonishment. As they fell upon me the expression that came into them would be difficult to describe; but her feelings could scarcely have been one whit more complicated than my own—for the wide eyes that looked into mine were those of Dian the Beautiful.

"Dian!" I cried. "Dian! Thank God that I came in time."

"You?" she whispered, and then she hid her face again; nor could I tell whether she were glad or angry that I had come.

Once more the dragon was sweeping toward us, and so rapidly that I had no time to unsling my bow. All that I could do was to snatch up a rock, and hurl it at the thing's hideous face. Again my aim was true, and with a hiss of pain and rage the reptile wheeled once more and soared away.

Quickly I fitted an arrow now that I might be ready at the next attack, and as I did so I looked down at the girl, so that I surprised her in a surreptitious glance which she was stealing at me; but immediately she again covered her face with her hands.

"Look at me, Dian," I pleaded. "Are you not glad to see me?"

She looked straight into my eyes.

"I hate you," she said, and then, as I was about to beg for a fair hearing she pointed over my shoulder. "The thipdar comes," she said, and I turned again to meet the reptile.

So this was a thipdar. I might have known it. The cruel bloodhound of the Mahars. The long-extinct pterodactyl of the outer world. But this time I met it with a weapon it never had faced before. I had selected my longest arrow, and with all my strength had bent the bow until the very tip of the shaft rested upon the thumb of my left hand, and then as the great creature darted toward us I let drive straight for that tough breast.

Hissing like the escape valve of a steam engine, the mighty creature fell turning and twisting into the sea below, my arrow buried completely in its carcass. I turned toward the girl. She was looking past me. It was evident that she had seen the thipdar die.

"Dian," I said, "won't you tell me that you are not sorry that I have found you?"

"I hate you," was her only reply; but I imagined that there was less vehemence in it than before—yet it might have been but my imagination.

"Why do you hate me, Dian?" I asked, but she did not answer me.

"What are you doing here?" I asked, "and what has happened to you since Hooja freed you from the Sagoths?"

At first I thought that she was going to ignore me entirely, but finally she thought better of it.

"I was again running away from Jubal the Ugly One," she said. "After I escaped from the Sagoths I made my way alone back to my own land; but on account of Jubal I did not dare enter the villages or let any of my friends know that I had returned for fear that Jubal might find it out. By watching for a long time I found that my brother had not yet returned, and so I continued to live in a cave beside a valley which my race seldom frequents, awaiting the time that he should come back and free me from Jubal.

"But at last one of Jubal's hunters saw me as I was creeping toward my father's cave to see if my brother had yet returned and he gave the alarm and Jubal set out after me. He has been pursuing me across many lands. He cannot be far behind me now. When he comes he will kill you and carry me back to his cave. He is a terrible man. I have gone as far as I can go, and there is no escape," and she looked hopelessly up at the continuation of the ledge twenty feet above us.

"But he shall not have me," she suddenly cried, with great vehemence. "The sea is there"—she pointed over the edge of the cliff—"and the sea shall have me rather than Jubal."

"But I have you now, Dian," I cried; "nor shall Jubal, nor any other have you, for you are mine," and I seized her hand, nor did I lift it above her head and let it fall in token of release.

She had risen to her feet, and was looking straight into my eyes with level gaze.

"I do not believe you," she said, "for if you meant it you would have done this when the others were present to witness it—then I should truly have been your mate; now there is no one to see you do it, for you know that without witnesses your act does not bind you to me," and she withdrew her hand from mine and turned away.

I tried to convince her that I was sincere, but she simply couldn't forget the humiliation that I had put upon her on that other occasion.

"If you mean all that you say you will have ample chance to prove it," she said, "if Jubal does not catch and kill you. I am in your power, and the treatment you accord me will be the best proof of your intentions toward me. I am not your mate, and again I tell you that I hate you, and that I should be glad if I never saw you again."

Dian certainly was candid. There was no gainsaying that. In fact I found candor and directness to be quite a marked characteristic of the cavemen of Pellucidar. Finally I suggested that we make some attempt to gain my cave, where we might escape the searching Jubal, for I am free to admit that I had no considerable desire to meet the formidable and ferocious creature, of whose mighty prowess Dian had told me when I first met her. He it was who, armed with a puny knife, had met and killed a cave bear in a hand-to-hand struggle. It was Jubal who could cast his spear entirely through the armored carcass of the sadok at fifty paces. It was he who had crushed the skull of a charging dyryth with a single blow of his war club. No, I was not pining to meet the Ugly One—and it was quite certain that I should not go out and hunt for him; but the matter was taken out of my hands very quickly, as is often the way, and I did meet Jubal the Ugly One face to face.

This is how it happened. I had led Dian back along the ledge the way she had come, searching for a path that would lead us to the top of the cliff, for I knew that we could then cross over to the edge of my own little valley, where I felt certain we should find a means of ingress from the cliff top. As we proceeded along the ledge I gave Dian minute directions for finding my cave against the chance of something happening to me. I knew that she would be quite safely hidden away from pursuit once she gained the shelter of my lair, and the valley would afford her ample means of sustenance.

Also, I was very much piqued by her treatment of me. My heart was sad and heavy, and I wanted to make her feel badly by suggesting that something terrible might happen to me—that I might, in fact, be killed. But it didn't work worth a cent, at least as far as I could perceive. Dian simply shrugged those magnificent shoulders of hers, and murmured something to the effect that one was not rid of trouble so easily as that.

For a while I kept still. I was utterly squelched. And to think that I had twice protected her from attack—the last time risking my life to save hers. It was incredible that even a daughter of the Stone Age could be so ungrateful—so heartless; but maybe her heart partook of the qualities of her epoch.

Presently we found a rift in the cliff which had been widened and extended by the action of water draining through it from the plateau above. It gave us a rather rough climb to the summit, but finally we stood upon the level mesa which stretched back for several miles to the main mountain range. Behind us lay the broad inland sea, curving upward in the horizonless distance to merge into the blue of the sky, so that for all the world it looked as though the sea lapped back to arch completely over us and disappear beyond the distant mountains at our backs—the weird and uncanny aspect of the seascapes of Pellucidar balk description.

At our right lay a dense forest, but to the left the country was open and clear to the plateau's farther verge. It was in this direction that our way led, and we had turned to resume our journey when Dian touched my arm. I turned to her, thinking that she was about to make peace overtures; but I was mistaken.

"Jubal," she said, and nodded toward the forest.

I looked, and there, emerging from the dense wood, came a perfect whale of a man. He must have been seven feet tall, and proportioned accordingly. He still was too far off to distinguish his features.

"Run," I said to Dian. "I can engage him until you get a good start. Maybe I can hold him until you have gotten entirely away," and then, without a backward glance, I advanced to meet the Ugly One. I had hoped that Dian would have a kind word to say to me before she went, for she must have known that I was going to my death for her sake; but she never even so much as bid me good-bye, and it was with a heavy heart that I strode through the flower-bespangled grass to my doom.

When I had come close enough to Jubal to distinguish his features I understood how it was that he had earned the sobriquet of Ugly One. Apparently some fearful beast had ripped away one entire side of his face. The eye was gone, the nose, and all the flesh, so that his jaws and all his teeth were exposed and grinning through the horrible scar.

Formerly he may have been as good to look upon as the others of his handsome race, and it may be that the terrible result of this encounter had tended to sour an already strong and brutal character. However this may be it is quite certain that he was not a pretty sight, and now that his features, or what remained of them, were distorted in rage at the sight of Dian with another male, he was indeed most terrible to see—and much more terrible to meet.

He had broken into a run now, and as he advanced he raised his mighty spear, while I halted and fitting an arrow to my bow took as steady aim as I could. I was somewhat longer than usual, for I must confess that the sight of this awful man had wrought upon my nerves to such an extent that my knees were anything but steady. What chance had I against this mighty warrior for whom even the fiercest cave bear had no terrors! Could I hope to best one who slaughtered the sadok and the dyryth single-handed! I shuddered; but, in fairness to myself, my fear was more for Dian than for my own fate.

And then the great brute launched his massive stone-tipped spear, and I raised my shield to break the force of its terrific velocity. The impact hurled me to my knees, but the shield had deflected the missile and I was unscathed. Jubal was rushing upon me now with the only remaining weapon that he carried—a murderous-looking knife. He was too close for a careful bowshot, but I let drive at him as he came, without taking aim.

My arrow pierced the fleshy part of his thigh, inflicting a painful but not disabling wound. And then he was upon me.

My agility saved me for the instant. I ducked beneath his raised arm, and when he wheeled to come at me again he found a sword's point in his face. And a moment later he felt an inch or two of it in the muscles of his knife arm, so that thereafter he went more warily.

It was a duel of strategy now—the great, hairy man maneuvering to get inside my guard where he could bring those giant thews to play, while my wits were directed to the task of keeping him at arm's length. Thrice he rushed me, and thrice I caught his knife blow upon my shield. Each time my sword found his body—once penetrating to his lung. He was covered with blood by this time, and the internal hemorrhage induced paroxysms of coughing that brought the red stream through the hideous mouth and nose, covering his face and breast with bloody froth. He was a most unlovely spectacle, but he was far from dead.

As the duel continued I began to gain confidence, for, to be perfectly candid, I had not expected to survive the first rush of that monstrous engine of ungoverned rage and hatred. And I think that Jubal, from utter contempt of me, began to change to a feeling of respect, and then in his primitive mind there evidently loomed the thought that perhaps at last he had met his master, and was facing his end.

At any rate it is only upon this hypothesis that I can account for his next act, which was in the nature of a last resort—a sort of forlorn hope, which could only have been born of the belief that if he did not kill me quickly I should kill him. It happened on the occasion of his fourth charge, when, instead of striking at me with his knife, he dropped that weapon, and seizing my sword blade in both his hands wrenched the weapon from my grasp as easily as from a babe.

Flinging it far to one side he stood motionless for just an instant glaring into my face with such a horrid leer of malignant triumph as to almost unnerve me—then he sprang for me with his bare hands. But it was Jubal's day to learn new methods of warfare. For the first time he had seen a bow and arrows, never before that duel had he beheld a sword, and now he learned what a man who knows may do with his bare fists.

As he came for me, like a great bear, I ducked again beneath his outstretched arm, and as I came up planted as clean a blow upon his jaw as ever you have seen. Down went that great mountain of flesh sprawling upon the ground. He was so surprised and dazed that he lay there for several seconds before he made any attempt to rise, and I stood over him with another dose ready when he should gain his knees.

Up he came at last, almost roaring in his rage and mortification; but he didn't stay up—I let him have a left fair on the point of the jaw that sent him tumbling over on his back. By this time I think Jubal had gone mad with hate, for no sane man would have come back for more as many times as he did. Time after time I bowled him over as fast as he could stagger up, until toward the last he lay longer on the ground between blows, and each time came up weaker than before.

He was bleeding very profusely now from the wound in his lungs, and presently a terrific blow over the heart sent him reeling heavily to the ground, where he lay very still, and somehow I knew at once that Jubal the Ugly One would never get up again. But even as I looked upon that massive body lying there so grim and terrible in death I could not believe that I, single-handed, had bested this slayer of fearful beasts—this gigantic ogre of the Stone Age.

Picking up my sword I leaned upon it, looking down on the dead body of my foeman, and as I thought of the battle I had just fought and won a great idea was born in my brain—the outcome of this and the suggestion that Perry had made within the city of Phutra. If skill and science could render a comparative pygmy the master of this mighty brute, what could not the brute's fellows accomplish with the same skill and science. Why all Pellucidar would be at their feet—and I would be their king and Dian their queen.

Dian! A little wave of doubt swept over me. It was quite within the possibilities of Dian to look down upon me even were I king. She was quite the most superior person I ever had met—with the most convincing way of letting you know that she was superior. Well, I could go to the cave, and tell her that I had killed Jubal, and then she might feel more kindly toward me, since I had freed her of her tormentor. I hoped that she had found the cave easily—it would be terrible had I lost her again, and I turned to gather up my shield and bow to hurry after her, when to my astonishment I found her standing not ten paces behind me.

"Girl!" I cried, "what are you doing here? I thought that you had gone to the cave, as I told you to do."

Up went her head, and the look that she gave me took all the majesty out of me, and left me feeling more like the palace janitor—if palaces have janitors.

"As you told me to do!" she cried, stamping her little foot. "I do as I please. I am the daughter of a king, and, furthermore, I hate you."

I was dumbfounded—this was my thanks for saving her from Jubal! I turned and looked at the corpse. "May be that I saved you from a worse fate, old man," I said, but I guess it was lost on Dian, for she never seemed to notice it at all.

"Let us go to my cave," I said, "I am tired and hungry."

She followed along a pace behind me, neither of us speaking. I was too angry, and she evidently didn't care to converse with the lower orders. I was mad all the way through, as I had certainly felt that at least a word of thanks should have rewarded me, for I knew that even by her own standards I must have done a very wonderful thing to have killed the redoubtable Jubal in a hand-to-hand encounter.

We had no difficulty in finding my lair, and then I went down into the valley and bowled over a small antelope, which I dragged up the steep ascent to the ledge before the door. Here we ate in silence. Occasionally I glanced at her, thinking that the sight of her tearing at raw flesh with her hands and teeth like some wild animal would cause a revulsion of my sentiments toward her; but to my surprise I found that she ate quite as daintily as the most civilized woman of my acquaintance, and finally I found myself gazing in foolish rapture at the beauties of her strong, white teeth. Such is love.

After our repast we went down to the river together and bathed our hands and faces, and then after drinking our fill went back to the cave. Without a word I crawled into the farthest corner and, curling up, was soon asleep.

When I awoke I found Dian sitting in the doorway looking out across the valley. As I came out she moved to one side to let me pass, but she had no word for me. I wanted to hate her, but I couldn't. Every time I looked at her something came up in my throat, so that I nearly choked. I had never been in love before, but I did not need any aid in diagnosing my case—I certainly had it and had it bad. God, how I loved that beautiful, disdainful, tantalizing, prehistoric girl!

After we had eaten again I asked Dian if she intended returning to her tribe now that Jubal was dead, but she shook her head sadly, and said that she did not dare, for there was still Jubal's brother to be considered—his oldest brother.

"What has he to do with it?" I asked. "Does he too want you, or has the option on you become a family heirloom, to be passed on down from generation to generation?"

She was not quite sure as to what I meant.

"It is probable," she said, "that they all will want revenge for the death of Jubal—there are seven of them—seven terrible men. Someone may have to kill them all, if I am to return to my people."

It began to look as though I had assumed a contract much too large for me—about seven sizes, in fact.

"Had Jubal any cousins?" I asked. It was just as well to know the worst at once.

"Yes," replied Dian, "but they don't count—they all have mates. Jubal's brothers have no mates because Jubal could get none for himself. He was so ugly that women ran away from him—some have even thrown themselves from the cliffs of Amoz into the Darel Az rather than mate with the Ugly One."

"But what had that to do with his brothers?" I asked.

"I forget that you are not of Pellucidar," said Dian, with a look of pity mixed with contempt, and the contempt seemed to be laid on a little thicker than the circumstance warranted—as though to make quite certain that I shouldn't overlook it. "You see," she continued, "a younger brother may not take a mate until all his older brothers have done so, unless the older brother waives his prerogative, which Jubal would not do, knowing that as long as he kept them single they would be all the keener in aiding him to secure a mate."

Noticing that Dian was becoming more communicative I began to entertain hopes that she might be warming up toward me a bit, although upon what slender thread I hung my hopes I soon discovered.

"As you dare not return to Amoz," I ventured, "what is to become of you, since you cannot be happy here with me, hating me as you do?"

"I shall have to put up with you," she replied coldly, "until you see fit to go elsewhere and leave me in peace, then I shall get along very well alone."

I looked at her in utter amazement. It seemed incredible that even a prehistoric woman could be so cold and heartless and ungrateful. Then I arose.

"I shall leave you *now*," I said haughtily, "I have had quite enough of your ingratitude and your insults," and then I turned and strode majestically down toward the valley. I had taken a hundred steps in absolute silence, and then Dian spoke.

"I hate you!" she shouted, and her voice broke—in rage, I thought.

I was absolutely miserable, but I hadn't gone far when I began to realize that I couldn't leave her alone there without protection, to hunt her own food amid the dangers of that savage world. She might hate me, and revile me, and heap indignity after indignity upon me, as she already had, until I should have hated her; but the pitiful fact remained that I loved her, and I couldn't leave her there alone.

The more I thought about it the madder I got, so that by the time I reached the valley I was furious, and the result of it was that I turned right around and went up that cliff again twice as fast as I had come down. I saw that Dian had left the ledge and gone within the cave, but I bolted right in after her. She was lying upon her face on the pile of grasses I had gathered for her bed. When she heard me enter she sprang to her feet like a tigress.

"I hate you!" she cried.

Coming from the brilliant light of the noonday sun into the semidarkness of the cave I could not see her features, and I was rather glad, for I disliked to think of the hate that I should have read there.

I never said a word to her at first. I just strode across the cave and grasped her by the wrists, and when she struggled, I put my arm around her so as to pinion her hands to her sides. She fought like a tigress, but I took my free hand and pushed her head back—I imagine that I had suddenly turned brute, that I had gone back a thousand million years, and was again a veritable caveman taking my mate by force—and then I kissed that beautiful mouth again and again.

"Dian," I cried, shaking her roughly, "I love you. Can't you understand that I love you? That I love you better than all else in this world or my own? That I am going to have you? That love like mine cannot be denied?"

I noticed that she lay very still in my arms now, and as my eyes became accustomed to the light I saw that she was smiling—a very contented, happy smile. I was thunderstruck. Then I realized that, very gently, she was trying to disengage her arms, and I loosened my grip upon them so that she could do so. Slowly they came up and stole about my neck, and then she drew my lips down to hers once more and held them there for a long time. At last she spoke.

"Why didn't you do this at first, David? I have been waiting so long."

"What!" I cried. "You said that you hated me!"

"Did you expect me to run into your arms, and say that I loved you before I knew that you loved me?" she asked.

"But I have told you right along that I love you," I said.

"Love speaks in acts," she replied. "You could have made your mouth say what you wished it to say, but just now when you came and took me in your arms your heart spoke to mine in the language that a woman's heart understands. What a silly man you are, David."

"Then you haven't hated me at all, Dian?" I asked.

"I have loved you always," she whispered, "from the first moment that I saw you, although I did not know it until that time you struck down Hooja the Sly One, and then spurned me."

"But I didn't spurn you, dear," I cried. "I didn't know your ways—I doubt if I do now. It seems incredible that you could have reviled me so, and yet have cared for me all the time."

"You might have known," she said, "when I did not run away from you that it was not hate which chained me to you. While you were battling with Jubal I could have run to the edge of the forest, and when I had learned the outcome of the combat it would have been a simple thing to have eluded you and returned to my own people."

"But Jubal's brothers—and cousins—" I reminded her, "how about them?"

She smiled, and hid her face on my shoulder.

"I had to tell you *something*, David," she whispered. "I must needs have *some* excuse for remaining near you."

"You little sinner!" I exclaimed. "And you have caused me all this anguish for nothing!"

"I have suffered even more," she answered simply, "for I thought that you did not love me, and I was helpless. I couldn't come to you and demand that my love be returned, as you have just come to me. Just now when you went away hope went with you. I was wretched, terrified, miserable, and my heart was breaking. I wept, and I have not done that before since my mother died," and now I saw that there was the moisture of tears about her eyes. It was near to making me cry myself when I thought of all that poor child had been through. Motherless and unprotected; hunted across a savage, primeval world by that hideous brute of a man; exposed to the attacks of the countless fearsome denizens of its mountains, its plains, and its jungles—it was a miracle that she had survived at all.

To me it was a revelation of the things my early forebears must have endured that the human race of the outer crust might survive. It made me very proud to think that I had won the love of such a woman. Of course she couldn't read or write; there was nothing cultured or refined about her as you judge culture and refinement; but she was the essence of all that is best in woman, for she was good, and brave, and noble, and virtuous. And she was all these things in spite of the fact that their observance entailed suffering and danger and possible death.

How much easier it would have been to have gone to Jubal in the first place! She would have been his lawful mate. She would have been queen in her own land—and it meant just as much to the cave woman to be a queen in the Stone Age as it does to the woman of today to be a queen now; it's all comparative glory any way you look at it, and if there were only half-naked savages on the outer crust today, you'd find that it would be considerable glory to be the wife of a Dahomey chief.

I couldn't help but compare Dian's action with that of a splendid young woman I had known in New York—I mean splendid to look at and to talk to. She had been head over heels in love with a chum of mine—a clean, manly chap—but she had married a broken-down, disreputable old debauchee because he was a count in some dinky little European principality that was not even accorded a distinctive color by Rand McNally.

Yes, I was mighty proud of Dian.

After a time we decided to set out for Sari, as I was anxious to see Perry, and to know that all was right with him. I had told Dian about our plan of emancipating the human race of Pellucidar, and she was fairly wild over it. She said that if Dacor, her brother, would only return he could easily be king of Amoz, and that then he and Ghak could form an alliance. That would give us a flying start, for the Sarians and the Amozites were both very powerful tribes. Once they had been armed with swords, and bows and arrows, and trained in their use we were confident that they could overcome any tribe that seemed disinclined to join the great army of federated states with which we were planning to march upon the Mahars.

I explained the various destructive engines of war which Perry and I could construct after a little experimentation—gunpowder, rifles, cannon, and the like, and Dian would clap her little hands, and throw her arms about my neck, and tell me what a wonderful thing I was. She was beginning to think that I was omnipotent although I really hadn't done anything but talk—but that is the way with women when they love. Perry used to say that if a fellow was one-tenth as remarkable as his wife or mother thought him, he would have the world by the tail with a downhill drag.

The first time we started for Sari I stepped into a nest of poisonous vipers before we reached the valley. A little fellow stung me on the ankle, and Dian made me come back to the cave. She said that I mustn't exercise, or it might prove fatal—if it had been a full-grown snake that struck me she said, I wouldn't have moved a single pace from the nest—I'd have died in my tracks, so virulent is the poison. As it was I must have been laid up for quite a while, though Dian's poultices of herbs and leaves finally reduced the swelling and drew out the poison.

The episode proved most fortunate, however, as it gave me an idea which added a thousandfold to the value of my arrows as missiles of offense and defense. As soon as I was able to be about again I sought out some adult vipers of the species which had stung me, and having killed them, I extracted their virus, smearing it upon the tips of several arrows. Later I shot a hyaenodon with one of these, and though my arrow inflicted but a superficial flesh wound the beast crumpled in death almost immediately he was hit.

We now set out once more for the land of the Sarians, and it was with feelings of sincere regret that we bade good-bye to our beautiful Garden of Eden, in the comparative peace and harmony of which we had lived the happiest moments of our lives. How long we had been there I did not know, for as I have told you, time had ceased to exist for me beneath that eternal noonday sun—it may have been an hour, or a month of earthly time; I do not know.

WE CROSSED THE RIVER and passed through the mountains beyond, and finally we came out upon a great level plain which stretched away as far as the eye could reach. I cannot tell you in what direction it stretched even if you would care to know, for all the while that I was within Pellucidar I never discovered any but local methods of indicating direction—there is no north, no south, no east, no west. *Up* is about the only direction which is well defined, and that, of course, is *down* to you of the outer crust. Since the sun neither rises nor sets there is no method of indicating direction beyond visible objects such as high mountains, forests, lakes, and seas.

The plain which lies beyond the white cliffs which flank the Darel Az upon the shore nearest the Mountains of the Clouds is about as near to direction as any Pellucidarian can come. If you happen not to have heard of the Darel Az, or the white cliffs, or the Mountains of the Clouds you feel that there is something lacking, and long for the good old understandable northeast or southwest of the outer world.

We had barely entered the great plain when we discovered two enormous animals approaching us from a great distance. So far were they that we could not distinguish what manner of beasts they might be, but as they came closer I saw that they were enormous quadrupeds, eighty or a hundred feet long, with tiny heads perched at the top of very long necks. Their heads must have been quite forty feet from the ground. The beasts moved very slowly—that is their action was slow—but their strides covered such a great distance that in reality they traveled considerably faster than a man walks.

As they drew still nearer we discovered that upon the back of each sat a human being. Then Dian knew what they were, though she never before had seen one.

"They are lidis from the land of the Thorians," she cried. "Thoria lies at the outer verge of the Land of Awful Shadow. The Thorians alone of all the races of Pellucidar ride the lidi, for nowhere else than beside the dark country are they found."

"What is the Land of Awful Shadow?" I asked.

"It is the land which lies beneath the Dead World," replied Dian; "the Dead World which hangs forever between the sun and Pellucidar above the Land of Awful Shadow. It is the Dead World which makes the great shadow upon this portion of Pellucidar."

I did not fully understand what she meant, nor am I sure that I do yet, for I have never been to that part of Pellucidar from which the Dead World is visible; but Perry says that it is the moon of Pellucidar—a tiny planet within a planet—and that it revolves about the earth's axis coincidently with the earth, and thus is always above the same spot within Pellucidar.

I remember that Perry was very much excited when I told him about this Dead World, for he seemed to think that it explained the hitherto inexplicable phenomena of nutation and the precession of the equinoxes.

When the two upon the lidis had come quite close to us we saw that one was a man and the other a woman. The former had held up his two hands, palms toward us, in sign of peace, and I had answered him in kind, when he suddenly gave a cry of astonishment and pleasure, and slipping from his enormous mount ran forward toward Dian, throwing his arms about her.

In an instant I was white with jealousy, but only for an instant; since Dian quickly drew the man toward me, telling him that I was David, her mate.

"And this is my brother, Dacor the Strong One, David," she said to me.

It appeared that the woman was Dacor's mate. He had found none to his liking among the Sari, nor farther on until he had come to the land of the Thoria, and there he had found and fought for this very lovely Thorian maiden whom he was bringing back to his own people.

When they had heard our story and our plans they decided to accompany us to Sari, that Dacor and Ghak might come to an agreement relative to an alliance, as Dacor was quite as enthusiastic about the proposed annihilation of the Mahars and Sagoths as either Dian or I.

After a journey which was, for Pellucidar, quite uneventful, we came to the first of the Sarian villages which consists of between one and two hundred artificial caves cut into the face of a great chalk cliff. Here to our immense delight, we found both Perry and Ghak. The old man was quite overcome at sight of me for he had long since given me up as dead.

When I introduced Dian as my wife he didn't quite know what to say, but he afterward remarked that with the pick of two worlds I could not have done better.

Ghak and Dacor reached a very amicable arrangement, and it was at a council of the head men of the various tribes of the Sari that the eventual form of government was tentatively agreed upon. Roughly, the various kingdoms were to remain virtually independent, but there was to be one great overlord, or emperor. It was decided that I should be the first of the dynasty of the emperors of Pellucidar.

We set about teaching the women how to make bows and arrows, and poison pouches. The young men hunted the vipers which provided the virus, and it was they who mined the iron ore, and fashioned the swords under Perry's direction. Rapidly the fever spread from one tribe to another until representatives from nations so far distant that the Sarians had never even heard of them came in to take the oath of allegiance which we required, and to learn the art of making the new weapons and using them.

We sent our young men out as instructors to every nation of the federation, and the movement had reached colossal proportions before the Mahars discovered it. The first intimation they had was when three of their great slave caravans were annihilated in rapid succession. They could not comprehend that the lower orders had suddenly developed a power which rendered them really formidable.

In one of the skirmishes with slave caravans some of our Sarians took a number of Sagoth prisoners, and among them were two who had been members of the guards within the building where we had been confined at Phutra. They told us that the Mahars were frantic with rage when they discovered what had taken place in the cellars of the building. The Sagoths knew that something very terrible had befallen their masters, but the Mahars had been most careful to see that no inkling of the true nature of their vital affliction reached beyond their own race. How long it would take for the race to become extinct it was impossible even to guess; but that this must eventually happen seemed inevitable.

The Mahars had offered fabulous rewards for the capture of any one of us alive, and at the same time had threatened to inflict the direst punishment upon whomever should harm us. The Sagoths could not understand these seemingly paradoxical instructions, though their purpose was quite evident to me. The Mahars wanted the Great Secret, and they knew that we alone could deliver it to them.

Perry's experiments in the manufacture of gunpowder and the fashioning of rifles had not progressed as rapidly as we had hoped—there was a whole lot about these two arts which Perry didn't know. We were both assured that the solution of these problems would advance the cause of civilization within Pellucidar thousands of years at a single stroke. Then there were various other arts and sciences which we wished to introduce, but our combined knowledge of them did not embrace the mechanical details which alone could render them of commercial, or practical, value.

"David," said Perry, immediately after his latest failure to produce gunpowder that would even burn, "one of us must return to the outer world and bring back the information we lack. Here we have all the labor and materials for reproducing anything that ever has been produced above—what we lack is knowledge. Let us go back and get that knowledge in the shape of books—then this world will indeed be at our feet."

And so it was decided that I should return in the prospector, which still lay upon the edge of the forest at the point where we had first penetrated to the surface of the inner world. Dian would not listen to any arrangement for my going which did not include her, and I was not sorry that she wished to accompany me, for I wanted her to see my world, and I wanted my world to see her.

With a large force of men we marched to the great iron mole, which Perry soon had hoisted into position with its nose pointed back toward the outer crust. He went over all the machinery carefully. He replenished the air tanks, and manufactured oil for the engine. At last everything was ready, and we were about to set out when our pickets, a long, thin line of which had surrounded our camp at all times, reported that a great body of what appeared to be Sagoths and Mahars were approaching from the direction of Phutra.

Dian and I were ready to embark, but I was anxious to witness the first clash between two fair-sized armies of the opposing races of Pellucidar. I realized that this was to mark the historic beginning of a mighty struggle for possession of a world, and as the first emperor of Pellucidar I felt that it was not alone my duty, but my right, to be in the thick of that momentous struggle.

As the opposing army approached we saw that there were many Mahars with the Sagoth troops—an indication of the vast importance which the dominant race placed upon the outcome of this campaign, for it was not customary with them to take active part in the sorties which their creatures made for slaves—the only form of warfare which they waged upon the lower orders.

Ghak and Dacor were both with us, having come primarily to view the prospector. I placed Ghak with some of his Sarians on the right of our battle line. Dacor took the left, while I commanded the center. Behind us I stationed a sufficient reserve under one of Ghak's head men. The Sagoths advanced steadily with menacing spears, and I let them come until they were within easy bowshot before I gave the word to fire.

At the first volley of poison-tipped arrows the front ranks of the gorilla-men crumpled to the ground; but those behind charged over the prostrate forms of their comrades in a wild, mad rush to be upon us with their spears. A second volley stopped them for an instant, and then my reserve sprang through the openings in the firing line to engage them with sword and shield.

The clumsy spears of the Sagoths were no match for the swords of the Sarian and Amozite, who turned the spear thrusts aside with their shields and leaped to close quarters with their lighter, handier weapons.

Ghak took his archers along the enemy's flank, and while the swords-men engaged them in front, he poured volley after volley into their un-protected left. The Mahars did little real fighting, and were more in the way than otherwise, though occasionally one of them would fasten its powerful jaws upon the arm or leg of a Sarian.

The battle did not last a great while, for when Dacor and I led our men in upon the Sagoth's right with naked swords they were already so demoral-ized that they turned and fled before us. We pursued them for some time, taking many prisoners and recovering nearly a hundred slaves, among whom was Hooja the Sly One.

He told me that he had been captured while on his way to his own land; but that his life had been spared in hope that through him the Mahars would learn the whereabouts of their Great Secret. Ghak and I were inclined to think that the Sly One had been guiding this expedition to the land of Sari, where he thought that the book might be found in Perry's possession; but we had no proof of this and so we took him in and treated him as one of us, although none liked him. And how he rewarded my generosity you shall presently learn.

There were a number of Mahars among our prisoners, and so fearful were our own people of them that they would not approach them unless completely covered from the sight of the reptiles by a piece of skin. Even Dian shared the popular superstition regarding the evil effects of exposure to the eyes of angry Mahars, and though I laughed at her fears I was willing enough to humor them if it would relieve her apprehension in any degree, and so she sat apart from the prospector, near which the Mahars had been chained, while Perry and I again inspected every portion of the mechanism.

At last I took my place in the driving seat, and called to one of the men without to fetch Dian. It happened that Hooja stood quite close to the doorway of the prospector, so that it was he who, without my knowledge, went to bring her; but how he succeeded in accomplishing the fiendish thing he did, I cannot guess, unless there were others in the plot to aid him. Nor can I believe that, since all my people were loyal to me and would have made short work of Hooja had he suggested the heartless scheme, even had he had time to acquaint another with it. It was all done so quickly that I may only believe that it was the result of sudden impulse, aided by a number of, to Hooja, fortuitous circumstances occurring at precisely the right moment.

All I know is that it was Hooja who brought Dian to the prospector, still wrapped from head to toe in the skin of an enormous cave lion which had covered her since the Mahar prisoners had been brought into camp. He deposited his burden in the seat beside me. I was all ready to get under way. The good-byes had been said. Perry had grasped my hand in the last, long farewell. I closed and barred the outer and inner doors, took my seat again at the driving mechanism, and pulled the starting lever.

As before on that far-gone night that had witnessed our first trial of the iron monster, there was a frightful roaring beneath us—the giant frame trembled and vibrated—there was a rush of sound as the loose earth passed up through the hollow space between the inner and outer jackets to be deposited in our wake. Once more the thing was off.

But on the instant of departure I was nearly thrown from my seat by the sudden lurching of the prospector. At first I did not realize what had happened, and presently it dawned upon me that just before entering the crust the towering body had fallen through its supporting scaffolding, and that instead of entering the ground vertically we were plunging into it at a different angle. Where it would bring us out upon the upper crust I could not even conjecture. And then I turned to note the effect of this strange experience upon Dian. She still sat shrouded in the great skin.

"Come, come," I cried, laughing, "come out of your shell. No Mahar eyes can reach you here," and I leaned over and snatched the lion skin from her. And then I shrank back upon my seat in utter horror.

The thing beneath the skin was not Dian—it was a hideous Mahar. Instantly I realized the trick that Hooja had played upon me, and the purpose of it. Rid of me, forever as he doubtless thought, Dian would be at his mercy. Frantically I tore at the steering wheel in an effort to turn the prospector back toward Pellucidar; but, as on that other occasion, I could not budge the thing a hair.

It is needless to recount the horrors or the monotony of that journey. It varied but little from the former one which had brought us from the outer to the inner world. Because of the angle at which we had entered the ground the trip required nearly a day longer, and brought me out here upon the sands of the Sahara instead of in the United States as I had hoped.

For months I have been waiting here for a white man to come. I dared not leave the prospector for fear I should never be able to find it again—the shifting sands of the desert would soon cover it, and then my only hope of returning to my Dian and her Pellucidar would be gone forever.

That I ever shall see her again seems but remotely possible, for how may I know upon what part of Pellucidar my return journey may terminate—and how, without a north or a south or an east or a west may I hope ever to find my way across that vast world to the tiny spot where my lost love lies grieving for me?

That is the story as David Innes told it to me in the goatskin tent upon the rim of the great Sahara Desert. The next day he took me out to see the prospector—it was precisely as he had described it. So huge was it that it could have been brought to this inaccessible part of the world by no means of transportation that existed there—it could only have come in the way that David Innes said it came—up through the crust of the earth from the inner world of Pellucidar.

I spent a week with him, and then, abandoning my lion hunt, returned directly to the coast and hurried to London where I purchased a great quantity of stuff which he wished to take back to Pellucidar with him. There were books, rifles, revolvers, ammunition, cameras, chemicals, telephones, telegraph instruments, wire, tools and more books—books upon every subject under the sun. He said he wanted a library with which they could reproduce the wonders of the twentieth century in the Stone Age and if quantity counts for anything I got it for him.

I took the things back to Algeria myself, and accompanied them to the end of the railroad; but from here I was recalled to America upon important business. However, I was able to employ a very trustworthy man to take charge of the caravan—the same guide, in fact, who had accompanied me on the previous trip into the Sahara—and after writing a long letter to Innes in which I gave him my American address, I saw the expedition head south.

Among the other things which I sent to Innes was over five hundred miles of double, insulated wire of a very fine gauge. I had it packed on a special reel at his suggestion, as it was his idea that he could fasten one end here before he left and by paying it out through the end of the prospector lay a telegraph line between the outer and inner worlds. In my letter I told him to be sure to mark the terminus of the line very plainly with a high cairn, in case I was not able to reach him before he set out, so that I might easily find it and communicate with him should he be so fortunate as to reach Pellucidar.

I received several letters from him after I returned to America—in fact he took advantage of every northward-passing caravan to drop me word of some sort. His last letter was written the day before he intended to depart. Here it is.

My DEAR FRIEND:

Tomorrow I shall set out in quest of Pellucidar and Dian. That is if the Arabs don't get me. They have been very nasty of late. I don't know the cause, but on two occasions they have threatened my life. One, more friendly than the rest, told me today that they intended attacking me tonight. It would be unfortunate should anything of that sort happen now that I am so nearly ready to depart.

However, maybe I will be as well off, for the nearer the hour approaches, the slenderer my chances for success appear.

Here is the friendly Arab who is to take this letter north for me, so good-bye, and God bless you for your kindness to me.

The Arab tells me to hurry, for he sees a cloud of sand to the south—

he thinks it is the party coming to murder me, and he doesn't want to be found with me. So good-bye again.

Yours,

DAVID INNES.

A year later found me at the end of the railroad once more, headed for the spot where I had left Innes. My first disappointment was when I discovered that my old guide had died within a few weeks of my return, nor could I find any member of my former party who could lead me to the same spot.

For months I searched that scorching land, interviewing countless desert sheiks in the hope that at last I might find one who had heard of Innes and his wonderful iron mole. Constantly my eyes scanned the blinding waste of sand for the rocky cairn beneath which I was to find the wires leading to Pellucidar—but always was I unsuccessful.

And always do these awful questions harass me when I think of David Innes and his strange adventures.

Did the Arabs murder him, after all, just on the eve of his departure? Or, did he again turn the nose of his iron monster toward the inner world? Did he reach it, or lies he somewhere buried in the heart of the great crust? And if he did come again to Pellucidar was it to break through into the bottom of one of her great inland seas, or among some savage race far, far from the land of his heart's desire?

Does the answer lie somewhere upon the bosom of the broad Sahara, at the end of two tiny wires, hidden beneath a lost cairn? I wonder.

THE LAND THAT
TIME FORGOT

...we have learned not to fire at any of the dinosaurs unless we can keep out of their reach for at least two minutes after hitting them in the brain or spine, or five minutes after puncturing their hearts—it takes them so long to die.

Contents

CHAPTER ONE

It must have been a little after three o'clock in the afternoon that it happened—the afternoon of June 3rd, 1916. It seems incredible that all that I have passed through—all those weird and terrifying experiences—should have been encompassed within so short a span as three brief months. Rather might I have experienced a cosmic cycle, with all its changes and evolutions for that which I have seen with my own eyes in this brief interval of time—things that no other mortal eye had seen before, glimpses of a world past, a world dead, a world so long dead that even in the lowest Cambrian stratum no trace of it remains. Fused with the melting inner crust, it has passed forever beyond the ken of man other than in that lost pocket of the earth whither fate has borne me and where my doom is sealed. I am here and here I must remain.

AFTER READING THIS FAR, my interest, which already had been stimulated by the finding of the manuscript, was approaching the boiling point. I had come to Greenland for the summer, on the advice of my physician, and was slowly being bored to extinction, as I had thoughtlessly neglected to bring sufficient reading matter. Being an indifferent fisherman, my enthusiasm for this form of sport soon waned; yet in the absence of other forms of recreation I was now risking my life in an entirely inadequate boat off Cape Farewell at the southernmost extremity of Greenland.

Greenland! As a descriptive appellation, it is a sorry joke—but my story has nothing to do with Greenland, nothing to do with me; so I shall get through with the one and the other as rapidly as possible.

The inadequate boat finally arrived at a precarious landing, the natives, waist-deep in the surf, assisting. I was carried ashore, and while the evening meal was being prepared, I wandered to and fro along the rocky, shattered shore. Bits of surf-harried beach clove the worn granite, or whatever the rocks of Cape Farewell may be composed of, and as I followed the ebbing tide down one of these soft stretches, I saw the thing. Were one to bump into a Bengal tiger in the ravine behind the Bimini Baths, one could be no more surprised than was I to see a perfectly good quart thermos bottle turning and twisting in the surf of Cape Farewell at the southern extremity of Greenland. I rescued it, but I was soaked above the knees doing it; and then I sat down in the sand and opened it, and in the long twilight read the manuscript, neatly written and tightly folded, which was its contents.

You have read the opening paragraph, and if you are an imaginative idiot like myself, you will want to read the rest of it; so I shall give it to you here, omitting quotation marks—which are difficult of remembrance. In two minutes you will forget me.

My home is in Santa Monica. I am, or was, junior member of my father's firm. We are shipbuilders. Of recent years we have specialized on submarines, which we have built for Germany, England, France and the United States. I know a sub as a mother knows her baby's face, and have commanded a score of them on their trial runs. Yet my inclinations were all toward aviation. I graduated under Curtiss, and after a long siege with my father obtained his permission to try for the Lafayette Escadrille. As a stepping stone I obtained an appointment in the American ambulance service and was on my way to France when three shrill whistles altered, in as many seconds, my entire scheme of life.

I was sitting on deck with some of the fellows who were going into the American ambulance service with me, my Airedale, Crown Prince Nobbler, asleep at my feet, when the first blast of the whistle shattered the peace and security of the ship. Ever since entering the U-boat zone we had been on the lookout for periscopes, and children that we were, bemoaning the unkind fate that was to see us safely into France on the morrow without a glimpse of the dread marauders. We were young; we craved thrills, and God knows we got them that day; yet by comparison with that through which I have since passed they were as tame as a Punch-and-Judy show.

I shall never forget the ashy faces of the passengers as they stampeded for their life belts, though there was no panic. Nobs rose with a low growl. I rose, also, and over the ship's side I saw not two hundred yards distant the periscope of a submarine, while racing toward the liner the wake of a torpedo was distinctly visible. We were aboard an American ship—which, of course, was not armed. We were entirely defenseless; yet without warning, we were being torpedoed.

I stood rigid, spellbound, watching the white wake of the torpedo. It struck us on the starboard side almost amidships. The vessel rocked as though the sea beneath it had been uptorn by a mighty volcano. We were thrown to the decks, bruised and stunned, and then above the ship, carrying with it fragments of steel and wood and dismembered human bodies, rose a column of water hundreds of feet into the air.

The silence which followed the detonation of the exploding torpedo was almost equally horrifying. It lasted for perhaps two seconds, to be followed by the screams and moans of the wounded, the cursing of the men and the hoarse commands of the ship's officers. They were splendid—they and their crew. Never before had I been so proud of my nationality as I was that moment. In all the chaos which followed the torpedoing of the liner no officer or member of the crew lost his head or showed in the slightest any degree of panic or fear. While we were attempting to lower boats, the submarine emerged and trained guns on us. The officer in command ordered us to lower our flag, but this the captain of the liner refused to do. The ship was listing frightfully to starboard, rendering the port boats useless, while half the starboard boats had been demolished by the explosion. Even while the passengers were crowding the starboard rail and scrambling into the few boats left to us, the submarine commenced shelling the ship. I saw one shell burst in a group of women and children, and then I turned my head and covered my eyes.

When I looked again to horror was added chagrin, for with the emerging of the U-boat I had recognized her as a product of our own shipyard. I knew her to a rivet. I had superintended her construction. I had sat in that very conning tower and directed the efforts of the sweating crew below when first her prow clove the sunny summer waters of the Pacific; and now this creature of my brain and hand had turned *Frankenstein*, bent upon pursuing me to my death.

A second shell exploded upon the deck. One of the lifeboats, frightfully overcrowded, swung at a dangerous angle from its davits. A fragment of the shell shattered the bow tackle, and I saw the women and children and the men vomited into the sea beneath, while the boat dangled stern up for a moment from its single davit, and at last with increasing momentum dived into the midst of the struggling victims screaming upon the face of the waters.

Now I saw men spring to the rail and leap into the ocean. The deck was tilting to an impossible angle. Nobs braced himself with all four feet to keep from slipping into the scuppers and looked up into my face with a questioning whine. I stooped and stroked his head.

"Come on, boy!" I cried, and running to the side of the ship, dived headforemost over the rail. When I came up, the first thing I saw was Nobs swimming about in a bewildered sort of way a few yards from me. At sight of me his ears went flat, and his lips parted in a characteristic grin.

The submarine was withdrawing toward the north, but all the time it was shelling the open boats, three of them, loaded to the gunwales with survivors. Fortunately the small boats presented a rather poor target, which, combined with the bad marksmanship of the Germans preserved their occupants from harm; and after a few minutes a blotch of smoke appeared upon the eastern horizon and the U-boat submerged and disappeared.

All the time the lifeboats had been pulling away from the danger of the sinking liner, and now, though I yelled at the top of my lungs, they either did not hear my appeals for help or else did not dare return to succor me. Nobs and I had gained some little distance from the ship when it rolled completely over and sank. We were caught in the suction only enough to be drawn backward a few yards, neither of us being carried beneath the surface. I glanced hurriedly about for something to which to cling. My eyes were directed toward the point at which the liner had disappeared when there came from the depths of the ocean the muffled reverberation of an explosion, and almost simultaneously a geyser of water in which were shattered lifeboats, human bodies, steam, coal, oil, and the flotsam of a liner's deck leaped high above the surface of the sea—a watery column momentarily marking the grave of another ship in this greatest cemetery of the seas.

When the turbulent waters had somewhat subsided and the sea had ceased to spew up wreckage, I ventured to swim back in search of something substantial enough to support my weight and that of Nobs as well. I had gotten well over the area of the wreck when not a half-dozen yards ahead of me a lifeboat shot bow foremost out of the ocean almost its entire length to flop down upon its keel with a mighty splash. It must have been carried far below, held to its mother ship by a single rope which finally parted to the enormous strain put upon it. In no other way can I account for its having leaped so far out of the water—a beneficent circumstance to which I doubtless owe my life, and that of another far dearer to me than my own. I say beneficent circumstance even in the face of the fact that a fate far more hideous confronts us than that which we escaped that day; for because of that circumstance I have met her whom otherwise I never should have known; I have met and loved her. At least I have had that great happiness in life; nor can Caspak, with all her horrors, expunge that which has been. So for the thousandth time I thank the strange fate which sent that lifeboat hurtling upward from the green pit of destruction to which it had been dragged—sent it far up above the surface, emptying its water as it rose above the waves, and dropping it upon the surface of the sea, buoyant and safe.

It did not take me long to clamber over its side and drag Nobs in to comparative safety, and then I glanced around upon the scene of death and desolation which surrounded us. The sea was littered with wreckage among which floated the pitiful forms of women and children, buoyed up by their useless life belts. Some were torn and mangled; others lay rolling quietly to the motion of the sea, their countenances composed and peaceful; others were set in hideous lines of agony or horror. Close to the boat's side floated the figure of a girl. Her face was turned upward, held above the surface by her life belt, and was framed in a floating mass of dark and waving hair. She was very beautiful. I had never looked upon such perfect features, such a divine molding which was at the same time human—intensely human. It was a face filled with character and strength and femininity—the face of one who was created to love and to be loved. The cheeks were flushed to the hue of life and health and vitality, and yet she lay there upon the bosom of the sea, dead. I felt something rise in my throat as I looked down upon that radiant vision, and I swore that I should live to avenge her murder.

And then I let my eyes drop once more to the face upon the water, and what I saw nearly tumbled me backward into the sea, for the eyes in the dead face had opened; the lips had parted; and one hand was raised toward me in a mute appeal for succor. She lived! She was not dead! I leaned over the boat's side and drew her quickly in to the comparative safety which God had given me. I removed her life belt and my soggy coat and made a pillow for her head. I chafed her hands and arms and feet. I worked over her for an hour, and at last I was rewarded by a deep sigh, and again those great eyes opened and looked into mine.

At that I was all embarrassment. I have never been a ladies' man; at

Leland-Stanford I was the butt of the class because of my hopeless imbecility in the presence of a pretty girl; but the men liked me, nevertheless. I was rubbing one of her hands when she opened her eyes, and I dropped it as though it were a red-hot rivet. Those eyes took me in slowly from head to foot; then they wandered slowly around the horizon marked by the rising and falling gunwales of the lifeboat. They looked at Nobs and softened, and then came back to me, filled with questioning.

"I—I—" I stammered, moving away and stumbling over the next thwart. The vision smiled wanly.

"Aye-aye, sir!" she replied faintly, and again her lids drooped, and her long lashes swept the firm, fair texture of her skin.

"I hope that you are feeling better," I finally managed to say.

"Do you know," she said after a moment of silence, "I have been awake for a long time! But I did not dare open my eyes. I thought I must be dead, and I was afraid to look, for fear that I should see nothing but blackness all about me. I am afraid to die! Tell me what happened after the ship went down. I remember all that happened before—oh, but I wish that I might forget it!" A sob broke her voice. "The beasts!" she went on after a moment. "And to think that I was to have married one of them—a lieutenant in the German navy."

Presently she resumed as though she had not ceased speaking. "I went down and down and down. I thought I should never cease to sink. I felt no particular distress until I suddenly started upward at ever-increasing velocity; then my lungs seemed about to burst, and I must have lost consciousness, for I remember nothing more until I opened my eyes after listening to a torrent of invective against Germany and Germans. Tell me, please, all that happened after the ship sank."

I told her, then, as well as I could, all that I had seen—the submarine shelling the open boats and all the rest of it. She thought it marvelous that we should have been spared in so providential a manner, and I had a pretty speech upon my tongue's end, but lacked the nerve to deliver it. Nobs had come over and nosed his muzzle into her lap, and she stroked his ugly face, and at last she leaned over and put her cheek against his forehead. I have always admired Nobs; but this was the first time that it had ever occurred to me that I might wish to be Nobs. I wondered how he would take it, for he is as unused to women as I. But he took to it as a duck takes to water. What I lack of being a ladies' man Nobs certainly makes up for as a ladies' dog. The old scalawag just closed his eyes and put on one of the softest "sugar-wouldn't-melt-in-my-mouth" expressions you ever saw and stood there taking it and asking for more. It made me jealous.

"You seem fond of dogs," I said.

"I am fond of this dog," she replied.

Whether she meant anything personal in that reply I did not know; but I took it as personal and it made me feel mighty good.

As we drifted about upon that vast expanse of loneliness it is not strange that we should quickly become well acquainted. Constantly we scanned the horizon for signs of smoke, venturing guesses as to our chances of rescue; but darkness settled, and the black night enveloped us without ever the sight of a speck upon the waters.

We were thirsty, hungry, uncomfortable, and cold. Our wet garments had dried but little and I knew that the girl must be in grave danger from the exposure to a night of cold and wet upon the water in an open boat, without sufficient clothing and no food. I had managed to bail all the water out of the boat with cupped hands, ending by mopping the balance up with my handkerchief—a slow and backbreaking procedure; thus I had made a comparatively dry place for the girl to lie down low in the bottom of the boat, where the sides would protect her from the night wind, and when at last she did so, almost overcome as she was by weakness and fatigue, I threw my wet coat over her further to thwart the chill. But it was of no avail; as I sat watching her, the moonlight marking out the graceful curves of her slender young body, I saw her shiver.

"Isn't there something I can do?" I asked. "You can't lie there chilled through all night. Can't you suggest something?"

She shook her head. "We must grin and bear it," she replied after a moment.

Nobbler came and lay down on the thwart beside me, his back against my leg, and I sat staring in dumb misery at the girl, knowing in my heart of hearts that she might die before morning came, for what with the shock and the exposure, she had already gone through enough to kill almost any woman. And as I gazed down at her, so small and delicate and helpless, there was born slowly within my breast a new emotion. It had never been there before; now it will never cease to be there. It made me almost frantic in my desire to find some way to keep warm the cooling lifeblood in her veins. I was cold myself, though I had almost forgotten it until Nobbler moved and I felt a new sensation of cold along my leg against which he had lain, and suddenly realized that in that one spot I had been warm. Like a great light came the understanding of a means to warm the girl. Immediately I knelt beside her to put my scheme into practice when suddenly I was overwhelmed with embarrassment. Would she permit it, even if I could muster the courage to suggest it? Then I saw her frame convulse shudderingly, her muscles reacting to her rapidly lowering temperature, and casting prudery to the winds, I threw myself down beside her and took her in my arms, pressing her body close to mine.

She drew away suddenly, voicing a little cry of fright, and tried to push me from her.

"Forgive me," I managed to stammer. "It is the only way. You will die of exposure if you are not warmed, and Nobs and I are the only means we can command for furnishing warmth." And I held her tightly while I called Nobs and bade him lie down at her back. The girl didn't struggle any more when she learned my purpose; but she gave two or three little gasps, and then she began to cry softly, burying her face on my arm, and thus she fell asleep.

CHAPTER TWO

Toward morning, I must have dozed, though it seemed to me at the time that I had lain awake for days, instead of hours. When I finally opened my eyes, it was daylight, and the girl's hair was in my face, and she was breathing normally. I thanked God for that. She had turned her head during the night so that as I opened my eyes I saw her face not an inch from mine, my lips almost touching hers.

It was Nobs who finally awoke her. He got up, stretched, turned around a few times and lay down again, and the girl opened her eyes and looked into mine. Hers went very wide at first, and then slowly comprehension came to her, and she smiled.

"You have been very good to me," she said, as I helped her to rise, though if the truth were known I was more in need of assistance than she; the circulation all along my left side seeming to be paralyzed entirely. "You have been very good to me." And that was the only mention she ever made of it; yet I know that she was thankful and that only reserve prevented her from referring to what, to say the least, was an embarrassing situation, however unavoidable.

Shortly after daylight we saw smoke apparently coming straight toward us, and after a time we made out the squat lines of a tug—one of those fearless exponents of England's supremacy of the sea that tows sailing ships into French and English ports. I stood up on a thwart and waved my soggy coat above my head. Nobs stood upon another and barked. The girl sat at my feet straining her eyes toward the deck of the oncoming boat. "They see us," she said at last. "There is a man answering your signal." She was right. A lump came into my throat—for her sake rather than for mine. She was saved, and none too soon. She could not have lived through another night upon the Channel; she might not have lived through the coming day.

The tug came close beside us, and a man on deck threw us a rope. Willing hands dragged us to the deck, Nobs scrambling nimbly aboard without assistance. The rough men were gentle as mothers with the girl. Plying us both with questions they hustled her to the captain's cabin and me to the boiler room. They told the girl to take off her wet clothes and throw them outside the door that they might be dried, and then to slip into the captain's bunk and get warm. They didn't have to tell me to strip after I once got into the warmth of the boiler room. In a jiffy, my clothes hung about where they might dry most quickly, and I myself was absorbing, through every pore, the welcome heat of the stifling compartment. They brought us hot soup and coffee, and then those who were not on duty sat around and helped me damn the Kaiser and his brood.

As soon as our clothes were dry, they bade us don them, as the chances were always more than fair in those waters that we should run into trouble with the enemy, as I was only too well aware. What with the warmth and the feeling of safety for the girl, and the knowledge that a little rest and food would quickly overcome the effects of her experiences of the past dismal hours, I was feeling more content than I had experienced since those three whistle blasts had shattered the peace of my world the previous afternoon.

But peace upon the Channel has been but a transitory thing since August, 1914. It proved itself such that morning, for I had scarce gotten into my dry clothes and taken the girl's apparel to the captain's cabin when an order was shouted down into the engine room for full speed ahead, and an instant later I heard the dull boom of a gun. In a moment I was up on deck to see an enemy submarine about two hundred yards off our port bow. She had signaled us to stop, and our skipper had ignored the order; but now she had her gun trained on us, and the second shot grazed the cabin, warning the belligerent tug captain that it was time to obey. Once again an order went down to the engine room, and the tug reduced speed. The U-boat ceased firing and ordered the tug to come about and approach. Our momentum had carried us a little beyond the enemy craft, but we were turning now on the arc of a circle that would bring us alongside her. As I stood watching the maneuver and wondering what was to become of us, I felt something touch my elbow and turned to see the girl standing at my side. She looked up into my face with a rueful expression. "They seem bent on our destruction," she said, "and it looks like the same boat that sunk us yesterday."

"It is," I replied. "I know her well. I helped design her and took her out on her first run."

The girl drew back from me with a little exclamation of surprise and disappointment. "I thought you were an American," she said. "I had no idea you were a—a—"

"Nor am I," I replied. "Americans have been building submarines for all nations for many years. I wish, though, that we had gone bankrupt, my father and I, before ever we turned out that *Frankenstein* of a thing."

We were approaching the U-boat at half speed now, and I could almost distinguish the features of the men upon her deck. A sailor stepped to my side and slipped something hard and cold into my hand. I did not have to look at it to know that it was a heavy pistol. "Tyke 'er an' use 'er," was all he said.

Our bow was pointed straight toward the U-boat now as I heard word passed to the engine room for full speed ahead. Instantly I grasped the brazen effrontery of the plucky English skipper—he was going to ram five hundred tons of U-boat in the face of her trained gun. I could scarce repress a cheer. At first the Germans didn't seem to grasp his intention. Evidently they thought they were witnessing an exhibition of poor seamanship, and they yelled their warnings to the tug to reduce speed and throw the helm hard to port.

We were within fifty feet of them when they awakened to the intentional menace of our maneuver. Their gun crew was off its guard; but they sprang to their piece now and sent a futile shell above our heads. Nobs leaped about and barked furiously. "Let 'em have it!" commanded the tug captain, and instantly revolvers and rifles poured bullets upon the deck of the submersible. Two of the gun crew went down; the other trained their piece at the waterline of the oncoming tug. The balance of those on deck replied to our small arms fire, directing their efforts toward the man at our wheel.

I hastily pushed the girl down the companionway leading to the engine room, and then I raised my pistol and fired my first shot at a Boche. What happened in the next few seconds happened so quickly that details are rather blurred in my memory. I saw the helmsman lunge forward upon the wheel, pulling the helm around so that the tug sheered off quickly from her course, and I recall realizing that all our efforts were to be in vain, because of all the men aboard, Fate had decreed that this one should fall first to an enemy bullet. I saw the depleted gun crew on the submarine fire their piece and I felt the shock of impact and heard the loud explosion as the shell struck and exploded in our bows.

I saw and realized these things even as I was leaping into the pilothouse and grasping the wheel, standing astride the dead body of the helmsman. With all my strength I threw the helm to starboard; but it was too late to effect the purpose of our skipper. The best I did was to scrape alongside the sub. I heard someone shriek an order into the engine room; the boat shuddered and trembled to the sudden reversing of the engines, and our speed quickly lessened. Then I saw what that madman of a skipper planned since his first scheme had gone wrong.

With a loud yelled command, he leaped to the slippery deck of the submersible, and at his heels came his hardy crew. I sprang from the pilothouse and followed, not to be left out in the cold when it came to strafing the Germans. From the engine room companionway came the engineer and stokers, and together we leaped after the balance of the crew and into the hand-to-hand fight that was covering the wet deck with red blood. Beside me came Nobs, silent now, and grim. Germans were emerging from the open hatch to take part in the battle on deck. At first the pistols cracked amidst the cursing of the men and the loud commands of the commander and his junior; but presently we were too indiscriminately mixed to make it safe to use our firearms, and the battle resolved itself into a hand-to-hand struggle for possession of the deck.

The sole aim of each of us was to hurl one of the opposing force into the sea. I shall never forget the hideous expression upon the face of the great Prussian with whom chance confronted me. He lowered his head and rushed at me, bellowing like a bull. With a quick side step and ducking low beneath his outstretched arms, I eluded him; and as he turned to come back at me, I landed a blow upon his chin which sent him spinning toward the edge of the deck. I saw his wild endeavors to regain his equilibrium; I saw him reel drunkenly for an instant upon the brink of eternity and then, with a loud scream, slip into the sea. At the same instant a pair of giant arms encircled me from behind and lifted me entirely off my feet. Kick and squirm as I would, I could neither turn toward my antagonist nor free myself from his maniacal grasp. Relentlessly he was rushing me toward the side of the vessel and death. There was none to stay him, for each of my companions was more than occupied by from one to three of the enemy. For an instant I was fearful for myself, and then I saw that which filled me with a far greater terror for another.

My Boche was bearing me toward the side of the submarine against which the tug still was pounding. That I should be ground to death between the two was lost upon me as I saw the girl standing alone upon the tug's deck, as I saw the stern high in air and the bow rapidly settling for the final dive, as I saw death from which I could not save her clutching at the skirts of the woman I now knew all too well that I loved.

I had perhaps the fraction of a second longer to live when I heard an angry growl behind us mingle with a cry of pain and rage from the giant who carried me. Instantly he went backward to the deck, and as he did so he threw his arms outwards to save himself, freeing me. I fell heavily upon him, but was upon my feet in the instant. As I arose, I cast a single glance at my opponent. Never again would he menace me or another, for Nobs' great jaws had closed upon his throat. Then I sprang toward the edge of the deck closest to the girl upon the sinking tug.

"Jump!" I cried. "Jump!" And I held out my arms to her. Instantly as though with implicit confidence in my ability to save her, she leaped over the side of the tug onto the sloping, slippery side of the U-boat. I reached far over to seize her hand. At the same instant the tug pointed its stern straight toward the sky and plunged out of sight. My hand missed the girl's by a fraction of an inch, and I saw her slip into the sea; but scarce had she touched the water when I was in after her.

The sinking tug drew us far below the surface; but I had seized her the moment I struck the water, and so we went down together, and together we came up—a few yards from the U-boat. The first thing I heard was Nobs barking furiously; evidently he had missed me and was searching. A single glance at the vessel's deck assured me that the battle was over and that we had been victorious, for I saw our survivors holding a handful of the enemy at pistol points while one by one the rest of the crew was coming out of the craft's interior and lining up on deck with the other prisoners.

As I swam toward the submarine with the girl, Nobs' persistent barking attracted the attention of some of the tug's crew, so that as soon as we reached the side there were hands to help us aboard. I asked the girl if she was hurt, but she assured me that she was none the worse for this second wetting; nor did she seem to suffer any from shock. I was to learn for myself that this slender and seemingly delicate creature possessed the heart and courage of a warrior.

As we joined our own party, I found the tug's mate checking up our survivors. There were ten of us left, not including the girl. Our brave skipper was missing, as were eight others. There had been nineteen of us in the attacking party and we had accounted in one way and another during the battle for sixteen Germans and had taken nine prisoners, including the commander. His lieutenant had been killed.

"Not a bad day's work," said Bradley, the mate, when he had completed his roll. "Only losing the skipper," he added, "was the worst. He was a fine man, a fine man."

Olson—who in spite of his name was Irish, and in spite of his not being Scotch had been the tug's engineer—was standing with Bradley and me. "Yis," he agreed, "it's a day's wor-rk we're after doin', but what are we goin' to be doin' wid it now we got it?"

"We'll run her into the nearest English port," said Bradley, "and then we'll all go ashore and get our V.C.'s," he concluded, laughing.

"How you goin' to run her?" queried Olson. "You can't trust these Dutchmen."

Bradley scratched his head. "I guess you're right," he admitted. "And I don't know the first thing about a sub."

"I do," I assured him. "I know more about this particular sub than the officer who commanded her."

Both men looked at me in astonishment, and then I had to explain all over again as I had explained to the girl. Bradley and Olson were delighted. Immediately I was put in command, and the first thing I did was to go below with Olson and inspect the craft thoroughly for hidden Germans and damaged machinery. There were no Germans below, and everything was intact and in shipshape working order. I then ordered all hands below except one man who was to act as lookout. Questioning the Germans, I found that all except the commander were willing to resume their posts and aid in bringing the vessel into an English port. I believe that they were relieved at the prospect of being detained at a comfortable English prison camp for the duration of the war after the perils and privations through which they had passed. The officer, however, assured me that he would never be a party to the capture of his vessel.

There was, therefore, nothing to do but put the man in irons. As we were preparing to put this decision into force, the girl descended from the deck. It was the first time that she or the German officer had seen each other's faces since we had boarded the U-boat. I was assisting the girl down the ladder and still retained a hold upon her arm—possibly after such support was no longer necessary—when she turned and looked squarely into the face of the German. Each voiced a sudden exclamation of surprise and dismay.

"Lys!" he cried, and took a step toward her.

The girl's eyes went wide, and slowly filled with a great horror, as she shrank back. Then her slender figure stiffened to the erectness of a soldier, and with chin in air and without a word she turned her back upon the officer.

"Take him away," I directed the two men who guarded him, "and put him in irons."

When he had gone, the girl raised her eyes to mine. "He is the German of whom I spoke," she said. "He is Baron von Schoenvorts."

I merely inclined my head. She had loved him! I wondered if in her heart of hearts she did not love him yet. Immediately I became insanely jealous. I hated Baron Friedrich von Schoenvorts with such utter intensity that the emotion thrilled me with a species of exaltation.

But I didn't have much chance to enjoy my hatred then, for almost immediately the lookout poked his face over the hatchway and bawled down that there was smoke on the horizon, dead ahead. Immediately I went on deck to investigate, and Bradley came with me.

"If she's friendly," he said, "we'll speak her. If she's not, we'll sink her—eh, Captain?"

"Yes, Lieutenant," I replied, and it was his turn to smile.

We hoisted the Union Jack and remained on deck, asking Bradley to go below and assign to each member of the crew his duty, placing one Englishman with a pistol beside each German.

"Half speed ahead," I commanded.

More rapidly now we closed the distance between ourselves and the stranger, until I could plainly see the red ensign of the British merchant marine. My heart swelled with pride at the thought that presently admiring British tars would be congratulating us upon our notable capture; and just about then the merchant steamer must have sighted us, for she veered suddenly toward the north, and a moment later dense volumes of smoke issued from her funnels. Then, steering a zigzag course, she fled from us as though we had been the bubonic plague. I altered the course of the submarine and set off in chase; but the steamer was faster than we, and soon left us hopelessly astern.

With a rueful smile I directed that our original course be resumed, and once again we set off toward merry England. That was three months ago, and we haven't arrived yet; nor is there any likelihood that we ever shall.

The steamer we had just sighted must have wirelessed a warning, for it wasn't half an hour before we saw more smoke on the horizon, and this time the vessel flew the white ensign of the Royal Navy and carried guns. She didn't veer to the north or anywhere else, but bore down on us rapidly. I was just preparing to signal her, when a flame flashed from her bows, and an instant later the water in front of us was thrown high by the explosion of a shell.

Bradley had come on deck and was standing beside me. "About one more of those, and she'll have our range," he said. "She doesn't seem to take much stock in our Union Jack."

A second shell passed over us, and then I gave the command to change our direction, at the same time directing Bradley to go below and give the order to submerge. I passed Nobs down to him, and following, saw to the closing and fastening of the hatch.

It seemed to me that the diving tanks never had filled so slowly. We heard a loud explosion apparently directly above us; the craft trembled to the shock, which threw us all to the deck. I expected momentarily to feel the deluge of inrushing water, but none came. Instead we continued to submerge until the manometer registered forty feet and then I knew that we were safe. Safe! I almost smiled. I had relieved Olson, who had remained in the tower at my direction, having been a member of one of the early British submarine crews, and therefore having some knowledge of the business. Bradley was at my side. He looked at me quizzically.

"What the devil are we to do?" he asked. "The merchantman will flee us; the war vessel will destroy us; neither will believe our colors or give us a chance to explain. We will meet even a worse reception if we go nosing around a British port—mines, nets and all of it. We can't do it."

"Let's try it again when this fellow has lost the scent," I urged. "There must come a ship that will believe us."

And try it again we did, only to be almost rammed by a huge freighter. Later we were fired upon by a destroyer, and two merchantmen turned and fled at our approach. For two days we cruised up and down the Channel trying to tell someone, who would listen, that we were friends; but no one would listen. After our encounter with the first warship I had given instructions that a wireless message be sent out explaining our predicament; but to my chagrin I discovered that both sending and receiving instruments had disappeared.

"There is only one place you can go," von Schoenvorts sent word to me, "and that is Kiel. You can't land anywhere else in these waters. If you wish, I will take you there, and I can promise that you will be treated well."

"There is another place we can go," I sent back my reply, "and we will before we'll go to Germany. That place is hell."

CHAPTER THREE

THOSE WERE ANXIOUS DAYS, during which I had but little opportunity to associate with Lys. I had given her the commander's room, Bradley and I taking that of the deck officer, while Olson and two of our best men occupied the room ordinarily allotted to petty officers. I made Nobs' bed down in Lys' room, for I knew she would feel less alone.

Nothing of much moment occurred for a while after we left British waters behind us. We ran steadily along upon the surface, making good time. The first two boats we sighted made off as fast as they could go; and the third, a huge freighter, fired on us, forcing us to submerge. It was after this that our troubles commenced. One of the diesel engines broke down in the morning, and while we were working on it, the forward port diving tank commenced to fill. I was on deck at the time and noted the gradual list. Guessing at once what was happening, I leaped for the hatch and slamming it closed above my head, dropped to the centrale. By this time the craft was going down by the head with a most unpleasant list to port, and I didn't wait to transmit orders to someone else but ran as fast as I could for the valve that let the sea into the forward port diving tank. It was wide open. To close it and to have the pump started that would empty it were the work of but a minute; but we had had a close call.

I knew that the valve had never opened itself. Someone had opened it—someone who was willing to die himself if he might at the same time encompass the death of all of us.

After that I kept a guard pacing the length of the narrow craft. We worked upon the engine all that day and night and half the following day. Most of the time we drifted idly upon the surface, but toward noon we sighted smoke due west, and having found that only enemies inhabited the world for us, I ordered that the other engine be started so that we could move out of the path of the oncoming steamer. The moment the engine started to turn, however, there was a grinding sound of tortured steel, and when it had been stopped, we found that someone had placed a cold chisel in one of the gears.

It was another two days before we were ready to limp along, half repaired. The night before the repairs were completed, the sentry came to my room and awoke me. He was rather an intelligent fellow of the English middle class, in whom I had much confidence.

"Well, Wilson," I asked, "what's the matter now?"

He raised his finger to his lips and came closer to me. "I think I've found out who's doin' the mischief," he whispered, and nodded his head toward the girl's room. "I seen her sneakin' from the crew's room just now," he went on. "She'd been in gassin' wit' the Boche commander. Benson seen her in there las' night, too, but he never said nothin' till I goes on watch tonight. Benson's sorter slow in the head, an' he never puts two an' two together till someone else has made four out of it."

If the man had come in and struck me suddenly in the face, I could have been no more surprised.

"Say nothing of this to anyone," I ordered. "Keep your eyes and ears open and report every suspicious thing you see or hear."

The man saluted and left me; but for an hour or more I tossed, restless, upon my hard bunk in an agony of jealousy and fear. Finally I fell into a troubled sleep. It was daylight when I awoke. We were steaming along slowly upon the surface, my orders having been to proceed at half speed until we could take an observation and determine our position. The sky had been overcast all the previous day and all night; but as I stepped into the centrale that morning I was delighted to see that the sun was again shining. The spirits of the men seemed improved; everything seemed propitious. I forgot at once the cruel misgivings of the past night as I set to work to take my observations.

What a blow awaited me! The sextant and chronometer had both been broken beyond repair, and they had been broken just this very night. They had been broken upon the night that Lys had been seen talking with von Schoenvorts. I think that it was this last thought which hurt me the worst. I could look the other disaster in the face with equanimity; but the bald fact that Lys might be a traitor appalled me.

I called Bradley and Olson on deck and told them what had happened, but for the life of me I couldn't bring myself to repeat what Wilson had reported to me the previous night. In fact, as I had given the matter thought, it seemed incredible that the girl could have passed through my room, in which Bradley and I slept, and that occupied by Olson and two others, and then carried on a conversation in the crew's room, in which von Schoenvorts was kept, without having been seen by more than a single man.

Bradley shook his head. "I can't make it out," he said. "One of those Germans must be pretty clever to come it over us all like this; but they haven't harmed us as much as they think; there are still the extra instruments."

It was my turn now to shake a doleful head. "There are no extra instruments," I told them. "They too have disappeared as did the wireless apparatus."

Both men looked at me in amazement. "We still have the compass and the sun," said Olson. "They may be after getting the compass some night; but they's too many of us around in the daytime fer 'em to get the sun."

It was then that one of the men stuck his head up through the hatchway and seeing me, asked permission to come on deck and get a breath of fresh air. I recognized him as Benson, the man who, Wilson had said, reported having seen Lys with von Schoenvorts two nights before. I motioned him on deck and then called him to one side, asking if he had seen anything out of the way or unusual during his trick on watch the night before. The fellow scratched his head a moment and said "No," and then as though it was an afterthought, he told me that he had seen the girl in the crew's room about midnight talking with the German commander, but as there hadn't seemed to him to be any harm in that, he hadn't said anything about it. Telling him never to fail to report to me anything in the slightest out of the ordinary routine of the ship, I dismissed him.

Several of the other men now asked permission to come on deck, and soon all but those actually engaged in some necessary duty were standing around smoking and talking, all in the best of spirits. I took advantage of the absence of the men upon the deck to go below for my breakfast, which the cook was already preparing upon the electric stove. Lys, followed by Nobs, appeared as I entered the centrale. She met me with a pleasant "Good morning!" which I am afraid I replied to in a tone that was rather constrained and surly.

"Will you breakfast with me?" I suddenly asked the girl, determined to commence a probe of my own along the lines which duty demanded.

She nodded a sweet acceptance of my invitation, and together we sat down at the little table of the officers' mess.

"You slept well last night?" I asked.

"All night," she replied. "I am a splendid sleeper."

Her manner was so straightforward and honest that I could not bring myself to believe in her duplicity; yet— Thinking to surprise her into a betrayal of her guilt, I blurted out: "The chronometer and sextant were both destroyed last night; there is a traitor among us." But she never turned a hair by way of evidencing guilty knowledge of the catastrophe.

"Who could it have been?" she cried. "The Germans would be crazy to do it, for their lives are as much at stake as ours."

"Men are often glad to die for an ideal—an ideal of patriotism, perhaps," I replied; "and a willingness to martyr themselves includes a willingness to sacrifice others, even those who love them. Women are much the same, except that they will go even further than most men—they will sacrifice everything, even honor, for love."

I watched her face carefully as I spoke, and I thought that I detected a very faint flush mounting her cheek. Seeing an opening and an advantage, I sought to follow it up.

"Take von Schoenvorts, for instance," I continued: "he would doubtless be glad to die and take us all with him, could he prevent in no other way the falling of his vessel into enemy hands. He would sacrifice anyone, even you; and if you still love him, you might be his ready tool. Do you understand me?"

She looked at me in wide-eyed consternation for a moment, and then she went very white and rose from her seat. "I do," she replied, and turning her back upon me, she walked quickly toward her room. I started to follow, for even believing what I did, I was sorry that I had hurt her. I reached the door to the crew's room just behind her and in time to see von Schoenvorts lean forward and whisper something to her as she passed; but she must have guessed that she might be watched, for she passed on.

That afternoon it clouded over; the wind mounted to a gale, and the sea rose until the craft was wallowing and rolling frightfully. Nearly everyone aboard was sick; the air became foul and oppressive. For twenty-four hours I did not leave my post in the conning tower, as both Olson and Bradley were sick. Finally I found that I must get a little rest, and so I looked about for someone to relieve me. Benson volunteered. He had not been sick, and assured me that he was a former R.N. man and had been detailed for submarine duty for over two years. I was glad that it was he, for I had considerable confidence in his loyalty, and so it was with a feeling of security that I went below and lay down.

I slept twelve hours straight, and when I awoke and discovered what I had done, I lost no time in getting to the conning tower. There sat Benson as wide awake as could be, and the compass showed that we were heading straight into the west. The storm was still raging; nor did it abate its fury until the fourth day. We were all pretty well done up and looked forward to the time when we could go on deck and fill our lungs with fresh air. During the whole four days I had not seen the girl, as she evidently kept closely to her room; and during this time no untoward incident had occurred aboard the boat—a fact which seemed to strengthen the web of circumstantial evidence about her.

For six more days after the storm lessened we still had fairly rough weather; nor did the sun once show himself during all that time. For the season—it was now the middle of June—the storm was unusual; but being from southern California, I was accustomed to unusual weather. In fact, I have discovered that the world over, unusual weather prevails at all times of the year.

We kept steadily to our westward course, and as the *U-33* was one of the fastest submersibles we had ever turned out, I knew that we must be pretty close to the North American coast. What puzzled me most was the fact that for six days we had not sighted a single ship. It seemed remarkable that we could cross the Atlantic almost to the coast of the American continent without glimpsing smoke or sail, and at last I came to the conclusion that we were way off our course, but whether to the north or to the south of it I could not determine.

On the seventh day the sea lay comparatively calm at early dawn. There was a slight haze upon the ocean which had cut off our view of the stars; but conditions all pointed toward a clear morrow, and I was on deck anxiously awaiting the rising of the sun. My eyes were glued upon the impenetrable mist astern, for there in the east I should see the first glow of the rising sun that would assure me we were still upon the right course. Gradually the heavens lightened; but astern I could see no intenser glow that would indicate the rising sun behind the mist. Bradley was standing at my side. Presently he touched my arm.

"Look, Captain," he said, and pointed south.

I looked and gasped, for there directly to port I saw outlined through the haze the red top of the rising sun. Hurrying to the tower, I looked at the compass. It showed that we were holding steadily upon our westward course. Either the sun was rising in the south, or the compass had been tampered with. The conclusion was obvious.

I went back to Bradley and told him what I had discovered. "And," I concluded, "we can't make another five hundred knots without oil; our provisions are running low and so is our water. God only knows how far south we have run."

"There is nothing to do," he replied, "other than to alter our course once more toward the west; we must raise land soon or we shall all be lost."

I told him to do so, and then I set to work improvising a crude sextant with which we finally took our bearings in a rough and most unsatisfactory manner; for when the work was done, we did not know how far from the truth the result might be. It showed us to be about 20° north and 30° west—nearly twenty-five hundred miles off our course. In short, if our reading was anywhere near correct, we must have been traveling due south for six days. Bradley now relieved Benson, for we had arranged our shifts so that the latter and Olson now divided the nights, while Bradley and I alternated with one another during the days.

I questioned both Olson and Benson closely in the matter of the compass; but each stoutly maintained that no one had tampered with it during his tour of duty. Benson gave me a knowing smile, as much as to say: "Well, you and I know who did this." Yet I could not believe that it was the girl.

We kept to our westerly course for several hours when the lookout's cry announced a sail. I ordered the *U-33*'s course altered, and we bore down upon the stranger, for I had come to a decision which was the result of necessity. We could not lie there in the middle of the Atlantic and starve to death if there was any way out of it. The sailing ship saw us while we were still a long way off, as was evidenced by her efforts to escape. There was scarcely any wind, however, and her case was hopeless; so when we drew near and signaled her to stop, she came into the wind and lay there with her sails flapping idly. We moved in quite close to her. She was the *Balmen* of Halmstad, Sweden, with a general cargo from Brazil for Spain.

I explained our circumstances to her skipper and asked for food, water and oil; but when he found that we were not German, he became very angry and abusive and started to draw away from us; but I was in no mood for any such business. Turning toward Bradley, who was in the conning tower, I snapped out: "Gun service on deck! To the diving stations!" We had no opportunity for drill; but every man had been posted as to his duties, and the German members of the crew understood that it was obedience or death for them, as each was accompanied by a man with a pistol. Most of them, though, were only too glad to obey me.

Bradley passed the order down into the ship, and a moment later the gun crew clambered up the narrow ladder and at my direction trained their piece upon the slow-moving Swede. "Fire a shot across her bow," I instructed the gun captain.

Accept it from me, it didn't take that Swede long to see the error of his way and get the red and white pennant signifying "I understand" to the masthead. Once again the sails flapped idly, and then I ordered him to lower a boat and come after me. With Olson and a couple of the Englishmen I boarded the ship, and from her cargo selected what we needed—oil, provisions and water. I gave the master of the *Balmen* a receipt for what we took, together with an affidavit signed by Bradley, Olson, and myself, stating briefly how we had come into possession of the *U-33* and the urgency of our need for what we took. We addressed both to any British agent with the request that the owners of the *Balmen* be reimbursed; but whether or not they were, I do not know.**

With water, food, and oil aboard, we felt that we had obtained a new lease of life. Now, too, we knew definitely where we were, and I determined to make for Georgetown, British Guiana—but I was destined to again suffer bitter disappointment.

Six of us of the loyal crew had come on deck either to serve the gun or board the Swede during our set-to with her; and now, one by one, we descended the ladder into the centrale. I was the last to come, and when I reached the bottom, I found myself looking into the muzzle of a pistol in the hands of Baron Friedrich von Schoenvorts—I saw all my men lined up at one side with the remaining eight Germans standing guard over them.

I couldn't imagine how it had happened; but it had. Later I learned that they had first overpowered Benson, who was asleep in his bunk, and taken his pistol from him, and then had found it an easy matter to disarm the cook and the remaining two Englishmen below. After that it had been comparatively simple to stand at the foot of the ladder and arrest each individual as he descended.

The first thing von Schoenvorts did was to send for me and announce that as a pirate I was to be shot early the next morning. Then he explained that the *U-33* would cruise in these waters for a time, sinking neutral and enemy shipping indiscriminately, and looking for one of the German raiders that was supposed to be in these parts.

He didn't shoot me the next morning as he had promised, and it has never been clear to me why he postponed the execution of my sentence. Instead he kept me ironed just as he had been; then he kicked Bradley out of my room and took it all to himself.

We cruised for a long time, sinking many vessels, all but one by gunfire,

---

*Late in July, 1916, an item in the shipping news mentioned a Swedish sailing vessel, *Balmen*, Rio de Janeiro to Barcelona, sunk by a German raider sometime in June. A single survivor in an open boat was picked up off the Cape Verde Islands, in a dying condition. He expired without giving any details.

but we did not come across a German raider. I was surprised to note that von Schoenvorts often permitted Benson to take command; but I reconciled this by the fact that Benson appeared to know more of the duties of a submarine commander than did any of the stupid Germans.

Once or twice Lys passed me; but for the most part she kept to her room. The first time she hesitated as though she wished to speak to me; but I did not raise my head, and finally she passed on. Then one day come the word that we were about to round the Horn and that von Schoenvorts had taken it into his fool head to cruise up along the Pacific coast of North America and prey upon all sorts and conditions of merchantmen.

"I'll put the fear of God and the Kaiser into them," he said.

The very first day we entered the South Pacific we had an adventure. It turned out to be quite the most exciting adventure I had ever encountered. It fell about this way. About eight bells of the forenoon watch I heard a hail from deck, and presently the footsteps of the entire ship's company, from the amount of noise I heard at the ladder. Someone yelled back to those who had not yet reached the level of the deck: "It's the raider, the German raider *Geier!*"

I saw that we had reached the end of our rope. Below all was quiet—not a man remained. A door opened at the end of the narrow hull, and presently Nobs came trotting up to me. He licked my face and rolled over on his back, reaching for me with his big, awkward paws. Then other footsteps sounded, approaching me. I knew whose they were, and I looked straight down at the flooring. The girl was coming almost at a run—she was at my side immediately. "Here!" she cried. "Quick!" And she slipped something into my hand. It was a key—the key to my irons. At my side she also laid a pistol, and then she went on into the centrale. As she passed me, I saw that she carried another pistol for herself. It did not take me long to liberate myself, and then I was at her side. "How can I thank you?" I started; but she shut me up with a word.

"Do not thank me," she said coldly. "I do not care to hear your thanks or any other expression from you. Do not stand there looking at me. I have given you a chance to do something—now do it!" The last was a peremptory command that made me jump.

Glancing up, I saw that the tower was empty, and I lost no time in clambering up, looking about me. About a hundred yards off lay a small, swift cruiser-raider, and above her floated the German man-of-war's flag.

A boat had just been lowered, and I could see it moving toward us filled with officers and men. The cruiser lay dead ahead. "My," I thought, "what a wonderful targ—"

I stopped even thinking, so surprised and shocked was I by the boldness of my imagery. The girl was just below me. I looked down at her wistfully. Could I trust her? Why had she released me at this moment? I must! I must! There was no other way. I dropped back below. "Ask Olson to step down here, please," I requested; "and don't let anyone see you ask him."

She looked at me with a puzzled expression on her face for the barest fraction of a second, and then she turned and went up the ladder. A moment later Olson returned, and the girl followed him. "Quick!" I whispered to the big Irishman, and made for the bow compartment where the torpedo tubes are built into the boat; here, too, were the torpedoes. The girl accompanied us, and when she saw the thing I had in mind, she stepped forward and lent a hand to the swinging of the great cylinder of death and destruction into the mouth of its tube. With oil and main strength we shoved the torpedo home and shut the tube; then I ran back to the conning tower, praying in my heart of hearts that the *U-33* had not swung her bow away from the prey. No, thank God!

Never could aim have been truer. I signaled back to Olson: "Let 'er go!" The *U-33* trembled from stem to stern as the torpedo shot from its tube. I saw the white wake leap from her bow straight toward the enemy cruiser. A chorus of hoarse yells arose from the deck of our own craft; I saw the officers stand suddenly erect in the boat that was approaching us, and I heard loud cries and curses from the raider. Then I turned my attention to my own business. Most of the men on the submarine's deck were standing in paralyzed fascination, staring at the torpedo. Bradley happened to be looking toward the conning tower and saw me. I sprang on deck and ran toward him. "Quick!" I whispered. "While they are stunned, we must overcome them."

A German was standing near Bradley—just in front of him. The Englishman struck the fellow a frantic blow upon the neck and at the same time snatched his pistol from its holster. Von Schoenvorts had recovered from his first surprise quickly and had turned toward the main hatch to investigate. I covered him with my revolver, and at the same instant the torpedo struck the raider, the terrific explosion drowning the German's command to his men.

Bradley was now running from one to another of our men, and though some of the Germans saw and heard him, they seemed too stunned for action.

Olson was below, so that there were only nine of us against eight Germans, for the man Bradley had struck still lay upon the deck. Only two of us were armed; but the heart seemed to have gone out of the Germans, and they put up but half-hearted resistance. Von Schoenvorts was the worst—he was fairly frenzied with rage and chagrin, and he came charging for me like a mad bull, and as he came he discharged his pistol. If he'd stopped long enough to take aim, he might have gotten me; but his pace made him wild, so that not a shot touched me, and then we clinched and went to the deck. This left two pistols, which two of my own men were quick to appropriate. The Baron was no match for me in a hand-to-hand encounter, and I soon had him pinned to the deck and the life almost choked out of him.

A half hour later things had quieted down, and all was much the same as before the prisoners had revolted—only we kept a much closer watch on von Schoenvorts. The *Geier* had sunk while we were still battling upon our deck, and afterward we had drawn away toward the north, leaving the survivors to the attention of the single boat which had been making its way toward us when Olson launched the torpedo. I suppose the poor devils never reached land, and if they did, they most probably perished on that cold and unhospitable shore; but I couldn't permit them aboard the *U-33*. We had all the Germans we could take care of.

That evening the girl asked permission to go on deck. She said that she felt the effects of long confinement below, and I readily granted her request. I could not understand her, and I craved an opportunity to talk with her again in an effort to fathom her and her intentions, and so I made it a point to follow her up the ladder. It was a clear, cold, beautiful night. The sea was calm except for the white water at our bows and the two long radiating swells running far off into the distance upon either hand astern, forming a great V which our propellers filled with choppy waves. Benson was in the tower, we were bound for San Diego and all looked well.

Lys stood with a heavy blanket wrapped around her slender figure, and as I approached her, she half turned toward me to see who it was. When she recognized me, she immediately turned away.

"I want to thank you," I said, "for your bravery and loyalty—you were magnificent. I am sorry that you had reason before to think that I doubted you."

"You did doubt me," she replied in a level voice. "You practically accused me of aiding Baron von Schoenvorts. I can never forgive you."

There was a great deal of finality in both her words and tone.

"I could not believe it," I said; "and yet two of my men reported having seen you in conversation with von Schoenvorts late at night upon two separate occasions—after each of which some great damage was found done us in the morning. I didn't want to doubt you; but I carried all the responsibility of the lives of these men, of the safety of the ship, of your life and mine. I had to watch you, and I had to put you on your guard against a repetition of your madness."

She was looking at me now with those great eyes of hers very wide and round.

"Who told you that I spoke with Baron von Schoenvorts at night, or any other time?" she asked.

"I cannot tell you, Lys," I replied, "but it came to me from two different sources."

"Then two men have lied," she asserted without heat. "I have not spoken to Baron von Schoenvorts other than in your presence when first we came aboard the *U-33*. And please, when you address me, remember that to others than my intimates I am Miss La Rue."

Did you ever get slapped in the face when you least expected it? No? Well, then you do not know how I felt at that moment. I could feel the hot, red flush surging up my neck, across my cheeks, over my ears, clear to my scalp. And it made me love her all the more; it made me swear inwardly a thousand solemn oaths that I would win her.

CHAPTER FOUR

FOR SEVERAL DAYS THINGS WENT ALONG in about the same course. I took our position every morning with my crude sextant; but the results were always most unsatisfactory. They always showed a considerable westing when I knew that we had been sailing due north. I blamed my crude instrument, and kept on. Then one afternoon the girl came to me.

"Pardon me," she said; "but were I you, I should watch this man

Benson—especially when he is in charge." I asked her what she meant, thinking I could see the influence of von Schoenvorts raising a suspicion against one of my most trusted men.

"If you will note the boat's course a half hour after Benson goes on duty," she said, "you will know what I mean, and you will understand why he prefers a night watch. Possibly, too, you will understand some other things that have taken place aboard."

Then she went back to her room, thus ending the conversation. 1 waited until half an hour after Benson had gone on duty, and then I went on deck, passing through the conning tower where Benson sat, and looking at the compass. It showed that our course was north by west—that is, one point west of north, which was, for our assumed position, about right. I was greatly relieved to find that nothing was wrong, for the girl's words had caused me considerable apprehension. I was about to return to my room when a thought occurred to me that again caused me to change my mind—and, incidentally, came near proving my death warrant.

When I had left the conning tower little more than a half hour since, the sea had been breaking over the port bow, and it seemed to me quite improbable that in so short a time an equally heavy sea could be deluging us from the opposite side of the ship—winds may change quickly, but not a long, heavy sea. There was only one other solution—since I left the tower, our course had been altered some eight points. Turning quickly, I climbed out upon the conning tower. A single glance at the heavens confirmed my suspicions; the constellations which should have been dead ahead were directly starboard. We were sailing due west.

Just for an instant longer I stood there to check up my calculations—I wanted to be quite sure before I accused Benson of perfidy, and about the only thing I came near making quite sure of was death. I cannot see even now how I escaped it. I was standing on the edge of the conning tower, when a heavy palm suddenly struck me between the shoulders and hurled me forward into space. The drop to the triangular deck forward of the conning tower might easily have broken a leg for me, or I might have slipped off onto the deck and rolled overboard; but fate was upon my side, as I was only slightly bruised. As I came to my feet, I heard the conning tower cover slam. There is a ladder which leads from the deck to the top of the tower. Up this I scrambled as fast as I could go; but Benson had the cover tight before I reached it.

I stood there a moment in dumb consternation. What did the fellow intend? What was going on below? If Benson was a traitor, how could I know that there were not other traitors among us? I cursed myself for my folly in going out upon the deck, and then this thought suggested another—a hideous one: who was it had really been responsible for my being here?

Thinking to attract attention from inside the craft, I again ran down the ladder and onto the small deck only to find that the steel covers of the conning tower windows were shut, and then I leaned with my back against the tower and cursed myself for a gullible idiot.

I glanced at the bow. The sea seemed to be getting heavier, for every wave now washed completely over the lower deck. I watched them for a moment, and then a sudden chill pervaded my entire being. It was not the chill of wet clothing, or the dashing spray which drenched my face; no, it was the chill of the hand of death upon my heart. In an instant I had turned the last corner of life's highway and was looking God Almighty in the face—the *U-33* was being slowly submerged!

It would be difficult, even impossible, to set down in writing my sensations at that moment. All I can particularly recall is that I laughed, though neither from a spirit of bravado nor from hysteria. And I wanted to smoke. Lord! how I did want to smoke; but that was out of the question.

I watched the water rise until the little deck I stood on was awash, and then I clambered once more to the top of the conning tower. From the very slow submergence of the boat I knew that Benson was doing the entire trick alone—that he was merely permitting the diving tanks to fill and that the diving rudders were not in use. The throbbing of the engines ceased, and in its stead came the steady vibration of the electric motors. The water was halfway up the conning tower! I had perhaps five minutes longer on the deck. I tried to decide what I should do after I was washed away. Should I swim until exhaustion claimed me, or should I give up and end the agony at the first plunge?

From below came two muffled reports. They sounded not unlike shots. Was Benson meeting with resistance? Personally it could mean little to me, for even though my men might overcome the enemy, none would know of my predicament until long after it was too late to succor me. The top of the conning tower was now awash. I clung to the wireless mast, while the great waves surged sometimes completely over me.

I knew the end was near and, almost involuntarily, I did that which I had not done since childhood—I prayed. After that I felt better.

I clung and waited, but the water rose no higher. Instead it receded. Now the top of the conning-tower received only the crests of the higher waves; now the little triangular deck below became visible! What had occurred within? Did Benson believe me already gone, and was he emerging because of that belief, or had he and his forces been vanquished? The suspense was more wearing than that which I had endured while waiting for dissolution. Presently the main deck came into view, and then the conning tower opened behind me, and I turned to look into the anxious face of Bradley. An expression of relief overspread his features.

"Thank God, man!" was all he said as he reached forth and dragged me into the tower. I was cold and numb and rather all in. Another few minutes would have done for me, I am sure, but the warmth of the interior helped to revive me, aided and abetted by some brandy which Bradley poured down my throat, from which it nearly removed the membrane. That brandy would have revived a corpse.

When I got down into the centrale, I saw the Germans lined up on one side with a couple of my men with pistols standing over them. Von Schoenvorts was among them. On the floor lay Benson, moaning, and beyond him stood the girl, a revolver in one hand. I looked about, bewildered.

"What has happened down here?" I asked. "Tell me!"

Bradley replied. "You see the result, sir," he said. "It might have been a very different result but for Miss La Rue. We were all asleep. Benson had relieved the guard early in the evening; there was no one to watch him—no one but Miss La Rue. She felt the submergence of the boat and came out of her room to investigate. She was just in time to see Benson at the diving rudders. When he saw her, he raised his pistol and fired point-blank at her, but he missed and she fired—and didn't miss. The two shots awakened everyone, and as our men were armed, the result was inevitable as you see it; but it would have been very different had it not been for Miss La Rue. It was she who closed the diving tank sea cocks and roused Olson and me, and had the pumps started to empty them."

And there I had been thinking that through her machinations I had been lured to the deck and to my death! I could have gone on my knees to her and begged her forgiveness—or at least I could have, had I not been

Anglo-Saxon. As it was, I could only remove my soggy cap and bow and mumble my appreciation. She made no reply—only turned and walked very rapidly toward her room. Could I have heard aright? Was it really a sob that came floating back to me through the narrow aisle of the *U-33*?

Benson died that night. He remained defiant almost to the last; but just before he went out, he motioned to me, and I leaned over to catch the faintly whispered words.

"I did it alone," he said. "I did it because I hate you—I hate all your kind. I was kicked out of your shipyard at Santa Monica. I was kicked out of California. I am an IWW. I became a German agent—not because I love them, for I hate them too—but because I wanted to injure Americans, whom I hated more. I threw the wireless apparatus overboard. I destroyed the chronometer and the sextant. I devised a scheme for varying the compass to suit my wishes. I told Wilson that I had seen the girl talking with von Schoenvorts, and I made the poor egg think he had seen her doing the same thing. I am sorry—sorry that my plans failed. I hate you."

He didn't die for a half hour after that; nor did he speak again—aloud; but just a few seconds before he went to meet his Maker, his lips moved in a faint whisper; and as I leaned close to catch his words, what do you suppose I heard? "Now—I—lay me—down—to—sleep—" That was all; Benson was dead. We threw his body overboard.

The wind of that night brought on some pretty rough weather with a lot of black clouds which persisted for several days. We didn't know what course we had been holding, and there was no way of finding out, as we could no longer trust the compass, not knowing what Benson had done to it. The long and the short of it was that we cruised about aimlessly until the sun came out again. I'll never forget that day or its surprises. We reckoned, or rather guessed, that we were somewhere off the coast of Peru. The wind, which had been blowing fitfully from the east, suddenly veered around into the south, and presently we felt a sudden chill.

"Peru!" snorted Olson. "When were yez after smellin' iceber-rgs off Peru?"

Icebergs! "Icebergs, nothin'!" exclaimed one of the Englishmen. "Why, man, they don't come north of fourteen here in these waters."

"Then," replied Olson, "ye're sout' of fourteen, me b'y."

We thought he was crazy; but he wasn't, for that afternoon we sighted a great berg south of us, and we'd been running north, we thought, for days. I can tell you we were a discouraged lot; but we got a faint thrill of hope early the next morning when the lookout bawled down the open hatch: "Land! Land northwest by west!"

I think we were all sick for the sight of land. I know that I was; but my interest was quickly dissipated by the sudden illness of three of the Germans. Almost simultaneously they commenced vomiting. They couldn't suggest any explanation for it. I asked them what they had eaten, and found they had eaten nothing other than the food cooked for all of us. "Have you drunk anything?" I asked, for I knew that there was liquor aboard, and medicines in the same locker.

"Only water," moaned one of them. "We all drank water together this morning. We opened a new tank. Maybe it was the water."

I started an investigation which revealed a terrifying condition—someone, probably Benson, had poisoned all the remaining water on the ship. It would have been worse, though, had land not been in sight. The sight of land filled us with renewed hope.

Our course had been altered, and we were rapidly approaching what appeared to be a precipitous headland. Cliffs, seemingly rising perpendicularly out of the sea, faded away into the mist upon either hand as we approached. The land before us might have been a continent, so mighty appeared the shoreline; yet we knew that we must be thousands of miles from the nearest western landmass—New Zealand or Australia.

We took our bearings with our crude and inaccurate instruments; we searched the chart; we cudgeled our brains; and at last it was Bradley who suggested a solution. He was in the tower and watching the compass, to which he called my attention. The needle was pointing straight toward the land. Bradley swung the helm hard to starboard. I could feel the *U-33* respond, and yet the arrow still clung straight and sure toward the distant cliffs.

"What do you make of it?" I asked him.

"Did you ever hear of Caproni?" he asked.

"An early Italian navigator?" I returned.

"Yes; he followed Cook about 1781. He is scarcely mentioned even by contemporaneous historians—probably because he got into political difficulties on his return to Italy. It was the fashion to scoff at his claims, but I recall reading one of his works—his only one, I believe—in which he described a new continent in the south seas, a continent made up of 'some strange metal' which attracted the compass; a rockbound, inhospitable coast, without beach or harbor, which extended for hundreds of miles. He could make no landing; nor in the several days he cruised about it did he see sign of life. He called it Caprona and sailed away. I believe, sir, that we are looking upon the coast of Caprona, uncharted and forgotten for two hundred years."

"If you are right, it might account for much of the deviation of the compass during the past two days," I suggested. "Caprona has been luring us upon her deadly rocks. Well, we'll accept her challenge. We'll land upon Caprona. Along that long front there must be a vulnerable spot. We will find it, Bradley, for we must find it. We must find water on Caprona, or we must die."

And so we approached the coast upon which no living eyes had ever rested. Straight from the ocean's depths rose towering cliffs, shot with brown and blues and greens—withered moss and lichen and the verdigris of copper, and everywhere the rusty ocher of iron pyrites. The cliff tops, though ragged, were of such uniform height as to suggest the boundaries of a great plateau, and now and again we caught glimpses of verdure topping the rocky escarpment, as though bush or jungle land had pushed outward from a lush vegetation farther inland to signal to an unseeing world that Caprona lived and joyed in life beyond her austere and repellent coast.

But metaphor, however poetic, never slaked a dry throat. To enjoy Caprona's romantic suggestions we must have water, and so we came in close, always sounding, and skirted the shore. As close in as we dared cruise, we found fathomless depths, and always the same undented coastline of bald cliff. As darkness threatened, we drew away and lay well off the coast all night. We had not as yet really commenced to suffer for lack of water; but I knew that it would not be long before we did, and so at the first streak of dawn I moved in again and once more took up the hopeless survey of the forbidding coast.

Toward noon we discovered a beach, the first we had seen. It was a narrow strip of sand at the base of a part of the cliff that seemed lower than any we had before scanned. At its foot, half buried in the sand, lay great boulders, mute evidence that in a bygone age some mighty natural force had crumpled Caprona's barrier at this point. It was Bradley who first called our attention to a strange object lying among the boulders above the surf.

"Looks like a man," he said, and passed his glasses to me.

I looked long and carefully and could have sworn that the thing I saw was the sprawled figure of a human being. Miss La Rue was on deck with us. I turned and asked her to go below. Without a word she did as I bade. Then I stripped, and as I did so, Nobs looked questioningly at me. He had been wont at home to enter the surf with me, and evidently he had not forgotten it.

"What are you going to do, sir?" asked Olson.

"I'm going to see what that thing is on shore," I replied. "If it's a man, it may mean that Caprona is inhabited, or it may merely mean that some poor devils were shipwrecked here. I ought to be able to tell from the clothing which is more near the truth."

"How about sharks?" queried Olson. "Sure, you ought to carry a knoife."

"Here you are, sir," cried one of the men.

It was a long slim blade he offered—one that I could carry between my teeth—and so I accepted it gladly.

"Keep close in," I directed Bradley, and then I dived over the side and struck out for the narrow beach. There was another splash directly behind me, and turning my head, I saw faithful old Nobs swimming valiantly in my wake.

The surf was not heavy, and there was no undertow, so we made shore easily, effecting an equally easy landing. The beach was composed largely of small stones worn smooth by the action of water. There was little sand, though from the deck of the *U-33* the beach had appeared to be all sand, and I saw no evidences of mollusca or crustacea such as are common to all beaches I have previously seen. I attribute this to the fact of the smallness of the beach, the enormous depth of surrounding water and the great distance at which Caprona lies from her nearest neighbor.

As Nobs and I approached the recumbent figure farther up the beach, I was appraised by my nose that whether man or not, the thing had once been organic and alive, but that for some time it had been dead. Nobs halted, sniffed and growled. A little later he sat down upon his haunches, raised his muzzle to the heavens and bayed forth a most dismal howl. I shied a small stone at him and bade him shut up—his uncanny noise made me nervous. When I had come quite close to the thing, I still could not say whether it had been man or beast. The carcass was badly swollen and partly decomposed. There was no sign of clothing upon or about it.

A fine, brownish hair covered the chest and abdomen, and the face, the palms of the hands, the feet, the shoulders and back were practically hairless. The creature must have been about the height of a fair-sized man; its features were similar to those of a man; yet had it been a man?

I could not say, for it resembled an ape no more than it did a man. Its large toes protruded laterally as do those of the semiarboreal peoples of Borneo, the Philippines, and other remote regions. The countenance might have been that of a cross between *Pithecanthropus*, the Java ape-man, and a daughter of the Piltdown race of prehistoric Sussex. A wooden cudgel lay beside the corpse.

Now this fact set me thinking. There was no wood of any description in sight. There was nothing about the beach to suggest a wrecked mariner. There was absolutely nothing about the body to suggest that it might possibly in life have known a maritime experience. It was the body of a low type of man or a high type of beast. In neither instance would it have been of a seafaring race. Therefore I deduced that it was native to Caprona— that it lived inland, and that it had fallen or been hurled from the cliffs above. Such being the case, Caprona was inhabitable, if not inhabited, by man; but how to reach the inhabitable interior! That was the question. A closer view of the cliffs than had been afforded me from the deck of the *U-33* only confirmed my conviction that no mortal man could scale those perpendicular heights; there was not a fingerhold, not a toehold, upon them. I turned away baffled.

Nobs and I met with no sharks upon our return journey to the submarine. My report filled everyone with theories and speculations, and with renewed hope and determination. They all reasoned along the same lines that I had reasoned—the conclusions were obvious, but not the water. We were now thirstier than ever.

The balance of that day we spent in continuing a minute and fruitless exploration of the monotonous coast. There was not another break in the frowning cliffs—not even another minute patch of pebbly beach. As the sun fell, so did our spirits. I had tried to make advances to the girl again; but she would have none of me, and so I was not only thirsty but otherwise sad and downhearted. I was glad when the new day broke the hideous spell of a sleepless night.

The morning's search brought us no shred of hope. Caprona was impregnable—that was the decision of all; yet we kept on. It must have been about two bells of the afternoon watch that Bradley called my attention to the branch of a tree, with leaves upon it, floating on the sea. "It may have been carried down to the ocean by a river," he suggested.

"Yes," I replied, "it may have; it may have tumbled or been thrown off the top of one of these cliffs."

Bradley's face fell. "I thought of that, too," he replied, "but I wanted to believe the other."

"Right you are!" I cried. "We must believe the other until we prove it false. We can't afford to give up heart now, when we need heart most. The branch was carried down by a river, and we are going to find that river." I smote my open palm with a clenched fist, to emphasize a determination unsupported by hope. "There!" I cried suddenly. "See that, Bradley?" And I pointed at a spot closer to shore. "See that, man!" Some flowers and grasses and another leafy branch floated toward us. We both scanned the water and the coastline. Bradley evidently discovered something, or at least thought that he had. He called down for a bucket and rope, and when they were passed up to him, he lowered the former into the sea and drew it in filled with water. Of this he took a taste, and straightening up, looked into my eyes with an expression of elation—as much as to say "I told you so!"

"This water is warm," he announced, "and fresh!"

I grabbed the bucket and tasted its contents. The water was very warm, and it was fresh, but there was a most unpleasant taste to it.

"Did you ever taste water from a stagnant pool full of tadpoles?" Bradley asked.

"That's it," I exclaimed, "—that's just the taste exactly, though I haven't experienced it since boyhood ; but how can water from a flowing stream taste thus, and what the dickens makes it so warm? It must be at least 70 or 80 Fahrenheit, possibly higher."

"Yes," agreed Bradley, "I should say higher; but where does it come from?"

"That is easily discovered now that we have found it," I answered. "It can't come from the ocean; so it must come from the land. All that we have to do is follow it, and sooner or later we shall come upon its source."

We were already rather close in; but I ordered the *U-33*'s prow turned inshore and we crept slowly along, constantly dipping up the water and tasting it to assure ourselves that we didn't get outside the freshwater current.

There was a very light offshore wind and scarcely any breakers, so that the approach to the shore was continued with little or no danger. We sounded constantly without finding bottom; yet though we were already quite close, we saw no indication of any indentation in the coast from which even a tiny brooklet might issue, and certainly no mouth of a large river such as this must necessarily be to freshen the ocean even two hundred yards from shore. The tide was running out, and this, together with the strong flow of the freshwater current, would have prevented our going against the cliffs even had we not been under power; as it was we had to buck the combined forces in order to hold our position at all. We came up to within twenty-five feet of the sheer wall, which loomed high above us. There was no break in its forbidding face. As we watched the face of the waters and searched the cliff's face, Olson suggested that the fresh water might come from a submarine geyser. This, he said, would account for its heat; but even as he spoke a bush, covered thickly with leaves and flowers, bubbled to the surface and floated off astern.

"Flowering shrubs don't thrive in the subterranean caverns from which geysers spring," suggested Bradley.

Olson shook his head. "It beats me," he said.

"I've got it!" I exclaimed suddenly. "Look there!" And I pointed at the base of the cliff ahead of us, which the receding tide was gradually exposing to our view. They all looked, and all saw what I had seen—the top of a dark opening in the rock, through which water was pouring out into the sea. "It's the subterranean channel of an inland river," I cried. "It flows through a land covered with vegetation—and therefore a land upon which the sun shines. No subterranean caverns produce any order of plant life even remotely resembling what we have seen disgorged by this river. Beyond those cliffs lie fertile lands and fresh water—perhaps, game."

"Yis sir," said Olson, "behoind the cliffs! Ye spoke a true word, sir— behoind!"

Bradley laughed—a rather sorry laugh, though. "You might as well call our attention to the fact, sir," he said, "that science has indicated that there is fresh water and vegetation on Mars."

"Not at all," I rejoined. "A U-boat isn't constructed to navigate space, but it is designed to travel below the surface of the water."

"You'd be after sailin' into that blank pocket?" asked Olson.

"I would, Olson," I replied. "We haven't one chance for life in a hundred thousand if we don't find food and water upon Caprona. This water coming out of the cliff is not salt; but neither is it fit to drink, though each of us has drunk it. It is fair to assume that inland the river is fed by pure streams, that there are fruits and herbs and game. Shall we lie out here and die of thirst and starvation with a land of plenty possibly only a few hundred yards away? We have the means for navigating a subterranean river. Are we too cowardly to utilize this means?"

"Be afther goin' to it," said Olson.

"I'm willing to see it through," agreed Bradley.

"Then under the bottom, wi' the best o' luck an' give 'em hell!" cried a young fellow who had been in the trenches.

"To the diving stations!" I commanded, and in less than a minute the deck was deserted, the conning tower covers had slammed to and the *U-33* was submerging—possibly for the last time. I know that I had this feeling, and I think that most of the others did.

As we went down, I sat in the tower with the searchlight projecting its seemingly feeble rays ahead. We submerged very slowly and without headway more than sufficient to keep her nose in the right direction, and as we went down, I saw outlined ahead of us the black opening in the great cliff. It was an opening that would have admitted a half-dozen U-boats at one and the same time, roughly cylindrical in contour—and dark as the pit of perdition.

As I gave the command which sent the *U-33* slowly ahead, I could not but feel a certain uncanny presentiment of evil. Where were we going? What lay at the end of this great sewer? Had we bidden farewell forever to the sunlight and to life, or were there before us dangers even greater than those which we now faced? I tried to keep my mind from vain imagining by calling everything which I observed to the eager ears below. I was the eyes of the whole company, and I did my best not to fail them. We had advanced a hundred yards, perhaps, when our first danger confronted us. Just ahead was a sharp right-angle turn in the tunnel. I could see the river's flotsam hurtling against the rocky wall upon the left as it was driven on by the mighty current, and I feared for the safety of the *U-33* in making so sharp a turn under such adverse conditions ; but there was nothing for it but to try it. I didn't warn my fellows of the danger—it could have but caused them useless apprehension, for if we were to be smashed against the rocky wall, no power on earth could avert the quick end that would come to us. I gave the command full speed ahead and went charging toward the menace. I was forced to approach the dangerous left-hand wall in order to make the turn, and I depended upon the power of the motors to carry us through the surging waters in safety. Well, we made it; but it was a narrow squeak. As we swung around, the full force of the current caught us and drove the stern against the rocks; there was a thud which sent a tremor through the whole craft, and then a moment of nasty grinding as the steel hull scraped the rock wall. I expected momentarily the inrush of waters that would seal our doom; but presently from below came the welcome word that all was well.

In another fifty yards there was a second turn, this time toward the left! but it was more of a gentle curve, and we took it without trouble. After that it was plain sailing, though as far as I could know, there might be most anything ahead of us, and my nerves were strained to the snapping point every instant. After the second turn the channel ran comparatively straight for between one hundred and fifty and two hundred yards. The waters grew suddenly lighter, and my spirits rose accordingly. I shouted down to those below that I saw daylight ahead, and a great shout of thanksgiving reverberated through the ship. A moment later we emerged into sunlit water, and immediately I raised the periscope and looked about me upon the strangest landscape I had ever seen.

We were in the middle of a broad and now sluggish river the banks of which were lined by giant, arboraceous ferns, raising their mighty fronds fifty, one hundred, two hundred feet into the quiet air. Close by us something rose to the surface of the river and dashed at the periscope. I had a vision of wide, distended jaws, and then all was blotted out. A shiver ran down into the tower as the thing closed upon the periscope. A moment later it was gone, and I could see again. Above the trees there soared into my vision a huge thing on batlike wings—a creature large as a large whale, but fashioned more after the order of a lizard. Then again something charged the periscope and blotted out the mirror. I will confess that I was almost gasping for breath as I gave the commands to emerge. Into what sort of strange land had fate guided us?

The instant the deck was awash, I opened the conning tower hatch and stepped out. In another minute the deck hatch lifted, and those who were not on duty below streamed up the ladder, Olson bringing Nobs under one arm. For several minutes no one spoke; I think they must each have been as overcome by awe as was I. All about us was a flora and a fauna as strange and wonderful to us as might have been those upon a distant planet had we suddenly been miraculously transported through ether to an unknown world. Even the grass upon the nearer bank was unearthly— lush and high it grew, and each blade bore upon its tip a brilliant flower— violet or yellow or carmine or blue—making as gorgeous a sward as human imagination might conceive. But the life! It teemed. The tall, fernlike trees were alive with monkeys, snakes, and lizards. Huge insects hummed and buzzed hither and thither. Mighty forms could be seen moving upon the ground in the thick forest, while the bosom of the river wriggled with living things, and above flapped the wings of gigantic creatures such as we are taught have been extinct throughout countless ages.

"Look!" cried Olson. "Would you look at the giraffe comin' up out o' the bottom of the say?" We looked in the direction he pointed and saw a long, glossy neck surmounted by a small head rising above the surface of the river. Presently the back of the creature was exposed, brown and glossy as the water dripped from it. It turned its eyes upon us, opened its lizardlike mouth, emitted a shrill hiss and came for us. The thing must have been sixteen or eighteen feet in length and closely resembled pictures I had seen of restored plesiosaurs of the lower Jurassic. It charged us as savagely as a mad bull, and one would have thought it intended to destroy and devour the mighty U-boat, as I verily believe it did intend.

We were moving slowly up the river as the creature bore down upon us with distended jaws. The long neck was far outstretched, and the four flippers with which it swam were working with powerful strokes, carrying it forward at a rapid pace. When it reached the craft's side, the jaws closed upon one of the stanchions of the deck rail and tore it from its socket as though it had been a toothpick stuck in putty. At this exhibition of titanic strength I think we all simultaneously stepped backward, and Bradley drew his revolver and fired. The bullet struck the thing in the neck, just above its body; but instead of disabling it, merely increased its rage. Its hissing rose to a shrill scream as it raised half its body out of water onto the sloping sides of the hull of the *U-33* and endeavored to scramble upon the deck to devour us. A dozen shots rang out as we who were armed drew our pistols and fired at the thing; but though struck several times, it showed no signs of succumbing and only floundered farther aboard the submarine.

I had noticed that the girl had come on deck and was standing not far behind me, and when I saw the danger to which we all were exposed, I turned and forced her toward the hatch. We had not spoken for some days, and we did not speak now; but she gave me a disdainful look, which was quite as eloquent as words, and broke loose from my grasp. I saw I could do nothing with her unless I exerted force, and so I turned with my back toward her that I might be in a position to shield her from the strange reptile should it really succeed in reaching the deck; and as I did so I saw the thing raise one flipper over the rail, dart its head forward and with the quickness of lightning seize upon one of the Germans. I ran forward, discharging my pistol into the creature's body in an effort to force it to relinquish its prey; but I might as profitably have shot at the sun.

Shrieking and screaming, the German was dragged from the deck, and the moment the reptile was clear of the boat, it dived beneath the surface of the water with its terrified prey. I think we were all more or less shaken by the frightfulness of the tragedy—until Olson remarked that the balance of power now rested where it belonged. Following the death of Benson we had been nine and nine—nine Germans and nine "Allies," as we called ourselves; now there were but eight Germans. We never counted the girl on either side, I suppose because she was a girl, though we knew well enough now that she was ours.

And so Olson's remark helped to clear the atmosphere, for the Allies at least, and then our attention was once more directed toward the river, for around us there had sprung up a perfect bedlam of screams and hisses and a seething caldron of hideous reptiles, devoid of fear and filled only with hunger and with rage. They clambered, squirmed and wriggled to the deck, forcing us steadily backward, though we emptied our pistols into them. There were all sorts and conditions of horrible things—huge, hideous, grotesque, monstrous—a veritable Mesozoic nightmare. I saw that the girl was gotten below as quickly as possible, and she took Nobs with her—poor Nobs had nearly barked his head off; and I think, too, that for the first time since his littlest puppyhood he had known fear; nor can I blame him. After the girl I sent Bradley and most of the Allies and then the Germans who were on deck—von Schoenvorts being still in irons below.

The creatures were approaching perilously close before I dropped through the hatchway and slammed down the cover. Then I went into the tower and ordered full speed ahead, hoping to distance the fearsome things;

but it was useless. Not only could any of them easily outdistance the *U-33*, but the further upstream we progressed the greater the number of our besiegers, until fearful of navigating a strange river at high speed, I gave orders to reduce and moved slowly and majestically through the plunging, hissing mass. I was mighty glad that our entrance into the interior of Caprona had been inside a submarine rather than in any other form of vessel. I could readily understand how it might have been that Caprona had been invaded in the past by venturesome navigators without word of it ever reaching the outside world, for I can assure you that only by submarine could man pass up that great sluggish river, alive.

We proceeded up the river for some forty miles before darkness overtook us. I was afraid to submerge and lie on the bottom overnight for fear that the mud might be deep enough to hold us, and as we could not hold with the anchor, I ran in close to shore, and in a brief interim of attack from the reptiles we made fast to a large tree. We also dipped up some of the river water and found it, though quite warm, a little sweeter than before. We had food enough, and with the water we were all quite refreshed; but we missed fresh meat. It had been weeks, now, since we had tasted it, and the sight of the reptiles gave me an idea—that a steak or two from one of them might not be bad eating. So I went on deck with a rifle, twenty of which were aboard the *U-33*. At sight of me a huge thing charged and climbed to the deck. I retreated to the top of the conning tower, and when it had raised its mighty bulk to the level of the little deck on which I stood, I let it have a bullet right between the eyes.

The thing stopped then and looked at me a moment as much as to say: "Why, this thing has a stinger! I must be careful." And then it reached out its long neck and opened its mighty jaws and grabbed for me; but I wasn't there. I had tumbled backward into the tower, and I mighty near killed myself doing it. When I glanced up, that little head on the end of its long neck was coming straight down on top of me, and once more I tumbled into greater safety, sprawling upon the floor of the centrale.

Olson was looking up, and seeing what was poking about in the tower, ran for an ax; nor did he hesitate a moment when he returned with one, but sprang up the ladder and commenced chopping away at that hideous face. The thing didn't have sufficient brainpan to entertain more than a single idea at once. Though chopped and hacked, and with a bullet hole between its eyes, it still persisted madly in its attempt to get inside the

tower and devour Olson, though its body was many times the diameter
of the hatch; nor did it cease its efforts until after Olson had succeeded in
decapitating it. Then two men went on deck through the main hatch, and
while one kept watch, the other cut a hind quarter off *Plesiosaurus olsoni*,
as Bradley dubbed the thing. Meantime Olson cut off the long neck, saying
that it would make fine soup. By the time we had cleared away the blood
and refuse in the tower, the cook had juicy steaks and a steaming broth
upon the electric stove, and the aroma arising from *P. olsoni* filled us all
with a hitherto unfelt admiration for him and all his kind.

CHAPTER FIVE

THE STEAKS WE HAD THAT NIGHT, and they were fine; and the following
morning we tasted the broth. It seemed odd to be eating a creature
that should, by all the laws of paleontology, have been extinct for
several million years. It gave one a feeling of newness that was almost
embarrassing, although it didn't seem to embarrass our appetites. Olson
ate until I thought he would burst.

The girl ate with us that night at the little officers' mess just back of
the torpedo compartment. The narrow table was unfolded; the four stools
were set out; and for the first time in days we sat down to eat, and for the
first time in weeks we had something to eat other than the monotony of
the short rations of an impoverished U-boat. Nobs sat between the girl
and me and was fed with morsels of the Plesiosaurus steak, at the risk of
forever contaminating his manners. He looked at me sheepishly all the
time, for he knew that no well-bred dog should eat at table; but the poor
fellow was so wasted from improper food that I couldn't enjoy my own
meal had he been denied an immediate share in it; and anyway Lys wanted
to feed him. So there you are.

Lys was coldly polite to me and sweetly gracious to Bradley and Olson.
She wasn't of the gushing type, I knew; so I didn't expect much from her
and was duly grateful for the few morsels of attention she threw upon the
floor to me. We had a pleasant meal, with only one unfortunate occurrence—when Olson suggested that possibly the creature we were eating
was the same one that ate the German. It was some time before we could
persuade the girl to continue her meal, but at last Bradley prevailed upon

her, pointing out that we had come upstream nearly forty miles since the Boche had been seized, and that during that time we had seen literally thousands of these denizens of the river, indicating that the chances were very remote that this was the same Plesiosaur. "And anyway," he concluded, "it was only a scheme of Mr. Olson's to get all the steaks for himself."

We discussed the future and ventured opinions as to what lay before us; but we could only theorize at best, for none of us knew. If the whole land was infested by these and similar horrid monsters, life would be impossible upon it, and we decided that we would only search long enough to find and take aboard fresh water and such meat and fruits as might be safely procurable and then retrace our way beneath the cliffs to the open sea.

And so at last we turned into our narrow bunks, hopeful, happy and at peace with ourselves, our livers and our God, to awaken the following morning refreshed and still optimistic. We had an easy time getting away—as we learned later, because the saurians do not commence to feed until late in the morning. From noon to midnight their curve of activity is at its height, while from dawn to about nine o'clock it is lowest. As a matter of fact, we didn't see one of them all the time we were getting under way, though I had the cannon raised to the deck and manned against an assault. I hoped, but I was none too sure, that shells might discourage them. The trees were full of monkeys of all sizes and shades, and once we thought we saw a manlike creature watching us from the depth of the forest.

Shortly after we resumed our course upstream, we saw the mouth of another and smaller river emptying into the main channel from the south—that is, upon our right; and almost immediately after we came upon a large island five or six miles in length; and at fifty miles there was a still larger river than the last coming in from the northwest, the course of the main stream having now changed to northeast by southwest. The water was quite free from reptiles, and the vegetation upon the banks of the river had altered to more open and parklike forest, with eucalyptus and acacia mingled with a scattering of tree ferns, as though two distinct periods of geologic time had overlapped and merged. The grass, too, was less flowering, though there were still gorgeous patches mottling the greensward; and lastly, the fauna was less multitudinous.

Six or seven miles farther, and the river widened considerably; before us opened an expanse of water to the farther horizon, and then we sailed out upon an inland sea so large that only the shoreline upon our side was visible to us. The waters all about us were alive with life. There were still a few reptiles; but there were fish by the thousands, by the millions.

The water of the inland sea was very warm, almost hot, and the atmosphere was hot and heavy above it. It seemed strange that beyond the buttressed walls of Caprona icebergs floated and the south wind was biting, for only a gentle breeze moved across the face of these living waters, and that was damp and warm. Gradually we commenced to divest ourselves of our clothing, retaining only sufficient for modesty; but the sun was not hot. It was more the heat of a steam room than of an oven.

We coasted up the shore of the lake in a northwesterly direction, sounding all the time. We found the lake deep and the bottom rocky and steeply shelving toward the center, and once when I moved straight out from shore to take other soundings we could find no bottom whatsoever. In open spaces along the shore we caught occasional glimpses of the distant cliffs, and here they appeared only a trifle less precipitous than those which bound Caprona on the seaward side. My theory is that in a far distant era Caprona was a mighty mountain—perhaps the world's mightiest mountain—and that in some titanic eruption volcanic action blew off the entire crest, blew thousands of feet of the mountain upward and outward and onto the surrounding continent, leaving a great crater; and then, possibly, the continent sank as ancient continents have been known to do, leaving only the summit of Caprona above the sea. The encircling walls, the central lake, the hot springs which feed the lake, all point to such a conclusion, and the fauna and the flora bear indisputable evidence that Caprona was once part of some great landmass.

As we cruised up along the coast, the landscape continued a more or less open forest, with here and there a small plain where we saw animals grazing. With my glass I could make out a species of large red deer, some antelope and what appeared to be a species of horse; and once I saw the shaggy form of what might have been a monstrous bison. Here was game aplenty! There seemed little danger of starving upon Caprona. The game, however, seemed wary; for the instant the animals discovered us, they threw up their heads and tails and went cavorting off, those farther inland following the example of the others until all were lost in the mazes of the distant forest. Only the great, shaggy ox stood his ground. With lowered head he watched us until we had passed, and then continued feeding.

About twenty miles up the coast from the mouth of the river we encountered low cliffs of sandstone, broken and tortured evidence of the great upheaval which had torn Caprona asunder in the past, intermingling upon a common level the rock formations of widely separated eras, fusing some and leaving others untouched.

We ran along beside them for a matter of ten miles, arriving off a broad cleft which led into what appeared to be another lake. As we were in search of pure water, we did not wish to overlook any portion of the coast, and so after sounding and finding that we had ample depth, I ran the *U-33* between headlands into as pretty a landlocked harbor as sailorman could care to see, with good water right up to within a few yards of the shore. As we cruised slowly along, two of the Germans again saw what they believed to be a man, or manlike creature, watching us from a fringe of trees a hundred yards inland, and shortly after we discovered the mouth of a small stream emptying into the bay. It was the first stream we had found since leaving the river, and I at once made preparations to test its water. To land, it would be necessary to run the *U-33* close in to the shore, at least as close as we could, for even these waters were infested, though not so thickly, by savage reptiles. I ordered sufficient water let into the diving tanks to lower us about a foot, and then I ran the bow slowly toward the shore, confident that should we run aground, we still had sufficient lifting force to free us when the water should be pumped out of the tanks; but the bow nosed its way gently into the reeds and touched the shore with the keel still clear.

My men were all armed now with both rifles and pistols, each having plenty of ammunition. I ordered one of the Germans ashore with a line, and sent two of my own men to guard him, for from what little we had seen of Caprona, or Caspak as we learned later to call the interior, we realized that any instant some new and terrible danger might confront us. The line was made fast to a small tree, and at the same time I had the stern anchor dropped.

As soon as the Boche and his guard were aboard again, I called all hands on deck, including von Schoenvorts, and there I explained to them that the time had come for us to enter into some sort of an agreement among ourselves that would relieve us of the annoyance and embarrassment of being divided into two antagonistic parts—prisoners and captors. I told them that it was obvious our very existence depended upon our unity of action, that we were to all intent and purpose entering a new world as far from the seat and causes of our own world war as if millions of miles of space and eons of time separated us from our past lives and habitations.

"There is no reason why we should carry our racial and political hatreds into Caprona," I insisted. "The Germans among us might kill all the English, or the English might kill the last German, without affecting in the slightest degree either the outcome of even the smallest skirmish upon the western front or the opinion of a single individual in any belligerent or neutral country. I therefore put the issue squarely to you all: shall we bury our animosities and work together with and for one another while we remain upon Caprona, or must we continue thus divided and but half armed, possibly until death has claimed the last of us? And let me tell you, if you have not already realized it, the chances are a thousand to one that not one of us ever will see the outside world again. We are safe now in the matter of food and water; we could provision the *U-33* for a long cruise; but we are practically out of fuel, and without fuel we cannot hope to reach the ocean, as only a submarine can pass through the barrier cliffs. What is your answer?" I turned toward von Schoenvorts.

He eyed me in that disagreeable way of his and demanded to know, in case they accepted my suggestion, what their status would be in event of our finding a way to escape with the *U-33*. I replied that I felt that if we had all worked loyally together we should leave Caprona upon a common footing, and to that end I suggested that should the remote possibility of our escape in the submarine develop into reality, we should then immediately make for the nearest neutral port and give ourselves into the hands of the authorities, when we should all probably be interned for the duration of the war. To my surprise he agreed that this was fair and told me that they would accept my conditions and that I could depend upon their loyalty to the common cause.

I thanked him and then addressed each one of his men individually, and each gave me his word that he would abide by all that I had outlined. It was further understood that we were to act as a military organization under military rules and discipline—I as commander, with Bradley as my first lieutenant and Olson as my second, in command of the Englishmen; while von Schoenvorts was to act as an additional second lieutenant and have charge of his own men. The four of us were to constitute a military court under which men might be tried and sentenced to punishment for infraction of military rules and discipline, even to the passing of the death sentence.

I then had arms and ammunition issued to the Germans, and leaving Bradley and five men to guard the *U-33*, the balance of us went ashore. The first thing we did was to taste the water of the little stream—which, to our delight, we found sweet, pure and cold. This stream was entirely free from dangerous reptiles, because, as I later discovered, they become immediately dormant when subjected to a much lower temperature than 70 degrees Fahrenheit. They dislike cold water and keep as far away from it as possible. There were countless brook trout here, and deep holes that invited us to bathe, and along the bank of the stream were trees bearing a close resemblance to ash and beech and oak, their characteristics evidently induced by the lower temperature of the air above the cold water and by the fact that their roots were watered by the water from the stream rather than from the warm springs which we afterward found in such abundance elsewhere.

Our first concern was to fill the water tanks of the *U-33* with fresh water, and that having been accomplished, we set out to hunt for game and explore inland for a short distance. Olson, von Schoenvorts, two Englishmen and two Germans accompanied me, leaving ten to guard the ship and the girl. I had intended leaving Nobs behind, but he got away and joined me and was so happy over it that I hadn't the heart to send him back. We followed the stream upward through a beautiful country for about five miles, and then came upon its source in a little boulder-strewn clearing. From among the rocks bubbled fully twenty ice-cold springs. North of the clearing rose sandstone cliffs to a height of some fifty to seventy-five feet, with tall trees growing at their base and almost concealing them from our view. To the west the country was flat and sparsely wooded, and here it was that we saw our first game—a large red deer. It was grazing away from us and had not seen us when one of my men called my attention to it. Motioning for silence and having the rest of the party lie down, I crept toward the quarry, accompanied only by Whitely. We got within a hundred yards of the deer when he suddenly raised his antlered head and pricked up his great ears. We both fired at once and had the satisfaction of seeing the buck drop; then we ran forward to finish him with our knives. The deer lay in a small open space close to a clump of acacias, and we had advanced to within several yards of our kill when we both halted suddenly and simultaneously. Whitely looked at me, and I looked at Whitely, and then we both looked back in the direction of the deer.

"Blime!" he said. "Wot is hit, sir?"

"It looks to me, Whitely, like an error," I said; "some assistant god who had been creating elephants must have been temporarily transferred to the lizard department."

"Hi wouldn't s'y that, sir," said Whitely; "it sounds blasphemous."

"It is no more blasphemous than that thing which is swiping our meat," I replied, for whatever the thing was, it had leaped upon our deer and was devouring it in great mouthfuls which it swallowed without mastication. The creature appeared to be a great lizard at least ten feet high, with a huge, powerful tail as long as its torso, mighty hind legs and short forelegs. When it had advanced from the wood, it hopped much after the fashion of a kangaroo, using its hind feet and tail to propel it, and when it stood erect, it sat upon its tail. Its head was long and thick, with a blunt muzzle, and the opening of the jaws ran back to a point behind the eyes, and the jaws were armed with long sharp teeth. The scaly body was covered with black and yellow spots about a foot in diameter and irregular in contour. These spots were outlined in red with edgings about an inch wide. The underside of the chest, body and tail were a greenish white.

"Wot s'y we pot the bloomin' bird, sir?" suggested Whitely.

I told him to wait until I gave the word; then we would fire simultaneously, he at the heart and I at the spine.

"Hat the 'eart, sir—yes, sir," he replied, and raised his piece to his shoulder.

Our shots rang out together. The thing raised its head and looked about until its eyes rested upon us; then it gave vent to a most appalling hiss that rose to the crescendo of a terrific shriek and came for us.

"Beat it, Whitely!" I cried as I turned to run.

We were about a quarter of a mile from the rest of our party, and in full sight of them as they lay in the tall grass, watching us. That they saw all that had happened was evidenced by the fact that they now rose and ran toward us, and at their head leaped Nobs. The creature in our rear was gaining on us rapidly when Nobs flew past me like a meteor and rushed straight for the frightful reptile. I tried to recall him, but he would pay no attention to me, and as I couldn't see him sacrificed, I, too, stopped and faced the monster. The creature appeared to be more impressed by Nobs than by us and our firearms, for it stopped as the Airedale dashed at it growling, and struck at him viciously with its powerful jaws.

Nobs, though, was lightning by comparison with the slow-thinking beast and dodged his opponent's thrust with ease. Then he raced to the rear of the tremendous thing and seized it by the tail. There Nobs made the error of his life. Within that mottled organ were the muscles of a Titan, the force of a dozen mighty catapults, and the owner of the tail was fully aware of the possibilities which it contained. With a single fillip of the tip it sent poor Nobs sailing through the air a hundred feet above the ground, straight back into the clump of acacias from which the beast had leaped upon our kill—and then the grotesque thing sank lifeless to the ground.

Olson and von Schoenvorts came up a minute later with their men; then we all cautiously approached the still form upon the ground. The creature was quite dead, and an examination resulted in disclosing the fact that Whitely's bullet had pierced its heart, and mine had severed the spinal cord.

"But why didn't it die instantly?" I exclaimed.

"Because," said von Schoenvorts in his disagreeable way, "the beast is so large, and its nervous organization of so low a caliber, that it took all this time for the intelligence of death to reach and be impressed upon the minute brain. The thing was dead when your bullets struck it; but it did not know it for several seconds—possibly a minute. If I am not mistaken, it is an Allosaurus of the Upper Jurassic, remains of which have been found in Central Wyoming, in the suburbs of New York."

An Irishman by the name of Brady grinned. I afterward learned that he had served three years on the traffic squad of the Chicago police force.

I had been calling Nobs in the meantime and was about to set out in search of him, fearing, to tell the truth, to do so lest I find him mangled and dead among the trees of the acacia grove, when he suddenly emerged from among the boles, his ears flattened, his tail between his legs and his body screwed into a suppliant S. He was unharmed except for minor bruises; but he was the most chastened dog I have ever seen.

We gathered up what was left of the red deer after skinning and cleaning it, and set out upon our return journey toward the U-boat. On the way

Olson, von Schoenvorts, and I discussed the needs of our immediate future, and we were unanimous in placing foremost the necessity of a permanent camp on shore. The interior of a U-boat is about as impossible and uncomfortable an abiding place as one can well imagine, and in this warm climate, and in warm water, it was almost unendurable. So we decided to construct a palisaded camp.

CHAPTER SIX

A S WE STROLLED SLOWLY BACK TOWARD THE BOAT, planning and discussing this, we were suddenly startled by a loud and unmistakable detonation.

"A shell from the *U-33!*" exclaimed von Schoenvorts.

"What can be after signifyin'?" queried Olson.

"They are in trouble," I answered for all, "and it's up to us to get back to them. Drop that carcass," I directed the men carrying the meat, "and follow me!" I set off at a rapid run in the direction of the harbor.

We ran for the better part of a mile without hearing anything more from the direction of the harbor, and then I reduced the speed to a walk, for the exercise was telling on us who had been cooped up for so long in the confined interior of the *U-33.* Puffing and panting, we plodded on until within about a mile of the harbor we came upon a sight that brought us all up standing. We had been passing through a little heavier timber than was usual to this part of the country, when we suddenly emerged into an open space in the center of which was such a band as might have caused the most courageous to pause. It consisted of upward of five hundred individuals representing several species closely allied to man. There were anthropoid apes and gorillas—these I had no difficulty in recognizing; but there were other forms which I had never before seen, and I was hard put to it to say whether they were ape or man. Some of them resembled the corpse we had found upon the narrow beach against Caprona's seawall, while others were of a still lower type, more nearly resembling the apes, and yet others were uncannily manlike, standing almost erect, being less hairy and possessing better shaped heads.

There was one among the lot, evidently the leader of them, who bore a close resemblance to the so-called Neanderthal man of La Chapelle-aux-Saints.

There was the same short, stocky trunk upon which rested an enormous head habitually bent forward into the same curvature as the back, the arms shorter than the legs, and the lower leg considerably shorter than that of modern man, the knees bent forward and never straightened. This creature and one or two others who appeared to be of a lower order than he, yet higher than that of the apes, carried heavy clubs; the others were armed only with giant muscles and fighting fangs—nature's weapons. All were males, and all were entirely naked; nor was there upon even the highest among them a sign of ornamentation.

At sight of us they turned with bared fangs and low growls to confront us. I did not wish to fire among them unless it became absolutely necessary, and so I started to lead my party around them; but the instant that the Neanderthal man guessed my intention, he evidently attributed it to cowardice upon our part, and with a wild cry he leaped toward us, waving his cudgel above his head. The others followed him, and in a minute we should have been overwhelmed. I gave the order to fire, and at the first volley six of them went down, including the Neanderthal man. The others hesitated a moment and then broke for the trees, some running nimbly among the branches, while others lost themselves to us between the boles. Both von Schoenvorts and I noticed that at least two of the higher, manlike types took to the trees quite as nimbly as the apes, while others that more nearly approached man in carriage and appearance sought safety upon the ground with the gorillas.

An examination disclosed that five of our erstwhile opponents were dead and the sixth, the Neanderthal man, was but slightly wounded, a bullet having glanced from his thick skull, stunning him. We decided to take him with us to camp, and by means of belts we managed to secure his hands behind his back and place a leash around his neck before he regained consciousness. We then retraced our steps for our meat, being convinced by our own experience that those aboard the *U-33* had been able to frighten off this party with a single shell—but when we came to where we had left the deer it had disappeared.

On the return journey Whitely and I preceded the rest of the party by about a hundred yards in the hope of getting another shot at something edible, for we were all greatly disgusted and disappointed by the loss of our venison. Whitely and I advanced very cautiously, and not having the whole party with us, we fared better than on the journey out, bagging two large antelope not a half mile from the harbor; so with our game and our prisoner we made a cheerful return to the boat, where we found that all were safe. On the shore a little north of where we lay there were the corpses of twenty of the wild creatures who had attacked Bradley and his party in our absence, and the rest of whom we had met and scattered a few minutes later.

We felt that we had taught these wild ape-men a lesson and that because of it we would be safer in the future—at least safer from them; but we decided not to abate our carefulness one whit, feeling that this new world was filled with terrors still unknown to us; nor were we wrong.

The following morning we commenced work upon our camp, Bradley, Olson, von Schoenvorts, Miss La Rue, and I having sat up half the night discussing the matter and drawing plans. We set the men at work felling trees, selecting for the purpose jarrah, a hard, weather-resisting timber which grew in profusion nearby. Half the men labored while the other half stood guard, alternating each hour with an hour off at noon. Olson directed this work. Bradley, von Schoenvorts and I, with Miss La Rue's help, staked out the various buildings and the outer wall. When the day was done, we had quite an array of logs nicely notched and ready for our building operations on the morrow, and we were all tired, for after the buildings had been staked out we all fell in and helped with the logging—all but von Schoenvorts. He, being a Prussian and a gentleman, couldn't stoop to such menial labor in the presence of his men, and I didn't see fit to ask it of him, as the work was purely voluntary upon our part. He spent the afternoon shaping a swagger stick from a branch of jarrah and talking with Miss La Rue, who had sufficiently unbent toward him to notice his existence.

We saw nothing of the wild men of the previous day, and only once were we menaced by any of the strange denizens of Caprona, when some frightful nightmare of the sky swooped down upon us, only to be driven off by a fusillade of bullets. The thing appeared to be some variety of pterodactyl, and what with its enormous size and ferocious aspect was most awe-inspiring. There was another incident, too, which to me at least was far more unpleasant than the sudden onslaught of the prehistoric reptile. Two of the men, both Germans, were stripping a felled tree of its branches. Von Schoenvorts had completed his swagger stick, and he and I were passing close to where the two worked.

One of the men threw to his rear a small branch that he had just chopped off, and as misfortune would have it, it struck von Schoenvorts across the face. It couldn't have hurt him, for it didn't leave a mark; but he flew into a terrific rage, shouting: "Attention!" in a loud voice. The sailor immediately straightened up, faced his officer, clicked his heels together and saluted. "Pig!" roared the Baron, and struck the fellow across the face, breaking his nose. I grabbed von Schoenvorts' arm and jerked him away before he could strike again, if such had been his intention, and then he raised his little stick to strike me; but before it descended the muzzle of my pistol was against his belly and he must have seen in my eyes that nothing would suit me better than an excuse to pull the trigger. Like all his kind and all other bullies, von Schoenvorts was a coward at heart, and so he dropped his hand to his side and started to turn away; but I pulled him back, and there before his men I told him that such a thing must never again occur—that no man was to be struck or otherwise punished other than in due process of the laws that we had made and the court that we had established. All the time the sailor stood rigidly at attention, nor could I tell from his expression whether he most resented the blow his officer had struck him or my interference in the gospel of the Kaiser breed. Nor did he move until I said to him: "Plesser, you may return to your quarters and dress your wound." Then he saluted and marched stiffly off toward the *U-33*.

Just before dusk we moved out into the bay a hundred yards from shore and dropped anchor, for I felt that we should be safer there than elsewhere. I also detailed men to stand watch during the night and appointed Olson officer of the watch for the entire night, telling him to bring his blankets on deck and get what rest he could. At dinner we tasted our first roast Caprona antelope, and we had a mess of greens that the cook had found growing along the stream. All during the meal von Schoenvorts was silent and surly.

After dinner we all went on deck and watched the unfamiliar scenes of a Capronian night—that is, all but von Schoenvorts. There was less to see than to hear. From the great inland lake behind us came the hissing and the screaming of countless saurians. Above we heard the flap of giant wings, while from the shore rose the multitudinous voices of a tropical jungle—of a warm, damp atmosphere such as must have enveloped the entire earth during the Paleozoic and Mesozoic eras. But here were intermingled the voices of later eras—the scream of the panther, the roar of the lion, the baying of wolves and a thunderous growling which we could attribute to nothing earthly but which one day we were to connect with the most fearsome of ancient creatures.

One by one the others went to their rooms, until the girl and I were left alone together, for I had permitted the watch to go below for a few minutes, knowing that I would be on deck. Miss La Rue was very quiet, though she replied graciously enough to whatever I had to say that required reply. I asked her if she did not feel well.

"Yes," she said, "but I am depressed by the awfulness of it all. I feel of so little consequence—so small and helpless in the face of all these myriad manifestations of life stripped to the bone of its savagery and brutality. I realize as never before how cheap and valueless a thing is life. Life seems a joke, a cruel, grim joke. You are a laughable incident or a terrifying one as you happen to be less powerful or more powerful than some other form of life which crosses your path; but as a rule you are of no moment whatsoever to anything but yourself. You are a comic little figure hopping from the cradle to the grave. Yes, that is our trouble—we take ourselves too seriously; but Caprona should be a sure cure for that." She paused and laughed.

"You have evolved a beautiful philosophy," I said. "It fills such a longing in the human breast. It is full, it is satisfying, it is ennobling. What wondrous strides toward perfection the human race might have made if the first man had evolved it and it had persisted until now as the creed of humanity."

"I don't like irony," she said; "it indicates a small soul."

"What other sort of soul, then, would you expect from 'a comic little figure hopping from the cradle to the grave'?" I inquired. "And what difference does it make, anyway, what you like and what you don't like? You are here for but an instant, and you mustn't take yourself too seriously."

She looked up at me with a smile. "I imagine that I am frightened and blue," she said, "and I know that I am very, very homesick and lonely." There was almost a sob in her voice as she concluded. It was the first time that she had spoken thus to me. Involuntarily I laid my hand upon hers where it rested on the rail.

"I know how difficult your position is," I said; "but don't feel that you are alone. There is—is one here who—who would do anything in the world for you," I ended lamely. She did not withdraw her hand, and she looked up into my face with tears on her cheeks and I read in her eyes the thanks her lips could not voice. Then she looked away across the weird moonlit landscape and sighed. Evidently her newfound philosophy had tumbled about her ears, for she was seemingly taking herself seriously. I wanted to take her in my arms and tell her how I loved her, and had taken her hand from the rail and started to draw her toward me when Olson came blundering up on deck with his bedding.

The following morning we started building operations in earnest, and things progressed finely. The Neanderthal man was something of a care, for we had to keep him in irons all the time, and he was mighty savage when approached; but after a time he became more docile, and then we tried to discover if he had a language. Lys spent a great deal of time talking to him and trying to draw him out; but for a long while she was unsuccessful. It took us three weeks to build all the houses, which we constructed close by a cold spring some two miles from the harbor.

We changed our plans a trifle when it came to building the palisade, for we found a rotted cliff nearby where we could get all the flat building stone we needed, and so we constructed a stone wall entirely around the buildings. It was in the form of a square, with bastions and towers at each corner which would permit an enfilading fire along any side of the fort, and was about one hundred and thirty-five feet square on the outside, with walls three feet thick at the bottom and about a foot and a half wide at the top, and fifteen feet high. It took a long time to build that wall, and we all turned in and helped except von Schoenvorts, who, by the way, had not spoken to me except in the line of official business since our encounter— a condition of armed neutrality which suited me to a T. We have just finished it, the last touches being put on today. I quit about a week ago and commenced working on this chronicle of our strange adventures, which will account for any minor errors in chronology which may have crept in; there was so much material that I may have made some mistakes, but I think they are but minor and few.

I see in reading over the last few pages that I neglected to state that Lys finally discovered that the Neanderthal man possessed a language. It is very meager, but still it is a spoken language. She has learned to speak it, and so have I, to some extent. It was he—his name he says is Am, or

Ahm—who told us that this country is called Caspak. When we asked him how far it extended, he waved both arms about his head in an all-including gesture which took in, apparently, the entire universe. He is more tractable now, and we are going to release him, for he has assured us that he will not permit his fellows to harm us. He calls us Galus and says that in a short time he will be a Galu. It is not quite clear to us what he means. He says that there are many Galus north of us, and that as soon as he becomes one he will go and live with them.

Ahm went out to hunt with us yesterday and was much impressed by the ease with which our rifles brought down antelope and deer. We have been living upon the fat of the land, Ahm having shown us the edible fruits, tubers and herbs, and twice a week we go out after fresh meat. A certain proportion of this we dry and store away, for we do not know what may come. Our drying process is really smoking. We have also dried a large quantity of two varieties of cereal which grow wild a few miles south of us. One of these is a giant Indian maize—a lofty perennial often fifty and sixty feet in height, with ears the size of a man's body and kernels as large as your fist. We have had to construct a second storehouse for the great quantity of this that we have gathered.

September 3, 1916: Three months ago today the torpedo from the *U-33* started me from the peaceful deck of the American liner upon the strange voyage which has ended here in Caspak. We have settled down to an acceptance of our fate, for all are convinced that none of us will ever see the outer world again. Ahm's repeated assertions that there are human beings like ourselves in Caspak have roused the men to a keen desire for exploration. I sent out one party last week under Bradley. Ahm, who is now free to go and come as he wishes, accompanied them. They marched about twenty-five miles due west, encountering many terrible beasts and reptiles and not a few manlike creatures whom Ahm sent away. Here is Bradley's report of the expedition:

Marched fifteen miles the first day, camping on the bank of a large stream which runs southward. Game was plentiful and we saw several varieties which we had not before encountered in Caspak. Just before making camp we were charged by an enormous woolly rhinoceros, which Plesser dropped with a perfect shot. We had rhinoceros steaks for supper. Ahm called the thing "Atis." It was almost a continuous battle from the time we left the fort until we arrived at camp. The mind of man can scarce conceive the plethora of carnivorous life in this lost world; and their prey, of course, is even more abundant.

The second day we marched about ten miles to the foot of the cliffs. Passed through dense forests close to the base of the cliffs. Saw manlike creatures and a low order of ape in one band, and some of the men swore that there was a white man among them. They were inclined to attack us at first; but a volley from our rifles caused them to change their minds. We scaled the cliffs as far as we could; but near the top they are absolutely perpendicular without any sufficient cleft or protuberance to give hand or foothold. All were disappointed, for we hungered for a view of the ocean and the outside world. We even had hope that we might see and attract the attention of a passing ship. Our exploration has determined one thing which will probably be of little value to us and never heard of beyond Caprona's walls—this crater was once entirely filled with water. Indisputable evidence of this is on the face of the cliffs.

Our return journey occupied two days and was as filled with adventure as usual. We are all becoming accustomed to adventure. It is beginning to pall on us. We suffered no casualties and there was no illness.

I had to smile as I read Bradley's report. In those four days he had doubtless passed through more adventures than an African big game hunter experiences in a lifetime, and yet he covered it all in a few lines. Yes, we are becoming accustomed to adventure. Not a day passes that one or more of us does not face death at least once. Ahm taught us a few things that have proved profitable and saved us much ammunition, which it is useless to expend except for food or in the last recourse of self-preservation. Now when we are attacked by large flying reptiles we run beneath spreading trees; when land carnivora threaten us, we climb into trees, and we have learned not to fire at any of the dinosaurs unless we can keep out of their reach for at least two minutes after hitting them in the brain or spine, or five minutes after puncturing their hearts—it takes them so long to die. To hit them elsewhere is worse than useless, for they do not seem to notice it, and we had discovered that such shots do not kill or even disable them.

September 7, 1916: Much has happened since last I wrote. Bradley is away again on another exploring expedition to the cliffs. He expects to be gone several weeks and to follow along their base in search of a point where they may be scaled. He took Sinclair, Brady, James, and Tippet with him. Ahm has disappeared. He has been gone about three days; but the most startling thing I have to record is that von Schoenvorts and Olson while out hunting the other day discovered oil about fifteen miles north of us beyond the sandstone cliffs. Olson says there is a geyser of oil there, and von Schoenvorts is making preparations to refine it. If he succeeds, we shall have the means for leaving Caspak and returning to our own world. I can scarce believe the truth of it. We are all elated to the seventh heaven of bliss. Pray God we shall not be disappointed.

I have tried on several occasions to broach the subject of my love to Lys; but she will not listen.

CHAPTER SEVEN

OCTOBER 8, 1916: This is the last entry I shall make upon my manuscript. When this is done, I shall be through. Though I may pray that it reaches the haunts of civilized man, my better judgment tells me that it will never be perused by other eyes than mine, and that even though it should, it would be too late to avail me. I am alone upon the summit of the great cliff overlooking the broad Pacific. A chill south wind bites at my marrow, while far below me I can see the tropic foliage of Caspak on the one hand and huge icebergs from the near Antarctic upon the other. Presently I shall stuff my folded manuscript into the thermos bottle I have carried with me for the purpose since I left the fort—Fort Dinosaur we named it —and hurl it far outward over the cliff top into the Pacific. What current washes the shore of Caprona I know not; whither my bottle will be borne I cannot even guess; but I have done all that mortal man may do to notify the world of my whereabouts and the dangers that threaten those of us who remain alive in Caspak—if there be any other than myself.

About the 8th of September I accompanied Olson and von Schoenvorts to the oil geyser. Lys came with us, and we took a number of things which von Schoenvorts wanted for the purpose of erecting a crude refinery. We went up the coast some ten or twelve miles in the *U-33*, tying up to shore near the mouth of a small stream which emptied great volumes of crude oil into the sea—I find it difficult to call this great lake by any other name. Then we disembarked and went inland about five miles, where we came upon a small lake entirely filled with oil, from the center of which a geyser of oil spouted.

On the edge of the lake we helped von Schoenvorts build his primitive refinery. We worked with him for two days until he got things fairly well started, and then we returned to Fort Dinosaur, as I feared that Bradley might return and be worried by our absence. The *U-33* merely landed those of us that were to return to the fort and then retraced its course toward the oil well. Olson, Whitely, Wilson, Miss La Rue, and myself disembarked, while von Schoenvorts and his German crew returned to refine the oil. The next day Plesser and two other Germans came down overland for ammunition. Plesser said they had been attacked by wild men and had exhausted a great deal of ammunition. He also asked permission to get some dried meat and maize, saying that they were so busy with the work of refining that they had no time to hunt. I let him have everything he asked for, and never once did a suspicion of their intentions enter my mind. They returned to the oil well the same day, while we continued with the multitudinous duties of camp life.

For three days nothing of moment occurred. Bradley did not return; nor did we have any word from von Schoenvorts. In the evening Lys and I went up into one of the bastion towers and listened to the grim and terrible night life of the frightful ages of the past. Once a sabertooth screamed almost beneath us, and the girl shrank close against me. As I felt her body against mine, all the pent love of these three long months shattered the bonds of timidity and conviction, and I swept her up into my arms and covered her face and lips with kisses. She did not struggle to free herself; but instead her dear arms crept up about my neck and drew my own face even closer to hers.

"You love me, Lys?" I cried.

I felt her head nod an affirmative against my breast. "Tell me, Lys," I begged, "tell me in words how much you love me."

Low and sweet and tender came the answer: "I love you beyond all conception."

My heart filled with rapture then, and it fills now as it has each of the countless times I have recalled those dear words, as it shall fill always until death has claimed me. I may never see her again; she may not know how

I love her—she may question, she may doubt; but always true and steady and warm with the fires of love my heart beats for the girl who said that night: "I love you beyond all conception."

For a long time we sat there upon the little bench constructed for the sentry that we had not as yet thought it necessary to post in more than one of the four towers. We learned to know one another better in those two brief hours than we had in all the months that had intervened since we had been thrown together. She told me that she had loved me from the first, and that she never had loved von Schoenvorts, their engagement having been arranged by her aunt for social reasons.

That was the happiest evening of my life; nor ever do I expect to experience its like; but at last, as is the way of happiness, it terminated. We descended to the compound, and I walked with Lys to the door of her quarters. There again she kissed me and bade me good night, and then she went in and closed the door.

I went to my own room, and there I sat by the light of one of the crude candles we had made from the tallow of the beasts we had killed, and lived over the events of the evening. At last I turned in and fell asleep, dreaming happy dreams and planning for the future, for even in savage Caspak I was bound to make my girl safe and happy. It was daylight when I awoke. Wilson, who was acting as cook, was up and astir at his duties in the cookhouse. The others slept; but I arose and followed by Nobs went down to the stream for a plunge. As was our custom, I went armed with both rifle and revolver; but I stripped and had my swim without further disturbance than the approach of a large hyena, a number of which occupied caves in the sandstone cliffs north of the camp. These brutes are enormous and exceedingly ferocious. I imagine they correspond with the cave hyena of prehistoric times. This fellow charged Nobs, whose Capronian experiences had taught him that discretion is the better part of valor—with the result that he dived head foremost into the stream beside me after giving vent to a series of ferocious growls which had no more effect upon *Hyaena spelaeus* than might a sweet smile upon an enraged tusker. Afterward I shot the beast, and Nobs had a feast while I dressed, for he had become quite a raw-meat eater during our numerous hunting expeditions, upon which we always gave him a portion of the kill.

Whitely and Olson were up and dressed when we returned, and we all sat down to a good breakfast. I could not but wonder at Lys' absence from the table, for she had always been one of the earliest risers in camp; so about nine o'clock, becoming apprehensive lest she might be indisposed, I went to the door of her room and knocked. I received no response, though I finally pounded with all my strength; then I turned the knob and entered, only to find that she was not there. Her bed had been occupied, and her clothing lay where she had placed it the previous night upon retiring; but Lys was gone. To say that I was distracted with terror would be to put it mildly. Though I knew she could not be in camp, I searched every square inch of the compound and all the buildings, yet without avail.

It was Whitely who discovered the first clue—a huge humanlike footprint in the soft earth beside the spring, and indications of a struggle in the mud. Then I found a tiny handkerchief close to the outer wall. Lys had been stolen! It was all too plain. Some hideous member of the ape-man tribe had entered the fort and carried her off. While I stood stunned and horrified at the frightful evidence before me, there came from the direction of the great lake an increasing sound that rose to the volume of a shriek. We all looked up as the noise approached apparently just above us, and a moment later there followed a terrific explosion which hurled us to the ground. When we clambered to our feet, we saw a large section of the west wall torn and shattered. It was Olson who first recovered from his daze sufficiently to guess the explanation of the phenomenon.

"A shell!" he cried. "And there ain't no shells in Caspak besides what's on the *U-33*. The dirty Germans are shellin' the fort. Come on!" And he grasped his rifle and started on a run toward the lake. It was over two miles, but we did not pause until the harbor was in view, and still we could not see the lake because of the sandstone cliffs which intervened. We ran as fast as we could around the lower end of the harbor, scrambled up the cliffs and at last stood upon their summit in full view of the lake. Far away down the coast, toward the river through which we had come to reach the lake, we saw upon the surface the outline of the *U-33*, black smoke vomiting from her funnel.

Von Schoenvorts had succeeded in refining the oil! The cur had broken his every pledge and was leaving us there to our fates. He had even shelled the fort as a parting compliment; nor could anything have been more truly Prussian than this leave-taking of the Baron Friedrich von Schoenvorts.

Olson, Whitely, Wilson, and I stood for a moment looking at one another. It seemed incredible that man could be so perfidious—that we had really seen with our own eyes the thing that we had seen; but when we returned to the fort, the shattered wall gave us ample evidence that there was no mistake.

Then we began to speculate as to whether it had been an ape-man or a Prussian that had abducted Lys. From what we knew of von Schoenvorts, we would not have been surprised at anything from him; but the footprints by the spring seemed indisputable evidence that one of Caprona's undeveloped men had borne off the girl I loved.

As soon as I had assured myself that such was the case, I made my preparations to follow and rescue her. Olson, Whitely, and Wilson each wished to accompany me; but I told them that they were needed here, since with Bradley's party still absent and the Germans gone it was necessary that we conserve our force as far as might be possible.

CHAPTER EIGHT

IT WAS A SAD LEAVE-TAKING as in silence I shook hands with each of the three remaining men. Even poor Nobs appeared dejected as we quit the compound and set out upon the well-marked spoor of the abductor. Not once did I turn my eyes backward toward Fort Dinosaur. I have not looked upon it since—nor in all likelihood shall I ever look upon it again. The trail led northwest until it reached the western end of the sandstone cliffs to the north of the fort; there it ran into a well-defined path which wound northward into a country we had not as yet explored. It was a beautiful, gently rolling country, broken by occasional outcroppings of sandstone and by patches of dense forest relieved by open, parklike stretches and broad meadows whereon grazed countless herbivorous animals—red deer, aurochs, and infinite variety of antelope and at least three distinct species of horse, the latter ranging in size from a creature about as large as Nobs to a magnificent animal fourteen to sixteen hands high. These creatures fed together in perfect amity; nor did they show any great indications of terror when Nobs and I approached. They moved out of our way and kept their eyes upon us until we had passed; then they resumed their feeding.

The path led straight across the clearing into another forest, lying upon the verge of which I saw a bit of white. It appeared to stand out in marked contrast and incongruity to all its surroundings, and when I stopped to examine it, I found that it was a small strip of muslin—part of the hem of a garment. At once I was all excitement, for I knew that it was a sign left by Lys that she had been carried this way; it was a tiny bit torn from the hem of the undergarment that she wore in lieu of the night-robes she had lost with the sinking of the liner. Crushing the bit of fabric to my lips, I pressed on even more rapidly than before, because I now knew that I was upon the right trail and that up to this point at least, Lys still had lived.

I made over twenty miles that day, for I was now hardened to fatigue and accustomed to long hikes, having spent considerable time hunting and exploring in the immediate vicinity of camp. A dozen times that day was my life threatened by fearsome creatures of the earth or sky, though I could not but note that the farther north I traveled, the fewer were the great dinosaurs, though they still persisted in lesser numbers. On the other hand the quantity of ruminants and the variety and frequency of carnivorous animals increased. Each square mile of Caspak harbored its terrors.

At intervals along the way I found bits of muslin, and often they reassured me when otherwise I should have been doubtful of the trail to take where two crossed or where there were forks, as occurred at several points. And so, as night was drawing on, I came to the southern end of a line of cliffs loftier than any I had before seen, and as I approached them, there was wafted to my nostrils the pungent aroma of woodsmoke. What could it mean? There could, to my mind, be but a single solution: man abided close by, a higher order of man than we had as yet seen, other than Ahm, the Neanderthal man. I wondered again as I had so many times that day if it had not been Ahm who stole Lys.

Cautiously I approached the flank of the cliffs, where they terminated in an abrupt escarpment as though some all-powerful hand had broken off a great section of rock and set it upon the surface of the earth. It was now quite dark, and as I crept around the edge of the cliff, I saw at a little distance a great fire around which were many figures—apparently human figures. Cautioning Nobs to silence, and he had learned many lessons in the value of obedience since we had entered Caspak, I slunk forward, taking advantage of whatever cover I could find, until from behind a bush I could distinctly see the creatures assembled by the fire. They were human and yet not human. I should say that they were a little higher in the scale of evolution than Ahm, possibly occupying a plane of evolution between that of the Neanderthal man and what is known as the Grimaldi race. Their features were distinctly negroid, though their skins were white. A considerable portion of both torso and limbs was covered with short hair, and their physical proportions were in many respects apelike, though not so much so as were Ahm's. They carried themselves in a more erect position, although their arms were considerably longer than those of the Neanderthal man. As I watched them, I saw that they possessed a language, that they had knowledge of fire and that they carried besides the wooden club of Ahm a thing which resembled a crude stone hatchet. Evidently they were very low in the scale of humanity, but they were a step upward from those I had previously seen in Caspak.

But what interested me most was the slender figure of a dainty girl, clad only in a thin bit of muslin which scarce covered her knees—a bit of muslin torn and ragged about the lower hem. It was Lys, and she was alive and so far as I could see, unharmed. A huge brute with thick lips and prognathous jaw stood at her shoulder. He was talking loudly and gesticulating wildly. I was close enough to hear his words, which were similar to the language of Ahm, though much fuller, for there were many words I could not understand. However I caught the gist of what he was saying —which in effect was that he had found and captured this Galu, that she was his and that he defied anyone to question his right of possession. It appeared to me, as I afterward learned was the fact, that I was witnessing the most primitive of marriage ceremonies. The assembled members of the tribe looked on and listened in a sort of dull and perfunctory apathy, for the speaker was by far the mightiest of the clan. There seemed no one to dispute his claims when he said, or rather shouted, in stentorian tones: "I am Tsa. This is my she. Who wishes her more than Tsa?"

"I do," I said in the language of Ahm, and I stepped out into the firelight before them. Lys gave a little cry of joy and started toward me, but Tsa grasped her arm and dragged her back.

"Who are you?" shrieked Tsa. "I kill! I kill! I kill!"

"The she is mine," I replied, "and I have come to claim her. I kill if you do not let her come to me." And I raised my pistol to a level with his heart. Of course the creature had no conception of the purpose of the strange little implement which I was poking toward him. With a sound that was half human and half the growl of a wild beast, he sprang toward me. I aimed at his heart and fired, and as he sprawled headlong to the ground, the others of his tribe, overcome by fright at the report of the pistol, scattered toward the cliffs—while Lys, with outstretched arms, ran toward me.

As I crushed her to me, there rose from the black night behind us and then to our right and to our left a series of frightful screams and shrieks, bellowings, roars and growls. It was the night-life of this jungle world coming into its own—the huge, carnivorous nocturnal beasts which make the nights of Caspak hideous. A shuddering sob ran through Lys' figure. "O God," she cried, "give me the strength to endure, for his sake!" I saw that she was upon the verge of a breakdown, after all that she must have passed through of fear and horror that day, and I tried to quiet and reassure her as best I might; but even to me the future looked most unpromising, for what chance of life had we against the frightful hunters of the night who even now were prowling closer to us?

Now I turned to see what had become of the tribe, and in the fitful glare of the fire I perceived that the face of the cliff was pitted with large holes into which the man-things were clambering. "Come," I said to Lys, "we must follow them. We cannot last a half hour out here. We must find a cave." Already we could see the blazing green eyes of the hungry carnivora. I seized a brand from the fire and hurled it out into the night, and there came back an answering chorus of savage and rageful protest; but the eyes vanished for a short time. Selecting a burning branch for each of us, we advanced toward the cliffs, where we were met by angry threats.

"They will kill us," said Lys. "We may as well keep on in search of another refuge."

"They will not kill us so surely as will those others out there," I replied. "I am going to seek shelter in one of these caves; nor will the man-things prevent." And I kept on in the direction of the cliff's base. A huge creature stood upon a ledge and brandished his stone hatchet. "Come and I will kill you and take the she," he boasted.

"You saw how Tsa fared when he would have kept my she," I replied in his own tongue. "Thus will you fare and all your fellows if you do not permit us to come in peace among you out of the dangers of the night."

"Go north," he screamed. "Go north among the Galus, and we will not harm you. Some day will we be Galus; but now we are not. You do not belong among us. Go away or we will kill you. The she may remain if she is afraid, and we will keep her; but the he must depart."

"The he won't depart," I replied, and approached still nearer. Rough and narrow ledges formed by nature gave access to the upper caves. A man might scale them if unhampered and unhindered, but to clamber upward in the face of a belligerent tribe of half-men and with a girl to assist was beyond my capability.

"I do not fear you," screamed the creature. "You were close to Tsa; but I am far above you. You cannot harm me as you harmed Tsa. Go away!"

I placed a foot upon the lowest ledge and clambered upward, reaching down and pulling Lys to my side. Already I felt safer. Soon we would be out of danger of the beasts again closing in upon us. The man above us raised his stone hatchet above his head and leaped lightly down to meet us. His position above me gave him a great advantage, or at least so he probably thought, for he came with every show of confidence. I hated to do it, but there seemed no other way, and so I shot him down as I had shot down Tsa.

"You see," I cried to his fellows, "that I can kill you wherever you may be. A long way off I can kill you as well as I can kill you nearby. Let us come among you in peace. I will not harm you if you do not harm us. We will take a cave high up. Speak!"

"Come, then," said one. "If you will not harm us, you may come. Take Tsa's hole, which lies above you."

The creature showed us the mouth of a black cave, but he kept at a distance while he did it, and Lys followed me as I crawled in to explore. I had matches with me, and in the light of one I found a small cavern with a flat roof and floor which followed the cleavage of the strata. Pieces of the roof had fallen at some long-distant date, as was evidenced by the depth of the filth and rubble in which they were embedded. Even a superficial examination revealed the fact that nothing had ever been attempted that might have improved the livability of the cavern; nor, should I judge, had it ever been cleaned out. With considerable difficulty I loosened some of the larger pieces of broken rock which littered the floor and placed them as a barrier before the doorway. It was too dark to do more than this. I then gave Lys a piece of dried meat, and sitting inside the entrance, we dined as must have some of our ancient forbears at the dawning of the age of man, while from below the open diapason of the savage night rose weird and horrifying to our ears. In the light of the great fire still burning we could see huge, skulking forms, and in the blacker background countless flaming eyes.

Lys shuddered, and I put my arm around her and drew her to me; and thus we sat throughout the hot night. She told me of her abduction and of the fright she had undergone, and together we thanked God that she had come through unharmed, because the great brute had dared not pause along the danger-infested way. She said that they had but just reached the cliffs when I arrived, for on several occasions her captor had been forced to take to the trees with her to escape the clutches of some hungry cave lion or saber-toothed tiger, and that twice they had been obliged to remain for considerable periods before the beasts had retired.

Nobs, by dint of much scrambling and one or two narrow escapes from death, had managed to follow us up the cliff and was now curled between me and the doorway, having devoured a piece of the dried meat, which he seemed to relish immensely. He was the first to fall asleep; but I imagine we must have followed suit soon, for we were both tired. I had laid aside my ammunition belt and rifle, though both were close beside me; but my pistol I kept in my lap beneath my hand. However, we were not disturbed during the night, and when I awoke, the sun was shining on the treetops in the distance. Lys' head had drooped to my breast, and my arm was still about her.

Shortly afterward Lys awoke, and for a moment she could not seem to comprehend her situation. She looked at me and then turned and glanced at my arm about her, and then she seemed quite suddenly to realize the scantiness of her apparel and drew away, covering her face with her palms and blushing furiously. I drew her back toward me and kissed her, and then she threw her arms about my neck and wept softly in mute surrender to the inevitable.

It was an hour later before the tribe began to stir about. We watched them from our "apartment," as Lys called it. Neither men nor women wore any sort of clothing or ornaments, and they all seemed to be about of an age; nor were there any babies or children among them. This was, to us, the strangest and most inexplicable of facts, but it recalled to us that though we had seen many of the lesser developed wild people of Caspak, we had never yet seen a child or an old man or woman.

After a while they became less suspicious of us and then quite friendly in their brutish way. They picked at the fabric of our clothing, which seemed to interest them, and examined my rifle and pistol and the ammunition in the belt around my waist. I showed them the thermos bottle, and when I poured a little water from it, they were delighted, thinking that it was a spring which I carried about with me—a never-failing source of water supply.

One thing we both noticed among their other characteristics: they never laughed nor smiled; and then we remembered that Ahm had never done so, either. I asked them if they knew Ahm; but they said they did not.

One of them said: "Back there we may have known him." And he jerked his head to the south.

"You came from back there?" I asked. He looked at me in surprise.

"We all come from there," he said. "After a while we go there." And this time he jerked his head toward the north. "Be Galus," he concluded.

Many times now had we heard this reference to becoming Galus. Ahm had spoken of it many times. Lys and I decided that it was a sort of original religious conviction, as much a part of them as their instinct for self-preservation—a primal acceptance of a hereafter and a holier state. It was a brilliant theory, but it was all wrong. I know it now, and how far we were from guessing the wonderful, the miraculous, the gigantic truth which even yet I may only guess at—the thing that sets Caspak apart from all the rest of the world far more definitely than her isolated geographic position or her impregnable barrier of giant cliffs. If I could live to return to civilization, I should have meat for the clergy and the layman to chew upon for years—and for the evolutionists, too.

After breakfast the men set out to hunt, while the women went to a large pool of warm water covered with a green scum and filled with billions of tadpoles. They waded in to where the water was about a foot deep and lay down in the mud. They remained there from one to two hours and then returned to the cliff. While we were with them, we saw this same thing repeated every morning; but though we asked them why they did it we could get no reply which was intelligible to us. All they vouchsafed in way of explanation was the single word *Ata*. They tried to get Lys to go in with them and could not understand why she refused. After the first day I went hunting with the men, leaving my pistol and Nobs with Lys, but she never had to use them, for no reptile or beast ever approached the pool while the women were there—nor, so far as we know, at other times.

There was no spoor of wild beast in the soft mud along the banks, and the water certainly didn't look fit to drink.

This tribe lived largely upon the smaller animals which they bowled over with their stone hatchets after making a wide circle about their quarry and driving it so that it had to pass close to one of their number. The little horses and the smaller antelope they secured in sufficient numbers to support life, and they also ate numerous varieties of fruits and vegetables. They never brought in more than sufficient food for their immediate needs; but why bother? The food problem of Caspak is not one to cause worry to her inhabitants.

The fourth day Lys told me that she thought she felt equal to attempting the return journey on the morrow, and so I set out for the hunt in high spirits, for I was anxious to return to the fort and learn if Bradley and his party had returned and what had been the result of his expedition. I also wanted to relieve their minds as to Lys and myself, as I knew that they must already have given us up for dead. It was a cloudy day, though warm, as it always is in Caspak. It seemed odd to realize that just a few miles away winter lay upon the storm-tossed ocean, and that snow might be falling all about Caprona; but no snow could ever penetrate the damp, hot atmosphere of the great crater.

We had to go quite a bit farther than usual before we could surround a little bunch of antelope, and as I was helping drive them, I saw a fine red deer a couple of hundred yards behind me. He must have been asleep in the long grass, for I saw him rise and look about him in a bewildered way, and then I raised my gun and let him have it. He dropped, and I ran forward to finish him with the long thin knife, which one of the men had given me; but just as I reached him, he staggered to his feet and ran on for another two hundred yards—when I dropped him again. Once more was this repeated before I was able to reach him and cut his throat; then I looked around for my companions, as I wanted them to come and carry the meat home; but I could see nothing of them. I called a few times and waited, but there was no response and no one came. At last I became disgusted, and cutting off all the meat that I could conveniently carry, I set off in the direction of the cliffs. I must have gone about a mile before the truth dawned upon me—I was lost, hopelessly lost.

The entire sky was still completely blotted out by dense clouds; nor was there any landmark visible by which I might have taken my bearings.

I went on in the direction I thought was south but which I now imagine must have been about due north, without detecting a single familiar object. In a dense wood I suddenly stumbled upon a thing which at first filled me with hope and later with the most utter despair and dejection. It was a little mound of new-turned earth sprinkled with flowers long since withered, and at one end was a flat slab of sandstone stuck in the ground. It was a grave, and it meant for me that I had at last stumbled into a country inhabited by human beings. I would find them; they would direct me to the cliffs; perhaps they would accompany me and take us back with them to their abodes—to the abodes of men and women like ourselves. My hopes and my imagination ran riot in the few yards I had to cover to reach that lonely grave and stoop that I might read the rude characters scratched upon the simple headstone. This is what I read:

HERE LIES JOHN TIPPET
ENGLISHMAN
KILLED BY TYRANNOSAURUS
10 SEP., A. D. 1916
R. I. P.

Tippet! It seemed incredible. Tippet lying here in this gloomy wood! Tippet dead! He had been a good man, but the personal loss was not what affected me. It was the fact that this silent grave gave evidence that Bradley had come this far upon his expedition and that he too probably was lost, for it was not our intention that he should be long gone. If I had stumbled upon the grave of one of the party, was it not within reason to believe that the bones of the others lay scattered somewhere near?

CHAPTER NINE

A S I STOOD LOOKING DOWN upon that sad and lonely mound, wrapped in the most dismal of reflections and premonitions, I was suddenly seized from behind and thrown to earth. As I fell, a warm body fell on top of me, and hands grasped my arms and legs. When I could look up, I saw a number of giant figures pinioning me down, while others stood about surveying me. Here again was a new type of man—a higher type than the primitive tribe I had just quitted. They were a taller people, too, with better-shaped skulls and more intelligent faces. There were less of the ape characteristics about their features, and less of the negroid, too. They carried weapons, stone-shod spears, stone knives, and hatchets—and they wore ornaments and breechcloths—the former of feathers worn in their hair and the latter made of a single snakeskin cured with the head on, the head depending to their knees.

Of course I did not take in all these details upon the instant of my capture, for I was busy with other matters. Three of the warriors were sitting upon me, trying to hold me down by main strength and awkwardness, and they were having their hands full in the doing, I can tell you. I don't like to appear conceited, but I may as well admit that I am proud of my strength and the science that I have acquired and developed in the directing of it—that and my horsemanship I always have been proud of. And now, that day, all the long hours that I had put into careful study, practice and training brought me in two or three minutes a full return upon my investment. Californians, as a rule, are familiar with jujitsu, and I especially had made a study of it for several years, both at school and in the gym of the Los Angeles Athletic Club, while recently I had had, in my employ, a Japanese man who was a wonder at the art.

It took me just about thirty seconds to break the elbow of one of my assailants, trip another and send him stumbling backward among his fellows, and throw the third completely over my head in such a way that when he fell his neck was broken. In the instant that the others of the party stood in mute and inactive surprise, I unslung my rifle—which, carelessly, I had been carrying across my back; and when they charged, as I felt they would, I put a bullet in the forehead of one of them. This stopped them all temporarily—not the death of their fellow, but the report of the rifle, the first they had ever heard. Before they were ready to attack me again, one of them spoke in a commanding tone to his fellows, and in a language similar but still more comprehensive than that of the tribe to the south, as theirs was more complete than Ahm's. He commanded them to stand back and then he advanced and addressed me.

He asked me who I was, from whence I came and what my intentions were. I replied that I was a stranger in Caspak, that I was lost and that my only desire was to find my way back to my companions. He asked where they were and I told him toward the south somewhere, using the Caspakian phrase which, literally translated, means "toward the beginning." His surprise showed upon his face before he voiced it in words. "There are no Galus there," he said. "You have lied. The Galus have turned you out."

"I tell you," I said angrily, "that I am from another country, far from Caspak, far beyond the high cliffs. I do not know who the Galus may be; I have never seen them. This is the farthest north I have been. Look at me—look at my clothing and my weapons. Have you ever seen a Galu or any other creature in Caspak who possessed such things?"

He had to admit that he had not, and also that he was much interested in me, my rifle and the way I had handled his three warriors. Finally he became half convinced that I was telling him the truth and offered to aid me if I would show him how I had thrown the man over my head and also make him a present of the "bang-spear," as he called it. I refused to give him my rifle, but promised to show him the trick he wished to learn if he would guide me in the right direction. He told me that he would do so tomorrow, that it was too late today and that I might come to their village and spend the night with them. I was loath to lose so much time; but the fellow was obdurate, and so I accompanied them. The two dead men they left where they had fallen, nor gave them a second glance—thus cheap is life upon Caspak.

These people also were cave dwellers, but their caves showed the result of a higher intelligence that brought them a step nearer to civilized man than the tribe next "toward the beginning." The interiors of their caverns were cleared of rubbish, though still far from clean, and they had pallets of dried grasses covered with the skins of leopard, lynx, and bear, while before the entrances were barriers of stone and small, rudely circular stone ovens. The walls of the cavern to which I was conducted were covered with drawings scratched upon the sandstone. There were the outlines of the giant red deer, of mammoths, of tigers and other beasts. Here, as in the last tribe, there were no children or any old people. The men of this tribe had two names, or rather names of two syllables, and their language contained words of two syllables; whereas in the tribe of Tsa the words were all of a single syllable, with the exception of a very few like *Atis* and *Galus*. The chief's name was To-jo, and his household consisted of seven females and himself. These women were much more comely, or rather less hideous than those of Tsa's people; one of them, even, was almost pretty, being less hairy and having a rather nice skin, with high coloring.

They were all much interested in me and examined my clothing and equipment carefully, handling and feeling and smelling of each article. I learned from them that their people were known as Band-lu, or spear-men; Tsa's race was called Sto-lu—hatchet-men. Below these in the scale of evolution came the Bo-lu, or club-men, and then the Alus, who had no weapons and no language. In that word I recognized what to me seemed the most remarkable discovery I had made upon Caprona, for unless it were mere coincidence, I had come upon a word that had been handed down from the beginning of spoken language upon earth, been handed down for millions of years, perhaps, with little change. It was the sole remaining thread of the ancient woof of a dawning culture which had been woven when Caprona was a fiery mount upon a great landmass teeming with life. It linked the unfathomable then to the eternal now. And yet it may have been pure coincidence; my better judgment tells me that it is coincidence that in Caspak the term for speechless man is *Alus*, and in the outer world of our own day it is *Alalus*.

The comely woman of whom I spoke was called So-ta, and she took such a lively interest in me that To-jo finally objected to her attentions, emphasizing his displeasure by knocking her down and kicking her into a corner of the cavern. I leaped between them while he was still kicking her, and obtaining a quick hold upon him, dragged him screaming with pain from the cave. There I made him promise not to hurt the she again, upon pain of worse punishment. So-ta gave me a grateful look; but To-jo and the balance of his women were sullen and ominous.

Later in the evening So-ta confided to me that she was soon to leave the tribe.

"So-ta soon be Kro-lu," she confided in a low whisper. I asked her what a Kro-lu might be, and she tried to explain, but I do not yet know if I understood her. From her gestures I deduced that the Kro-lus were a people who were armed with bows and arrows, had vessels in which to cook their food and huts of some sort in which they lived, and were accompanied by animals. It was all very fragmentary and vague, but the idea seemed to be that the Kro-lus were a more advanced people than the Band-lus. I pondered a long time upon all that I had heard, before sleep came to me. I tried to find some connection between these various races that would explain the universal hope which each of them harbored that some day they would become Galus. So-ta had given me a suggestion; but the resulting idea was so weird that I could scarce even entertain it; yet it coincided with Ahm's expressed hope, with the various steps in evolution I had noted in the several tribes I had encountered and with the range of type represented in each tribe. For example, among the Band-lu were such types as So-ta, who seemed to me to be the highest in the scale of evolution, and To-jo, who was just a shade nearer the ape, while there were others who had flatter noses, more prognathous faces and hairier bodies. The question puzzled me. Possibly in the outer world the answer to it is locked in the bosom of the Sphinx. Who knows? I do not.

Thinking the thoughts of a lunatic or a dope fiend, I fell asleep; and when I awoke, my hands and feet were securely tied and my weapons had been taken from me. How they did it without awakening me I cannot tell you. It was humiliating, but it was true. To-jo stood above me. The early light of morning was dimly filtering into the cave.

"Tell me," he demanded, "how to throw a man over my head and break his neck, for I am going to kill you, and I wish to know this thing before you die."

Of all the ingenuous declarations I have ever heard, this one copped the proverbial bun. It struck me as so funny that, even in the face of death, I laughed. Death, I may remark here, had, however, lost much of his terror for me. I had become a disciple of Lys' fleeting philosophy of the valuelessness of human life. I realized that she was quite right—that we were but comic figures hopping from the cradle to the grave, of interest to practically no other created thing than ourselves and our few intimates.

Behind To-jo stood So-ta. She raised one hand with the palm toward me—the Caspakian equivalent of a negative shake of the head.

"Let me think about it," I parried, and To-jo said that he would wait until night. He would give me a day to think it over; then he left, and the women left—the men for the hunt, and the women, as I later learned from So-ta, for the warm pool where they immersed their bodies as did the shes of the Sto-lu. "Ata," explained So-ta, when I questioned her as to the purpose of this matutinal rite; but that was later.

I must have lain there bound and uncomfortable for two or three hours when at last So-ta entered the cave. She carried a sharp knife—mine, in fact, and with it she cut my bonds.

"Come!" she said. "So-ta will go with you back to the Galus. It is time that So-ta left the Band-lu. Together we will go to the Kro-lu, and after that the Galus. To-jo will kill you tonight. He will kill So-ta if he knows that So-ta aided you. We will go together."

"I will go with you to the Kro-lu," I replied, "but then I must return to my own people 'toward the beginning.'"

"You cannot go back," she said. "It is forbidden. They would kill you. Thus far have you come—there is no returning."

"But I must return," I insisted. "My people are there. I must return and lead them in this direction."

She insisted, and I insisted; but at last we compromised. I was to escort her as far as the country of the Kro-lu and then I was to go back after my own people and lead them north into a land where the dangers were fewer and the people less murderous. She brought me all my belongings that had been filched from me—rifle, ammunition, knife, and thermos bottle, and then hand in hand we descended the cliff and set off toward the north.

For three days we continued upon our way, until we arrived outside a village of thatched huts just at dusk. So-ta said that she would enter alone; I must not be seen if I did not intend to remain, as it was forbidden that one should return and live after having advanced this far. So she left me. She was a dear girl and a stanch and true comrade—more like a man than a woman. In her simple barbaric way she was both refined and chaste. She had been the wife of To-jo. Among the Kro-lu she would find another mate after the manner of the strange Caspakian world; but she told me very frankly that whenever I returned, she would leave her mate and come to me, as she preferred me above all others. I was becoming a ladies' man after a lifetime of bashfulness!

At the outskirts of the village I left her without even seeing the sort of people who inhabited it, and set off through the growing darkness toward the south. On the third day I made a detour westward to avoid the country of the Band-lu, as I did not care to be detained by a meeting with To-jo. On the sixth day I came to the cliffs of the Sto-lu, and my heart beat fast as I approached them, for here was Lys. Soon I would hold her tight in my arms again; soon her warm lips would merge with mine. I felt sure that she was still safe among the hatchet people, and I was already picturing the joy and the love-light in her eyes when she should see me once more as I emerged from the last clump of trees and almost ran toward the cliffs.

It was late in the morning. The women must have returned from the pool; yet as I drew near, I saw no sign of life whatever. "They have remained longer," I thought; but when I was quite close to the base of the cliffs, I saw that which dashed my hopes and my happiness to earth. Strewn along the ground were a score of mute and horrible suggestions of what had taken place during my absence—bones picked clean of flesh, the bones of manlike creatures, the bones of many of the tribe of Sto-lu; nor in any cave was there sign of life.

Closely I examined the ghastly remains fearful each instant that I should find the dainty skull that would shatter my happiness for life; but though I searched diligently, picking up every one of the twenty-odd skulls, I found none that was not the skull of a creature but slightly removed from the ape. Hope, then, still lived. For another three days I searched north and south, east and west for the hatchet-men of Caspak; but never a trace of them did I find. It was raining most of the time now, and the weather was as near cold as it ever seems to get on Caprona.

At last I gave up the search and set off toward Fort Dinosaur. For a week—a week filled with the terrors and dangers of a primeval world—I pushed on in the direction I thought was south. The sun never shone; the rain scarcely ever ceased falling. The beasts I met with were fewer in number but infinitely more terrible in temper; yet I lived on until there came to me the realization that I was hopelessly lost, that a year of sunshine would not again give me my bearings; and while I was cast down by this terrifying knowledge, the knowledge that I never again could find my Lys, I stumbled upon another grave—the grave of William James, with its little crude headstone and its scrawled characters recording that he had died upon the 13th of September—killed by a saber-toothed tiger.

I think that I almost gave up then. Never in my life have I felt more hopeless or helpless or alone. I was lost. I could not find my friends. I did not even know that they still lived; in fact, I could not bring myself to believe that they did. I was sure that Lys was dead. I wanted myself to die, and yet I clung to life—useless and hopeless and harrowing a thing as it had become. I clung to life because some ancient, reptilian forbear had clung to life and transmitted to me through the ages the most powerful motive that guided his minute brain—the motive of self-preservation.

At last I came to the great barrier cliffs; and after three days of mad effort—of maniacal effort—I scaled them. I built crude ladders; I wedged sticks in narrow fissures; I chopped toeholds and fingerholds with my long knife; but at last I scaled them. Near the summit I came upon a huge cavern. It is the abode of some mighty winged creature of the Triassic—or rather it was. Now it is mine. I slew the thing and took its abode. I reached the summit and looked out upon the broad gray terrible Pacific of the far-southern winter. It was cold up there. It is cold here today; yet here I sit watching, watching, watching for the thing I know will never come— for a sail.

CHAPTER TEN

ONCE A DAY I DESCEND to the base of the cliff and hunt, and fill my stomach with water from a clear cold spring. I have three gourds which I fill with water and take back to my cave against the long nights. I have fashioned a spear and a bow and arrow, that I may conserve my ammunition, which is running low. My clothes are worn to shreds. Tomorrow I shall discard them for leopard skins which I have tanned and sewn into a garment strong and warm. It is cold up here. I have a fire burning, and I sit bent over it while I write; but I am safe here. No other living creature ventures to the chill summit of the barrier cliffs. I am safe, and I am alone with my sorrows and my remembered joys—but without hope. It is said that hope springs eternal in the human breast; but there is none in mine.

I am about done. Presently I shall fold these pages and push them into my thermos bottle. I shall cork it and screw the cap down tight, and then I shall hurl it as far out into the sea as my strength will permit. The wind is offshore; the tide is running out; perhaps it will be carried into one of those numerous ocean currents which sweep perpetually from pole to pole and from continent to continent, to be deposited at last upon some inhabited shore. If fate is kind and this does happen, then, *for God's sake, come and get me!*

It was a week ago that I wrote the preceding paragraph, which I thought would end the written record of my life upon Caprona. I had paused to put a new point on my quill and stir the crude ink (which I made by crushing a black variety of berry and mixing it with water) before attaching my signature, when faintly from the valley far below came an unmistakable sound which brought me to my feet, trembling with excitement, to peer eagerly downward from my dizzy ledge. How full of meaning that sound was to me you may guess when I tell you that it was the report of a firearm! For a moment my gaze traversed the landscape beneath until it was caught and held by four figures near the base of the cliff—a human figure held at bay by three hyaenodons, those ferocious and bloodthirsty wild dogs of the Eocene. A fourth beast lay dead or dying nearby.

I couldn't be sure, looking down from above as I was; but yet I trembled like a leaf in the intuitive belief that it was Lys, and my judgment served to confirm my wild desire, for whoever it was carried only a pistol, and thus had Lys been armed. The first wave of sudden joy which surged through me was short-lived in the face of the swift-following conviction that the one who fought below was already doomed. Luck and only luck it must have been which had permitted that first shot to lay low one of the savage creatures, for even such a heavy weapon as my pistol is entirely inadequate against even the lesser carnivora of Caspak. In a moment the three would charge! a futile shot would but tend more greatly to enrage the one it chanced to hit; and then the three would drag down the little human figure and tear it to pieces.

And maybe it was Lys! My heart stood still at the thought, but mind and muscle responded to the quick decision I was forced to make. There was but a single hope—a single chance—and I took it. I raised my rifle to my shoulder and took careful aim. It was a long shot, a dangerous shot, for unless one is accustomed to it, shooting from a considerable altitude is most deceptive work. There is, though, something about marksmanship which is quite beyond all scientific laws.

Upon no other theory can I explain my marksmanship of that moment. Three times my rifle spoke—three quick, short syllables of death. I did not take conscious aim; and yet at each report a beast crumpled in its tracks!

From my ledge to the base of the cliff is a matter of several thousand feet of dangerous climbing; yet I venture to say that the first ape from whose loins my line has descended never could have equaled the speed with which I literally dropped down the face of that rugged escarpment. The last two hundred feet is over a steep incline of loose rubble to the valley bottom, and I had just reached the top of this when there arose to my ears an agonized cry—"Bowen! Bowen! Quick, my love, quick!"

I had been too much occupied with the dangers of the descent to glance down toward the valley; but that cry which told me that it was indeed Lys, and that she was again in danger, brought my eyes quickly upon her in time to see a hairy, burly brute seize her and start off at a run toward the nearby wood. From rock to rock, chamoislike, I leaped downward toward the valley, in pursuit of Lys and her hideous abductor.

He was heavier than I by many pounds, and so weighted by the burden he carried that I easily overtook him; and at last he turned, snarling, to face me. It was Kho of the tribe of Tsa, the hatchet- men. He recognized me, and with a low growl he threw Lys aside and came for me. "The she is mine," he cried. "I kill! I kill!"

I had had to discard my rifle before I commenced the rapid descent of the cliff, so that now I was armed only with a hunting knife, and this I whipped from its scabbard as Kho leaped toward me. He was a mighty beast, mightily muscled, and the urge that has made males fight since the dawn of life on earth filled him with bloodlust and the thirst to slay; but not one whit less did it fill me with the same primal passions. Two abysmal beasts sprang at each other's throats that day beneath the shadow of earth's oldest cliffs—the man of now and the man-thing of the earliest, forgotten then, imbued by the same deathless passion that has come down unchanged through all the epochs, periods and eras of time from the beginning, and which shall continue to the incalculable end—woman, the imperishable Alpha and Omega of life.

Kho closed and sought my jugular with his teeth. He seemed to forget the hatchet dangling by its aurochs-hide thong at his hip, as I forgot, for the moment, the dagger in my hand. And I doubt not but that Kho would easily have bested me in an encounter of that sort had not Lys' voice awakened within my momentarily reverted brain the skill and cunning of reasoning man. "Bowen!" she cried. "Your knife! Your knife!"

It was enough. It recalled me from the forgotten eon to which my brain had flown and left me once again a modern man battling with a clumsy, unskilled brute. No longer did my jaws snap at the hairy throat before me; but instead my knife sought and found a space between two ribs over the savage heart. Kho voiced a single horrid scream, stiffened spasmodically and sank to the earth. And Lys threw herself into my arms. All the fears and sorrows of the past were wiped away, and once again I was the happiest of men.

With some misgivings I shortly afterward cast my eyes upward toward the precarious ledge which ran before my cave, for it seemed to me quite beyond all reason to expect a dainty modern belle to essay the perils of that frightful climb. I asked her if she thought she could brave the ascent, and she laughed gayly in my face.

"Watch!" she cried, and ran eagerly toward the base of the cliff. Like a squirrel she clambered swiftly aloft, so that I was forced to exert myself to keep pace with her. At first she frightened me; but presently I was aware that she was quite as safe here as was I. When we finally came to my ledge and I again held her in my arms, she recalled to my mind that for several weeks she had been living the life of a cave girl with the tribe of hatchet-men. They had been driven from their former caves by another tribe which had slain many and carried off quite half the females, and the new cliffs to which they had flown had proven far higher and more precipitous, so that she had become, through necessity, a most practiced climber.

She told me of Kho's desire for her, since all his females had been stolen and of how her life had been a constant nightmare of terror as she sought by night and by day to elude the great brute. For a time Nobs had been all the protection she required; but one day he disappeared—nor has she seen him since. She believes that he was deliberately made away with; and so do I, for we both are sure that he never would have deserted her. With her means of protection gone, Lys was now at the mercy of the hatchet-man; nor was it many hours before he had caught her at the base of the cliff and seized her; but as he bore her triumphantly aloft toward his cave, she had managed to break loose and escape him.

"For three days he has pursued me," she said, "through this horrible world. How I have passed through in safety I cannot guess, nor how I have always managed to outdistance him; yet I have done it, until just as you discovered me. Fate was kind to us, Bowen."

I nodded my head in assent and crushed her to me. And then we talked and planned as I cooked antelope steaks over my fire, and we came to the conclusion that there was no hope of rescue, that she and I were doomed to live and die upon Caprona, Well, it might be worse! I would rather live here always with Lys than to live elsewhere without her; and she, dear girl, says the same of me; but I am afraid of this life for her. It is a hard, fierce, dangerous life, and I shall pray always that we shall be rescued from it—for her sake.

That night the clouds broke, and the moon shone down upon our little ledge; and there, hand in hand, we turned our faces toward heaven and plighted our troth beneath the eyes of God. No human agency could have married us more sacredly than we are wed. We are man and wife, and we are content. If God wills it, we shall live out our lives here. If He wills otherwise, then this manuscript which I shall now consign to the inscrutable forces of the sea shall fall into friendly hands. However, we are each without hope. And so we say good-bye in this, our last message to the world beyond the barrier cliffs.

(*Signed*) BOWEN J. TYLER, JR.
LYS LA R. TYLER.

Edgar Rice Burroughs: Master of Adventure

The creator of the immortal characters Tarzan of the Apes and John Carter of Mars, EDGAR RICE BURROUGHS is one of the world's most popular authors. Mr. Burroughs' timeless tales of heroes and heroines transport readers from the jungles of Africa and the dead sea bottoms of Barsoom to the miles-high forests of Amtor and the savage inner world of Pellucidar, and even to alien civilizations beyond the farthest star. Mr. Burroughs' books are estimated to have sold hundreds of millions of copies, and they have spawned 60 films and 250 television episodes.

About Edgar Rice Burroughs, Inc.

Founded in 1923 by Edgar Rice Burroughs, one of the first authors to incorporate himself, EDGAR RICE BURROUGHS, INC., holds numerous trademarks and the rights to all literary works of the author still protected by copyright, including stories of Tarzan of the Apes and John Carter of Mars. The company oversees authorized adaptations of his literary works in film, television, radio, publishing, theatrical stage productions, licensing, and merchandising. Edgar Rice Burroughs, Inc., continues to manage and license the vast archive of Mr. Burroughs' literary works, fictional characters, and corresponding artworks that has grown for over a century. The company is still owned by the Burroughs family and remains headquartered in Tarzana, California, the town named after the Tarzana Ranch Mr. Burroughs purchased there in 1919 that led to the town's future development.

In 2015, under the leadership of President James Sullos, the company relaunched its publishing division, which was founded by Mr. Burroughs in 1931. With the publication of new authorized editions of Mr. Burroughs' works and brand-new novels and stories by today's talented authors, the company continues its long tradition of bringing tales of wonder and imagination featuring the Master of Adventure's many iconic characters and exotic worlds to an eager reading public.

Visit **EdgarRiceBurroughs.com** for more information.

The only fan organization to be personally approved by Edgar Rice Burroughs, The Burroughs Bibliophiles is the largest ERB fan club in the world, with members spanning the globe and maintaining local chapters across the United States and in England.

Also endorsed by Burroughs, *The Burroughs Bulletin*, the organization's official publication, features fascinating articles, essays, interviews, and more centered on the rich history and continuing legacy of the Master of Adventure. The Bibliophiles also annually sponsors the premier ERB fan convention.

Regular membership dues include:

- *Four issues of* The Burroughs Bulletin
- The Gridley Wave *newsletter in PDF*
- *The latest news in ERB fandom*
- *Information about the annual ERB fan convention*

For more information about the society and membership, visit **BurroughsBibliophiles.com** or The Burroughs Bibliophiles Facebook page, or email the Editor at BurroughsBibliophiles@gmail.com.

Call (573) 647-0225
or mail
318 Patriot Way,
Yorktown, Virginia
23693-4639, USA.

EDGAR RICE BURROUGHS AUTHORIZED LIBRARY™

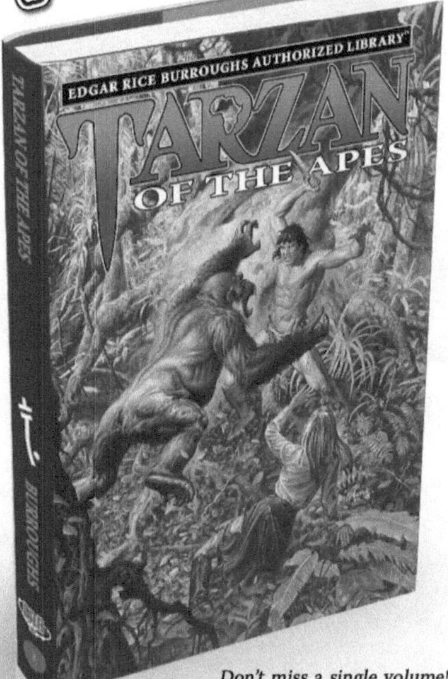

COLLECT EVERY VOLUME!

For the first time ever, the Edgar Rice Burroughs Authorized Library presents the complete literary works of the Master of Adventure in handsome uniform editions. Published by the company founded by Burroughs himself in 1923, each volume of the Authorized Library is packed with extras and rarities not to be found in any other edition. From cover art and frontispieces by legendary artist Joe Jusko to forewords and afterwords by today's authorities and luminaries to a treasure trove of bonus materials mined from the company's extensive archives in Tarzana, California, the Edgar Rice Burroughs Authorized Library will take you on a journey of wonder and imagination you will never forget.

Don't miss a single volume! Sign up for email updates at ERBurroughs.com to keep apprised of all 80-plus editions of the Authorized Library as they become available.

1. TARZAN OF THE APES
2. THE RETURN OF TARZAN
3. THE BEASTS OF TARZAN
4. THE SON OF TARZAN
5. TARZAN AND THE JEWELS OF OPAR
6. JUNGLE TALES OF TARZAN
7. TARZAN THE UNTAMED
8. TARZAN THE TERRIBLE
9. TARZAN AND THE GOLDEN LION
10. TARZAN AND THE ANT MEN
11. TARZAN, LORD OF THE JUNGLE
12. TARZAN AND THE LOST EMPIRE
13. TARZAN AT THE EARTH'S CORE
14. TARZAN THE INVINCIBLE
15. TARZAN TRIUMPHANT
16. TARZAN AND THE CITY OF GOLD
17. TARZAN AND THE LION MEN
18. TARZAN AND THE LEOPARD MEN
19. TARZAN'S QUEST
20. TARZAN THE MAGNIFICENT
21. TARZAN AND THE FORBIDDEN CITY
22. TARZAN AND THE FOREIGN LEGION
23. TARZAN AND THE MADMAN
24. TARZAN AND THE CASTAWAYS

THE JOURNEY BEGINS AT ERBURROUGHS.COM

ERB INC.

Edgar Rice Burroughs, Inc.
Edgar Rice Burroughs JIGSAW PUZZLE
Warlord of Mars
Edgar Rice Burroughs
Dejah Thoris
TARZAN
LORD OF THE LOUISIANA JUNGLE
Joe Jusko's Art of Edgar Rice Burroughs
A whole universe of ERB collectibles, including books, T-shirts, DVDs, statues, puzzles, playing cards, dust jackets, art prints, and MORE!
Your one-stop destination for all things ERB!

Edgar Rice Burroughs
The Master of Adventure

TARZAN
VINTAGE CLASSICS!
SOAP!
ENTER THE
EDGAR RICE BURROUGHS
UNIVERSE
ERB
INC.

www.ingramcontent.com/pod-product-compliance
Lightning Source LLC
Chambersburg PA
CBHW061610210726
48287CB00001B/63